ASTRODON

VICTORIA RIVERA

First published in the United States by Prosey Books, an imprint of Pocketful of Prosey LLC.

Cover art by TrifBookDesign
Maps and interior art by Daniel Brown
Layout, typography, and formatting by Victoria Rivera

www.toririv.com

First published June 8, 2025
Second Edition

For Rocco and Bellamy,
my very own little dinos.

Note From Author

This story is inspired by real-world places and the things, people, and languages in them. However, it is neither historical fiction nor an alternate history of Earth. It takes place in a unique setting that also includes dinosaurs and other prehistoric creatures from various geological time periods (as well as special breeds, hybrids, and a few fictional species). I have obviously taken creative license with the overall concept and many details, and simplified a few items for better readability, but I hope readers will feel as excited about this fantasy world as I do. I wanted to write a story that incorporates my passion for dinosaurs and my love of Latin America; this is my ode to both.

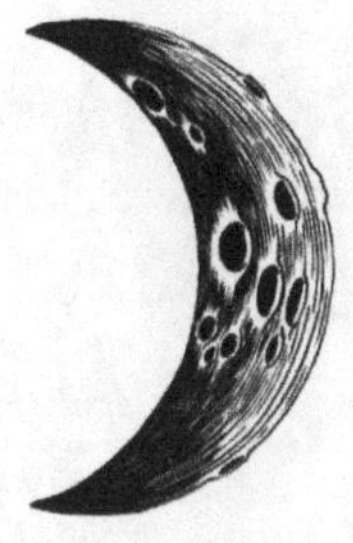

Some parts of this novel may deal briefly
with sensitive subject matter.

....

For a detailed list of content warnings, please visit:
www.toririv.com/cw

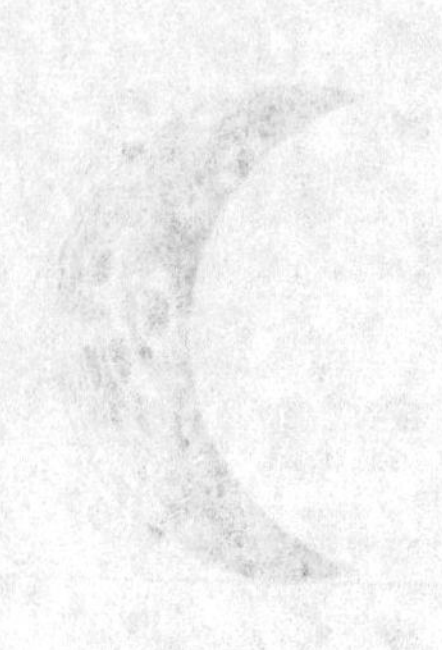

RUNAQA
GULF OF WAYAQA
Lake Weqe
TISQU
Masi
Silver City
Willkapampa Mountains
Port Sach'ara
Port Anqas
ALETA
RUHPARIY
QHUSI
Urubamba Mountains
SUMAQ
Volcanic Region
QOLQE
Ñansa
Lake Waylla
KANTUTA BAY
Lake Umiña
YUPA
UNU
Huandoy
ALLPA
Lake Sillu
AMACHAKUNA
Tukukuq
Pirqa Mountains
GULF OF ALLPA
Mt. Wiru
ANQAS OCEAN
Murkroot
THE TAIL

GLOSSARY

CONTINENT

RUNAQA *(roo-NAH-kuh)*

TERRAINS

SUMAQ *(SOO-mahk)*

UNU *(OOH-noo)*

QOLQE *(KOHL-kay)*

ALLPA *(AHL-puh)*

TISQU *(TISS-koo)*

CAPITALS

QHUSI *(KOO-see)*

YUPA *(YOO-puh)*

RUPHARIY *(roo-PAR-ee)*

AMACHAKUNA *(ah-mah-chuh-KOO-nuh)*

ALETA *(ah-LAY-tuh)*

OTHER

THE TAIL

MURKROOT

THE VERDANT REACH

PAKASQA *(pah-KAHSS-kuh)*

ÑIQAY ARENA *(NYEE-kahy)*

HUANDOY *(WAHN-doy)*

QORA *(KOR-uh)*

NINAN *(NIH-non)* | **APO-KIMSA** *(AH-poh KIM-suh)*

OLLAN *(OH-lun)*

PAQARI *(pah-KAR-ee)*

KONDOR *(KOHN-dor)*

QHAPAQ APO *(KAH-pahk AH-poh)*

QHAPAQ IZHI *(KAH-pahk EE-see)*

QUYA URPI *(KOO-yuh OORP-ee)*

QUYA ILLARI *(KOO-yuh ih-LAR-ee)*

KUY *(KOO-ee)*

REQ *(rek)*

WAYRA *(WAHY-ruh)*

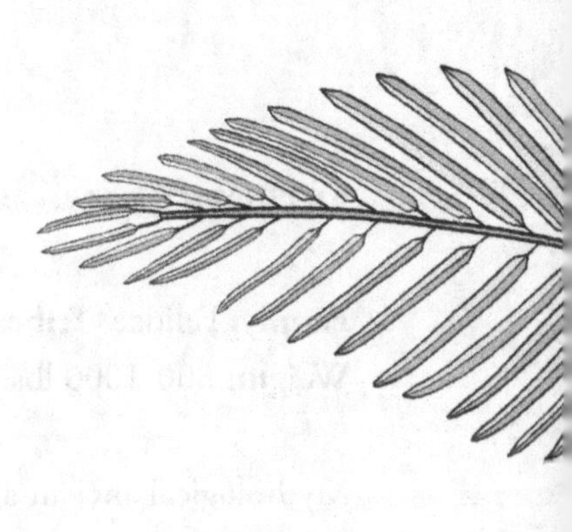

GORGO *(GOR-goh)*

PIDRU *(PIH-droo)*

TAMYA *(TAHM-yuh)*

HAKAN *(HAH-kahn)*

RIMAQ *(RIH-mahk)*

ANKU *(AHN-koo)*

ELDERBOUGH RAPHI *(ELL-dur-baow RAH-pee)*

ELDERBOUGH MALLKI *(ELL-dur-baow MAHL-kee)*

ELDERBOUGH LLUTA *(ELL-dur-baow LYOO-tuh)*

ELDERBOUGH K'ULLU *(ELL-dur-baow kuh-OOL-ooh)*

SURI *(SOO-ree)*

CHINBO *(CHIN-boh)*

MIYIL *(MEE-yeel)*

RUKA *(ROO-kuh)*

UTURUNKU *(ooh-too-ROON-kooh)*

ASTRODON *(AS-troh-don)*

Family: Felidae **Tribe:** Smilodontini **Length:** 10-12 ft
Weight: 800-1000 lbs

Mythological ancient ancestor of the smilodon species; a large
sabertoothed cat with glowing teeth. The first of its kind is
often believed to be an avatar from the High World, who took
the form of a powerful feline imbued with celestial power.

Allpan Encyclopedia of Cryptozoology

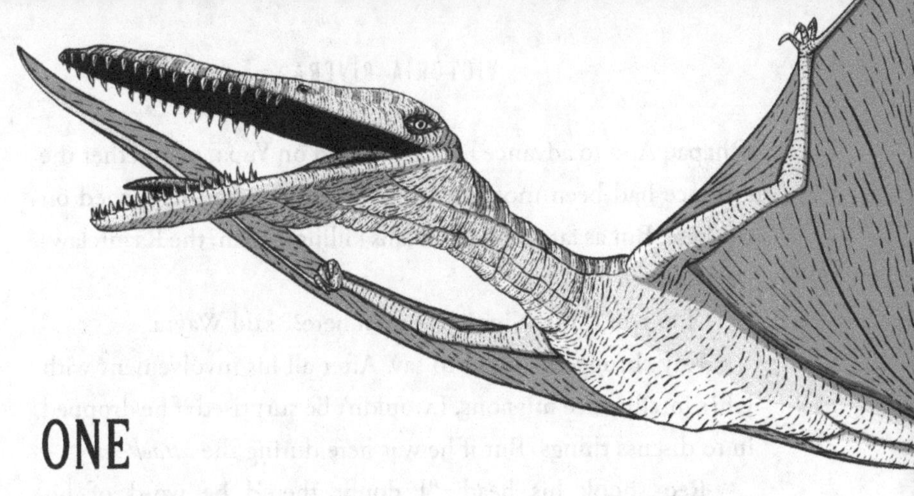

ONE

THE RAZORCLAWS OBSERVED THE CITADEL from a small mountain overlooking the Unuvian capital. Kuy, Wayra, Req, and Gorgo, along with their pteranodons, watched distantly as Sumaqi guards patrolled the outer walls, whose blocks sustained huge breaks where additional military personnel filtered in and out performing various tasks.

One of the tasks was to dispose of the blue-uniformed corpses that lay everywhere.

"I heard Qhapaq Apo sent ankylosaurs to get through," Kuy said. "With double-sized tail clubs as battering rams."

There were no dinosaurs on the premises, however—no members of the Sauroguard that had allowed the Sumaqi qhapaq to conquer this place, only the aftermath of its presence.

The chronicles had detailed the vicious battle, the retaliation against Qhapaq Izhi after he had sent a human unit to destroy the Sauroguard breeding and training base in the Aquchay Desert of Tisqu two days earlier.

Additional news had begun to circulate, that the Unuvians had been responsible for the capture of the Third Prince, Apo-Kimsa Kallpa (known by Venture fans as "Ninan"), from his royal wedding. Sources claimed he had been brutally executed. It was unclear whether this alleged act had been what had spurred

Qhapaq Apo to advance his Sauroguard on Yupa, or whether the advance had been motivated purely by what had happened on the base. But as far as the Unuvians killing Ninan, the Razorclaws knew better.

"Do you think Ninan was even here?" said Wayra.

Kuy shrugged. "Hard to say. After all his involvement with Izhi's intelligence missions, I wouldn't be surprised if he dropped in to discuss things. But if he was here during the *attack* ..."

Req shook his head. "I doubt there'd be word of his 'execution' by the Unuvians if his father got a hold of him. Ninan had to have gotten out of reach before then. Either way, I don't buy it for a second that anyone managed to capture him from the wedding."

Wayra sighed and tucked her chin-length hair behind one ear. "Everyone's saying Izhi hired some pirates to do the job, but there's no way a few lowborn nautical thieves could've taken him that easy, right?"

"Right," Gorgo said through a grumble. "I've gone up against him myself and had my hindquarters handed to me. He's a force with his fists." The burly young man rolled his eyes.

As far as anyone knew, Qhapaq Izhi was still free, and in hiding. Meanwhile, Qhapaq Achik of Tisqu remained loyal to Sumaq (despite the sabotage of the wedding that would have legally united their two Terrains), as did Qolqe (already legally allied through the marriage of Qhapaq Apo to his third wife, Ninan's mother).

"So much for working directly with Izhi on new military strategies."

Req fiddled with the group's three remaining dominite crystals, only one of which still had a particularly strong purple glow, intriguing the pteranodons. "Where do we go now?"

The group had intended to leave Sumaq just after Qora had headed off for Allpa, but had been delayed as Wayra finished up arrangements for someone to care for her reptiles on Mount Qaqra. It was a good thing, too, or the Razorclaws might have arrived at the citadel with very unfortunate timing—and not made it out alive.

Wayra twisted her lips. "Maybe Qora had the right idea. Maybe Allpa is the place to be."

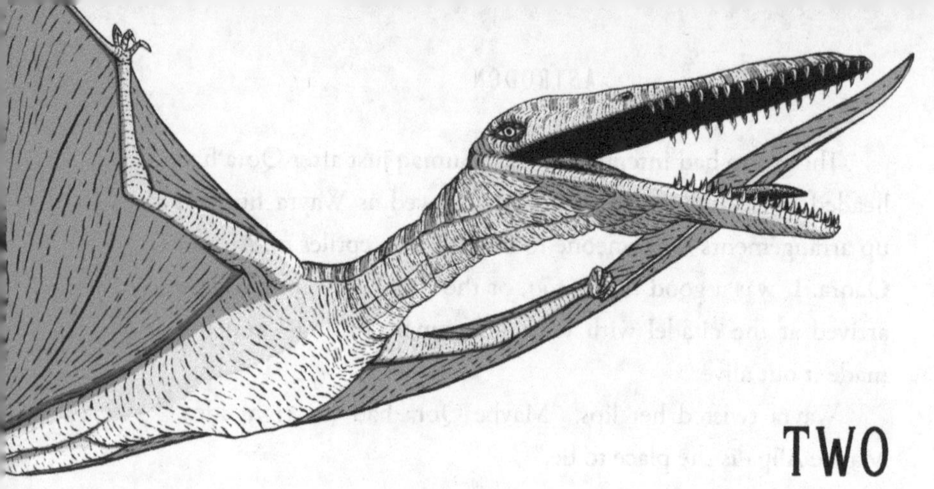

TWO

NINAN HATED THAT EVERY DESCENT from air travel seemed to bear so much weight now. He seemed, more often than not, to be landing in situations that held his heart in a vise grip: descending on Kallpa House to raid his own home and steal pterobeast arks; descending on Thak to face the community that had once harbored him in his exile before he had been forced to reveal his true identity without warning; descending on Unu just before the Sauroguard had attacked the citadel; descending on Allpa in hopes of finally finding Qora, only to learn that she had yet again moved on.

This morning, he would descend on the Allpan region of Wiñay, where his friends from Thak were starting their quinoa crops anew in this foreign land, all because his father had threatened their safety for leverage against him.

Even from here, at least a mile away, the acres of bare, half-tilled soil caught his notice.

"Looks like they've already begun their work," said Qora's mamáy, who sat beside her two sons on the gondola bench.

Paqari, who sat on the opposite side, glanced up from a book titled *Geometry in Stellar Patterns* and hummed in acknowledgement of the sight.

Quya Urpi had explained the plan for these crops. Her

own agriculturists had been developing a heat-tolerant variety of quinoa with a shorter growing season. They were a little late for this *particular* growing season, as plants in Sumaq were already sprouting their fourth leaves, but there was still time for successful growth if the workers began immediately. The crops would require mulch to keep water from evaporating too quickly from the soil (as they were still in the dry season, which would end within the next two months), and plants would need to be spaced further apart to allow more air circulation between them. Irrigation techniques were in place to provide extra water. Pest control was in full force, as this climate made vegetation more susceptible to insects. But despite Allpa's rough climate, Urpi had selected this location in the coolest region of her Terrain, close to one of the Kuchuna River tributaries. She expected lower yields for the first few years until the farmers could establish a standard production method.

"You're sure you wouldn't rather stay at Qhispina House?" Ninan asked Qora's mamáy.

The woman patted the top of the large trunk beside her. "We have everything we really need in here. And I don't want the boys to forget how to work. I'm grateful for the quya's generosity, but we belong in the countryside."

"As long as there's a good market within a couple of miles," Hakan said, scraping the blade of his whittling knife against a rough, wooden figurine of an alpaca. His voice broke a little on the last word, not for emotion but for his changing vocal cords.

The boy wasn't much older than Tamya, Ninan realized. Ninan knew that the girl who had once been an adoptive sister would welcome Qora's brothers and see that they had friends in the community, and for that he was glad.

Rimaq, who was only nine, peered over the rim of the

gondola. "Look at the water ..."

A sickle-shaped body of water sat next to the river tributary, like a little irregular lake.

Paqari stopped reading again to see briefly. "It's left behind from a meander," she told him. "The water eroded the land at the neck and started flowing straight, then cut off the curve. It's called a 'bow lake.'"

Ninan observed the bow lake, feeling a bit too much like it. He wasn't sure whether it was his cut-off heritage or the rift between himself and Pidru or his distance from Qora (who still thought he had married Paqari) that made this geological feature resonate with him, but he wondered if a heavy rain could ever reconnect it to the river, or if it would simply dry up and disappear. That was all he felt capable of doing in this moment—drying up and disappearing.

He rubbed his shoulder, where the afterburn of Tuko's claws still irritated his skin; the little pteromorph had been through a lot, and had still managed to stick close to Ninan even during high-speed aerial pursuits. After the chaos of the *Velosaura* tour and Ninan's near-execution at Qhapaq Izhi's citadel, there had been nothing to do but let Tuko retire to the Qhispina House pteriary where he could enjoy daily meals of tiger beetles and mangoes, and bathe in the fountain. Quya Urpi had been fascinated by such a pliable creature and more than happy to add him to her collection. He was certainly no average reptile; after all, he'd had a part in uncovering the Sauroguard training base, not to mention in saving Ninan's life.

Additional credit went to the Second Princess of Tisqu. Glancing at Paqari, Ninan still couldn't believe she'd gone all the way to Unu to help him. If she hadn't arrived at the last minute, he wasn't sure how he would have escaped his father's guards. Even now, her demeanor didn't match her actions, as she stared morosely at the pages of her book with no apparent enthusiasm for the place they were going—and yet, she had accepted Ninan's invitation to come along to see the quinoa farmers and bid farewell to Qora's family. He squinted, as though this would help him understand her better, but … he remained at a loss. Who could guess what went on in that head of hers? He hadn't expected her to have been the evil mastermind behind the pirates that had attacked the *Velosaura*, or the staged attack on the royal wedding, or the mixup at the masquerade, or the terminonatators off the eastern coast of Phapa, and yet, she'd planned each of those things without ever having triggered Ninan's suspicion.

He took a deep breath to calm his nerves as the group neared the croplands where he would have to see Pidru again. His last encounter with Pidru had been tense, to say the least. Ninan couldn't blame his friend—the friend that had been more of a brother to him than his two brothers by blood—for resenting him. Ninan had spent almost a year in Thak without anyone knowing he was really the Third Prince of Sumaq (*former* prince at the time), a secret that had been revealed by the end of the Venture and which had cost the entire community their safety so that Ninan would comply with the arranged marriage to Paqari. Ninan had managed to get the community members to Allpa for a fresh start, but they'd had to leave behind the land they'd known and loved their whole lives.

Qora's mamáy patted Ninan's hand. "They will forgive you eventually. I know they will."

A sting formed behind Ninan's eyes. By now, the woman knew everything that had led to this point. The previous evening, he'd met her with apologies, with tears he hadn't expected to shed. And like the mother she was—although she wasn't his own—she'd embraced him and comforted him and said she was glad to finally know him. The next several hours had been an exchange of information, during which Ninan had learned more details about Ollan's sudden return, as well as the devastating news of Sakay's death, and then he had shared certain details of his past as well as his perspective on the events surrounding the *Velosaura* tour and his intentions for the near future. She knew the weight of this visit, along with most of the other things that weighed on him today.

He forced a smile for her and whispered, "Thank you."

⟩⟩⟩

The grassy plains were vast and mostly golden but with a faint hue of green. The grasses seemed to undulate in the wind, which was subtle but for this visual clue, made more prominent by the flapping of the pterobeast's enormous wings when it swooped in descent.

The land seemed boundless, both wild and serene. Only a few trees were scattered throughout the stretch, standing like sentinels, while birds and small flyers soared between them. Wild gallimimus sprinted in herds, covering the distance in elegant cooperation.

And then the earth was bare in perfectly cut patches, its grasses shorn from its dirt, dotted with farmers guiding their iguanodon-drawn plows to carve long furrows for seed.

Everyone on the ground looked up as the pterobeast and gondola approached the cluster of homes, which were rough and still under construction but which would provide sufficient shelter even before they were complete. Already Ninan could tell that these homes were a great improvement from those back in Thak—some of these even had a second story for the families with children—despite their simplicity. A crew of builders was putting up the last outer wall of an additional house, where the Kanchayas would stay.

A large dinoshelter and warehouse stood along the fringes, while iguanodons drank from troughs in the connected paddock.

Many of the people below were wearing new work trousers and durable roughspun shirts instead of threadbare tunics. Tamya and her mamáy were among them, also well attired, with a flush of nourishment in their cheeks.

It seemed Quya Urpi had provided more than just an opportunity to work her land. How good the quality of work could be, Ninan thought, when workers were respected and cared for. That was something these people had never known. Still, they would likely never see their homeland in Sumaq again.

Ninan didn't see Pidru, but he caught sight of Kunaq, Tika, and Yaku, the bandits that had helped him orchestrate his plan to get his friends to safety, working among the others while they waited for him to retrieve them. The "arks"—and the eighteen pterobeasts required to carry such enormous gondolas—were back at Qhispina House (after having dropped the farmers here) along with the two pteranodons belonging to Tika and Kunaq respectively, as there was no pteriary out here to care for them. Ninan had likewise left Yaku's pteranodon (which he had borrowed to fly to Unu and on which he'd flown to Allpa shortly afterward) among the others.

Just before the gondola struck the ground, Ninan stood and gripped the rim. The others stood too, in anticipation of the landing. Immediately the community members bowed to Ninan and Paqari.

The pilot opened the exit panel.

Paqari gestured for Ninan to go first, so, after a pause, he stepped out.

The people stared at him as though waiting for instruction, but he had none to give. He wasn't sure how to go about this reunion. He didn't know what to say or how to act.

When the silence and the lack of motion seemed too heavy to bear, Ninan opened his mouth to ask that they stand up straight and treat him as an equal, but before he could, Tamya came forward. She glanced over her shoulder at her mamáy, who made no point to dissuade her. She locked eyes with Ninan for a moment, then wrapped her arms around him.

Releasing a pent-up breath, Ninan let her sink into him, embracing her in return.

"I missed you," she muttered against his chest.

"I missed you too," he told her.

Tamya's mamáy soon followed, embracing him as well.

Slowly, the others stood. Some of the men came to shake his hand.

"Thank you for bringing us here," said one of the older women. "It has been an adjustment, but we are grateful."

Ninan felt his emotional fortitude return, and finally he found the energy to speak up.

"This is Paqari Huapaya, Second Princess of Tisqu." He indicated the princess, who stepped out of the gondola and acknowledged everyone with a brief nod. "And this is the mother and younger brothers of Qora Kanchaya, the fifth quinquennial Venture champion." The three members of Qora's family stepped out and smiled.

"I'm sorry I couldn't accompany you here at first," Ninan added. "My business in Unu was something I thought vital to preventing the start of my father's war, but I'm afraid I was too late. I witnessed firsthand the monsters my father has created. Unfortunately this is only the beginning. But you have a much better chance to thrive here on this land. In the meantime, I will be working with Quya Urpi and the rebel network to fight back. For now, you will be safe here."

After everyone took a minute or so to digest his words, Tamya told Qora's family, "Welcome to Wiñay. Let us show you to your new home," and motioned for them to follow her and her mamáy while two young men went to unload the trunk of their belongings.

The three bandits came forward now, greeting Ninan and Paqari.

"Nice to see you again, Your Highnesses," said Kunaq. "Although I must say, I'm surprised to see the two of you together, after all that money and effort spent trying to get away from each other."

Paqari rolled her eyes.

"We've actually had a decent time here," Tika told them. "Although we're looking forward to getting back to Tisqu to spend some of that gold." She winked at Ninan.

As much as Ninan wanted to reminisce about helping the bandits raid Qhapaq Apo's treasury, he couldn't ignore the urge to go looking for Pidru. "If you're all set to return to Qhispina House for your transportation, I'll be happy to take you. Just allow me a few minutes, would you?"

Several little girls swarmed Paqari. "Your hair is so long and pretty," one said, and "Your dress is my favorite color," said another, and "Do you have your own gondola?" another asked. The princess tensed, at first, at their sudden attention, but then began to speak to them as though they were any other girls with whom she might associate.

"Coconut oil," she said, twirling the end of one of her loose curls around her manicured finger. "It keeps the strands strong and smooth. And thank you. Yes, I quite like this color as well, a gift from the quya, and I've never worn this material before but it's very lightweight and comfortable in your climate. My gondolas are triangular—it's more aerodynamic for the windy weather we often get along the coasts of the islands."

With Paqari now occupied, and Qora's family off getting settled in, Ninan slipped away to find his friend.

꙳꙳꙳

To Ninan's surprise, he hadn't had to look beyond the dinoshelter to locate Pidru.

The boy was sifting out ruck from one of the stalls and barely looked over to see that someone had entered. Pidru's gaze lingered on Ninan for only a moment, and then he continued his work.

"I don't expect you to forgive me," Ninan told him.

"Good," Pidru muttered.

Ninan waited several seconds, then said, "You could at least talk to me, though."

"You want to talk?" Pidru plunged his pitchfork into the straw and gripped the handle upright. "Fine. I'll talk. Should I talk about how you were ripped from our midst one day without warning? How Tamya and my mamáy and I were so worried— and were helpless to do anything about it? How your name showed up on the Venture competitors list and how I hoped it was a coincidence but followed the competition religiously each day to see whether you lived or died? How, on the last day,

12

before a champion was even named, armed officers arrived and snatched me from my bed and flew me to Qhusi and kept me chained and gagged until some calculated moment when they dragged me to the qhapaq's menagerie only for me to realize that you were no ordinary boy, but a prince of Sumaq—and that the brother I had taken in had kept this massive secret from me for a *year*? And how then, when I was taken back to Thak, a unit of the qhapaq's guards followed, and from then on patrolled the community, the fields, the outskirts, with their weapons trained on us every second? And all the while, those words repeated over and over in my mind: 'What will it be, Apo-Kimsa?'" He scoffed. "That was the last thing I heard your father say to you. Your father the *qhapaq*. Calling you Apo-Kimsa, the name you should have told me that night when I first brought you into my home."

"You're right. I should have."

"I never even heard your response. When he asked you, 'What will it be, Apo-Kimsa?' I never knew what you told him. Because, while you were standing there like a stunned troodon looking down the shaft of a hunting arrow, they dragged me away. They took me straight home—except it wasn't home anymore; from then on, it was a prison yard. It wasn't until three days later that the news came of your engagement, announced at the Venture homecoming ceremony and word carried to Thak by courier, that I knew whether we would be safe. Although, even then, I wasn't sure how long it would last, if you would really go through with the *Velosaura* tour or whether you might rebel and provoke your father's anger, and then we'd all be dead in an instant."

Ninan's stomach hardened into a knot. He pressed his lips together. "I never imagined my going to Thak would have done that to you," he assured him. "I never had the faintest idea that my father would send Mullu to find me, let alone put me in the Venture and try to make me a prince again. I thought once he stripped me of my heritage and abandoned me in the wilderness that he was done with me for good. You have to understand that. I didn't tell you who I was because I simply didn't think it mattered anymore. Legally speaking, I was not a prince. Legally speaking, I was no longer a Kallpa. I was no one. If I had known what would become of Thak, I never would have agreed to stay with you. I swear it." He paused for a moment and thought. "Except, there's one thing I don't regret … and that's the fact that you'll never have to sow another quinoa seed for my father. Yes I regret that you've had to start over after all you've already planted back in Sumaq, and I regret that the homes here—however improved—are not the homes you were raised in. I regret that I lied to you all, that I caused you to worry for me, that you were taken in the night to make *me* cooperate, and that you have lived for so many months with a threat hanging over you because of me. But not for one second do I regret removing you from my father's reach. You can hate me until the end of time, but for that, I'm not sorry."

Pidru spun to face away from Ninan and kicked the stall door, which swung fast on its hinges and slammed into the stall beside it, startling a hidden rhabdodon who honked in response. He grunted as he pulled at his own hair. "Why is it always like this with you?"

"Like what?"

"Like … I so badly want to hate you, to preserve some sense of rage toward you, but then you just …"

Ninan hesitated. "I'm sorry …"

"That's just it. You really mean it. I know that. You've never done anything but try to help. And things go wrong sometimes when you're around—or when you're not around, but because of you—but then you come back trying to make it right, and you quite literally go above and beyond"—he gestured wildly, pointing up and flourishing a hand, as if to demonstrate the arks Ninan had stolen to fly everyone across borders—"and somehow we're actually better off for having known you. Just like when you wouldn't come out to the fields because you couldn't keep up, and I'd want to scream at you for not carrying your share of the load. But then you showed up with a bloody nose and a handful of silvers—not to mention ointment for my blisters and squash cakes for all the children. Like some saintly benefactor that everyone can't help but love."

When Pidru's eyes welled, so did Ninan's.

That's all Ninan had wanted—love, community, family. A brother who actually cared for him. He'd found that in Thak. And then his father had managed to take that away too.

Pidru dropped his pitchfork with a clatter and embraced Ninan.

It took Ninan a few seconds to mentally catch up to the gesture after all the anger that had preceded it, but then he reciprocated.

"Ruck," Pidru muttered over Ninan's shoulder. "I was so worried about what they might have done to you, when you first left."

Ninan cracked a wan little smile. "You were worried about me?"

Pidru drew back and picked up his pitchfork again, wiping his eyes with the back of his wrist. "Of course I was. Gods."

They stood facing each other quietly for a minute, and then Ninan said, "I have to leave again."

Pidru nodded. "Guess I shouldn't be surprised. Where to this time?"

"The Tail."

"The Tail? Why?"

With a heavy heart, Ninan explained everything. He told Pidru about his feelings for Qora—things he hadn't had time to explain when he'd gone to Thak with the arks to evacuate everyone—and all that they'd been through during the Venture and also the past month at sea, reiterating the part about working with Qhapaq Izhi and how it had led to finding the Aquchay base, which had allowed Izhi's unit to attack and in turn had spurred Qhapaq Apo to advance on Unu with the Sauroguard. He described the horrors of each reptile that he'd encountered, and his narrow escape thanks to the princess. Pidru barely knew about the existence of the Sauroguard from Ninan's brief warning before insisting everyone board the arks; news of the battle at the citadel would not yet have arrived to this new community.

"Spirits …" Pidru murmured. "I'm sorry I was so angry with you for so long. I had no idea."

"You couldn't have known," Ninan told him. "But now my father occupies Unu's capital, and the only military we have is what Allpa can provide, which won't be enough against those mutant reptiles. Qora has already gone to the Tail on the quya's authority, looking for giant theropods to help us fight. That's why I'm going too; I have to get to her."

Pidru absentmindedly sifted a bit of ruck. "How do you know there are *any* giant theropods down there, let alone enough to fight a war?"

"There's a reason the Venture competitors had to face a spinosaur at the end. It didn't come from Quya Urpi's southern lands; she's confirmed those that live below the Pirqas aren't nearly that large."

"You think your father sourced it from even further south …"

Ninan nodded. "Eggs. Possibly more than a decade ago. But from all I've seen so far, he hasn't utilized dinosaurs like that in high numbers. I believe the spinosaur was only for experimental purposes, and then he saw fit to include it as a sort of homage to the terrenal emblem when Sumaq became Venture host."

"His Sauroguard utilizes smaller reptiles, then."

"For the most part. He appears to be more focused on what they can do, rather than on size. Swarms of moderately sized demons. He is, however, accelerating their maturation somehow, and giving them features that couldn't possibly be achieved with traditional crossbreeding. So right now, our only hope to overcome his dinosaurs is with something bigger. We're working on other tactics too, of course; the quya is training more of her sabertoothed cats, and I hope to soon reconnect with members of a rebel network that specializes in unconventional tactics."

Pidru curled his fingers around the handle of his pitchfork. "When do you leave?"

"Tomorrow morning."

"Well," Pidru said with a sigh, "you're a fugitive—yet again. It only makes sense that you remain on the move."

Smiling faintly, Ninan said, "Maybe one day I'll have a moment to stay still."

Before humankind, there was the dinosaur. And the dinosaurs did walk upon the earth and had dominion over all. Humankind came forth only by the mercy of our Great Reptilian Lords, and therefore we do honor them in this life and the next.

***Concords of the Verdant Reach*, Section 1, Verse 1**

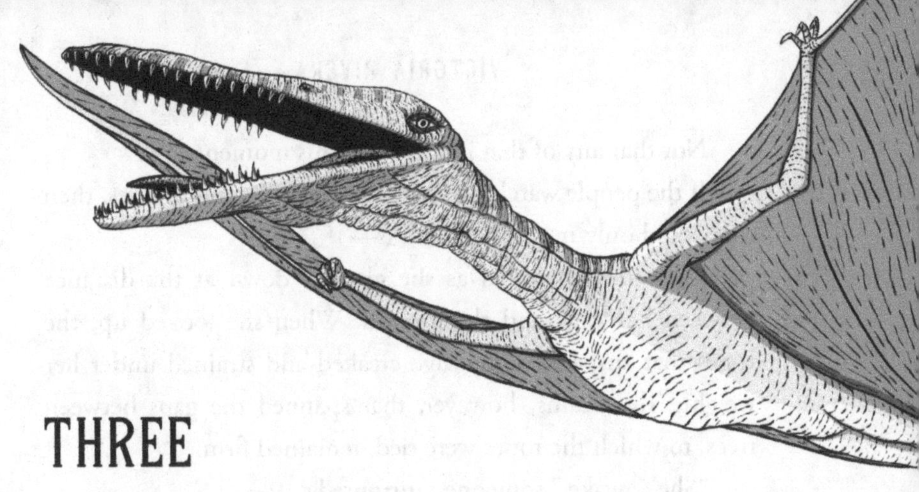

THREE

WHEN QORA STARTLED AWAKE, the view before her—a brooding conifer forest with structures all up and down the trees connected by ropes and bridges—began to swing back and forth.

No.

Wait.

The *view* was steady; it was Qora who swung back and forth.

Beyond a network of wooden crosspieces that implied she was trapped inside a kind of rounded, oversized birdcage, people had begun to gather along the rope bridges that were suspended between the trees around her. The majority of these people wore tints of grayish blue for their tunics and blouses, tawny-brown pants, and a variety of accessories made of dark woolly fur— indicative of whatever apparently limited pigment sources they had down here and strange animals Qora had yet to see.

The palette of skin tones was even more curious than their clothing. While some of them were darker like most of the people of Runaqa, many were pale, some even with light brown hair. Others were a mix of dark and light, an array of shades. The Kastillans must have had more influence here, Qora thought. In such a small region, with a smaller population, these people might not have had the means to drive out the foreigners quickly the way the Five Terrains had.

Not that any of that mattered in this moment.

If the people watching Qora were standing on bridges, then that could only mean that *she* was—

Her stomach roiled as she glanced down at the distance between her cage and the ground. When she looked up, the ropes that suspended the cage creaked and strained under her weight. The beams, however, that spanned the gaps between trees, to which the ropes were tied, remained firm.

"She's awake," someone murmured.

"It's about to start," said someone else.

"She doesn't look dangerous though …"

More whispers erupted from among the crowds.

Qora's pulse kicked up. How had she ended up here?

She tried to think.

How long had it been since she and Ollan had left Allpa, with two guards and a pilot in a pterobeast gondola? It seemed like only yesterday that she was at Qhispina House, talking to the quya about their plans. Quya Urpi would use the information Sakay had sacrificed himself to get, and send scouts to the two nearest military encampments listed on the papyr—Camp Ñansa and Camp Wood Ridge—to see what other hybrid dinosaurs might threaten the peace in Runaqa. Camp Kawsay was up near Sumaq's border with Qolqe and would be the least immediate threat.

Then Qora and Ollan had departed with the travel team Urpi had assigned them. They'd flown over the Pirqas, noting the distinct chill in the air. The mountains had been majestic, with bits of melting snow on top that fed the waters that flowed from them. And after that, they'd crossed the lush countryside, with meadows and clusters of trees, where larger theropods roamed.

Quya Urpi had been right that those theropods were not as

large as the spinosaur from the Venture—Qhapaq Apo had surely sourced it from somewhere else—but never in Qora's life had she seen so many dinosaurs that size in one place. Giganotosaurs and allosaurs and tyrannosaurs in full herds, with patterned feathers and powerful legs. If they were dying out, as the quya had said, Qora couldn't imagine how crowded these lands must have looked a hundred years earlier.

Then the group had flown over Mount Wiru, said to be sacred for its many colors (red for its oxidized iron-bearing minerals, green for its ferromagnesian minerals, yellow for its limonites, white for its quartzose sandstone) which had somehow formed into distinct stripes. It was no wonder people trekked to it with such reverence, or that Qora had seen several of those pilgrims trailing like ticks on the worn path that led there.

When the group had flown into Tail territory, the forests had grown thick and dark, with hundreds of thousands of evergreen trees sprawling in all directions.

Shortly thereafter, what had appeared to be a swoop of small flyers had risen from the branches and flown alongside the gondola. But Qora had quickly realized that these were not pterosaurs of any kind, or even birds.

Meganeuras, Qora had thought, recalling the creatures from a compendium of insects. Enormous dragonflies, almost as big as a rhamphorhynchus, with purplish bodies like batons, and an iridescent sheen on their papyr-thin wings.

They had buzzed with a kind of self-generated electricity and then, with a fuzzy snap, released a cloud of shimmering particles into the air—as though the particles had been clinging to their wings with the same kind of faint energy that could make two pieces of fabric stick together for a moment, dispelled like a tiny crackle of invisible lightning.

Qora hadn't been able to keep herself from inhaling those particles, and then everything had gone dreamlike.

What had happened after that should have made her panic: the two people coming up and flanking the gondola in pedal-powered flying contraptions made of wood and muslin, then one of those people blowing into a small wooden instrument that made a high-pitched noise. With that, the pterobeast had seemed to fall under the man's control, following him and his companion into a downward turn.

It was like Wayra's animal calls, Qora had thought, only instead of *mimicking* the pterobeast, it had stimulated the pterobeast's deeper brain senses. He had led it to a hidden clearing and encouraged it to land, and then at least a dozen other tree-dwelling people had thronged the gondola and separated Qora and Ollan from their guards and pilot, taking them off in separate directions. But despite all that, Qora had watched everything unfold with an eerie sense of calm, and then that calmness within her mind had relaxed her body, forcing it to cave to its natural fatigue after weeks of turmoil and days of constant waking terror. Her eyelids had gone heavy, and that was the last she remembered.

The fear of Qhapaq Apo's Sauroguard swarming Allpa, the agony of Sakay's death, the sting of Ninan's marriage to Paqari ... all of it had dissipated into a tranquil darkness. Now, she had emerged to *this*.

She had been stripped of her green jacket and her crossbow, and she wasn't sure what she was looking at.

Visually following the beams above, Qora caught sight of a platform supporting a larger, cubical cage that held several people. She squinted to see into it, to make out the face of the young man at the front.

Ollan.

Her brother gripped the bars and met her eyes. "Qora!"

He, along with the pilot and guards, seemed to be reluctantly waiting their turn for … whatever this was.

The ropes of Qora's cage were secured on brackets that were fastened to the structures on the trees. Qora observed the structures more carefully. The buildings wrapped around each tree in multiple levels, some with stairs that spiraled the trunks and led down to the forest floor. Most of the structures had open-air windows, and some had balconies. They seemed to go on for miles in every direction, all connected to one another through additional bridges and what looked like a cable-and-harness system where people could attach themselves and coast at a slight angle to a lower level.

Qora wondered how Allpan explorers had managed to get a glimpse of these people without ending up in a cage like she had. Perhaps because they had trekked into the region on foot. They could have observed from hidden vantage points, taken their notes, and gone. Qora and Ollan's arrival in the gondola had probably been too conspicuous—threatening, even. Not something that would slip easily past defenses. But of course there simply hadn't been time to be too strategic. The continent was in a state of emergency, and everyone needed to know.

"Please!" Qora cried to anyone who might listen. "We have important information!"

Several people muttered among themselves in response.

Before Qora could call out again, a low rumbling cut her off. Her muscles tensed at the sound—the *too-familiar* sound—and her ears began to throb.

The crowd applauded and the tree branches jostled and the ground vibrated.

Slowly, Qora turned her head and then allowed her gaze to fall. She curled her trembling fingers as she stared at the enormous creature below.

A fine pattern of pale-green scales covered its body, striped with bands of darker green. A row of tiny spikes ran down the crown of its head.

Although Qora dangled several feet above it, it pointed its snout upward. Its hot breath wafted over her skin, sending shivers through her core.

Not again, she thought, squeezing her eyes closed for a moment while she steadied her breath. Memories of the spinosaurus flashed across her mind—that same enormity, that same sinister look in its similarly amber eyes, and Qora within its reach and at its mercy.

"Release her to the giga!" someone shouted.

The giganotosaur roared, rattling Qora's bones.

"I haven't done anything wrong!" she cried. "We're not here to hurt anyone—we just came to warn you! Your people aren't safe, and we need your help. Please!"

"Let her go!" Ollan demanded

Flailing its head at her, the giganotosaur roared again, inciting the crowd to cheer.

Qora looked around desperately. If she could just get out of this cage, maybe she could climb to safety. She took note of several climbing holds and vertically placed nets that reminded her of the *Velosaura*'s ratlines—although none appeared to reach any of the bridges or balconies on which most people safely stood.

Suddenly it felt as though she were back in the Venture—not only because of the monster, but because of the setup, because of the apparent sport of it all.

"They want me to think I can avoid the giga ..." Qora lamented to herself. *But I'm not meant to get far.*

Just enough to make her try to stay out of its reach. Not enough to help her actually survive.

A man in a full-length woolly brown coat came to the forefront of the highest balcony, level with where Qora's cage dangled like bait for the giganotosaur. "Gather anyone else who cares to witness the execution of these invaders!" He announced. "In one hour, we'll make the drop."

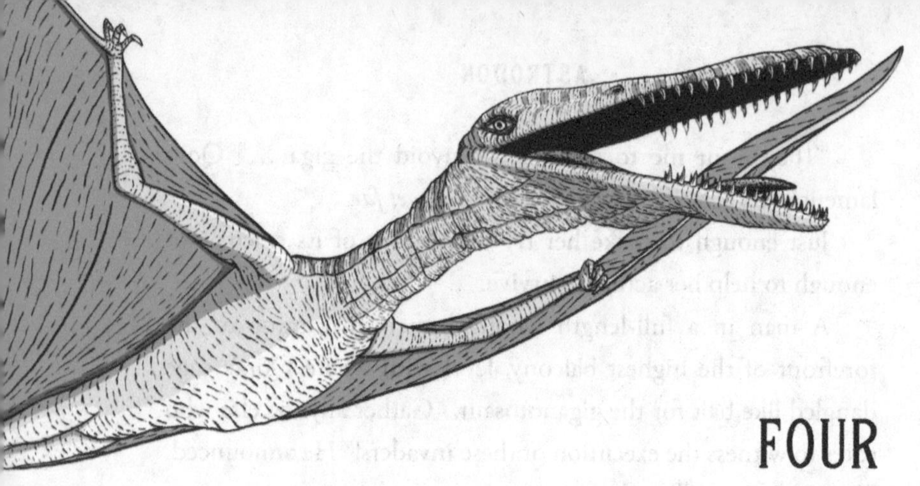

FOUR

PAQARI HAD TO READ THE SAME PASSAGE three times because she couldn't seem to concentrate.

Astronomers utilize a method called parallax, *a type of triangulation, in which they observe a single star from opposite points in the earth's journey around the sun to measure the star's shift against more distant "background" stars. Stars that appear to be side by side in fact exist on separate planes.*

She sighed and closed the book, gazing out at the landscape from the gondola, eager to get back to Qhispina House and peruse the quya's library in peace. Perhaps fiction this time, she thought—something a bit lighter. Although she made a point to consume educational materials for at least one hour each day. But her mind was tired for some reason. She couldn't think why; not with the constant lack of stimulating conversation around here.

Ninan had, for the most part, been silent and brooding as he longed to see the champion, as he mourned Sakay, and as he mulled over the tension between him and his friends. Then, the young girls in Wiñay had only cared to talk about the luxuries of Paqari's royalborn life, while Paqari had in fact desired to know more about the agricultural process of establishing quinoa crops in a new climate. She didn't have an interest in farming, per se, although the development of seed variations, the mineral ratios in the soil, and the irrigation methods fascinated her. Or maybe it was the puzzling out of the solution to making something grow where it naturally would not—the challenge of agricultural engineering. Similarly, Qhapaq Apo's creation of unnatural reptiles—while abhorrent—was fascinating to her as well.

The bandits whom Paqari had hired to sabotage her wedding had now joined her and Ninan in the gondola, with plans to return to Tisqu as soon as possible (once they retrieved their reptiles from the Qhispina House pteriary).

The princess thought, briefly, what it would be like to return to Tisqu after all this. She couldn't believe she'd dared to leave her homeland, despite the fact that she'd considered it often. Her father had given her reason enough—treating her like "damaged goods," sending her beloved watchman to a faraway city and ensuring him a wife, trying to force her to marry Ninan to secure ties with Sumaq. Her mother hadn't been much better, always pinching her flesh to prove she'd been eating too much, and insisting she raise her chin to elongate her "too-short" neck.

It had taken her nineteen years of such treatment to finally take the leap, but the urge had come on strongly and suddenly once the bandits had told her of Ninan's heroic acts to save his friends, and then once she'd learned that the Sauroguard had been on its way to attack Unu. Her legs still ached from all the time she'd spent on the back of that pteranodon, flying for hours to try and warn the prince. She was grateful to have found refuge with the quya, who supplied her with good food, a comfortable bed, plenty of books, lovely clothes, and her new favorite perfume (which reminded her of her grandmother) that smelled of night-lady orchids.

Ninan rested his chin on his hand, with his elbow propped

against the gondola rim.

Paqari rolled her eyes at the prince's melancholy pose and turned her attention to the pterobeast's descent as it neared the rust-colored plaster walls of the Qhispina House castle.

They were close enough that all the details of the smilodon-mouth tunnel at the base of the castle's motte were clearly visible. The river that flowed through that tunnel glinted in the full sun, which had already warmed the air substantially.

Grassland sprawled on both sides of the castle grounds, divided by the water. A few outbuildings—a reptiliary for reptestrian training, an armory, a laboratorium—complemented the castle itself, with a stone wall separating the grounds from the land beyond.

Guards patrolled the walls, each with a pair of armored smilodons. It had been growing dark and too difficult to see them when Paqari and Ninan had arrived the previous evening, but now the sabertoothed cats stood out with their large furry bodies and their regal posture.

A minute later, the gondola connected with the paved landing circle at the top of the pteriary tower, delivering the two royalborns and the three bandits back to their original place of refuge. Upon landing, however, one of the household attendants immediately approached.

"Your Highnesses," said the woman. "I'm sorry to disturb you, but there are some people here you might be interested to see."

))))

Taking what appeared to be a late breakfast at the outdoor dining area on the balcony terrace were four individuals whom Paqari did not recognize, but with whose descriptions she was familiar enough at this point to guess their identities. Ninan had gone on about them for a good half hour yesterday.

They now sat at a table covered in a spread of oviraptor eggs, dinohyus sausages, tiny melons, and crystal glasses filled with guava juice.

There was a tall and narrow man, a tall muscular man, a young woman with shoulder-length hair, and a short man with wild eyes. All wore flyer-riding gear, with goggles around their necks or pushed up onto the tops of their heads.

"Razorclaws?" Paqari said of the unexpected guests.

"Gods in the High World." The girl stood and came to Ninan, throwing her arms around him.

"Wayra," Ninan breathed. His eyes welled as he embraced her and looked at the others over her shoulder. He must have been thinking of Sakay, Paqari realized, that the group was short a member.

"Have you been here all this time?" Wayra pulled back to look at him.

Ninan shook his head. "Only since yesterday. It's a long story. What are you doing here?"

"We were hoping to find Qora. After the citadel attack in Unu, we weren't sure where else to go."

"I guess we all had the same idea," Ninan said solemnly.

The other Razorclaws greeted Ninan in turn, the last being the largest, who only grunted his acknowledgement and offered a stiff handshake.

Wayra turned to Paqari and bowed. "Your Highness. I'm Wayra Mamani." Then she gestured at the men, one by one. "This is Kuy, Req, and Gorgo. Kuy coordinates our missions and gathers new recruits; Req is an elementalist; and Gorgo is our strong-arm."

The men bowed as well.

"It's a pleasure to meet you," said Paqari. "I hope you don't hold it against me that my father supports this war."

"And I hope you don't hold it against *us*," Wayra countered, "that we attacked your father's ally and benefactor in the Aquchay."

"If I did, I wouldn't be here."

"And neither would I," Ninan said. "The princess hired these bandits"—he indicated Kunaq, Yaku, and Tika, and stepped out of the way to introduce them—"to swoop in and disrupt the wedding before we could combine our blood for the marital vow. And then she came after me when my father advanced on the Unuvian capital, where I was staying when it happened."

"I *knew* you weren't abducted," said Req.

"Actually he *asked* to be abducted," Tika replied. "Which was a brilliant escape plan, if you ask me."

"Brilliant," Wayra agreed through a breath. "But I have to admit I never would have suspected the princess to be behind the sabotage. No offense, Your Highness."

Paqari shrugged. "I prefer it when people underestimate me. The outcome is always in my favor."

"Bandits?" Kuy returned to Ninan's earlier statement with interest, directing his attention to Kunaq. "Do you run with any particular crew?"

"We're not formally organized," Kunaq told him. "Not like you—no crew name or assigned roles. I picked up a few strays over the years, mostly kids with no place to go, and we've done what we had to, to get by. Knowing the dark underbellies of most Tisquvian major cities gave us the skills to start taking jobs for money now and then, and the fact that we don't already have a reputation makes it easier to slip past authorities' notice."

Paqari nodded at the bandit's words, remembering how she had only found out about him and his companions by following a thread of rumors. While the Tisquvian Guard had been on high alert for any activity related to *known* crime organizations, these bandits had been able to come out of nowhere and wreak havoc on the wedding with ease.

"Are you staying long?" Wayra asked the bandits.

"We're headed back to the hideout this afternoon," Tika told her.

"That's too bad," Wayra said. "We could use more people like you in our network. And Quya Urpi needs all the help she can get. It's a terrible burden to be the last Terrain standing in a war like this."

"Where is the quya, anyway?" Ninan asked.

"She went to retrieve her messages," Req explained. "Apparently she's been aggressively corresponding with potential allies since yesterday and raking in whatever news is available as far as where Qhapaq Apo might strike next—assuming he doesn't come straight for Amachakuna now. We arrived not long before you did, and she welcomed us and offered this meal with her apologies, but said she would return soon."

"Well, I'm starving," said Yaku, taking a seat at the table and serving himself a pair of dinohyus sausages.

Paqari couldn't deny that the scent of the food was making her stomach squirm in anticipation. For once there were none of her own attendants nearby to slap her hand away, or limit what she could put on her plate.

As everyone else took a seat and the Razorclaws resumed eating, Paqari joined them, listening in as they shared the details of the past couple of days—the results of the attack on the base, the hybrids that had terrorized the citadel, delivering the quinoa farmers to Wiñay.

Nearly a half hour later, the quya arrived, flanked by two attendants who followed her onto the terrace, with a pet smilodon in tow. She held a document made of thick, rolled papyr. She didn't bother with any formalities.

"I'm glad you're all here in one place," she said. "Although I'm not glad for the message I must convey."

"Your Majesty." Paqari nodded at her to continue.

"I've received word from Qhapaq Apo. He describes 'immense grief' for his 'murdered son'"—she glanced meaningfully at Ninan—"and claims that 'enemy forces' continue to 'assault' his encampments. He says that as resistance grows toward his attempts to protect the people of Runaqa with his Sauroguard, the gods have ordained him to take control of the discord throughout the Terrains by unifying them once and for all. Along with this document, he has included a cession agreement; if we do not sign, he will come for us as he did for Unu, with full force. We have one moon cycle."

Crowns of gold have sharp points,
and press heavily upon the head.

Tisquvian proverb

FIVE

NINAN GRIPPED THE EDGE OF THE TACTICAL TABLE in Quya Urpi's war room, making his knuckles pale. Paqari stood beside him, along with the Razorclaws and the bandits, with the quya and her chief marshal and other military strategists on the opposite end. A topographical map covered the large tabletop between them, with markers for several locations within the visual representation of Sumaq along its border with Unu.

Looking over the markers—which indicated a few of the military encampments where Qhapaq Apo was keeping Sauroguard reptiles—Ninan's stomach soured. Sakay had died so that they could know where to place those markers. While that information was vital, it didn't seem enough in this moment to justify the loss of him; a life for a few tiny red flags. Especially since there was no guarantee those reptiles hadn't been moved in the past forty-eight hours.

"The only reason," Urpi said, "that Apo is allowing so much time before he advances is because of the lengthy legal preparations required for a peaceful transfer of sovereignty. There is much to consider as far as determining which laws, customs, and traditions will be retained and which will be abolished. He knows that it's in his best interest to retain some of these things, to ensure a more cooperative populace as well as to continue to

34

reap the benefits of trade and resources from this region. Taking Allpa by force must be his last resort, although it's clear he would have no difficulty nor any reservations in doing so."

There was no doubt in Ninan's mind that this was true. What had happened in Unu, according to his father's additional wording in the letter, had been a "tragic but necessary sacrifice for the prosperity of the countless future generations of Runaqa." Qolqe had already signed a cession agreement, and Tisqu was in the process of becoming a protectorate (although the quya had said she suspected that the island Terrain would easily be converted to a vassal state and that Qhapaq Apo would soon gain full control of it).

With that in mind, there had barely been any discussion over whether Allpa would cede or stand and fight. While it was tempting, the idea of giving up control in order to keep the peace, everyone here knew that there would not be true peace in the New Empire. Thus, it was a matter of figuring out how to fight back without getting trampled like field mice under a herd of stampeding gallimimus.

It was going to be a delicate process, especially since Qhapaq Apo had made it clear in his terms that any aggression against his forces—attacks on bases, encampments, or on Kallpa House— would result in an immediate counterattack and occupation, and that his cession request was an act of grace and mercy for which Allpa should be exceedingly grateful.

"The Allpan Guard cannot compete," the quya continued. "Not with the Sumaqi Guard to begin with, and certainly not with the Sauroguard. We must devise a plan to overcome them by some other means. As of right now, we would need a miracle just to *survive* them. But I pray that between all your brilliant minds and mine, we can find methods to outwit them. Currently, the

Venture champion and her brother are on a mission to the Tail to seek whatever assistance our neighbors are willing to offer, particularly in the way of giant dinosaurs—although we have yet to determine how we might move or utilize them—in addition to any strategies or tactics we have not yet considered. We have also discussed the possibility of utilizing the larger theropods from southern Allpa, although they aren't substantially larger than megaraptors, and unlike the qhapaq, we know no mystical means for enhancing or accelerating reptilian growth, unless his dominite crystals have managed to accomplish that."

"I don't believe they have, Your Majesty," Wayra told her. "I believe it's a combination of aquafern for hydration retention and a concentrated nutritional diet with high levels of augendium extract. Highborn breeders use these methods sometimes, although it's considered unethical, and most—even with their money—can only afford to do it for short periods of time. The qhapaq, on the other hand, would be able to keep it up long term. But it's painful for reptiles to grow at rates like that, and even still it could take up to six months to see a significant size increase in a reptile that normally reaches full size within ten to fifteen years."

"So even if we tried to follow in his cruel footsteps," Kuy concluded, "we still wouldn't have enough time to grow our own defensive monsters."

"Right," the quya agreed. "Although we do have a significant number of trained smilodons that can provide some defense. Based on rough estimates, I would say we have about one-tenth of the Sauroguard's numbers, although we can't be sure until we perform reconnaissance."

"That's not exactly reassuring," said Paqari.

The quya nodded. "However, I've seen a single smilodon tear

through a full gang of wild velociraptors, and I also happen to know that the larger breeds can go head to head with a baryonyx and come out on top—we had a problem with illegal 'beast fights' a few years back, but the information is useful at least—so I'm confident we won't need a one-to-one ratio in that regard. But that doesn't guarantee success, of course, particularly when the Sauroguard reptiles tend to possess special features. So we must mobilize the Allpan Guard as well—every fighter we've got."

"What about your fighters on raptorback?" Paqari asked. "What will prevent the qhapaq from using his dominite to control their mounts?"

"Fool's silver," Wayra interjected. "Sakay knew someone trying to sell it as counterfeit silver, but we learned it can make reptiles resistant to dominite energy. It comes from the Qolqese desert. The megaraptors will need to ingest it."

"Excellent," said Urpi. "Let's follow up on that and obtain as much as possible. But we'll have to be discreet; with Qolqe's loyalty to Apo, they can't know what we're using it for." She gestured at the topographical map. "As far as gathering more intelligence, the champion has brought me a document listing a few Sauroguard encampments, and I've sent agents to the two locations that are likely to pose the most immediate threat: Ñansa and Wood Ridge. They'll be looking at numbers, breeds, and features."

Kuy leaned forward. "The Razorclaws can scout the other two locations, if you'd like, Your Majesty."

"Or," Yaku chimed in, after a moment of whispering with the other two bandits, "the Razorclaws can take one of the locations and we'll take the other."

Ninan furrowed his brow. "I thought you were going back to Tisqu."

"We were," said Tika, "but the more we discuss all this, the more it's clear that it's not something we can just fly away from. Now that we know for a fact that Qhapaq Apo has Tisqu as a protectorate, and that he's intent on taking Allpa, this affects everyone in Runaqa."

Kunaq gave a brief nod of agreement. "Whatever we can do to help."

"Thank you," the quya said. "In that case, the three of you will go to Kawsay, and the Razorclaws will go to Wayaqa. With all locations covered simultaneously, we can get reports back with speed and give us more time to assess the information and prepare against what's coming."

"If it's alright, though," Req said, "I would prefer to stay and share what I know of dominite with your elementalists. Qhapaq Izhi was hoping to break down the formula and recreate it for his own supply—an effort I had been working on as well, independently—and I think we should follow his example. Even more so, now that he's in hiding and his citadel is occupied by Sumaqi forces."

"What do you require?" Urpi asked. "And what do you know so far?"

"I need skyrock in the purest form you can provide, to continue testing, and a full laboratorium. So far I only know that the elements in dominite are identical to those of skyrock, reordered. I've been trying to determine the catalyst, but it could be anything—a specific temperature, another element, a magnetic field, agitation, a combination of multiple conditions—and all I can do is keep testing different environments and conditions until one of them works."

"Alright. You can stay. I'll get you set up to start working this afternoon. Anyone else? Let's utilize our strengths."

Wayra raised her hand. "Maybe I should go with the prince and princess to the Tail. Although I haven't worked with theropods of that size, I think much of my expertise on reptiles in general is adaptable, and would be useful there to figure out whether it's possible to coordinate them."

"Done. You'll leave with the royalborns first thing in the morning."

That only left Kuy and Gorgo as the "Razorclaws" but Ninan supposed they didn't need all of them just to get a basic idea of whether the encampment was operational and how many reptiles might be there.

"It's good," the quya added, "that Qora will have additional support in the Tail. As it is, I worry her plea will fall on deaf ears."

Req reached into his trouser pocket and withdrew three faintly glowing purple crystals. He re-pocketed two of them but handed the brightest one to Ninan. "Take that to her. Once the people see what it can do, they'll know she's sincere—and that this is serious."

Ninan stared into the glow, then looked back up at Req. "You're a godsend."

"I know." Req smiled flatly.

The team discussed a few more details and then Urpi said, "My legislative council will analyze the cession agreement while Marshal Hatun prepares the Allpan Guard. We will fortify our borders and major cities with every resource. As for the rest of you: You have your marching orders. Let's prepare to fight."

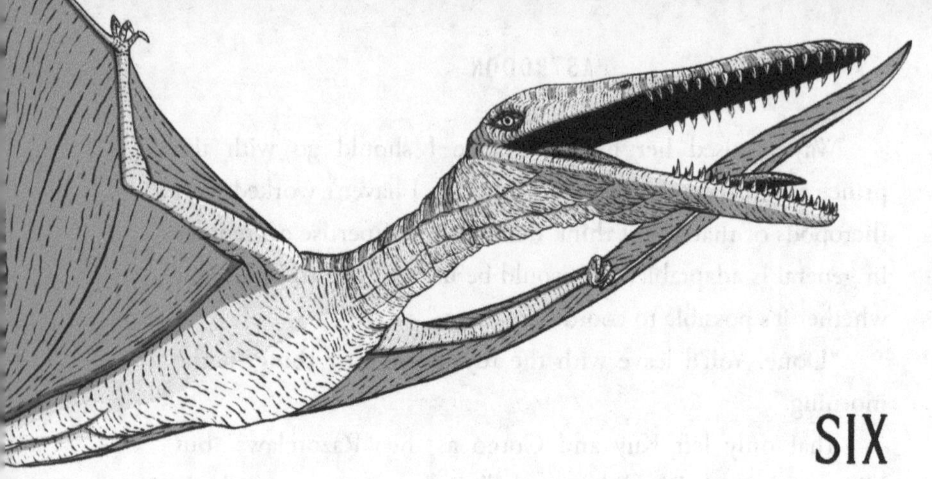

SIX

NEARLY AN HOUR PASSED and still no one would listen.

"I'm not a royalborn," Qora insisted.

"Then why did you arrive in a gondola belonging to one of the qhapaqs?" a man called from the bridge directly in front of her.

"I told you, there's a quya who's working *against* the qhapaqs. I'm helping her."

"What would a quya want with you, if you're no one important?" a woman asked with a sneer.

Qora pressed her face up to a gap in the cage. "I'm the champion of an interterrenal competition called the Venture. Competitors are required to travel through dangerous lands for weeks, seeking a prize guarded by monstrous dinosaurs. I had to fight off a spinosaurus—"

"Then this should be no problem for you," said the man in the full-length woolly coat, who appeared to be the moderator for this event. Whispers throughout the crowd implied he was called "The Penalizer."

Qora was about to say that the spinosaurus had come from these very lands when Ollan shouted, "She's barely eighteen. This is *vile*. I'll go instead!"

"It hardly matters," said the Penalizer. "Everyone in your

party will have their chance against the giga eventually. No need to squabble over who goes first or last."

"Is this seriously how you treat young women?" Ollan demanded.

"Unlike some of the people from your lands, here we do not consider either sex to be the weaker," the Penalizer told him. "Besides, we found more weapons on this girl than on any of you that we captured."

Qora remembered the way she'd filled her new green jacket with daggers and bolts. It had seemed a waste not to take advantage of every compartment that her mother had sewn in when she'd made the jacket; after all, this was wildly unfamiliar territory, and there had been no knowing for certain what would come up.

The group had even brought firesticks (similar to the ones used in the Venture to send up pyrotechnic location signals) in case they were to get separated. Now something like that seemed foolish.

"Is everyone ready to see the show?" the Penalizer shouted.

The people on the bridges and balconies cheered.

Ollan tried to scream over them but they drowned him out.

Qora's blood ran cold.

This was really happening.

Gods. The line of monsters waiting to tear into her seemed never ending—and more often than not, it wasn't the dinosaurs that were the worst of them.

Then everyone began to stomp and clap and chant in unison.

Drop! The! Cage!

Drop! The! Cage!

Drop! The! Cage!

Ollan continued to scream protests and strain the

components of his own cage, although Qora wasn't sure what he thought he would do even if he could manage to break out. He would still be high in the air on that platform, with nothing but a dangerous drop to where the giganotosaur waited. When his efforts failed him, Ollan slipped his legs through the bars so that they dangled enticingly. The giga jerked its head in Ollan's direction, sniffing the air and taking a step toward him.

"Ollan, don't—" Qora started.

But before she could say another word, the Penalizer loosened the control rope and dropped her cage. She braced herself to crash, but the cage stopped several feet short of the ground with a violent jerk. Qora gasped when the giga's face swept into view. Thankfully its arms weren't as long as a spinosaur's, but they weren't short like a tyrannosaur's either. It swatted at the cage, claws coming between bars at Qora's shoulder.

The swatting motion sent the cage swinging away, at which point Qora scrambled to the far side of it, leaving more space between her and the bars that separated her from the giga.

Before the cage swung back, the giga had already parted its enormous jaws.

Qora cringed and shrieked as the jaws came down on the bars, cutting through the wood with ease, the giga's hot breath flowing over her. Its fangs were each more than a foot long, dripping with saliva, mere inches from impaling her—but once again its force against the cage sent Qora swinging backward.

The giga roared as though this were horribly inconvenient.

With only seconds to make her move, Qora scrambled toward the new opening, crawling to the outside of the cage and pulling herself up to the top, where she grabbed hold of the suspending rope just as the cage swung like a pendulum and returned to the giga's vicinity.

Spectators shouted—encouragements, in some cases, but mostly insults—and stomped in rhythm. Ollan continued shouting and trying to claw his way out of his cage to distract the very indifferent giganotosaur.

But Qora didn't have a chance to dwell on any of that as she planted her feet on the top of the cage and braced her entire body against the rope.

The giga snapped its jaws at her but only took another chunk out of the cage before Qora shifted her weight to change the direction of the swinging arc and lengthen it until the amplitude allowed her to get close to a set of climbing holds attached to one of the adjacent trees.

She reached out.

Her fingers brushed the handhold but she couldn't grasp it.

The giga swatted and snapped at her again as she swung across its path. And once again she shifted her weight to increase the amplitude, swinging herself harder to reach the climbing holds.

This time she could feel the energy building. She could do it—she was certain.

But this time, the giga gave chase, stomping after the swinging cage and snapping at her from directly behind.

The climbing holds came within reach.

She gripped one of them with all the strength she could muster.

She released the rope and the cage, letting both fall to the giga's jaws and splinter between them as she gripped a second handhold.

She scraped the soles of her boots against the bark seeking purchase until both feet came down separately and gracelessly on other protrusions to stabilize her.

Panting, she spared a glance over her shoulder to see the giga crushing the remnants of the cage beneath its enormous feet. It roared at her audacity—and so did the spectators.

Suddenly a group of additional, uniformed people pushed through to the front of one of the balconies, all wearing long-sleeved green tunics and woolly vests, with wood-carved medallions strung around their necks and each bearing strange gauntlet-mounted weapons on one wrist.

One man in particular headed up the group, holding up a hand as if to try and silence the cacophony, although few paid attention. He observed the scene, eyebrows knit together.

The Penalizer shouted down at Qora. "Your resilience is impressive. At this point, I would like to offer you a weapon, to see whether you can withstand the giga even longer."

Qora climbed higher on the holds until she was positioned above the giga's head, but that didn't stop the reptile from snapping its jaws at her feet.

Would these people really allow her a weapon?

She shouldn't have been surprised. What was it about humankind that made them so eager for bloodsport? Not only to send others off to the mouths of monsters, but to watch them desperately try to escape? Her chest heaved and her heart hammered and her veins seemed to be filled with fire.

She'd be a fool not to use a weapon if she was allowed one. And yet …

Memories of the spinosaur spilled into her mind—the way she and Ninan had stood on the ruins barely out of its reach, the way her bolts had gotten stuck between its thick scales without penetrating them, the way she had dropped to the ground and the reptile had locked its eyes on her ready to charge, the way she had known there would be only one place her bolts might actually break through.

Remembering the sight of the blinded spinosaur sent waves of nausea through her belly. She'd had a weapon that day, and what had she done with it? Protected herself and Ninan, sure, but she'd also gone against everything she believed when it came to her treatment of the reptiles—or any creatures, for that matter—in the wild. What she had done was inhumane. Cruel. Despicable. Not a quick and painless death, but a prolonged torture.

"No," she bit out. "I won't accept your weapons."

The leader of the uniformed group whispered something to his companions.

"One of your own, then, perhaps?" The Penalizer offered.

Qora shook her head.

She almost regretted it when the giga's teeth scraped her heels, but she quickly drew up her legs and clung more fiercely to the tree.

"I need you to believe me when I say I only came here with good intentions," she told him. "That spinosaur that I fought in the Venture … I believe it came from the Tail. You know the Terrains have stolen your eggs before—and that won't be the last they steal from you. We have the same enemy, and when he comes for you, your meganeuras and your flying contraptions won't be enough to stop him. A war is already raging, and the qhapaq who started it won't stop until he controls every square inch of land on this continent!"

Finally the crowds quieted enough that Qora didn't have to shout at full volume.

But Ollan took over with, "You think you're better than those monsters up north?" He'd managed to snap one of the cage bars and was working on another as he spoke. "You're just like them, sacrificing people for sport! You're bloodthirsty monsters, and if you don't listen to us, you deserve what you get!"

This incited the people to uproar again, some of them hurling random objects at Ollan's cage along with their curses and swears.

For a moment, Qora closed her eyes, trying to block out the noise, to concentrate on her breathing, to think of what to do next. As she did, the tree trunk shook. Warily, she glanced down. The giga thrust its head against the tree, rattling the sprigs of green needles, pressuring the wood of the structure built onto it above where Qora clung. Another thrust made Qora slip.

She scratched at the bark as she slid down, scraping her arms. Snagging on several of the climbing holds—although she was unable to fully grip them—slowed her fall, with timing that sent her tumbling to the forest floor just after the giga had drawn back in preparation for another strike against the tree. On her back, she gazed up at the towering beast. She crawled backwards on her elbows, although it was no use to try and get out of harm's way now.

Her heart seized as the giga's jaws widened over her and came down.

She covered her face with her forearms as tears of defeat formed in her eyes.

Then a high-pitched, almost inaudible noise struck her ears.

The giga raised its head and roared for a moment, turning toward the sound.

Qora gasped for breath and peered between her arms, catching a glimpse of the uniformed leader leaning over the balcony, with his wooden medallion pressed to his lips. It was then that Qora realized it wasn't a medallion—or at least not *just* a medallion—but an instrument not unlike what those people had used when the gondola had first arrived, to entice the pterobeast to follow them and land.

Everyone groaned and booed the man.

"Gladewarden Sacha!" The Penalizer shouted from his separate balcony. "This is a blatant violation of my penalizing authority."

The giga stood and waited, to Qora's utter shock, and she slowly got to her feet.

This "gladewarden"—whatever that was—lowered his instrument and shook his head. "You've taken this too far. I think the girl has proven she's no threat to us. Besides ... I have questions for the foreigners. And I can't ask them anything if they're dead."

⟫⟫⟫

Gladewardens—what seemed to be members of some sort of local peacekeeping organization—ushered Qora and her brother and their three companions to a different area several bridge-lengths away from the giganotosaur site, and then into a structure that spanned the distance across eight trees. The structure was the equivalent of a municipal building Qora might have seen in Qhusi, Sumaq's capital, where legal matters or city meetings might occur, only it was mounted high up near the canopy.

The gladewardens separated Qora from Ollan, and Ollan from the others, to "question them individually," leaving Qora alone with the one whose instrumental sound had saved her at the last second. Gladewarden Sacha, the Penalizer had called him.

Qora waited numbly with her arms wrapped around herself, scrapes bleeding, in a large room with a wooden floor and wooden walls and a high ceiling that had several shafts open to the sky to let the light in. Despite what she'd just experienced, her attention fell to the gauntlet-mounted weapon on the gladewarden's wrist. It was like a miniature crossbow with no stock, and with what would have been a foregrip that instead ran along a bracer on his forearm. There was a sort of lever on it, and a bar that extended forward at an angle and came around the front of the gladewarden's hand, something he could grip in a fist—a trigger, perhaps.

"What's your name?" said the gladewarden.

"Qora," she told him.

"Just 'Qora'?"

"Qora Kanchaya."

"Nice to meet you. I'm Kondor Sacha. And where in the Five Terrains do you come from, specifically?"

"Do you know the Terrains well enough for that to matter?" She said it flatly, not quite defiantly, unsure why she would risk provoking the man who had kept her from being bitten in half by a dinosaur. Despite whatever mercy Kondor had shown, she supposed she was still angry over being forced to relive one of her worst nightmares.

"We've got maps here. We know the basics of the landscape, the general industries of each region. But mainly, I'm just curious. I need to know everything about you."

She stared up into his strange eyes, analyzing their grayish tone. His skin was so pale, but not in a sickly way; this seemed to simply be its natural color, and lightly flushed at the cheeks from the chill in the air. She guessed he was in his early twenties and that he likely stood close to six feet tall. His wavy, light brown hair was cut short although it was long enough to tuck behind his ears, and he had the shadow of a beard along his jaw.

Finally, she said, "I'm from Sumaq. Is this how you handle

everyone who happens to stumble onto your land? Throw them to the reptiles?"

"You hardly 'stumbled onto' it in your royal gondola. Not to mention you were all armed, from what I'm told, and with uniformed guards. Anyway, it wasn't on my authority, or the authority of the gladewardens in general. It was our border patrol that apprehended you. But we do have a treaty," Kondor reminded her.

"A treaty that neither I, nor my brother, nor our guards or pilot, violated. We came peacefully. We took nothing. We didn't even have the chance to seek a landing spot before we were rerouted from the air."

"We've seen your royalborn gondolas before," he explained. "Nothing good has ever come from one of those. The patrol was being vigilant."

"What happened to the people who came from the Five Terrains before?"

He raised an eyebrow. "I think you know."

"You fed them to that giga?"

He shrugged. "One of the gigas. Or a spino. Sometimes a tyrannosaur, although people don't find it quite as sporting when the arms don't reach the cage."

"You're despicable. All of you." It might have been people working for Qhapaq Apo, sure, but it wasn't about whether they deserved it; it was about the people here taking such pleasure in watching others die like that.

"Hey—I stopped it, remember? I'm not a fan of that process. I'm a gladewarden; I prefer a much more methodical approach to dealing with intruders, which is why I'm questioning you right now instead of letting the giga finish you off."

"So even with gladewardens to enforce the law, the Penalizer can just do whatever he wants?"

"If border patrol hands over a criminal, yes. Basically. Once that process has occurred, it's a bit unconventional for me to interfere, although I have the right to question his judgment if I choose, so I did."

"Because you felt sorry for me?"

"In part. I can't say watching a young girl get chewed up in front of me doesn't rub me the wrong way. I would have stopped it regardless. But what really got me was the fact that you didn't accept a weapon."

Qora scoffed. "What's that got to do with anything?"

He sighed and gestured for her to sit. She glanced behind her at a long bench and, after a moment, took a seat as instructed.

Kondor pulled up a heavy chair and took a seat facing her. "This is the thing your people don't seem to understand."

"What thing?"

"Even if you had said yes, the Penalizer wouldn't have given you anything to fight back with."

"So it was a trick, then."

"A test," he clarified. "We don't harm the dinosaurs here, Qora Kanchaya. For all intents and purposes, we treat them better than we do ourselves. We don't hunt or eat them. We don't use them for labor. We don't even ride them recreationally. They're sacred. Practically gods—which is why nobody had a problem sacrificing you to one of them."

Qora frowned. "Your faith in my word is based on my refusal to use a weapon against the giganotosaur?"

"Right."

She wondered what he would say if she told him how things had ended with the spinosaur. Or how many rhamphos and troodons she'd taken home for meat over the years. "But you know I come from a place where dinosaurs are *not* sacred. Certain things that I've done would be considered a serious crime to you." Surely he understood that she was not without dinosaur blood on her hands in some form or another.

"I believe you showed a sense of integrity, regardless. Enough to earn you the opportunity to be heard, at least. Anyway, I'm not a fanatic like a lot of my community. Some of us hold more progressive views. There's an entire movement in favor of utilizing the dinosaurs, arguing that it can be done in an ethical way that still holds them in high regard *and* can improve our industries. Personally, I don't put much stock in religion in general, let alone one that considers reptiles our superiors. Respect the earth, respect the animals, respect others; that's what I believe. But there are nuances, and I'm not here to tell you what will happen to your soul. You do have to be careful what you say to anyone else around here, though."

"I've already said everything I came to say. The whole continent—including the Tail—is in danger, but if you help us fight, my qhapaq's war won't ever come close to touching your land or your people. Or your sacred dinosaurs."

Kondor chuckled. "Help you fight?" He folded his arms and chuckled again. "How would we do that? Our numbers are nothing compared to even your smallest Terrain. All we have for battle weapons are wooden bows. We wouldn't know the first thing about war; we're not a violent people."

Not violent? The blood on her own arms and cheeks said otherwise. Qora narrowed her eyes at him.

"I didn't say they don't have a savage sense of justice," he added. "But if we're being technical, the *giganotosaur* was the one who attacked you. So unless you want *him* to help you fight, there's not much we can do for you."

With a dead-serious glare, Qora replied, "That's exactly what I want."

Still mid-chuckle from his own joke, he suddenly went silent. "Sorry—what?"

"I want the giganotosaur. And all his friends. Whatever allosaurs, tyrannosaurs, or spinosaurs you have on hand. I didn't come here to ask for your people to fight on the front lines; I came for permission to use your reptiles, and for any aid you're willing to provide in transporting the reptiles to Allpa."

Kondor gaped at her. "Kid, I think you hit your head too hard when you fell down from that tree. Did you not hear anything I said? My people would die a thousand deaths before they'd let you turn their dinosaurs into weapons in a war between nations they despise. They'll drop you from another cage just for asking, and I won't be able to stop it this time. That's not even considering the fact that herding giant theropods over the Pirqas—or any long distance—would be damn near impossible."

"I have some ideas for the logistics of moving the dinosaurs."

He threw up his hands. "Well, in that case ..."

Qora sighed and leaned forward. "Look, if your people are so concerned with dinosaur treatment, then you should know my qhapaq has made an abomination of every reptile he's been able to get his hands on. He's bred thousands of them with ungodly mutations, and he's developed a way to control and enslave them as his personal army. That alone should stir your people to fight."

"A dinosaur *army*?" Kondor tilted his head analytically at her. "Seriously, you must be concussed."

"Fine. Don't believe me. But Qhapaq Apo knows you have resources; that much is clear or he wouldn't have sent people down here to take samples from you—which you know he did, because you told me you threw them to your theropods. My guess is he wants your big dinosaurs' marrow, for its rapid healing properties. He'll bring his reptile army to take over the Tail, and then you'll see I'm not lying. By then, it will be too late."

"Again: Treaty."

"Sure, the treaty between the Tail and the Five Terrains. There won't be any treaty between you and the *new empire* he creates once he's taken all the Terrains for himself. He's only got one left to go."

Kondor groaned and rubbed the stubble along his jaw, then pressed his lips together and stared at her for a moment.

"You can wait for him to show up," Qora told him, "or you can listen to me and prepare your people in advance. Better yet, you can help us fight this war on Allpan soil so it never reaches your trees."

"Let's say I'm taking you seriously," said Kondor. "Even if you're right and we're in danger, I'm not someone who can do anything about it. I'm a senior gladewarden for the local outfit here in Murkroot—that's it. My job is to keep the peace, not make decisions about international conflict."

"So who has a say in these kinds of things?"

"You'd have to talk to the elderboughs. The council of eight that governs the Tail. Assuming the chief gladewarden of Murkroot agrees to let you and your companions go free after questioning. The council operates in the Verdant Reach."

"How do I get there?"

"It's half a day away on foot. Not to mention they're going to think you're crazy, if they'll agree to meet with you at all."

"I'm guessing you won't let me use the pterobeast I came in with to fly there? Because of 'ethical' reasons?"

"First of all, it's dinosaurs that are sacred, not pterosaurs— we do eat pterosaurs on occasion—and if we had any as big as yours down here, we might use them for transport like you do. Secondly, if you think the reaction to your flight arrival was bad before, you don't want to know what the Verdant Reach sentries will do to you. The elderboughs are highly protected, and if it looks like you somehow managed to force your way past border patrol to get further inland, they'll deem you highly aggressive and shoot you down on sight. And our archers are no joke."

"What about one of your winged contraptions?"

"You mean the skykes? None holds more than one person, and training to fly them safely takes weeks."

She nodded her understanding and stood. "On foot it is."

"Limbs above …" Kondor remarked. "You don't even know the area."

"Then give me a map. Or a guide, if someone's willing. I can pay, if my golds are any good to you."

"They're not. Our economy is trade based and only for certain types of goods. As far as metal, gold is too soft to be useful to us."

Qora bit her lip. "So, no map, then?"

Rolling his eyes, Kondor stood to match her, looking down at her. "I'll talk to the chief gladewarden on your behalf—if for no other reason than to make you fully understand that your mission here is futile. That's the best I can do."

"I accept."

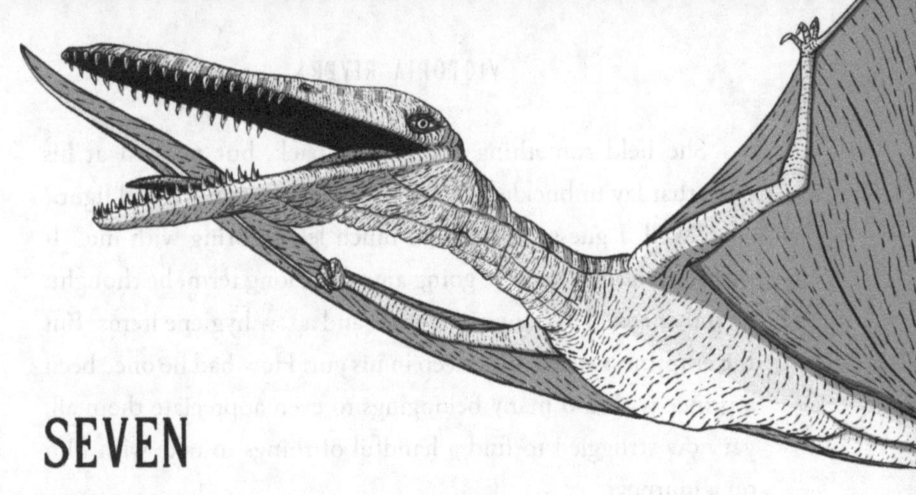

SEVEN

WAKING NOISES BEGAN TO FILL THE GUEST CORRIDOR of Qhispina House before the sun had so much as peeked up over the eastern horizon. Ninan groaned and rolled over in the large bed, wanting to remain inside the canopied darkness for the next six months rather than get up and face everything that was coming.

His mind had spun restlessly in his dreams. The dreams had been vague and hard to remember, but they'd managed to keep him from a full recovery of his energy. Still, despite Ninan's fatigue, his heart raced at the thought of seeing Qora soon, and that was enough to jolt him to action.

Attendants had already lit the corridor sconces, filling the space with golden light. The Razorclaws and bandits popped into one another's rooms, made conversation, and prepared their saddlebags for travel.

Ninan only had what had been packed into the saddlebag before the raid on Kallpa House—a half-empty cannon of hushdust, some rope, a few small tools and weapons—and the new clothes that the staff here had provided him when he'd arrived with Paqari. As he stared at the scant personal belongings, Paqari rapped her knuckles on the frame of his open bedroom door.

She held something behind her back, but nodded at his pack that lay unbuckled on the bed. "You certainly travel light."

"Well, I guess I don't have much left to bring with me." It wasn't as though he were going anywhere long term, he thought; he only needed a change of clothes and a few hygiene items. But the emptiness struck him deep in his gut. How had he once been a prince with too many belongings to even appreciate them all, yet now struggled to find a handful of things to take with him on a journey?

"Hmm," said the princess. "Maybe I can help with that."

She came forward and laid two things on the bedspread: a white dagger and a small guitar—his charango.

Just like that, Ninan's eyes welled. He ran his fingertips over the albino dilophosaur dinoleather that sheathed the serrated-tooth blade his mother had given him before the Venture. Then he picked up the charango, with the domed sound box and its carved scaly texture against his chest while he plucked the strings. After half a melancholy melody, he put a flat hand on the strings directly over the mouth—which had a circle of pearled teeth around the rim—to silence it, and looked at Paqari. "How did you get these?"

"You left them in your room at Huapaya House. Before the wedding. Remember?"

Of course, he thought. As far as he had known that day, that's where he would have been living for the foreseeable future.

"After you made your escape," she added, "most people believed you'd been abducted, but some thought you might have been responsible for the attack—that you were working directly with the 'pirates.' My father was going to order a search of your things to look for evidence. But I got there first."

Ninan shook his head. "I can't believe you did that for me."

"I meant what I said when I told you that neither of us is alone in the burdens we bear as royalborns. There are things about my life that only someone like you could ever understand, and the same for you with me. And … perhaps I felt a certain sense of guilt over the blame placed on you when I was the one to hire the bandits."

"*There* it is."

She rolled her eyes. "Anyway. I'm glad I could lift your spirits with these … keepsakes."

"Thank you," he told her. "You have no idea what this means to me. If I liked you better, I'd kiss you."

"We barely dodged that requirement as it is," she replied with a grimace. "Don't sour my stomach before I've even had breakfast."

))))

Ninan of course wouldn't be taking the charango with him—he would leave it within the safety of Qhispina House— but he packed the dagger, happy to have a piece of his mother with him. He only wished he could talk to her, send her a letter at least. But he couldn't risk it. If nothing else, he knew she was under the protection of the marital blood oath between her and his father. With that, she couldn't be punished for Ninan's crimes, even though she'd been the one to bear him.

After everyone had gathered their necessary supplies and eaten a few bites of the spread of food the quya's culinarium had provided, they began to load up the flyers at the top of the pteriary. The bandits each prepared their individual pteranodons, as did Kuy and Gorgo, while Ninan, Paqari, and Wayra waited for a pterobeast gondola. Packs contained mostly clothing, travel food, and weapons. Paqari, however, had also asked permission to borrow a few books from Quya Urpi, one of which she was flipping through while the handlers finished attaching gondola straps to the pterobeast's harness.

Highways in the Sky: A Study on Bird Migration Patterns was embossed on the cover with gold foil lettering.

"Of all the books you could have chosen, you pick something dry like that," Ninan mused.

She had access to the quya's vast library and yet she chose to read something that sounded like a scholastic requirement for a post-secondary field of study.

Paqari didn't look up from the page. "I actually read this one a few years ago. It was a different edition, but equally fascinating. Some birds sleep in the air—did you know? They can 'lock' their wings and simply glide for hours without expending energy. Others eat enough to double or triple their body weight before seasonal departures."

Ninan quirked a brow. "Didn't you say something last night about looking for a 'light read'? I thought you'd picked up one of those fictional suspense novels instead. *The Shadows of Laqu?*"

"*The Shadows of Laqha,*" she corrected. "And I did. But I finished it."

"When?"

"After I went to my room. Sometimes I like to read by lantern light in bed. It helps me relax and fall asleep."

"Wasn't that book some sort of murder mystery?"

The princess shrugged. "What does that matter?"

Ninan could only stare at her with a concerned expression.

Wayra laughed and said, "Leave her alone. A woman's taste in literature is not up for judgment. Anyway, I might want to take a look at *Highways in the Sky* when she's done with it." She looked to Paqari for approval. "If you don't mind, of course."

"I don't mind in the least. I suppose I shouldn't be surprised, considering your work with reptiles. You know, birds and theropod dinosaurs are said to have a common ancestor."

"Pterosaurs, too," said Wayra. "Although that must be obvious from the wings."

"If you want to take a look at this one in the meantime"—Paqari withdrew another book from her pack, titled *The Realm of the Fierce*—"it's about apex predators. I also borrowed this one that catalogues and describes carnivorous plants, and another suspense novel." She held up *Raptorial Green* and *The Haunting of Pteroclaw Heights*.

Wayra grinned and accepted *The Realm of the Fierce*.

Paqari waved the other two in front of Ninan. "It wouldn't hurt you to fill your mind with something other than angst."

After a moment, he released a huff and snatched *Raptorial Green* from her and allowed the attendants to usher him into the gondola. The young women filtered in behind him.

Req had come to see everyone off.

They all bid each other farewell and godsspeed. Ninan didn't want to think about whether they would see one another again; at this point, there was always a possibility that they wouldn't, but in order to preserve his sanity he blocked it out of his mind. Right now, he could only focus on his current task: getting this dominite crystal to Qora and securing the assistance of the Tail.

)))

Despite being a royalborn and having traveled to many places over the years, Ninan was certain he had never spent so much time in the air—or covered so much ground—as he had in the past month, even worse in the past few days alone. Multiple hours of flight was starting to seem normal.

In the early stages of this particular flight, he enjoyed some of the Allpan scenery, with the continued stretches of grassland leading up to the foothills of the Pirqas, which were rough and rocky and as big as some of the Willkapampa Mountains extending from Qhusi northward. There were only a few visible passes through the Pirqas, mostly on the eastern and western sides where the peaks were smaller, and they looked treacherous. The small city of Tukukuq lay just south of the pass on the west side, which then led to a clear route that Ninan assumed had been created for pilgrimages to the famed Mount Wiru.

It was somewhere around this part of the journey that he finally cracked open *Raptorial Green* and read about pitcher plants that could lure insects and small animals with an intoxicating scent, leading them to fall into a vessel full of digestive enzymes. He shuddered.

While he was grateful that Paqari had had this voracious appetite for knowledge, as it had been helpful in deciphering the botanical clues that had led Izhi and the Razorclaws to the Sauroguard base on Tisqu Isle, some of it was much more disturbing than he'd expected.

Deeper still into the Allpan south, they flew over open spaces full of large theropods. Wayra stared down at them, remarking on their sizes and colors. They were only half to three-quarters as big as the Venture spinosaurus, Ninan could say with certainty (having stood in the shadow of that beast more times than he cared to admit) but remarkable nonetheless.

After that he nodded off, half-waking repeatedly as his head drooped toward his chest and startled him back to consciousness.

When the group was close enough to see Mount Wiru,

Wayra shook Ninan and pointed up ahead.

Instantly Ninan went to the far edge of the gondola to observe, standing and bracing himself on one of the harness ropes.

The far-off, soft-pointed peaks showed distinct bands of color—like a woven cloth. He focused as the pterobeast neared the site and tried to pick out as many colors as he could.

Brownish red, then a slightly purer and more vibrant red. Pale, dusty green. Golden yellow. Faded pink. White. Beige.

"Gods, it's beautiful," whispered Ninan.

"I don't understand why the people make such a long trek from Tukukuq," said Paqari, who had put her book down for a moment. "Why don't they just build a city *here*."

Ninan was surprised she didn't launch into a lecture on the mountain's mineral composition.

"Probably because a city would ruin it," said Wayra. "You know how people can be."

"It's been declared sacred ground," Ninan told them. "I heard one of the Allpan diplomats mention that once. Although I've never seen it in person until today. Now I understand why they keep it isolated from civilization. Wayra's right; people would ruin it."

Getting closer, groups of people had made camp along its outskirts, stopping short of the mountain itself. Some seemed to have gone merely to view the incredible sight, while others appeared to be kneeling in prayer toward it. Ninan couldn't remember all the details of the legend that explained the beautiful phenomenon, but he knew it had something to do with discord among the early inhabitants of the earth, and how Sky Mother and Light Father had come together and gathered the earth spirits at this otherwise desolate mountain to infuse it with these hues as a symbol of harmony and peace.

Now more than ever, he thought, the world—at least *his* world—needed peace and harmony. He wasn't one to hold much faith, of course, in the vague entities that many people believed were in control of humankind; he couldn't understand the logic in a force that supposedly governed everything and yet simultaneously seemed to allow everything to run rampant. Qora, however, had that sort of faith. He recalled the night she'd shown him her glowing mushrooms, considering them a gift from Sky Mother. "Sky Mother looks after us," she had said.

Ninan remained fully alert from this point onward. Passing Mount Wiru meant that they were more than halfway to the border, and soon they would fly over the Q'aytucha Isthmus that connected the rest of Runaqa to the small peninsula in the south.

He tried to distract himself again using the book—*Found in nutrient-poor environments like acidic bogs, sandy soils, or tropical rainforests, these plants have evolved to extract nutrients from unlikely sources*—but all he could think of was Qora, whether she had made it safely to the Tail, whether there had been any delays or conflicts, whether the people had been receptive to her. It wasn't enough to know that she'd made it out of the Aquchay and to Qhispina House alive; he needed to see her in person, to touch her face. He reached into his pocket and felt the edges of the dominite crystal, eager to reveal to the people of the Tail what was at stake.

During the final hour or so of flight, the grasses below turned greener and more lush, and trees began to dot the ground—small deciduous trees, and then conifers too—and soon those trees grew closer together in bunches and larger clusters, until the way ahead was predominantly evergreen forest with increasing density the further one looked outward. The elevation varied, with rare sections of rock protruding from the canopy—the only places where trees did not dominate every surface. Across the distance, several wooden platforms appeared to be floating above the trees, too, although Ninan imagined they must be attached to structures that dipped between branches below to hold them up.

What was more, Ninan realized, was that the trees here were significantly taller than any he had ever seen, and much more robust. It was difficult to tell for sure from this height, but he would have guessed that they were easily taller than any dinosaur known to exist, including any sauropods and their exceedingly long necks.

On both sides of the green, the oceans glistened, taking up more of the view as the edges of the continent curved inward to a narrow neck.

"This is it," said the gondola pilot.

Everyone was standing now, bracing the gondola rim and staring out with rapt attention.

"The isthmus is less than three miles wide," Paqari informed them. "There's been talk of cutting a canal for centuries, but it's never been done. No one seems to think it's worth the effort or expense just to save a bit of time."

"Well it's not really near any major oceanic trade routes," Ninan said. "And Runaqa is a relatively small continent. It's hardly in anyone's way."

"I'm sure the people of the Tail were resistant to the canal," said Wayra.

Paqari cocked her head. "If there *were* a canal, I'd guess it would be right about …" She leaned over the rim a bit, waiting for the gondola to progress forward, then drew an imaginary line in the air over the narrowest strip of land. "Here."

And that imaginary line would have been the official border

between Allpa and the Tail.

Not ten seconds later, a mass of small flyers emerged from the treetops. No—*flying creatures*, but not flyers. Ninan flinched at their sudden appearance, particularly as they rose higher and came close to the gondola.

Wayra ducked at first, then slowly raised herself back up, relaxing as the creatures settled into a peaceful flight in parallel. "What are they?"

"Our approach may have startled them out of their nests," said the pilot. "But … I'm not sure what they are."

Ninan observed their features. They each possessed two pairs of wings—translucent ones, that shimmered with each wingbeat. Their bodies were long and narrow, thicker at the front and tapering slightly down the length.

Insects, Ninan thought. They were like enormous insects. *Enormous dragonflies.*

"They're meganeuras," said Paqari.

They emitted a soft, crackling hum as they moved through the air.

The meganeuras were quite a sight, but Ninan had a sinking feeling in his stomach, watching the way they surrounded the gondola. The pterobeast that carried the group paid them no notice, soaring yards above them all.

Paqari shrugged. "They're probably curious. I'm sure they don't see gondolas often—or pterobeasts. As far as I know, there won't be any flyers as large as ours down here, so they must be trying to figure out what it is, whether it's a threat."

That made sense, Ninan supposed. Pterobeasts were bred by the Old Empire to be magnificent and fierce and gigantic, and certainly weren't found that way in nature. But the purplish meganeuras didn't seem intimidated by this pterobeast at all.

"They're gorgeous," Wayra admitted, a bit wary in her stance but stretching out to get a better look at them. "Look how they sparkle."

It was then that Ninan fixated on the meganeuras' wings, observing that they had a sort of dusting of iridescent particles on the surface.

"Wait." Paqari squinted. "Those are …"

The meganeuras drew closer to the gondola passengers, maintaining an eerie circular formation.

"Spores!" Paqari instantly covered her mouth and nose.

Not fully understanding but also not doubting her expertise, Ninan and Wayra covered their own noses and mouths just as the crackling hum around them cut to silence with a snap.

The shimmering particles discharged into the air, forming a cloud that engulfed the passengers.

The pilot and guards, who had not protected their airways, coughed and sneezed, trying to waft away the cloud, which had already begun to dissipate under the force of the pterobeast's wingflaps and quick movement through the air.

Everyone waited to see what would happen.

A moment passed, and then the pilot gazed around at the others with a witless half-grin, while the guards looked at one another with bleary eyes and furrowed brows.

Wayra dared to uncover her lower face. "What's … going on?"

Ninan waved a hand in front of the pilot, but the pilot reacted with only a brief flick of his eyes and then continued to stare dreamily at nothing.

"They're under the influence." Paqari took a guard by the shoulders and shook her gently, snapping twice for attention, but to no avail.

"You said those were *spores?*" Ninan glanced backward at

their flight path as though he might see remnants of the particles still floating back there. A few of them caught the light just right, but were faint and few now. The meganeuras seemed to have returned to wherever they'd come from.

Paqari nodded. "From a bristle fungus called xyloscale. The meganeuras' wings have a certain magnetic quality ... something to do with electrical charge that they control through a fluid in their wing-veins ... that can hold the spores and later disperse them at will as a defense mechanism. The xyloscale spores allow the meganeuras to protect themselves, and the meganeuras spread the spores so that the xyloscale can reproduce. I had only seen ink-drawings in ecological works—so you'll forgive my delay in identifying what I was looking at—but the spores clearly have a stupefying effect." She gestured at the pilot, who had slumped down to the gondola floor and didn't seem to know fully where he was. "I believe it's fatal to certain animals. I hope that's not the case for humans."

A high-pitched sound—subtle, barely audible—rang in Ninan's ear, prompting him to turn toward it. When he did, another set of wings—flat and pale and geometrically cut—began to ease upward into his view, carrying a sort of wooden framework controlled by a young man whose feet worked at a set of rotary pedals. The man held a wood-carved whistle between his lips.

"What in the Five Terrains ..." Ninan whispered.

On the opposite side of the gondola, another man emerged in a similar contraption.

Wayra and Paqari screamed.

"Looks like a few didn't inhale!" said the second man.

The first ignored him, however, blowing his whistle again.

For some reason the pterobeast veered to follow the sound as the man changed course and led it down into the trees.

Wayra's eyes went wide with understanding: That sound was stimulating the pterobeast somehow, enticing it. She brought her hands together to form a sound chamber, interlacing specific fingers to control pitch and timbre, then blew forcefully into them to emit the simulation of a pterobeast call.

Again, the pterobeast shifted its flight path in response.

But as the man continued to use his whistle, the pterobeast favored the higher pitch, ignoring Wayra.

"They're trying to take us somewhere," Paqari said. "The meganeuras were supposed to subdue us. But the three of us, at least, can fight back." She cast an exasperated look at the guards and pilot, all of whom were sitting dazed at their charges' feet.

It wasn't lost on Ninan that he and Wayra would be in the same position, were it not for Paqari's quick assessment of the situation before the spores had dispersed.

Then a wave of nausea hit him.

Qora.

If this was some kind of border patrol assigned to capture foreigners, that meant Qora and Ollan had probably been met with the same treatment. He gripped one of the harness ropes to steady himself against his dizzying thoughts.

Was this really how the people of the Tail reacted to anyone who crossed their borders? If that were the case, Ninan was certain they would not respond kindly to a request for help. They might even—

He swallowed hard to fight back the bile that crept up his throat.

Assault. Torture. Kill.

Paqari grabbed his face and forced him to look at her. "Hey. I know what you're thinking. But Qora doesn't go down easy;

you know that."

Gathering himself, he nodded. "You're right. And I can't go down easy either."

"*That's* the Ninan we need right now," she told him. "Stay focused."

He lifted a crossbow from the male guard and aimed it, zoning in on one of the flying contraptions. Wayra followed his example and readied the female guard's crossbow beside him as the pterobeast took the gondola into a descent.

Together, they began to shoot.

The contraption's wings—although they could hardly be called wings, as they were more like very taut sails, or kite skins— were quite large, blocking Ninan's and Wayra's view of the pilots, who now flew side by side as they led the pterobeast onward.

But the bolts punctured the material of those wings, at least. As new holes emerged from each shot, the contraptions began to wobble and lose altitude quickly. What had been a smooth descent quickly became turbulent.

Despite the inconvenience, the first man continued to blow his whistle, luring the pterobeast downward.

"Ruck," Ninan muttered. "We're still going down with them."

The treetops came level with the gondola, which dropped into a clearing behind the contraption pilots. The contraptions landed with hasty and ungraceful maneuvers, one of them full-on crashing into the surrounding trees—but its pilot leapt from the seat before impact and rolled onto the ground.

A dozen uniformed people—rangers of some sort, Ninan figured—waited below. Ninan only had a flash of a second to take in the fact that many had pale physical features, and that they all wore bluish-gray military-type fatigues and held recurve bows at the ready.

The second the gondola touched down, Ninan climbed out and lunged at the first fallen pilot. Ninan picked up the man by the fabric of his jumpsuit uniform and maneuvered him into a reverse chokehold (which doubled as a human shield). Then he drew out his serrated-tooth dagger and held it to the man's neck.

"Stand down," Ninan told the rangers. "Or your friend dies."

His heart pounded furiously as he faced the heads of a dozen arrows. He pressed the dagger's serrations gently into the flesh of the man's neck, and hoped no one knew just how badly he was bluffing.

The other rangers had stashed their weapons in favor of capturing Wayra, Paqari, the two guards, and the gondola pilot, and tending to the second fallen contraption pilot. The gondola pilot and two guards complied with dazed expressions, while Paqari scowled at her captor but didn't fight him, and Wayra struggled against hers while shouting, "Get your hands *off* of me!"

A woman who appeared to be in charge of the rangers shouted at the contraption pilots: "How did this happen, wingmen? They're *all* supposed to be tranced!"

The "wingman" that was not in Ninan's grasp simply sighed and said, "We don't know. The 'neuras hazed 'em good—no reason it shouldn't have worked."

"That's because you don't know who you're dealing with," Wayra gritted out. She nodded at Paqari. "This is a Tisquvian *princess*." Then she nodded at Ninan. "And he's a Sumaqi prince *and* a Venture survivor."

"Your titles and accolades mean nothing to us," said one of the rangers. "All you mainlanders think you can come down here and take whatever you want—and we're just supposed to let you?" He spat on the ground.

"We're not here to take anything," Ninan insisted. "If you've had other mainlanders down here, that only means that what we came to tell you is true."

"And what's that?" said the head ranger.

"That war is coming," Paqari said firmly. "A kind of war you never could have imagined—and even your treaty won't protect you this time."

"That's what the others said too," the pilot rasped from behind Ninan's dagger.

Ninan loosened his grip a bit. "Others …"

"Yesterday."

As Ninan glanced down at his blade, where a tiny stain of red marked one of the serrations, his chest tightened. The arrows trained on him would do much worse, but … this wasn't who he wanted to be. Especially not if he and Paqari and Wayra had come to warn the Tail about a tyrant. If he hurt this man, he would only be representing a similar evil.

He released the wingman and sheathed his blade.

The wingman scrambled away, joining the other Tailfolk.

Ninan raised both hands in surrender. "Those 'others' are our friends. We truly mean you no harm. If we're being fair here, your wingmen attacked us first—and it's reasonable that we should defend ourselves, isn't it?"

The head ranger looked to what appeared to be her second in command. They exchanged a glance.

"Your friends were handed over to the regional Penalizer," the head ranger informed him. "I can't guarantee they're even alive."

Ninan squeezed the hilt of his sheathed dagger, feeling like all his blood was rushing to his head.

Not now, he thought. *Not when I'm* this *close to finding them.* He clenched his teeth for a moment, telling himself not to panic just yet. Qora had taken down a spinosaurus, not to mention plenty of grown men during the Venture. Paqari was right; Qora wasn't one to go down easy. And she was with her brother, whose military training gave him a good chance at survival too.

Depending on what they'd had to face, Ninan had to believe Qora and Ollan could at least buy themselves some time until he and Paqari and Wayra found them.

He heaved a couple of heavy breaths before he asked, "But … there's a chance?"

"A slim one," said the second in command. "You can see for yourself when you get there." He turned to one of the other rangers. "Strip him of any other weapons he might have."

The ranger obeyed, taking Ninan's dagger and patting him down until he came upon a small ridge in Ninan's pocket. He took out the dominite crystal. "What's this?"

Before Ninan could respond, several small flyers emerged from wherever they'd been perched in the trees and swarmed the ranger.

The ranger shrieked and covered his head. Other rangers prepared to shoot down the flyers but then everyone paused, gaping when the flyers landed.

Cautiously, the ranger relaxed and lowered his arms, holding out the glowing, purple crystal as if in demonstration. In a perfect ring around him, the flyers—mostly rhamphorhynchuses and a couple of microraptors—stared up at the crystal in a trance. Within a matter of seconds, a sciurumimus and a few wild compies had joined the ring too.

"What on the gods' green earth …" the head ranger whispered.

Ninan lifted his chin. "That's only a taste of what my father has planned for the reptiles of Runaqa. So you'd really better take me to my friends now. We have important news to deliver—together."

A single evergreen among broadleafs will find fault with himself
at the change of seasons, but he is not out of sync; he is merely
out of place.

Excerpt from *The Forest Philosophies*

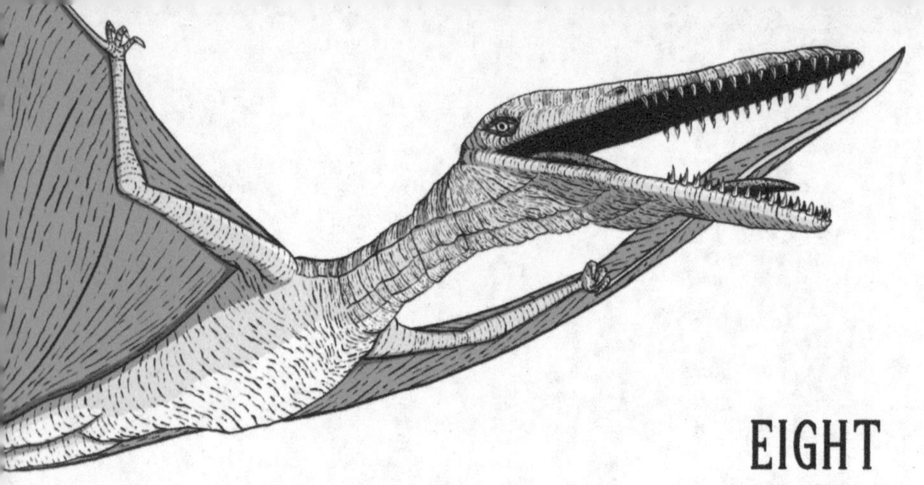

EIGHT

OLLAN SAT UP, PANTING. The wooden bed frame under him creaked at his abrupt motion, but he froze, clenching the edges, and observed his surroundings: a long room in a building high off the ground, a window through which he could see the forest of dark evergreen trees and the other structures built among them. The guards and gondola pilot were asleep in beds beside him, in a long row of beds that lined both sides of the room. Curtains hung between beds but most were pushed open. He had vague memories of someone checking him for bodily harm and urging him to lie down. Strangers occupied other beds sporadically. "Let's get you to the infirmary," someone had said the night before.

It was already a good three hours into the morning now, based on the position of the sun, but those spores—that's what Ollan had been told they were, once the gladewardens had released him and his companions—apparently took several days to completely pass through the body, and in the meantime could leave victims in need of extra sleep. What Ollan remembered to have been Qora's bed was empty at the moment, but her voice carried from somewhere outside the walls, arguing with someone. Everything smelled of conifer needles and pitch and damp tree bark.

Having gotten a better handle on the situation, Ollan lay back, waiting for the pounding of his heart to slow. He was still on edge—and reasonably so—from the previous day's events, having nearly lost his sister to a raging giganotosaur. Gods, would she never *not* be at the mercy of some monster or another? And with him unable to do anything to help her? First it had been the sailbeast that had incapacitated him. During the Venture, he hadn't even known it was his sister who competed, only felt some odd connection to her that he couldn't explain until after he'd had his memory restored. And yesterday he'd been unable to claw his way out of that cage to get to her. If it hadn't been for the gladewarden's interference, would Qora have actually managed to survive this time?

He didn't want to think about it. What kind of brother was he, constantly letting her get into situations like that—looking on helplessly because he couldn't manage to make himself useful?

He pressed a hand to his chest and took a deep breath. For an instant, he had experienced a sensation too similar to what he'd felt waking in the cage, and likewise not so different from when he'd regained consciousness after the sailbeast had attacked him more than four years ago. Disorientation, confusion … panic.

Somehow his body managed to feel heavy and drowsy, yet full of anxious energy at the same time. He could have slept for another four hours, but also he couldn't fathom sitting still a moment longer.

He climbed out of the bed, trembling from the mix of chemicals in his brain, and made for the door, coming out onto a wide walkway where Tailfolk were milling about.

Qora stood with Gladewarden Sacha, crossing her arms.

"Oh good," said the gladewarden. "You're awake. Pack up whatever you'll need for a day's journey. We'll be leaving in a few minutes."

"'We'?" Ollan repeated.

"The gladewarden is taking us to the Verdant Reach," said Qora.

Ollan rubbed his eyes and blinked a few times, trying to recall what that was. The Tail's ruling council of eight—the elderboughs—and their location among all these tree cities. Yes. Right. The Verdant Reach. A journey on foot, to take their news to someone who might actually be able to do something about it, provided they would believe them.

The gladewardens had questioned Ollan and Qora and their traveling companions individually the previous afternoon. Ollan had been unable to convince his interrogator of anything other than his complete lack of sanity, but Qora had gotten through to Gladewarden Sacha, such that he had agreed to speak to the chief gladewarden and request permission for the foreigners to travel out of region (considering the circumstances and the potential threat). But the chief gladewarden had been reluctant and requested the night to think it over. And so, the foreigners had been allowed a brief meal of some strange root-vegetable stew and a bed in the infirmary to recover in for the night, and they had all retired before sundown, brains still fogged over from the spores.

"To my dismay," the gladewarden clarified. "Since I was the one who made the request for you, the chief thought I would be the best person to accompany you." A scowl twisted his lips.

"It's only half a day," Qora reminded him.

"Half a day *each way*. And it's a waste of time, like I told you. The elderboughs are not easily convinced of anything. The only reason you had any sway with *me* is because I watched you risk your life with my own eyes—and I would hope you wouldn't do something so foolish without good reason. But you better have some earth-shattering speech prepared for them, because it's going to take a miracle to make them consider an alliance with the very people their ancestors have always strived to avoid."

"Well," she replied, "we've got a long walk ahead of us. I'll have plenty of time to choose my words."

Ollan watched his sister wearily, knowing she wasn't even close to finished with this mission, regardless of what the gladewarden was saying. That didn't stop him from wanting her to leave well enough alone, though—from wanting to beg her to go back to Allpa with him right now and forget this whole thing. He'd assumed that since these people kept to themselves they would be less prone to violence, but if he'd had any idea what had awaited him and Qora here, he would have never agreed to this. Not when he was ruck at keeping her safe. The fact that she had changed so much in the past few years (despite being the same as always) left him lost as to his role with her; she didn't seem to need him like she once had, and he couldn't help but feel superfluous.

Gladewarden Sacha sighed and adjusted his woolly vest. "Alright then. Let's get going."

Ollan quickly gathered a few things into a pack. He and Qora opted to leave the guards and pilot behind and allow them some rest, then followed the gladewarden to the edge of Murkroot, which was where the structures seemed to end—at least for now—and where a perpetual bridge extended into the trees like a raised wooden road.

It was plank after plank after plank, wider here with foot traffic moving both ways as people carried large baskets or pushed covered carts. As with everything else, the walkway was attached to the trees, keeping out of reach while large dinosaurs roamed below—which was logical, Ollan thought, noting several very large piles of ruck on the ground—and winding on for an indeterminate number of miles. The dinosaurs appeared to simply live below, as the quya had said, prowling and nesting and sometimes calling to one another. A few people had gone down and were moving around among them, without conflict. It seemed only within the Penalizer's domain that the dinosaurs showed any signs of aggression; otherwise, they went about their own business.

He could only think how Wayra would lose her mind if she could see them, study them. The wooden whistle medallion—a "whistlemute," Kondor had explained, as it was so subtle as to almost be mute—the people used for luring and enticing them reminded Ollan of Wayra's ability to approximate reptilian sounds, which was another thing she would surely find fascinating, were she here. As it was, he realized he might never see her again. Who could say how the war across Runaqa would leave things? A small pang struck his heart, although he wasn't sure why. He hardly knew the girl. It must have just been the way of things in times of conflict, to get a sudden sense of lost opportunity for things or people one might not think twice about in times of peace and safety.

The gladewarden paused, as if to allow them a moment to process everything. Then he said, "Ready?"

Qora offered him a cheeky smile. "After you, gladewarden."

He rolled his eyes. "You can just call me Kondor. And try to keep up."

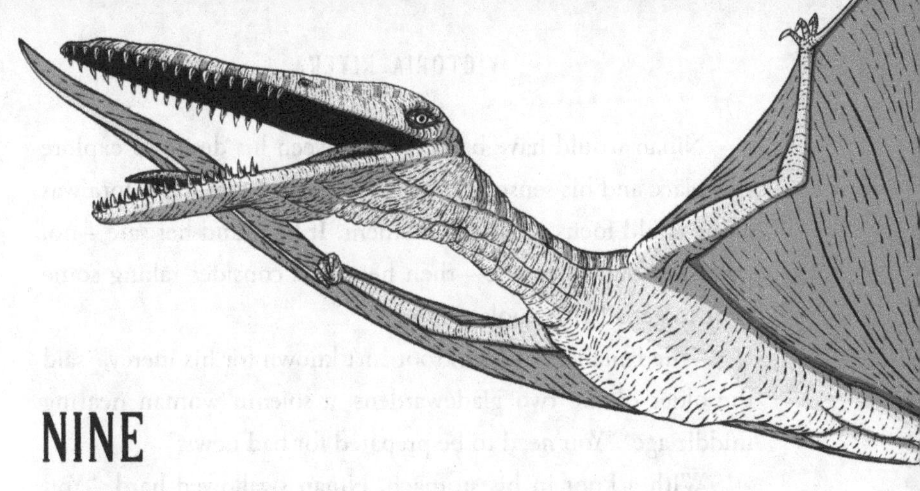

NINE

THE CITY OF MURKROOT was unlike anything Ninan had ever seen. He gaped at the elaborate structures built up in the trees—shops and homes and municipal buildings—and the wide walkways and bridges that allowed throngs of people to move all over.

Wayra was leaning so far over one of the railings, Ninan worried she might fall as she pointed at each species of the giant theropods thundering below.

"Look at those giganotosaurs," she breathed. "They're *enormous* ..."

Paqari cautiously examined the brown shag of a full-length coat hanging from one of the outdoor vendors' stands, and wrinkled her nose. "What's this made of? Why is it so coarse?"

A pair of gladewardens ushered them onward, although it was difficult not to want to stop every few minutes to observe or touch something. Border patrol had turned Ninan's party over to one of the local peacekeeping units, who would take them to speak to the chief gladewarden of the last-known location of Qora and Ollan.

"Gods ..." said Wayra. "I never could have imagined how beautiful these dinosaurs would be. And there are *so many*. And these people, they just live above them *all the time*."

Ninan would have been torn between his desire to explore this place and his sense of urgency to get to Qora, but Qora was all he could focus on at the moment. If he found her safe—no, *when* he found her safe—then he might consider taking some time to get a better look around.

"The Penalizer of Murkroot isn't known for his mercy," said the older of the two gladewardens, a solemn woman nearing middle age. "You need to be prepared for bad news."

With a knot in his stomach, Ninan swallowed hard. "You really just throw people into an enclosure with those … those …" He couldn't even say it. How many times was a person expected to face a giant theropod head-to-head in one lifetime?

That has to be to her advantage, Ninan thought. *It has to.* Of all the ways they could have tried to punish her, at least with this she would have had some idea what she was doing, some chance at survival.

For now, Ninan had agreed to allow the people of the Tail to keep the quya's pterobeast grounded at the border, to avoid causing fear among the citizens. Those flying machines—skycycles or skykes, as the people called them—were no good for multi-passenger travel, apparently. So on foot they went, hurrying over this wood-plank sort-of road.

Finally, they reached a place called Deadwood Pit. It was an enclosure within a tightly woven net of ropes surrounding the open space between several trees, with a gate on one side large enough to fit a spinosaur, and an empty, crushed cage dangling from a rope fixed in a pulley system to thick crossbeams. Instantly, Ninan's fists curled.

The gladewardens introduced Ninan, Paqari, and Wayra to a burly man in a full-length woolly coat like the one Paqari had been scrutinizing earlier. His beard was congruent with his attire, and Ninan wondered how that woolly beard would feel on his knuckles as they slammed into it hard enough to make the man's jaw crack.

"Yes," said the Penalizer, taking a swig of something sour-smelling from a little ceramic jug. "They were delivered to me yesterday. We dropped the cage before noon."

Blood boiling, Ninan lunged at the man with one fist pulled back ready to go. Paqari and Wayra, however, each took one of his arms and held him in place.

"You're supposed to be showing good faith," Paqari reminded him in a sharp whisper.

Ninan rolled his shoulders and huffed as tears of rage bit him from behind the eyes. With his heart pounding, he waited for the man to elaborate, each second like a full minute in his mind. "What happened to her?" he demanded.

"Soon as Grimjaw—that's what we call the giga—broke open the cage"—the man pointed his jug—"the girl used the swing motion to pull back, then climbed out before the return. She got on top, held onto the rope for a bit, then jumped to the climbing holds. Eventually she ended up on her back and we thought she was a goner, but then Gladewarden Sacha came to ruin all the fun. He called off the giga, saying he wanted to question the intruders."

Ninan released a pent-up breath. "So she's *alright*?" He still couldn't let himself fully relax. Not until he heard it from the Penalizer's mouth.

"Well, yeah. Of course she's alright. Do I look happy? If I did, then you'd have a problem. But that damned gladewarden thinks he can just walk up to the pit and put an end to—" His head snapped to the side and a splash of blood flew out from between his teeth.

The force of the blow traveled down Ninan's wrist and arm. Before he could even shake out his hand, the gladewardens wrenched him back.

"Hey, hey, hey!" called another man approaching from the adjacent walkway. He wore a gladewarden's uniform, but also a brimless cap on his head that set him apart from the others. The man frowned and raised a weapon attached to his wrist—was that a small *crossbow*?—that he aimed at Ninan's chest. "What's going on here?"

"Apologies," Paqari told him. "I'm afraid my friend was overcome with emotion, as he's just learned from your Penalizer that his girlfriend was nearly fed to your giganotosaur. Surely you can understand his reaction."

The Penalizer spat more blood. "Chief," he said, acknowledging the man.

"We caught some new foreigners," said the female gladewarden, indicating Ninan and his friends. "Except this time, border patrol says we're supposed to let them live. They made an impressive display, it seems."

"I'm Murkroot's chief gladewarden," the capped man told them. "You're here after the girl and her brother, then. You got separated from them?"

"Not exactly." Ninan flexed his fingers, still tingling from the punch. He scowled at the Penalizer.

"We were worried for their safety," said Wayra.

"Well …" The chief gladewarden adjusted his cap. "I can't speak to their safety at the moment, or where exactly they are. But I can assure you that when they left a little while ago, both were intact and unharmed—physically, at least."

It took much of Ninan's strength not to strike the chief too.

"Left?" said Paqari.

"The girl was persuasive. Managed to catch the attention of one of my senior gladewardens and convince him to advocate on her behalf. He took them to see the elderboughs."

"What's an elderbough?" Wayra asked.

"They govern our lands. Eight of them, each overseeing a different region. They'll be the ones with the authority to decide what aid we might be willing to give—but everyone has told your friends not to get their hopes up. I only let Gladewarden Sacha escort them because I trust his judgment. If he thinks a cause is worthy, he's usually right. That doesn't mean the elderboughs will agree, though."

One of the younger male gladewardens spoke up now: "I think when they see what this group has to show them, they might be more … open minded."

"We need to catch up to them," Ninan said. His pulse thrummed at the amount of time they were wasting here.

The chief gladewarden scratched his chin. "First … show me what you've got."

☽☽☽

When the group had learned that it would take half a day to get to the Verdant Reach—and that they were at least an hour behind their friends—Ninan had insisted on retrieving the pterobeast and gondola.

"We've already explained," said a gladewarden, "that it's too aggressive. The sentries will shoot you right out of the air, no questions asked. They don't use meganeuras. They've got long-range bows, and they're sharp as blades. You fly that thing over *any* of our cities and you'll regret it, but the Verdant Reach sentries are ten times more vigilant."

"Why can't you vouch for us?" Ninan asked.

"What—fly over alongside you screaming 'Don't shoot!' as we go? That's not how it works. The sentries would have no guarantee that we weren't simply foreigners posing as border patrol on commandeered skykes, or that we weren't working under duress. It's a security measure that has kept us safe for centuries now. Nothing is allowed past the borders if we can help it, and when someone does make it, they're vetted on the spot. Anyone deemed dangerous goes into a giga pit, and anyone deemed safe enough for the time being doesn't go anywhere without an escort. Descending aerial travelers don't make it to the ground alive."

Ninan clenched his jaw. "Alright, then. When can we leave?"

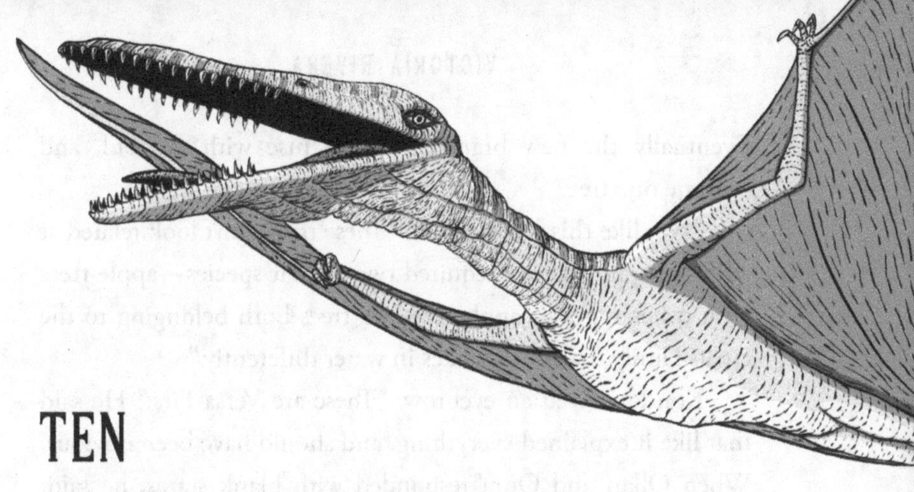

TEN

FOR PERHAPS A QUARTER MILE (or at least what felt like it), there had been only more trees, with no structures built onto them besides the walkway, but soon Ollan and Qora and Kondor had passed through a section where new branches grew from the tree trunks in a jarring way. These branches had pale, splotched bark, and sprouted leaves rather than needle sprigs, while plump orbs dangled from them.

People lined the walkways that ran along rows of the strange growths, pruning them and harvesting the fruits.

Ollan stopped in his tracks to observe.

Qora stopped too. "It's …"

Kondor took a moment to realize his charges had fallen behind, then slowly turned to look at them.

"An orchard?" Ollan said.

Kondor frowned as he glanced around. "This?" He pointed at one section of branches where rows of red leaves grew. "Yes. What else would it be?"

"It's growing from the other trees," Qora noted.

"Your people don't graft?" said Kondor.

Ollan had seen orchards before in the rural districts of Qhusi. He was familiar with the concept of grafting—in which branches from one tree could be cut off and attached to another.

Eventually the new branches would fuse with the old, and become one tree.

"Not like this," Ollan said. "These trees don't look related at all. I thought grafting required two similar species—apple trees with other types of apple trees, or trees both belonging to the citrus family. Each kind takes in water differently."

Kondor raised an eyebrow. "These are Versa Firs." He said that like it explained everything, and should have been obvious. When Ollan and Qora responded with blank stares, he said, "They accept just about any graft and adjust water and nutrient intake to the needs of the new branches."

Ollan approached one of the grafted branches and brushed his fingers over the leaves.

"Every Tail city," Kondor added, "grafts a few species of fruit or nuts on their outskirt trees, and trades with other cities. That's how we get variety."

As they continued, Kondor's explanation proved to be true. They passed through several other small cities with grafted branches leading up to or extending past them—growing cherries and lucuma and custard apples, inqa walnuts and cañihua, and special cool-weather varieties of cacao. Another, however, did not have any grafts but was instead known for its sap, with hundreds of surrounding trees tapped as workers retrieved buckets attached to the bark that had been collecting it to make syrup.

"What about grains?" Ollan asked. "If you operate up high, then it must be hard to cultivate crops—quinoa, maize, wheat."

"Beyond the forests there are plots of land reserved for crops—and true orchards as well, which is where the grafted branches come from. But they take a significant effort to protect from trampling—large pointed palisades, constant guarding, that sort of thing. They're rare, and it's expensive to trade for portions of grain yields. More often we just grind up varieties of nut flours. Some people also make work of going down to the ground to forage for root vegetables, which can provide other flours and starches, and bring them back up to trade. With those, and small pterosaur eggs as binders, we make breads and pastries very similar to what grains can do."

"Fascinating," Qora said.

After several more miles, Kondor took Ollan and Qora to a resting point with a view. A ramp leading up from the walkway spiraled toward the treetops, ending in a platform that rested fully above the trees in the open air and sunlight. Looking out from there, more platforms like these were visible dotting the canopy, many with other travelers stopped to rest and presumably to confirm orientation, others with garden beds sprouting flowers or stabilized vines that grew peppers, tomatoes, squashes and gourds, and legumes.

Now that he thought about it, Ollan had seen these platforms from the gondola, all spread out in the distance, and it had been unclear just what they were—there had been fewer close to the border—made worse by the fact that the spores had overcome his senses and left him without the ability to think on it with any amount of clarity. It had been much like his memory loss four years ago, with the visions before him so close and yet also mentally out of reach. He shook his head, hoping he never had to feel anything like that again.

Continuing the journey, they moved through an area where the trees grew over mountains, with bits of rock jutting from the earth. As the surface beneath the trees inclined, so too did the wooden walkway, and within minutes Ollan and Qora were huffing and had broken a sweat. They paused once again to rest, but this time the overlook remained beneath the treetops, with a relatively clear view of the forest floor with all its ferns and thickets.

Qora startled at the movement of several large, four-legged creatures that disturbed the ferns. They each had thick hair and a nasal horn to rival that of a triceratops. "What are those?"

"Woolly rhinos." Kondor pinched the material of his vest—the same dark brown shag texture that coated the rhinos on the ground.

They stood less than half as high as a tyrannosaur, although their horns were thick enough to serve as a solid defense against anything that might prey upon them.

"You hunt them?" Ollan asked.

"Not really," Kondor replied. "Mostly we leave them for the dinosaurs to eat. They like the woolly things—rhinos, mammoths, ground sloths. It all makes for a good bounty. We take what's left for coats and textiles. The majority of our meat, when we get it, comes from small pterosaurs."

"You don't have especially large flyers here," Ollan noted.

"Ironically enough, no. While our other creatures are large, anything with wings—at least within the wooded cities—is small enough for amateur hunters to handle. I believe our largest flyers would be the pterodactyls along the coasts."

"Well those should be big enough to carry off a grown man, at least," Qora suggested knowingly.

Kondor quirked a brow. "Not these ones. They're two hundred pounds *maybe*."

In contrast, Ollan recalled the fictionist retellings of the Venture that had described the events in which Qora had inadvertently summoned Sumaqi pterodactyls, calling them "five-hundred-pound air-beasts ravenous for human flesh."

"And they only eat fish," Kondor added.

"I guess it's no surprise that you've built your flying machines, then," Qora said. "With no other means of transportation. Or do you ride the mammals, at least? Like the rhinos?"

Kondor nodded. "On occasion. But we don't like to play with the dinosaurs' food. We only ride mammoths and rhinos on the ground—not up here on the bridges or walkways—and in the more rural areas, where the crops are grown."

More rural? Ollan thought. As if any of this could get more rural ...

"Although we're more likely to ride mammoths," Kondor explained. "But those are bulkier and they prefer more open spaces. They're good for tilling soil and moving cargo loads. You might see some at the Verdant Reach. Otherwise, skycycles are best for emergency long-distance travel—and for targeting foreign aircraft."

Qora scowled at him, and then the three of them kept moving.

When another couple of hours had passed, Qora asked, "Do you think there's anything I can do to get the elderboughs to trust me?"

Scratching the shadow of his facial hair, Kondor said, "Not really. Our people are defensive, if you haven't noticed. The elderboughs make sure of that. Ever since the Kastillan Invasion. While most of Runaqa was immediately resistant to the foreign presence, our leaders felt that we might benefit mutually. We let them stay. And then it became clear that they were slowly depleting our resources and turning our people to little more than slaves. It was too late to drive them out the way the rest of the continent had; they were ingrained into our communities, into our blood ..."

Ollan observed Kondor's pale skin and larger stature with more scrutiny now. He hadn't thought much before on the history that made some of the Tailfolk different.

"Let's just say that's when we started our sacrificial traditions," Kondor told them. "The Kastillans didn't respect our land or our reptiles. So we revolted, and fed their high-ranking leaders to the gigas and the tyrannos. Soon, there was no one left who was strong enough to resist us, and the rest of them fled. People here are still divided about the families that have more Kastillan blood; after all, it was our fathers and grandfathers who were killed to set everyone free from their oppression."

"That certainly would make things complicated," Qora said quietly.

Kondor scoffed. "Anyway. You can see why we aren't eager to trust strangers. The elderboughs are reluctant to change, in general. Like I mentioned before, some people have wanted to explore the idea of utilizing the dinosaurs more—in farming, or in transportation as you do—in a kind of symbiosis. We accept resources from the earth, from Sky Mother and the earth spirits, so why not the dinosaurs too? But the elderboughs refuse. Unfortunately, I believe they will refuse to listen to you as well. Although I do wish you luck."

They went on in silence for a while, and just as Ollan fixated on a strange tree up ahead, Kondor slowed and pointed it out.

The tree was hollow inside, and the exterior shell of bark was gray with a unique texture—like hardened vines all twisted together with gaps between them.

"This is what the elderboughs fear," Kondor said.

"Stranglers." Ollan identified it as a type of parasitic plant.

Kondor nodded. "The Kastillans called them 'matapalos,' or 'tree killers.'"

"No doubt the Kastillans admired the metaphorical technique," Qora said.

"The matapalo is actually a tree itself," Kondor told them. "When its windblown seeds land in the crooks of other trees, they send down fine little roots that lengthen until they reach the soil. Then those roots take hold. The air roots grow thicker and stronger, wrapping around the host tree, climbing so that its own branches can grow and sprout leaves up where the light is. Over time, it cuts off the host tree from its nutrition sources and takes its place in the canopy. The host tree dies, then rots to nothing while the matapalo is left standing … like this."

Qora appeared to analyze its features. "The elderboughs think that's what foreigners will do to the Tail."

"It took centuries to rebuild what we lost," said Kondor. "To establish the peace and the social systems we have in place today."

"But that's the point," Ollan argued. "The elderboughs' fears are real, and logical. That"—Ollan gestured at the hollow tree—"is *exactly* what Qhapaq Apo will do to you once he's established dominance over the rest of Runaqa. My sister and I aren't the threat your leaders are trying to avoid; in fact, we may be the only ones who can help you prevent it."

"I believe you," said Kondor. "But I don't think they're going to see it that way. They think if we can remain isolated in all ways from the Terrains—and other outside forces—we'll be safe. It's *letting others in*, trusting them, taking them at their word, that scares the elderboughs. To do as you say, to fight your qhapaq, we'll have to let more of you in and trust you. Worse, fighting may require some of us to *leave* with you. That's no small request."

Ollan stretched his neck and took a deep breath. He

wished wholeheartedly that there were some way to prove to the elderboughs that the world, as all Runaqans knew it, was essentially ending. But if no one from the Tail was willing to leave to see it for themselves—to witness firsthand the reptilian forces gathered at Qhapaq Apo's encampments now that Sakay had ensured they could find more—it would be difficult to make anyone see reason. And to wait for the Sauroguard to show up here would be too late. All he and Qora could do was press on, and pray the elderboughs would listen.

"Thank you for your insight." Qora's tone was sincere, but firm. "Still, I'm going to make my request because, as our mamáy says, 'The only way to *guarantee* that a seed won't grow in rocky soil … is to never plant it there.'"

Ollan couldn't help but smile a little. How many times had Qora rolled her eyes at their mamáy's words? Now she was repeating them in the same tone.

Kondor shook his head and sighed. "I still say you're concussed, kid."

"You want me to prove my mental state?" she said. "Give me one of those weapons and I'll hit a rhampho right between the eyes."

The gladewarden glanced at the small crossbow attached to his forearm. "This? It's a regulation wristbow. Only gladewardens can wear them."

Ollan's and Qora's weapons were still being held back in Murkroot and Ollan knew that his sister, like him, must have felt naked without them. She'd gotten her jacket back, but with empty pockets.

Qora frowned at Kondor. "Sure. We'll see."

One for the stomp,
Two for the claw,
Three for the one who evades the jaw.

A common Penalizer's rhyme*

*Sometimes also spoken metaphorically prior to meeting with the elderboughs

ELEVEN

DOZENS OF WALKWAYS CONVERGED on the Verdant Reach from all directions. Here, the structures in the trees were built so large they spanned the distance between entire rows of tree trunks. The buildings all ran together, as with many big cities, some holding multiple dwellings with shared walls, others hosting shops and service centers and civic buildings like what Qora and Ollan had seen in other cities along the way, only more expansive. The walkways were as busy as the city streets of Qhusi, Qora thought, just high above the ground. She peered over the railing at the hundreds of giant theropods that wandered below, and paused to watch them, tightening her grip on the length of wood that separated her from a deadly fall.

The theropods came in all patterns and colors. Most of the giganotosaurs were the same pale green as the one Qora had battled the previous day, with dark stripes down their bodies and tiny spikes along the crowns of their heads. The tyrannosaurs came in shades of yellows with black spots. Several spinosaurs also prowled the area, many with blackish skin and red sails, while others had sails that were orange or even purple, and they waded in and out of a deep river that cut through the woods.

Qora took a slow, cleansing breath at the sight of them. They had those familiar amber eyes—just like the ones she'd pierced with bolts in a desperate move—a rhythm in their gait that reminded her all too well of the Venture spinosaur thundering after her, gaining on her. Her belly churned with the memories, with the guilt of what she'd done, with a lingering fear that made her shudder.

Ollan laid a hand on her shoulder. "Don't think about it. It won't help anything."

"It might," she said. "I mean … it's part of the reason I'm here, isn't it? Because Qhapaq Apo stole a spinosaur from these lands. Because he used it for experimental breeding. Because those experiments killed people. Because the continuation of those experiments is going to wipe out the Five Terrains, and then the Tail too."

"Well, I can't argue with *that*."

"It felt like I was fighting a monster during the Venture. But looking at these reptiles … how they live in harmony … how the people here don't fear them …" She shook her head. "That spinosaur was a victim to the qhapaq as much as everyone he sent to fight it."

Ollan watched the dinosaurs for a moment with her. "Then let's make sure the qhapaq has to face the ones he's wronged."

Kondor, who had been waiting patiently for them to have their moment, motioned for them to continue.

With him, they pushed through the hordes of people, nearing the city center and finally coming to an elaborate archway made of thousands of twisty branches covered in moss and climbing vines. Other gladewardens guarded the entry point, but only stopped to check documents for those entering with large quantities of goods to sell.

Once inside, a long lead-up drew Qora's gaze to a particularly immense tree. It must have been fifty feet in diameter, with branches so thick they were more like several trunks fused together.

"Spirits," she whispered. "That tree is as big as a building."

"And we treat it as such," Kondor told her. "That's the Arboreal Spire, where the elderboughs convene daily."

"Inside of it?" Ollan asked.

"The branches surround a sort of nexus, forming an open space between them. It's one of the last of its kind—a Hatunsu Fir. In ancient times, trees like that one covered these lands, but apparently climate shifts caused a lot of them to die out."

Kondor led them to the "spire," where he spoke to a few other gladewardens who were handling visitors, and then he told Qora and Ollan it would be a bit of a wait while other hearings took place. The line of visitors consisted of builders in conflict over resources, vendors looking to expand trade, people requesting new travel routes, and citizens petitioning for the right to use smaller dinosaurs for labor (just as Kondor had mentioned during Qora's interrogation).

But eventually two gladewardens came to retrieve the three of them, and ushered them into the spire.

The quadruple-wide walkway led between the branches which, Qora thought once again, were like trees themselves, draped in decorative vinery and moss like the archway leading into the heart of the city. Dozens of gladewardens patrolled the entrance. As the senior gladewarden—a counterpart to Kondor that appeared much more grandiose both in posture and attire— accepted a papyr on which they had put down their names, and stepped aside to allow them to pass.

A wooden floor spanned the distance across the interior of the Arboreal Spire, set into the space to create a flat surface. Qora walked single file between Kondor (ahead of her) and Ollan (behind her), stepping onto a runner made of some type of jute that had dinosaurs and floral shapes woven onto it. Lanterns—with amber "glass" that looked to be made from dried and polished tree resin—dangled from the branches (which curved inward overhead like a vented ceiling) to provide additional lighting in the dim environment. Spectators and attendants looked up at the visitors, loitering the way highborns sometimes did at Kallpa House courts to socialize or gain favor from the qhapaq or his quyas. On the far side, eight people sat behind a long table mounted on a dais, which of course was also made of wood, on high-backed wooden chairs. It was one of the few ways their hall resembled that of other Runaqan public figures.

A series of ropes and rolled sheets of canvas rimmed the interior like furled ship sails, and Qora followed the lines visually, determining that these could perhaps be deployed in a tent-like fashion to create shelter from rain or wind if needed.

An attendant came forward. "Welcome to the Arboreal Spire." She looked at the elderboughs, then read from a papyr. "Your Verdancies, I present to you Gladewarden Kondor Sacha of Murkroot, and Qora Kanchaya and Ollan Kanchaya of the Terrain of Sumaq. The foreigners have been vetted by Murkrootian law enforcement, and come bearing news of great importance from the Five Terrains." She stepped aside.

Then Kondor stepped aside too, leaving Qora to face the council directly.

Four women and four men sat in an alternating pattern along the table. Although they were only visible from the waist up, the men wore what appeared to be long tunics and woolly cloaks; they varied in age but each had a noteworthy beard. The women wore tunic-collar dresses with draping sleeves, and shawl-capes of that same woolly material, and strings of wooden-beaded necklaces in multiple layers, with long hair in many styles—in loose curls, in braids, swept back and up. All eight wore polished-wood headpieces with teeth embedded along the top (perhaps from dinosaurs that had died of natural causes, Qora imagined).

"The elderboughs will hear you now," said the attendant from the sidelines.

Qora eased forward. Ollan came to stand beside her, taking her hand and squeezing it.

"Your … uh … Verdancies …" Qora's mouth suddenly went dry, parching her throat along with it. She should have been used to dealing with royalborns (or their equivalents) by now, after all her time spent at Kallpa House as Qhapaq Apo's champion, but this was different. This was not only a foreign land, it was one that shared very little with the one she was used to in terms of custom and tradition. "Thank you for seeing me on such short notice. I'm … aware that my nationality—my terrenality—might come as a bit of a shock, but I want you to know that I am only intruding on your land because, well … because something terrible is happening on mine."

One of the female elderboughs leaned forward. Her hair was practically the color of fire, something Qora had never seen before in person. "While we sympathize with those affected by foreign conflict, I must tell you without hesitation that we will have nothing to do with it. So if that's why you're here …"

Qora shook her head. "No, Your Verdancy. I mean … Yes, the Terrains are experiencing conflict, but it's more than that. It will affect the Tail as well—without a doubt. Gladewarden Sacha has already told me repeatedly that I represent a lost cause and that the Tail will not likely acknowledge my pleas, but—"

"Then why are you here?" said the burliest of the four men,

his beard pale and wiry and his eyes a piercing blue that sent shivers up Qora's spine.

"Because evil is contagious," she replied in a voice too quiet for her own liking. "And I'm sorry but … your people are not immune. The treaty that has protected you for centuries will be dissolved along with the dissolution of the Five Terrains. My qhapaq has begun a war that now puts most of the other Terrains under his rule, and now he is one step away from restoring the Old Empire that preceded your agreement. He's been scouting the Tail for at least a decade; he knows the value of what you have here. His spies have stolen large theropod eggs and used them in nefarious breeding programs. He has created abominable creatures—thousands of them—by some means we don't yet fully understand, and he's developed mystical crystals that can force reptiles to act against their own wills to do his bidding."

"Mystical … *crystals* …" another female elderbough repeated, turning the words over analytically on her tongue. Her hair was dark but her skin was milky.

"We don't believe in magic or mysticism," said a male elderbough, whose beard was twisted into four distinct sections and held in place by wooden beads like the ones his female fellow-oligarchs wore around their necks. "You aren't the first to come here with incredible tales of impossible forces. The Kastillans fed our ancestors similar lies—of fire-breathing monsters, or witches who could imbue objects with power, or kings who could turn objects to gold with the touch of a finger. We aren't easily convinced of such things."

"I wish it were only fiction," Qora told them. "But it's real. I say 'mystical' because right now we can't explain it, although I believe there is an explanation—some elemental manipulation rooted in science. Except … what matters in this moment is that my people have fallen prey to the dinosaur army our qhapaq has created. No human army can survive against it. And once he's finished with the Terrains, he'll come for you too."

Another woman leaned forward, her features not dissimilar to the people Qora knew from Sumaq. She pointed a long-nailed finger at Qora. "Why should we believe you? We have had peace for hundreds of years, with little to no contact with the Terrains. Why this now? What has changed?"

"The qhapaq believes he is destined to reunite the Terrains under one empire. He thinks it's his divine right."

"And?" said the red-haired woman. "He is no different from other qhapaqs. They *all* think they're divinely appointed and entitled. For this reason, we have kept ourselves separate; we have no desire to associate with the likes of your royalborns."

"He's the first to discover the power to finally accomplish the task," Qora clarified. "What his forefathers could not do, he now has the *means* to do. That's what sets him apart."

"Let's say," said a tanned male elderbough, "that what you're saying is true. What is it you want of *us*? You have more potential soldiers in one corner of your Terrain than we do on this whole peninsula. You can't possibly want us to join your fight—not that we would. But I'm curious. What could we possibly do for you?"

Qora looked at Kondor, who winced in advance of what he surely knew she was about to say. She didn't blame him for being embarrassed to be the one to escort her here; it did sound crazy.

Ollan squeezed Qora's hand again and gave a reassuring nod.

"We need your dinosaurs."

There was only a brief pause before the redhead burst into laughter. The others chuckled in disbelief, exchanging glances.

"You need our ... " the blond elderbough scoffed. "You

think a gang of wild theropods—however large they may be—can stamp out a trained army?"

"Size is our only advantage," said Qora. "If you can help us, that is."

"You said your qhapaq can control the dinosaurs," the redhead reminded her. "What would stop him from controlling ours?"

"We have a sort of antidote."

The woman rolled her eyes. "Of course. I should have assumed. A magical problem requires a magical solution."

"But the war, as of now, as I understand," said the blond elderbough, "is taking place far away. How would you presume to get them in the same location?"

Qora bit her lip. "To be honest, I hadn't fully worked that out yet. But you know much more about them than I do, so maybe you could—"

"Alright," said the man on the far end, who had been watching with minimal reaction this whole time. "I think we've entertained this nonsense long enough. We'll alert our border patrols to be more vigilant, should the need arise to take defensive measures. Otherwise, your conflicts are your own, Miss Kanchaya." He flicked a hand at the attendant. "Please remove these people from the Spire."

The attendant offered a sympathetic look and moved to guide Qora away.

"Wait!" Qora said to the elderboughs. "You have to trust me! I know it sounds unbelievable, but I've seen the reptile armies with my own eyes! I've watched them train, watched them under the influence of the crystals"—she shrugged off the gladewardens that approached her when she evaded the attendant's guidance—"and witnessed unnatural mutations. Some of them can *shift their skin* to camouflage. Who knows what else they might be able to do? There'll be no stopping them—"

The gladewardens had her by the arms now and she struggled. Ollan tried to reason with them, but more gladewardens came to suppress him too. Meanwhile, Kondor kept saying, "Don't fight it, Qora, just do what they say. Just *do what they say.*"

She flailed until she broke loose, rushing back toward the dais, stumbling and landing on her knees, but she persisted. "If you care about the dinosaurs at all, you'll help stop this! If you care about your people—about humankind—you'll *listen*—"

A gladewarden caught her again and pulled her arms back behind her and she cried out. Ollan broke loose then and struck the gladewarden, causing a swarm of additional gladewardens to subdue them both.

"This kind of force is completely unnecessary!" Kondor argued, pushing into the mass, although none of the other gladewardens paid him any attention.

Spectators and attendants murmured with increasing volume while the elderboughs shouted for everyone to maintain order.

Somewhere in all this chaos, another commotion broke out near the Spire's entrance. The gladewardens who had converged on Qora and Ollan had left the entrance with little security.

"Let them go!" demanded a voice that made Qora freeze.

At first, the gladewardens began to divide their ranks to address the potential threat, but then they froze too.

Everyone fell silent.

Still in an oppressive grasp, Qora managed to push up to her feet and crane her neck to see better.

It wasn't the words that had struck everyone—it couldn't have been.

Slowly, the crowd parted.

The elderboughs stood, in turn, and gaped.

Qora's breath caught in her throat.

Moving toward the dais, as if in a ceremonial procession, was Ninan. He held a dominite crystal high above his head, its glow made all the more prominent by the dim space.

All around him—and behind him, too, trailing him—were at least a dozen small reptiles with their gazes fixed on the crystal. More reptiles that had been perched within the branches of the Arboreal Spire flew toward him, one flyer landing on his shoulder, but he didn't flinch.

Paqari and Wayra were with him, sticking close. The princess swatted at the reptiles that got in her way, while Wayra scooped up a compy in her arms.

Ninan stopped short of where Qora stood, stealing her breath with his defiant stance.

"Let them go," he said again.

The elderboughs exchanged glances.

The blond elderbough nodded at the gladewardens holding Qora and Ollan captive. "You heard the boy. Release them."

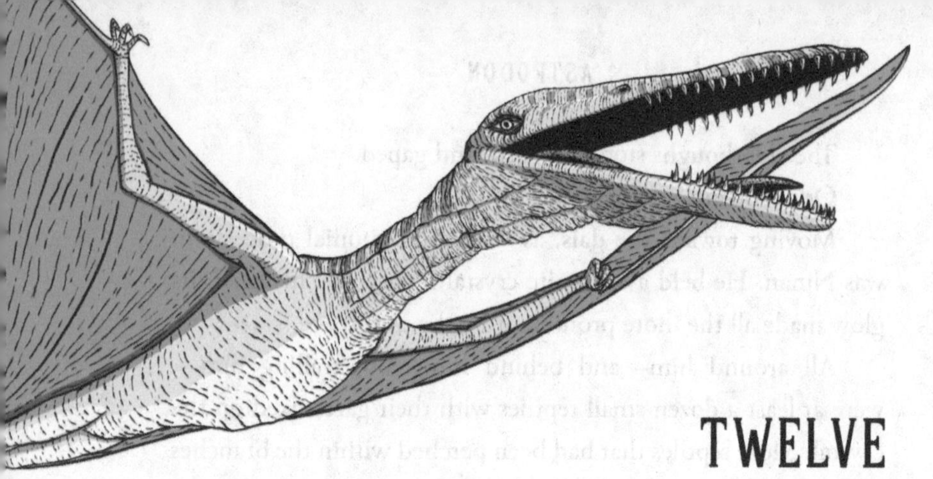

TWELVE

PAQARI STILL COULDN'T GET OVER THE ODDITY of this place. In a matter of hours, she had entered and been immersed in an entirely new world, in which the people lived high in the trees like woodland creatures and wore the skins of the ugliest mammals she had ever laid eyes upon.

Now she stood in what she supposed was the more rustic equivalent of a reception hall, where the oligarchs of this land were dressed like the personifications of the earth spirits. She wrinkled her nose.

She had to fight her way up to where Ninan stood facing the dais, because there were so many transfixed little reptiles on the ground that there was scarcely room to walk. It was, however, a nice reprieve from the reptiles' attention on *her*; they'd been oddly drawn to her since she'd landed, as though she had a particular smell they had liked, and it was only when Ninan had brought out the dominite that they'd focused elsewhere. *Little demons.*

Meanwhile, Wayra was so busy getting her fill of all the unique species that the gravity of the situation didn't seem to weigh on her. She cooed at the two feathered compies she now held, while an archaeopteryx clung to her sleeve and a sciurumimus climbed across her shoulders—although the sciurumimus was really just

104

using her as a stepping stone to get to Ninan, and leapt off of her promptly.

Qora cast a pained but grateful gaze at Ninan, and it was then that Paqari realized Qora had no idea what had transpired at the wedding. For all Qora likely knew, Paqari and Ninan were married—making this encounter more awkward, if that were even possible. She would have to explain later, and what a relief it would be to finally resolve this unintentional love triangle.

The elderboughs stared at Ninan, fixated on the crystal like the reptiles were, only for a different reason. Whatever Qora had done to anger them now appeared to be irrelevant in the midst of this fascinating power.

"So, what the Kanchaya girl says is true ..." remarked an elderbough with long curls of hair in a reddish hue Paqari could only describe as "otherworldly." Tiny, pigmented dots covered the woman's face—kind of like the spotted patterns on some reptiles' scales, Paqari thought.

"Clearly," Paqari muttered. Of course she didn't know what Qora had said, exactly, but she assumed it had had something to do with the qhapaq controlling dinosaurs and so on and so forth. It was just like Qora to recklessly thrust herself into danger like that without anything to catch her fall. If Qora had waited but a single day, the Razorclaws could have given her the crystal before she had ever set foot in this primitive place, and the elderboughs would have known immediately that she'd been telling the truth.

However, Paqari did think there was something to be said for spontaneity, for acting fast without overthinking the end result. She herself had only done this once, really—when she'd left Tisqu to go after Ninan—and while she had never been so terrified in her life, she had also never felt so free. Still, there were few things as satisfying as a well-calculated scheme.

"I wouldn't have brought her here," said one of the gladewardens, stepping forward, "if I thought she was lying."

Paqari looked the man up and down, with his light brown hair and pale eyes. He must have been the one from Murkroot that the people had mentioned—Gladewarden Kondor Sacha—the one who had been assigned to escort the Kanchayas to this hearing. He was awfully confident for a man wearing woolly rhino skin as a vest. His tight lips and crossed arms and the way he rubbed the back of his neck led the princess to believe this was some kind of *inconvenience* for him, even though he probably ought to be grateful to be in the presence of his leaders, not to mention royalborns and a celebrity from the Five Terrains. If he only knew how revered the champion was, or that under other circumstances he would be required to bow to Paqari and Ninan.

"Not that I wanted to be the one to trek *all the way here* on short notice," the gladewarden added, "but I do believe her."

"May I see the crystal?" said a male elderbough with braids in his beard.

When Ninan moved toward him, so did all the reptiles, and as he transferred the crystal to the elderbough, he transferred the attention of the reptiles too.

The elderbough twitched at the sudden shift, but examined the dominite nonetheless. "Where does it come from?"

"It's made from skyrock," Ninan told him. "From the elements of the meteorites that fell long ago."

"Those which have been used to influence the behavior of reptiles in the Terrains ..." said the woman with the bespeckled complexion.

The blond elderbough said, "But the legendary sky rocks have only *repelled* reptiles, have they not? Persuaded them through fear of punishment by exposure to its effects? *This*, on the other hand …"

"This changes everything," Ninan said firmly.

He and Qora locked eyes for a moment, forcing Paqari to roll hers. Goodness, these two were annoying. So much pining, such enduring loyalty. Resentfully, she wondered if any man would ever look at *her* that way—although she certainly didn't want Ninan to be the one to do it, and was glad he had found a way off the jetty before she'd been forced into a blood oath with him. But even the watchman, whom Paqari's father had removed from her life, had never directed such an intense gaze at her—what she wouldn't give for another moment with him regardless—although perhaps that kind of intensity was not meant for young women like her, with fathers who could shatter the objects of their delicate affections in a single command. Then again, she had extracted herself from her father's grasp once and for all, and in that she felt hopeful.

"You should also know," said Ninan, "that the qhapaq who will unleash this power on Runaqa … is my father."

Despite the whispers that had erupted since the revelation of the crystal, the place went silent again.

"You're a prince," another female elderbough concluded.

"I'm sure my title no longer belongs to me now that I have openly defied my father's authorities and am actively working against his cause. And I hope that speaks to you—to how serious this is—that a royalborn would abandon his comforts and his homeland and risk his life to tell you this. I'm not the only one, either." He gestured at Paqari. "This is a princess of Tisqu."

Paqari raised her chin, unwilling to bow to authorities that weren't her own, but acknowledging them nonetheless with her expression. "The Sauroguard was bred on my islands, and then

I witnessed some of its forces in the capital of Unu shortly after the destruction they caused there. In time, they will consume everything."

"I saw pterosaurs spit acid that could corrode stone," Ninan told them. "And velociraptors that could climb like spiders. And ankylosaurs with double-sized club-tails battering citadel walls. That's only the beginning. There are other mutated species, I guarantee it, with features we can't yet imagine. Something that goes far beyond selective breeding. Something unnatural and ungodly."

"And the qhapaq can captivate each one of them with the dominite crystals," Paqari said. "There's no limit to what he can make them do."

Qora paled at the information. She cleared her throat and refocused her attention on the elderboughs. "I know this is unprecedented. I know we're asking the world of you. But you have to understand by now that that world—the one in which we stop the qhapaq, and in which you remain free and safe—depends on your help."

They watched her silently for a moment and passed the dominite crystal among themselves for further observation, wary but intrigued by the effect it continued to have on the reptiles that had gathered over the dais (some of which were on the table now).

No longer carrying any compies, since both had followed the other reptiles toward the crystal, Wayra went to Ollan and embraced him, then Qora.

A dark-haired elderbough handed off the crystal to the man beside her, then said, "And who are you, Miss Kanchaya, that you have taken it upon yourself to bring us this news? If you are not a royalborn like your friends ..."

"In a deadly competition, I managed to come out the

winner," Qora told her. "I was forced to fight for my life against a spinosaur, and I'm ashamed to say that it died by my hand when it tried to kill me." She bowed her head. "This is the kind of place we come from, ruled by a man who plays with the lives of people and dinosaurs alike. This is the pattern we must put to an end." Slowly, she lifted her eyes to meet theirs, and straightened her shoulders. "I've seen one of your matapalo trees—the stranglers. Qhapaq Apo has already dropped his seeds here. In you, he sees a tree that is taking up space in the canopy that could be his. His roots will grow and choke you out, and nothing will be left but an empty shell, and all that you love and care for will have rotted away. Sumaq has already created an alliance with Tisqu, bullied Qolqe into compliance, and occupied Unu; now they threaten Allpa, the final independent Terrain …"

"Whose quya has one moon cycle to sign a cession agreement," Ninan interjected, "or must face the Sauroguard."

At this information, Qora went almost as pale as some of the elderboughs. Ollan's nostrils flared briefly.

Finally, Qora choked out, "Your giant theropods are Runaqa's last hope."

The elderboughs silently looked at one another, some with doubtful glances, but the crystal gleamed, washing them in purple hues. Somehow, they seemed to communicate a sort of agreement because the red-haired woman stood and addressed Qora. "We will perform an appeal to the dinosaurs. Because it is you who has brought this question to their feet, and you in whom we must trust as we make this decision, you will stand as envoy."

When the skies rumble, it is only the roar of our Reptilian Lords.

The Book of Vertitude, Chapter 1, Verse 7

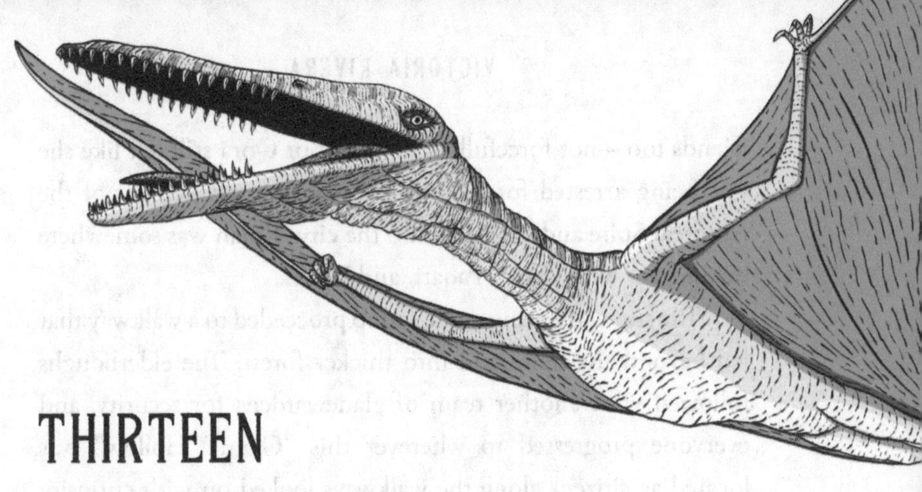

THIRTEEN

"ENVOY?" QORA REPEATED.

Her mind was still racing from everything that had happened in the past few minutes—from Ninan's unexpected arrival, to learning about the cession agreement, to the elderboughs' sudden change of heart toward her claims.

While she was grateful that Ninan had brought the dominite, she couldn't deny it was overwhelming to have him here with Paqari—his new *wife*—during such a pivotal conversation with the elderboughs. It hit her in the chest like a dagger, with a similar sense of finality (the immediate death of whatever hope she might have maintained about him, and whatever hope she'd had about the Sauroguard's limitations).

And then, the thought of more hybrid dinosaurs with unprecedented skills and features wreaking havoc on the Terrains.

She swallowed against the lump forming in her throat.

In addition to all that, now it sounded as though the elderboughs expected her to ask the dinosaurs *themselves* whether they would be willing to join the fight against Qhapaq Apo.

"Cancel all other audiences," the red-haired elderbough told the attendants. Then to the Spire gladewardens, she said, "Take Miss Kanchaya to Giants' Hollow."

Gladewardens swarmed Qora again, and her brother and

friends too—not forcefully this time, but Qora still felt like she was being arrested for a crime as they escorted her out of the Arboreal Spire and back out into the city. Ninan was somewhere behind her with Ollan, Paqari, and Wayra.

The sun was setting as the group proceeded to a walkway that led beyond the Spire and into thicker forest. The elderboughs followed with another team of gladewardens for security, and everyone progressed to wherever this "Giants' Hollow" was located as citizens along the walkways looked on with curiosity (and many gathered to follow along and witness whatever was about to happen while the news of Qora's outrageous request spread among them).

Kondor caught up to Qora, huffing.

"What's going on?" she asked him in a harsh whisper. "What did the elderbough mean when she said I have to 'stand as envoy'?"

"They're taking you down to a place where the people commune with the dinosaurs."

"'Down'? As in … on the *ground*?" When he nodded, she said, "Do you remember what happened *last time* I was on the ground?"

"There's no need to panic. It's not like Deadwood Pit. You've seen how gentle these other dinosaurs are. They won't hurt you. I mean … probably."

"*Probably?*"

"The dinosaurs at Deadwood Pit are trained to accept humans as offerings. They understand that a cage in the clearing means food. Others … they don't care. They have plenty to eat out here. Like I've said, we live out of their way as a matter of respect, not fear."

Qora took a deep breath to calm herself.

They crossed several bridges and then proceeded down a spiraling staircase that wrapped one of the thicker tree trunks. As they neared the ground, they came closer and closer to eye level with dozens of giant theropods, which sniffed vaguely in the humans' direction but otherwise ignored them.

Meanwhile, new flyers emerged as nocturnal conditions precipitated, clinging to the bark of the trees. The majority of these flyers had rounded wings with splotchy patterns, and rounded heads, and eyeballs like big black marbles. They were like giant moths, Qora thought—except it was clear from the patagial membranes that they were some species of pterosaur.

Qora cringed. "What are those?"

Kondor glanced around until he realized what she was talking about. "Vesperoptylus. 'Vespers.' Their eyes are best suited to darkness, so they run rampant in the evenings and during the night. They're harmless."

The black eyes seemed to watch her as the group descended, making this all the more eerie.

When they reached the bottom, they followed a trail of stones embedded in the soil until they arrived at a clearing that featured a slab of concrete painted with white symbols. A raised platform came up from the center with a few steps leading to its surface.

More attendants arrived, as if from nowhere, one of them carrying a basket with several large, rounded objects that were either dinosaur eggs Qora had never seen before, or some kind of exotic melon. They were dark red, with an exterior covered in a thick, bumpy texture.

"Scutefruit," Kondor told her before she could ask. "It's the only plant the carnivorous dinosaurs will eat—and only if they're in the mood. You will offer it to them, and if they accept, it means they accept your appeal."

Her brows pulled together.

"The whole ceremony's a load of ruck," he whispered. "Pure superstition. Basically a game of chance, dependent on the dinosaurs' whims. But if you're lucky—"

An attendant dropped one of the melons into Qora's arms. She sank under its weight, but the attendant bolstered her and urged her toward the central platform.

"What happens if they don't accept?" Qora asked.

A group of woolly-coated people quickly arranged themselves in a semicircle around where Qora stood, each holding what appeared to be a pteroleather drum by a strap around the neck. They raised mallets and began to pound out a rhythm.

The red-haired elderbough pressed a wooden whistle to her lips and blew into it, emitting a warbling noise. It wasn't the elevated pitch of whatever the border patrol had used. Qora wasn't sure what the difference was, only that different pitches must be used for different purposes.

Wayra stared at the elderbough with fascination. Surely it was a more accurate cry than what Wayra could produce by shaping her own hands.

A moment later, thunderous footfalls came shaking the trees, and Qora couldn't tell whether the vibrations in her chest were more from the dinosaurs' marching, from the incessant drumbeats, or from her own erratic heart.

Giant theropods appeared at the clearing—*Giants' Hollow*, Qora remembered—lumbering toward her.

She turned up her face to focus on their towering height.

The first to reach her was a spinosaurus.

She held her breath as she tilted her head back to look at its long snout. As if that weren't positioned high enough, its back-sail rose even higher, membranes as red as hot lava.

A low, purring growl emanated from its throat as its jaws parted. Its claws curled inward at the ends of its arms, and Qora imagined those claws encircling her neck like a sickle and decapitating her with no effort at all.

Slowly she released her breath, shuddering as the spinosaur neared. She tightened her hold on the scutefruit, almost forgetting why she had it.

Ninan and Ollan both struggled against gladewardens to try to interfere, but Kondor told them, "Don't be fools. If you want her to live, you'll control yourselves."

Paqari muttered something to Wayra about how the Tailfolk were a bunch of "brutish backlanders."

At least five other giant theropods of various species gathered behind.

"Make your request," said the red-haired elderbough. "Then provide the offering."

When the spinosaur lowered its head to her level, Qora stared into its amber eyes.

What was she supposed to say? "Please come fight the unnatural monsters in the north"? "Protect us from our tyrant qhapaq"? These weren't things a spinosaur could possibly understand.

"Make your request," the elderbough repeated more forcefully.

Qora's chin trembled as she opened her mouth, hoping the words would come to her. "I ..." She gasped when the spinosaur dipped its head even lower, mere inches from her face, its fangs shimmering with saliva and its breath fetid. *This is ridiculous,* she thought. *The others aren't scared. All these people, just standing here, not even fazed?* But her fear wasn't logical; it was visceral.

This beast was the stuff of nightmares that had plagued her since the Venture. "I'm here to …" She closed her eyes. Maybe if she didn't have to look at it, that would help. "I'm here to tell you that … that … the dinosaurs of my homeland are … under the influence of a horrible man. They're … being bred in unnatural ways, forced to do the bidding of someone who does not care for their wellbeing … or for the wellbeing of humankind. We …" She opened her eyes to find the spinosaur watching her with something almost like curiosity, and its patient stillness made her relax a bit. It was just an animal, albeit an abnormally large one, and it could have already bitten her in half so easily … but hadn't. "We need your help. We need your strength and your power. I don't know how we're going to do this, and there's no guarantee it will work, but my qhapaq won't stop until he's taken every inch of this continent for himself and for what he believes is his divine empire. You and your kind are not safe, and neither are the rest of us. So … please …" She swallowed, then shakily raised the offering. "Will you help us?"

The spinosaur huffed at her, blowing her hair back with its breath. Its jaws wrenched apart and came down fast. Qora flinched and nearly dropped the melon but she held firm as the spinosaur's teeth came together, sending streams of liquid down her arms. For an instant the sight and the sensation made her heart seize—a seemingly bloody mess, but with no pain. The liquid was cold and sticky, and carried bits of fruit pulp which, although they resembled human gore, smelled sweet and tart.

The melon rind broke into pieces that slipped out of her grasp and struck the platform, sending splatters of more scutefruit juice across the concrete and onto her boots.

All around her the people broke into solemn applause. Solemn, Qora realized, because even though she had succeeded in making this offering to the spinosaur, it really only meant one thing: They were going to war.

ↄↄↄ

A blur of motion had followed the success of Qora's appeal: attendants rolling more scutefruit onto the platform, another spinosaur and two tyrannosaurs and a giganotosaur and an allosaur catching the melons in their mouths and breaking them and spilling juice, the spectators—whose numbers seemed to have quadrupled since the initial curiosity above ground— murmuring and chattering over what would come next, all of Qora's friends rushing toward her.

Qora found herself in Ollan's arms and she buried her face in his shoulder and cried. Her tears fell with relief, with the chemicals flowing through her body in the wake of everything.

Finally she raised her head and wiped her eyes, and the two of them seemed to simultaneously become aware of Ninan waiting patiently, but with an anxious pinch in his brows. Paqari and Wayra parted to make way for him, and Ollan released her.

Qora supposed Ninan still cared for her, whatever his marital status now. It was only odd that Paqari seemed to be so accommodating, especially after how she and Qora had left things that night below decks on the *Velosaura*.

As Ninan reached toward her, however, the drums beat again several times, and then the blond elderbough raised his voice to say, "Now that our fate has been decided, we will dine together to discuss our plan of action. May the foreigners be our guests, and join us on the East Banquet Balcony at once."

And just like that, gladewardens and attendants ushered everyone back up to the trees and paraded them through the city. Qora hardly had a moment to breathe with everyone who came to introduce themselves and ask her about where she'd come from.

"Do you really live in the Five Terrains?" someone asked.

"Is it true everyone builds their homes right on the ground?" said another.

"There aren't *any* spinosaurs there?"

"Everyone's saying you flew across our border on a giant pterosaur."

"Is there really going to be a war?"

She did her best to answer all of them. Thankfully her friends fielded some of the other questions.

Several minutes later they arrived at the banquet balcony. Already scents of roasted root vegetables and nut-flour breads and pterosaur meat permeated the air. Long tables ran the length of the space, with more resin-glass lanterns hanging from overhead tree branches. Attendants laid out wooden plates, bowls, and cups, and wood-carved utensils.

A separate table, set perpendicular to the first, was laid for the elderboughs.

The area filled with people, most of whom seemed to be of higher rank—based on their woolly articles of clothing and beaded accessories—as they passed on the news of the foreigners, the war, and the strange request that the dinosaurs had approved. Qora didn't have a moment's pause in the midst of the continued questioning, but eventually, Ninan caught her eye and came to interrupt.

"Apologies," he told the group of people surrounding her. "But I need to speak with Miss Kanchaya. I promise I'll bring her right back." He cast a wary look at the gladewardens, all of whom were much more relaxed now and engaged in other conversations.

Qora tensed when he took her hand and led her away. She struggled to keep up with his hurried pace, as he was likely trying to get away before anyone else noticed they were gone. They crossed a bridge and descended a single level and then took a narrow passage that followed the curve of some rocky protrusions, and finally Ninan pulled her into an overlook where a spring of water cascaded down the rocks. Hanging moss curtained them off from the walkways, forming a natural alcove. There was just enough fading sunlight to set the space dimly aglow, and Qora braced herself on the railing while she observed the view.

Ninan watched her quietly. "I asked Gladwarden Sacha if there was a place where you and I could talk in private. He gave me directions here."

She turned her attention toward him. "You don't have to do this. We're old enough that we can accept the reality of the situation without having to talk through it. I already said my goodbyes to you at Port Waqta. I knew what would happen after I left. It will take time, of course, to not feel so …"

"Qora." He leaned in close and cupped her cheek. "I didn't marry Paqari."

Her pulse kicked up. "What?"

"You left Sumaq so quickly … There are so many things you still don't know. Paqari staged an attack on our wedding; I took advantage and bribed one of the attackers to take me away and make it look like an abduction. Then, with some help, I was able to move my friends from Thak to safety, and immediately afterward I flew to Unu to warn Izhi that my father was planning to advance on the capital."

Qora searched his face for proof of sincerity, because what he was saying was insane. "Quya Urpi told me you sent your friends to her, but I didn't realize you'd evacuated them in person; I thought you'd hired a special team or something to help you take care of that. And if you were in Unu after the wedding, then you must've ..."

Ninan nodded gravely. "I was there when the Sauroguard reached the citadel."

"That's how you were able to witness the ... the dinosaurs you described. The acid-spitters and the climbing velociraptors."

He nodded again.

Still hesitant, but reminding herself it was alright now, she slipped her arms around his waist and pulled him against her. He reciprocated, delicately at first, then tightened his hold.

"That must have been so horrifying," she said into his shoulder, her voice breaking as she imagined thousands of dinosaurs on the horizon.

They held each other for several minutes, chests colliding in slow breaths.

"I'm sorry about Sakay," he told her.

Her eyes welled at that, but she was relieved to know he knew. The fact that she'd lost Sakay had been bad enough, but having to break the news to someone else who cared about him would have been worse.

She pulled back and swiped at one of her bottom eyelids.

He swiped gently at the other. "I followed you to Allpa."

"You did?"

"Well, first I hoped to find you and the Razorclaws in Unu with Izhi. But I should have gone to Allpa first. We had the same idea—seeking refuge with the quya. After speaking to Izhi, I had plans to meet my friends at Qhispina House and make sure they arrived safely, but then my father captured me at the citadel before I could leave. He tried to kill me. I managed to fight off his guards but he had me cornered, with more guards on the way. Then Paqari came out of nowhere; she flew in and got me out of there. I told her I had to find you, to get to you as soon as I could, and we went to Allpa together."

"But ... how were you able to get to me *here*? How did you get past the meganeuras? And the giganotosaur?"

"The princess recognized the spores in time for us to protect ourselves. As soon as we landed, I used the crystal to show the border patrol we were on a mission of great importance. The gladewardens of Murkroot told me where you and your brother were headed, and we followed as fast as we could. They told me you would be in a whole other kind of Deadwood Pit, trying to convince the elderboughs of the truth of what's happening in the Terrains—so I knew we had to hurry. We ran most of the way."

Qora's eyes welled again, wondering what would have happened if he hadn't burst in with a horde of little reptiles on his heels and their eyes locked on that dominite crystal. "Thank you."

He wiped her eyes again and stared at her tenderly. "The people in the Terrains needed you to succeed. But more than that ... Qora ... I would do *anything* for you."

"Ninan ..." she whispered, shaking her head. "Spirits. I ... I just ..."

Ninan took both her hands in his. "What is it?"

"Sometimes I still think that you only believe you feel certain things for me because of the Venture. Because that experience bonded us in a way nothing else could have. And then after all those months apart, the absence of each other, the forbidden feelings. All of that was enough to create the illusion—"

"Don't say anything like that again. Don't you *dare* say it—because it's not true. You were everything to me, not only because you stunned me from the moment I met you—stunned me with your fire and your scathing words, and later stunned me with your tenacity and your kindness—but because you saw something in me. I may have thought I was pretending to be someone else, but I wasn't. You knew me as I really was, without the weight of my heritage, all that 'honor' stripped away, leaving me bare. And don't think for an instant that I would have risked it all for any other girl. It was *you* I couldn't walk away from. It was you I couldn't bear to compete with anymore—and you I would have lost to anyway. I still can't—and won't—walk away."

"Ninan ..."

"I'm not forbidden to be here with you now, am I? I'm not married, and I'm not engaged anymore, and no one is telling me I can't have you. There's no distance between us, nothing keeping us apart, nothing to make me long for the unattainable. Free and clear, I'm standing here in front of you. Free and clear, I want you. Free and clear, I *love* you—"

With that, Qora's emotions overwhelmed her and she grasped the front of his shirt and drew him to her until his lips met hers. She felt him smile against her mouth. He slid his hands up the back of her neck and into her hair.

Gods, she had longed to let herself feel these things fully, and now she could. She really could. She said it to herself over and over. *It's alright.* Even though everything was falling apart in the world around them, they at least had managed to fall together—although she didn't feel she had fallen so much as she felt she had jumped, and that somehow in the process she had sprouted wings.

He lifted her and she braced herself on his shoulders, wrapping her legs around his waist, because a simple kiss wasn't enough; she wanted to hold onto him with her whole body. And even though she didn't feel small enough for him to carry her easily, he seemed to find the strength to do it.

After several minutes, he set her down, both of them panting, and tucked her now-messy hair behind her ear, and then kissed her once more softly, stroking her chin with his thumb.

The skin of his fingers was rough, and she knew from having held his hand a few minutes ago that his palms were rough too. His knuckles were scarred from fighting—and spirits, how he could fight, with both the grace of autumn leaves dancing on the wind and the striking force of a tyrannosaur's footfalls. But despite how rough and vicious he was capable of being, he was also kind and compassionate and—with her, at least—gentle. He had been prepared to give his life over to the marital order of royalborns, to live a lie for his foreseeable future, so that the attack on the Sauroguard base could move forward. And, failing that, he had gone straight to rescue his friends, betraying his household and his father, to once again lose his title and become a fugitive and a traitor so that he could fight for what was right.

Somehow, even with a father like Qhapaq Apo, and with all the neglect and abuse he had faced, he still knew how to love and be loyal.

Now he fought for the cause against the New Empire, and if it hadn't been for him, Qora might have ended up in another cage. It pained her to think she had felt even the slightest temptation to not go after him that night when the pterodactyls had snatched him up during the Venture. Learning to trust had been a difficult process for her, but when it came to Ninan, she hadn't been able to *keep* herself from trusting him. Maybe that was why the revelation of his true identity had been so painful. But she didn't care anymore. No matter where he'd come from, he was just … Ninan. That was all he'd ever proven to be. And it was perfect.

"I love you too," she told him breathlessly.

His mouth broke into a crooked grin. "You know, I always enjoyed being around you even when you hated me. But I have to admit … I like this better."

FOURTEEN

NINAN'S PROMISE TO BRING QORA "right back" to the banquet was one he had broken all too easily. Even after several minutes in the glowy darkness by the spring, he simply didn't want to return to a group of unfamiliar people all vying for Qora's attention—or, he supposed, for his own, since he'd shown up with a crystal bearing mystical powers that everyone wanted to better understand.

On their way back, he couldn't help pulling her aside a few more times to relish new displays of affection, the likes of which were so much more intense now that there was nothing holding them back. There were no secrets between them anymore, no rules or arrangements or positions of power. They didn't have to hide or pretend or resist. He took her lips again and again, and he held her as close as he could.

Alas, he was also keenly aware that if he and Qora were to have any sort of future together, they would have to get on with the business of making their homeland a safe place to exist. And so, reluctantly, they found their way to the banquet balcony, where their friends were moving to take seats among the Tailfolk as attendants carried wooden trays of food and set them on the table.

There were fruit platters, herb salads, stuffed mushrooms,

roasted tubers with mince-nut garnish, flatbreads, pterosaur breast strips and drumsticks in a honey glaze, ptero-egg custard, and several other items Ninan was not sure of.

Ollan paused when Ninan and Qora arrived, with a sort of wary glare on his face. Ninan had, after all, been gone in the dark with the guy's sister for an indeterminate purpose, so Ninan knew he shouldn't be surprised. Boldly, he slipped his fingers between Qora's and locked their hands together as Ollan approached.

"Everything alright?" Ollan asked tightly.

Qora managed a small smile. "I think that's fairly obvious."

Wayra came over a second later, observed the scene, and said, "Oh good, I'm so glad we can all stop holding our breaths about you two." She placed a supportive hand on Ollan's shoulder and he seemed to relax a bit.

Ninan wasn't sure what Qora had told her brother about him, but he knew Qora hadn't gone unscathed by a few of his choices.

"My sister apparently trusts you," Ollan said, "So … I'll *choose* to trust you too. I know you've … sacrificed a lot, and for that I thank you."

"It's nothing," Ninan insisted.

Ollan nodded, then glanced at Wayra, who was still touching him, and his face flushed.

Then Paqari, who had approached without anyone's notice, cleared her throat. "Did I miss something?"

Immediately Qora released Ninan and threw her arms around the princess.

Paqari's eyebrows pulled together as she stiffly tolerated the embrace. "Now I'm *certain* I've missed something."

Qora pulled back. "You saved Ninan."

"Oh, that? Spirits … Don't be dramatic. He's the one who wriggled his way out from under an executioner and fought multiple guards—the showoff." She rolled her eyes. "I merely provided the getaway flight."

"Still …" Qora said.

"Well, you're welcome, I suppose."

"And …" Qora chewed the inside of her cheek. "Especially after the last time you and I saw each other. The night in Qaqakuna when we—"

Paqari put a finger to Qora's lips. "No, no. I won't hear a word about that. I've already explained to your beloved prizefighter that you both played right into my hands. My fury was only a ruse, a mere *fragment* of the schemes I concocted to try and sabotage my engagement. I will admit, I was surprised to find myself a bit wounded when I discovered what you might deem your 'betrayal,' but only because … well … I had grown to like you. And because you had heard about the disgraces of my past and didn't scrutinize me for it. You were a friend—not like those society girls and their fair-weather favor. I don't take that lightly." She clasped her hands at her waist. "If anyone should apologize for deceit, it ought to be me. If anyone should express gratitude, it ought to be me as well."

Now it was her turn, after some hesitance, to offer an embrace, which Qora tearily accepted.

ꓷꓷꓷ

Of all the long tables, Ninan and his friends were invited to sit with the elderboughs at the foremost table perpendicular to the rest.

After a few bites of honey-glazed pterosaur and stuffed

mushrooms, Ninan almost forgot why he was in this foreign land. The flavor was earthy and wholesome, and the way it felt when it hit his stomach lulled him into a state of bliss. Between that and having Qora by his side, he could happily pretend disaster wasn't lurking north of the Pirqas.

Over the course of the meal, Ninan actually learned some of the elderboughs' names. The woman with the red hair was Elderbough Raphi. The robust man with blond hair and his beard in a single braid was Elderbough Mallki. Then there was Elderbough K'ullu and Elderbough Lluta. Others were harder to keep track of, but he would try to remember what he could.

Once everyone had had the chance to partake of some of their meal, Elderbough Raphi stood and clapped her hands twice so that everyone took notice. "Thank you all for communing here tonight. I know that this is quite an unusual situation; we do not often encounter foreigners, much less invite them to dine with us or lend them our ears in matters beyond our borders. But as many of you have witnessed, we may soon be at the mercy of a power unlike anything we've ever seen—a power that is not only a threat to our people but an affront to our faith. As even more of you have witnessed, the dinosaurs have agreed to our intervention in the war."

Ninan still couldn't wrap his head around the idea of asking the dinosaurs' permission, and better yet, considering their acceptance of the strange scutefruit to be their 'reply,' although he wasn't about to complain. The method had provided the answer he had wanted to hear, and it had left Qora standing in one piece.

"Now," said Elderbough Raphi, "we must discuss how we will go about participating—with minimal impact on our lands, resources, people, and dinosaurs. Everyone is welcome to offer an opinion. Please respect your peers."

Elderbough Lluta spoke up. "We must send representatives of the Tail back to the Terrains to assess the severity. Two elderboughs, at least, and perhaps a few gladewardens for protection. With a personal witness to those conditions, we may be able to better formulate a plan."

"Agreed," said Elderbough Raphi.

One of the higher-ranking individuals from the next table raised a hand and said, "We need to send out a recruitment order for able-bodied adults and juveniles to be trained on skycycles, to support border patrol."

"And expand the meganeura program," said another.

Paqari set down her eating utensils calmly and told them, "You really ought to harvest those spores yourselves, too, you know. Sure, the meganeuras deploy them well, but imagine if you were to collect and aim them at a specific target using a projectile weapon?"

Kondor raised an eyebrow. "Where does a young royalborn lady like yourself get an idea like that?"

Ninan smiled. "She's *full* of ideas like that." He suddenly grew exhilarated by the thought of Paqari putting her diabolical skills to use against the Sumaqi Guard.

"Qhapaq Apo is committing biological warfare," Paqari explained, "by using reptiles against us. It's only logical that we think in kind, that we outwit him with similar—and even more clever—maneuvers. I should think an officer of your training, Gladewarden Sacha, would easily come to a similar conclusion." She turned up her nose.

Kondor scoffed. "Don't take offense, princess. I was only surprised to hear it coming from *you*."

"Because you assume that I'm a sheltered sort of dullard

without anything useful to contribute to a conversation like this?"

"Forgive me," Kondor said, "if I mistook your perpetual side-eyed scowl as contempt, and figured you for someone who would prefer to be lounging in the halls of your stone castle—while servants comb your hair—than you would in the company of these ... What was it I heard you whisper to your friend? These 'brutish backlanders'?"

She narrowed her eyes at him. "I was only referring to the gladewardens who forced my dear friend into the vicinity of several enormous dinosaurs. And with the way *you're* speaking to *me*, I can't say the sentiment was out of line."

Elderbough Raphi interjected to say, "I believe I told you to be *respectful* to your peers ..."

Ignoring her, Kondor smirked and leaned forward. "I don't know how they do things in the Terrains, princess, but it's clear you're not that much better than us, otherwise you wouldn't be here begging for our help."

Ninan tensed at the back and forth. Spirits, was this what it had been like for everyone on the *Velosaura* tour when he and Qora had argued over meals? He gently squeezed Qora's knee under the table.

"It's easy to maintain a government whose jurisdiction barely covers the area of a palm frond," Paqari shot back. "Come up north for a few days and you'll find that while our governments are highly flawed, we also inhabit a wide world full of vibrant cultures and grand innovations that put your little peninsula to shame."

"Paqari ..." Qora said with a warning glare.

The group had barely gotten the Tail to agree to this, and now the princess was insulting the whole nation.

"Yes, *that* I would like to see," Kondor said doubtfully.

"Wonderful," Elderbough Raphi cut in again. "Then you will go with our representatives to see it for yourself."

"I beg your pardon, Your Verdancy?" said Kondor.

"It seems you're taken with the princess and her native land. It's only fitting that you travel there with her."

Paqari sighed and picked up her wooden fork, poking at the tuber in front of her.

Kondor shook his head. "Your Verdancy, I appreciate your consideration; however, that's not really—"

"No further arguments, gladewarden," said the elderbough. "And we will waste no more time on petty disagreements. What other resources does the opposing force already have for battle? Miss Kanchaya?"

"Quya Urpi uses smilodons as part of her Guard, and she's training more as we speak. We're also working on importing fool's silver—the antidote for resisting the influence of dominite that I mentioned earlier—and our friend, along with the quya's elementalists, is working on trying to create our own dominite, along with other chemical-based defenses. Otherwise, it's blades and bows as usual, Your Verdancy. And of course whatever you can offer."

"Aside from the dinosaurs," said Elderbough K'ullu, "the skycycles, and the meganeura ... our people are sharpshooters. With pterosaurs as our main source of meat, the small flyers here are fast and furious; but our hunters know how to get a clean shot every time. We can put additional focus on ammunition production to prepare."

Qora nodded.

"Speaking of dinosaurs," said Kondor, who now spoke with a hint of resentment, "I think that *they* really ought to be the main point of discussion here. Don't you all?"

"He's right," said a woman with a woolly rhino stole around her neck. "I keep hearing everyone say the dinosaurs are going to fight against this 'Sauroguard,' but … how exactly are we supposed to get them to battle? Or are we waiting, gods forbid, for the war to come to *us*?"

Several people began to murmur at that, rising in volume until Wayra put two fingers in her mouth and whistled loud enough to cut through the noise.

"Thank you," Elderbough Raphi told Wayra once everyone had quieted again. "Yes, that is the main problem to solve, isn't it? As far as we elderboughs are concerned, we will not wait for the war to reach us. We will do everything possible to keep it in the Terrains. Thus, we must send our dinosaurs northward."

"But … how?" said a female gladewarden.

"How indeed." Elderbough Mallki looked pointedly at Ninan, Qora, Paqari, Ollan, and Wayra.

"We'll have to migrate them," Qora said.

"Migrate them?" A male gladewarden repeated. "They don't migrate. They're not birds."

"Actually," Paqari said, "they are more closely related than you might think. I was just discussing this with Wayra before we left. Dinosaurs and birds share a common ancestor."

"I think you mean *pterosaurs* and birds, princess." Kondor raised a pterosaur drumstick and took a bite.

Paqari offered him a blatantly false smile. "Yes, pterosaurs and birds *also* share a common ancestor, gladewarden. Thank you for the additional, albeit irrelevant, information. However, even though theropods don't have wings like pterosaurs—and certain winged dinosaurs—their heritage is the same. They come from a group of diapsid reptiles that existed hundreds of millions of years ago. Some of them evolved to have wings, while others like your giganotosaurs and tyrannosaurs did not. But if you've ever seen a bird without feathers, the resemblance to theropods is striking."

Kondor licked his teeth.

"What are you suggesting, then?" asked the female gladewarden. "We try to tap in to some ancient feature buried in their minds?"

"Dinosaurs use specific vocalizations," Wayra confirmed, "to communicate and work together as a group. It's usually for hunting, but if we observe them carefully, we can catalog the sounds they use and their meanings. Then we just have to recreate those sounds, maybe with instruments like your whistlemutes."

"Speak to them in their language ..." Ollan concluded.

Wayra nodded. "Exactly."

"And then you can just ... tell them what to do?" The male gladewarden frowned.

"Once we can understand them, and they can understand us," Wayra explained, "that will allow us to find out how much influence we have over them. At this point, it's all going to be experimental. But in my experience, most animals are willing to cooperate as long as they're treated with respect, they understand what's being asked of them, and they receive benefits in return. And, if in the case of ancient migration instincts, they are able to find some sense of coordination that we could use to our advantage, we'll be off to a good start."

"What about all the travel logistics, though?" said Elderbough Lluta. "Speed, distance, energy requirements?"

"Well that's just simple math," said Qora. "How fast can a giganotosaur comfortably walk, and for how long, before it needs to rest? How many pounds of meat does it consume per day? Then we map the distance, keeping the terrain in mind, and plan resources accordingly."

"If we're going to treat this like a migration," Paqari added, "then it might be helpful to consider a preparation method called 'hyperphagia.' It's when birds consume two to three times their normal intake before departure, typically with a high-fat diet to increase fat stores and provide more energy for the journey."

Kondor furrowed his brows like she was speaking a different language.

Wayra nodded along. "Most of the reptiles I've worked with have that capability—to store fat during times when prey is abundant. Although it's triggered seasonally. They sense the weather changes and they know to anticipate that some of the other animals will start to hibernate and soon be unavailable for consumption. I'm not sure how we would trigger that instinct artificially. I don't think whistlemute communication would work."

"It's hormonal," Paqari clarified. "Plants release volatile organic compounds in response to changes in temperature and humidity, and those compounds trigger certain hormones in animals that affect behavior."

The woman in the woolly stole inclined her head. "You mean like the etherpines?"

"I'm afraid I'm not as well versed in the specific trees in your region," said Paqari. "Are you referring to the ones with the reddish bark?"

Kondor swallowed another bite of meat. "She's referring to a type of tree that gives off a strong scent when the weather starts to get cold. We all associate it with the season. People like the smell so much they call it 'ether.'"

Ninan thought it was already fairly "cold" here, but based

on the presence of so many woolly creatures—like the rhinos he'd seen on the way to the Verdant Reach—he supposed it could get worse.

Elderbough Mallki raised an eyebrow. "The dinosaurs do become more aggressive in their hunting efforts around that time," he noted.

"Is there a way to synthesize that smell?" Ninan asked.

"Extracting the essential oils, maybe, and diffusing them?" said Qora.

"That's certainly a possibility," said Elderbough Raphi. "We'll take the idea to our arborists and determine the best method for extraction and diffusion. If we can induce hyperphagia, then the dinosaurs will be well prepared to leave. However, I still have concerns about energy requirements along the way. There is no guarantee of good hunting grounds coinciding with dinosaur feeding times. And we can't transport however many thousands of pounds of raw rhino meat for multiple days without spoilage."

"What about dry-cured meat?" someone suggested.

Kondor shook his head. "That would take weeks—months, even—to cure the amount of meat they would need. Not to mention it would be heavy to transport, and slow everything down."

"Actually," Qora said, "I was thinking … we could bring a herd of live woolly rhinos with us."

Everyone stared at her.

Ninan took a second to process the idea.

"Won't the dinosaurs eat them prematurely?" said Elderbough K'ullu.

"We could herd them separately," said Wayra. "Keep them a mile or two behind. Or ahead? And they eat plants, right? So they'll eat whatever grass, moss, or shrubs are available."

"Yes. That's a good idea," said Ollan.

Someone asked about the fool's silver "antidote" that would protect against dominite, and how it would be administered. Qora explained that once the dinosaurs arrived at Qhispina House, there would be plenty of time to lace their drinking water prior to battle.

There were a few other logistics to discuss, such as how to round up the rhinos, what sleeping arrangements might look like, and who would participate.

The conversation continued back and forth for another half hour or so, slowly winding down, and finally everyone finished their meals and dispersed for the night.

The elderboughs provided a guest house for Ninan and his friends. It was a cabin filled with bunks, but clean and supplied with fresh linens and pterosaur-feather pillows. Paqari grumbled about having to share space with everyone else but ended up being the first to fall asleep before anyone had even extinguished the lanterns.

Ninan curled up in the same bed with Qora, holding her until she drifted off. Although he himself was quite tired, his mind continued to spiral around everything he'd just learned and all the planning left to do. After what must have been an hour of lying wide awake, he slipped out onto the porch.

A few resin-glass lanterns remained lit on other porches and along the walkways, but otherwise the woods were dark. Endless rows of trees. Although the air was crisp and piney, Ninan craved something more open.

A set of stairs led upward and away from the porch, and Ninan followed them until he broke through the canopy and stepped onto the viewing platform. The sky above was clear and the stars were abundant.

He took a deep, cleansing breath as he looked up.

Several minutes later, Qora came up too.

"What are you doing up here?" she asked. "Couldn't you sleep?"

"Not really," he admitted.

She came to him and they lay down together on their backs.

Ninan traced a constellation in the air with his fingertip, pointing out the mouth of the astrodon and its individual teeth. "That's why smilodon teeth can cut through anything—because smilodons are descendants of the astrodons, whose teeth were made of burning starlight."

"I never thought of stars as burning," Qora said. "But someone told me once that the sun itself is a star, only much closer to us than the others."

"Yes, Paqari went on about that for a while on the way here," Ninan said. "From where we sit, stars are just pretty little lights, but up close they're enormous beyond comprehension— and hot enough to burn a man to ash in an instant. Apparently astronomers have learned all this by charting them and tracking their movements and using something called 'parallax.' And for how small the sun appears in the sky compared to the earth, it couldn't possibly heat the whole thing unless it was actually very big, but since it doesn't *look* big, that means it has to be far away. It's crazy. But don't tell the princess I was paying attention to her lecture, though; her ego's big enough as it is."

Qora laughed. "I think she's earned it."

"I guess I can't blame her for being interested in all that. So many things in our world don't make sense; studying them can help. That's why I like to look at the star patterns—because it's a way to make sense of them. I mean, I know they're just shapes people made up a long time ago, but it's nice to recognize something in the void."

They stared at the sky for a while, pondering this idea more deeply, and then Qora pointed to another cluster of stars. "There's 'Raptoriva in Flight.'"

Ninan got quiet all of a sudden, then smiled slowly. "That reminds me … There's something you should know."

Qora inclined her head toward his. "What?"

"When I went back to Kallpa House, to steal the arks … When the bandits and I were taking off, and I knew it might be the last time I ever set foot on the castle grounds … I looked back over the tiers, at the gardens and the paddocks … and … I saw her."

"You saw …" Qora pursed her lips like she was too afraid to say it, in case it wasn't what she was thinking.

"I saw the raptoriva. *Your* raptoriva."

She looked at him like she didn't believe it.

"It's true," he said. "She'd broken free from her tether somehow. And then she flew to the edge of the gorge and just … leapt."

Now Qora covered her mouth, eyes brimming.

"The raptoriva soared to the other side, where no one could reach her."

Qora nestled against Ninan's chest and let her tears fall onto his shirt. "I loosened the tether before I left Sumaq. I didn't know if she understood. I'm so glad you saw her."

"It was like you were there with me." He cradled her head and stroked her hair.

"I wish I could have *actually* been with you. I know it must have been so hard to leave Kallpa House behind."

"It was and it wasn't. It was my home once, but it was mostly unhappy. If it had been happy, I wouldn't have ever put myself in a position to be banished from it."

Ninan recalled all the nights he'd gone out with a group of highborn young men who were only his "friends" in the loosest sense of the word, a default social circle based on the limited number of noble families in the city. There had always been some sort of gathering at one of their estates, or at the manor of one of their parents' associates—and there had always been too much pisco and not enough supervision.

Not all Sumaqi highborns were loyal to the qhapaq, however, and when Ninan had unintentionally found himself at a secret assembly of those with intent to overthrow his father, it had been too late to escape before the raid. The so-called friend that had led him there had been too inebriated to think twice about involving the son of the monarch, and Ninan had been too inebriated to realize his father's chief attendant had been tailing him—due to a habit Ninan had made of staying out late and drinking too much and spending golds at gambling parlors, as plenty of overprivileged young men were wont to do. His father would have tried to cover up Ninan's "involvement," without a doubt, except that too many people had witnessed him there, not only the traitors but everyone in the streets as law officers had led him out. Thus, the only thing for the qhapaq to do had been to make an example of his own son. Spite may have played a part in Ninan's public shaming as well, after months of his rogue behavior embarrassing Kallpa House.

Ninan detailed all of this to Qora for the first time, having realized she'd never heard the full story. There had been enough information circulated about him to give most people the gist, but no one really knew what had happened or why.

"A year later, my father found me and summoned me for the Venture, and the rest is history."

Vespers lurked in the treetops, their black eyes reflecting moonlight, and flapped their moth-like wings now and then.

"He's treated you as nothing but a piece on his game board," Qora lamented.

"And you as well."

She nodded. "We can't let him win. Whatever we do, we can't let him win."

Ninan held her close and breathed her in and tried not to think about what it was going to take to stop his father. But together they had defeated monsters before; he had to believe they could do it again. This time they had more friends and allies than they could count. And this time, it might be their last chance.

FIFTEEN

UNAY: They called me "traitor," and for many years I believed it to befit me. Now I say unto you that some traitors are the most loyal of all, but merely born into the wrong household.

Echoes in the Void, Act II, Scene IV

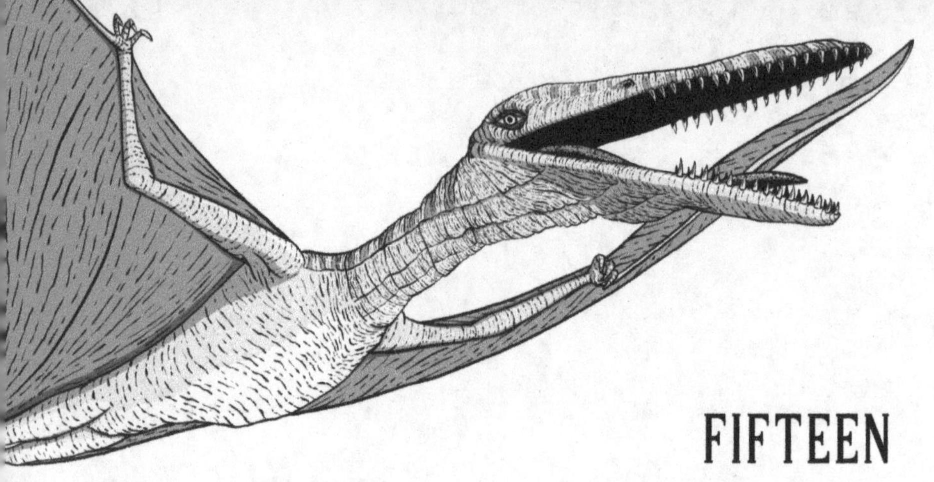

FIFTEEN

OLLAN HUNG BACK as the group came within a mile of returning to Murkroot. The trek back from the Verdant Reach had seemed to go by more quickly than their journey there the previous day, probably because the novelty of the grafted orchards and treehouse-buildings and unusual creatures had somewhat worn off, although that didn't stop Ollan from gawking at newly notable details as they went.

He watched Wayra play with another feathered compy by dropping small pieces of almond bread behind her to lure it along. She had already spent half the time with a sciurumimus around her neck like a scarf, while also trying to perfect mimicking the whistle of blue-capped tanager birds using her usual cupped-hands-and-interlocking-fingers method. Then Kondor had allowed her to try his whistlemute, and her eyes had lit up like two fireflies as she'd explored the shape and holes that produced the sound. "It's not mimicking any reptilian sound, though," she noted. "And yet, it means something to them ..."

Kondor shrugged. "I think somewhere in our ancient history, people figured out that reptiles like that pitch, so they made an instrument of it."

Along the way, the group had picked up an additional gladewarden from just outside the Verdant Reach, named

Anku—the other besides Kondor who would be going to Allpa—who was partial to giganotosaurs and had spent at least a half hour discussing them with Wayra. "The teeth are serrated rather than conical, so it kills its prey with more of a slicing motion instead of a crushing one" and "It's the fastest among the giants" and "Its brain is probably the smallest of its peers." Ollan wasn't sure why this made him tense; he'd had plenty of time to talk to Wayra and hadn't come up with a single interesting thing to say, so what did he expect?

She happened to glance backwards once and he forced a smile before Anku drew her attention to a pack of gigas making noises down below.

Ollan sighed and stuffed his hands into his pockets and tried to appreciate the fresh, piney scent of the air; it was different from the woods where he and Qora used to go shooting—sharper, and more fragrant.

By the time they reached Murkroot, the citizens were in a frenzy over Elderbough Raphi and Elderbough Mallki, who had arrived ahead of everyone else. Apparently they, with their status, had utilized a long-range zipline trolley system that had allowed them to cross significant sections of distance (particularly those descending from higher terrain like the Verdant Reach) much more quickly.

The elderboughs took time to greet the population while the local gladewardens retrieved Quya Urpi's pterobeasts and gondolas from the border patrol and readied them for departure. The guards and pilots that had come with each gondola separately were now well rested and ready to return home. All confiscated weapons and supplies were returned to the foreigners.

The passengers were instructed to load the gondolas as evenly as possible, each with two attendants and a pilot, one gladewarden, one elderbough, and half the visitors from the Terrains. Qora, Ninan, and Paqari boarded the first, followed by Kondor, who seemed intent on the second gondola but lost his place when Anku—still talking to Wayra—boarded it before he could. Ollan was already seated on the second gondola too and could have traded places with Kondor, he supposed, but he wasn't enthusiastic about watching his little sister and Ninan together for the entire ride, and for some reason the idea of Kondor and Paqari trapped in a confined space struck him as an opportunity for entertainment.

His instinct didn't disappoint, as Paqari immediately made herself comfortable with a small stack of books, flicking through to find a specific page in *The Haunting of Pteroclaw Heights*, at which point Kondor remarked, "Apparently the princess doesn't think we're good enough company for her."

Without looking up, she replied, "It must be quite emasculating for you to lose a woman's attention to fictional characters."

He took a seat and draped an arm lazily on the gondola rim, gazing out at the forest. "I think your preference for fictional characters says more about *your mental state* than it does about my confidence."

"And *I* think"—she turned the next page abruptly—"it says a lot about the state of men in this world that books are so often preferable to human interaction. Open one sometime; you might learn a thing or two. In fact, here …" The princess took the top book from her pile and extended it to him. "You might actually improve your manners from this one."

He scoffed without accepting it. "Oh?"

"Yes," the princess told him with a smug smile. "It discusses the social dynamics between carnivorous reptiles—and we all know that would be a step up for you."

Qora chuckled but snatched the book away. "Alright. No more fighting today, please. We've got a long afternoon ahead of us."

Paqari pursed her lips, then reluctantly went back to her suspense novel while Kondor scowled from the other side of the gondola.

With a heavy sigh, Qora laid her head on Ninan's shoulder.

It was still so strange for Ollan to see his sister like this. Even after all she had experienced, after the trials she'd braved. He knew she was more than capable of handling herself in all kinds of situations. But he would always feel the need to look out for her.

Several minutes later, the elderboughs arrived. Elderbough Mallki joined the first gondola while Elderbough Raphi joined the second. And then they were off, while citizens bid them all farewell from below.

〉〉〉

Ollan spent the first leg of the trip tuning out Anku's ongoing remarks about the landscape.

"Limbs above! Can you believe all this has *always* been out here? The isthmus is glorious—the sea on both sides! How open these spaces are! The mountains are practically *bare*. What a riveting way to travel."

Elderbough Raphi watched calmly, but with a dedicated gaze that hinted at her enjoyment. "This panorama is quite breathtaking, I must admit."

The first gondola flew several yards ahead, the passengers' conversations inaudible, but Qora and Ninan leaned over one side to see smaller theropods roaming the ground along a rocky ridge while Elderbough Mallki appeared to be pointing out others in the distance and discussing them with the attendants. Kondor kept his arms folded and his expression tight, but constantly snuck glances in different directions with a subtly craned neck. Paqari kept to her books, for the most part, pausing only once in a while to take in a view.

When the gondolas passed over Mount Wiru, Anku nearly lost his mind. "Incredible! I've heard the story about this—passed on from our ancestors—but never did I imagine it was *real.*"

Wayra smiled. "I didn't realize your people knew about it."

"Well, if you go back far enough in our history, we weren't always so separate from the rest of the continent. It stands to reason we shared some of these places, or at least traveled through them," Anku said.

Then he launched into a description of the tale he had heard as a child, about a girl named Chayaynin who had gone on a quest to reach the end of a rainbow where it was said that she could request her heart's desire. After weeks of arduous travel and facing many monsters and demons, she finally reached the mountaintop where the end of the rainbow had originally appeared, only to discover that it was both invisible and intangible, and she died of heartbreak on the spot. But the gods, to honor her efforts, infused the mountain with a rainbow of colors so that all future venturers who came seeking a rainbow's end would truly find one.

Ollan silently marveled at how different cultures tried to explain the same phenomenon. In Sumaq, it was something about a symbol of harmony created by Sky Mother and Light Father. To the Tailfolk, it was a literal rainbow made solid.

Crossing over the Pirqas generated new conversations about

the logistics of moving the giant theropods through such rough terrain, but a route to the west looked viable depending on the weather, and anyway there were many other details to work out before they would reach this point so they must take it one step at a time.

Then Anku asked Wayra for a demonstration of her reptile-sound mimicry and she formed her hands into a shape that allowed her to recreate the sound of a rhamphorhynchus, which drew a small flock of the little flyers up out of the scant trees and had them swirling around the gondola for several seconds before they realized the humans were of no interest to them and returned to their perches.

After all the excitement, Anku finally sat down to rest and soon began to snooze in an upright position, lulled by the gondola's rocking motion and the gentle breeze created by pterobeast wingflaps.

Wayra came to sit by Ollan. "You've been awfully quiet today."

He huffed. "Am I ever loud?"

"No, I guess you're not. But ..." She shrugged. "I don't know. You seem *quieter*. Trailing behind everyone, sitting in the corner by yourself, not saying much."

"It's been a long week. A lot's happened. Everything around me is different." He gestured at the region through which they were flying. "Well, actually, everything around me has *been* different, for a few years now. I guess nothing is familiar when you can't remember the past." He forced a laugh to lighten things once he processed what a heavy thing he'd said, but it was too late.

"And when you finally did remember, you went home to find that everything had changed while you were gone."

As soon as Wayra followed his gaze to Qora, Ollan realized he'd been staring at his sister. He'd left Qora at thirteen, and returned to find her a young woman, a Venture champion, a rebel conspiring against the qhapaq.

"I can't imagine what that must have been like for you," Wayra added softly. "Like … going to sleep and waking up in a different time. Missing so much. Years gone, as if in a blink."

Tears stabbed at Ollan's eyes but he held them back. "It's fine. I didn't mean to bring it up like that. Sorry." He raked his fingers through his hair.

"Don't be sorry. I asked."

"Sure, but we're all dealing with things. My sister's traumatized from the Venture, to say the least. The prince and princess are both wanted traitors by now, who can never go back to their old lives. And you … well, I guess I don't really know that much about you … but I know you lost a close friend recently, and that you left everything behind to come and help this cause."

"I don't have it nearly as bad as the rest of you," she told him. "No?"

"I'm not important enough to be considered a fugitive, and for the most part I've been able to avoid danger," she said. "I was raised on paddocks. Both my parents trained cargo reptiles and mounts; that's how they met, working for the same beastlord in the Northern Reach. They still live out there. I tell everyone they're dead so no one will go looking for them to punish me because of what I do with the Razorclaws, but they're doing well."

"But … you don't ever get to see them."

"Once in a while I make a visit. I disguise myself and cover my tracks. The distance is difficult, of course, but all things considered, I'm very lucky. Just look at the other Razorclaws: Kuy grew up on the streets after his father was imprisoned for substance trafficking and his mother overdosed on pachyrhine; Gorgo ran away from an abusive home when he was barely an adolescent; Req's mother—a professor at the Qhusi Academy of Elements—died from an explosion in her laboratorium. And then of course there's Sakay's fate ..." At that, her eyes turned glossy.

"Nothing's ever easy, is it?" Ollan said.

Wayra cleared her throat. "Sometimes I think we're given just enough to want to fight for it. Not enough to thrive."

"Enough to survive, and little more," Ollan agreed. "That's what it felt like when I couldn't remember. Like ... I could sense vague faces or hear distant voices on the fringes of my mind. I knew I *had* a past, and people I cared about, and that's what allowed me to keep living ... in hopes that I would one day get the full sense of it all again. But in the moment, I always felt sort of ... hollow."

"What did you do," Wayra asked, "all that time when you were gone?"

"Worked in the mines."

"That's it? Just 'worked in the mines'? Didn't you have a community? Friends?" She hesitated, then added, "Lovers?"

"I went for drinks with the other miners sometimes. Had a few brief ... attachments. But, it's hard to connect to anything in front of you when you don't know what's behind. Roots before branches, you know."

"That sounds very ... lonely."

"I was biding my time, I think."

"How so?"

"Hoping my mind would eventually heal." Ollan cracked a knuckle. "When I first got there, I was wounded badly and had to see a physician. But when I couldn't answer many of his questions, he explained that my head injuries had caused brain damage and memory loss. He said there was no guarantee, but if I did manage to recover anything, it would take time. In the meantime, he advised me to find work and try to live a normal life—as much as possible. So that's what I did."

"'Enough to survive.'"

Ollan nodded. "Otherwise I would only think about all the things that kept drifting into my mind—the half memories. It was like blurred vision; my eyes wouldn't focus no matter what I did. I remembered a girl—Qora—screaming at me in the woods, but I could never remember who she was or the words she was saying. I had the strongest feeling she was screaming my name, which made it so much worse because *that*, at the very least, I should have been able to recall. My own name."

"Did *any* memories start coming back for you, like the physician said they might? Filling in some of the blanks?"

"Sometimes the smells or the sights at the market in the nearest city would stoke my memories, and I would think maybe I was getting a better picture. But usually it only made me … *feel* things. I would feel sad, and not know why. Because of Qora's favorite foods, or dye like what my mother would use, or figurines similar to what I had taught my younger brothers to carve. Except I couldn't make the connection. Sometimes I'd seek out those feelings hoping they'd help me have a breakthrough, other times I'd avoid them because they were too painful."

"Have you told Qora any of this?" Wayra asked.

Ollan shook his head. "She's asked me before, although she is careful not to press me too much. But I think it would only hurt her to know more, to think of me suffering. She would blame herself. She would think she should have known somehow, and been able to track me down. Or she'd say she never should have let me get dragged off to begin with, like she could have actually stopped it. I don't want her feeling that way."

Wayra inclined her head. "You're a good brother."

"Well, I don't know about that. I'm not doing much for her lately."

"You are, though. You're giving her space. You're trying to protect her peace. I can tell you want what's best for her. Just … don't isolate yourself in the process."

He sighed. "I'll try not to."

〉〉〉

When the pterobeasts landed the gondolas at Qhispina House, the Razorclaws were there to greet them, along with Quya Urpi herself and a couple of pet smilodons that had wandered out with her.

The quya and the rebels stood firmly like soldiers, Ollan thought—and he had seen plenty of soldiers lined up—hands clasped, faces still.

Qhispina House attendants met the gondolas first to escort the elderboughs and gladewardens onto the platform.

Urpi came forward and bowed her head. "What a great honor that you have traveled all this way. I am Urpi Qhispina, quya of the Terrain of Allpa. Welcome."

The elderboughs and gladewardens bowed in return, all looking a bit wary of the big cats.

"I am Elderbough Raphi Chapra of Woodborough, and this is Elderbough Mallki Apaza of Thornbriar. We govern with a council of eight from the Verdant Reach, over the whole of the Tail. We appreciate your hospitality and, I must say"—she gazed up at the castle—"the honor is ours."

"These are two of our gladewardens," said Elderbough Mallki, going on to introduce the two men by name and briefly explaining the role of a gladewarden in the tree-dwelling society.

The quya introduced the three Razorclaws who were with her, summarizing their recent endeavors and mentioning the bandits who were still scouting the encampment in Kawsay. Then she addressed everyone else—Ollan, Qora, Ninan, Paqari, and Wayra. "I am grateful for your safe return, and for all that you have done to create the opportunity for this union. When we have a moment, I want to know *everything*. At this time, however, I'm afraid I must once again meet your arrival with dire news."

"What do you mean?" said Wayra.

Ollan's stomach lurched.

"My spies have returned," Urpi told them, "and informed me that the encampments at Ñansa and Wood Ridge are abandoned. They've scouted the surrounding areas but found no other evidence of Sauroguard activity. They believe the reptiles were either relocated, or that perhaps it was those reptiles that Apo used to take Unu's capital, and that they are now stationed somewhere in Unu."

"That makes sense," said Ninan. "There will of course be more camps beyond the four where my father sent the reptiles from the Aquchay base. But …"

"What about Camp Wayaqa?" Qora asked Kuy and Gorgo. "Did you find anything there?"

Kuy said, "We didn't make it to Wayaqa. We barely even got to the western peaks of Huandoy when we found something else."

"Another encampment in Unu?" Ollan guessed.

Gorgo nodded.

"And … what did you see there?" Qora asked.

"You'd have to see it to believe it," Kuy replied. "It's probably best if we show you."

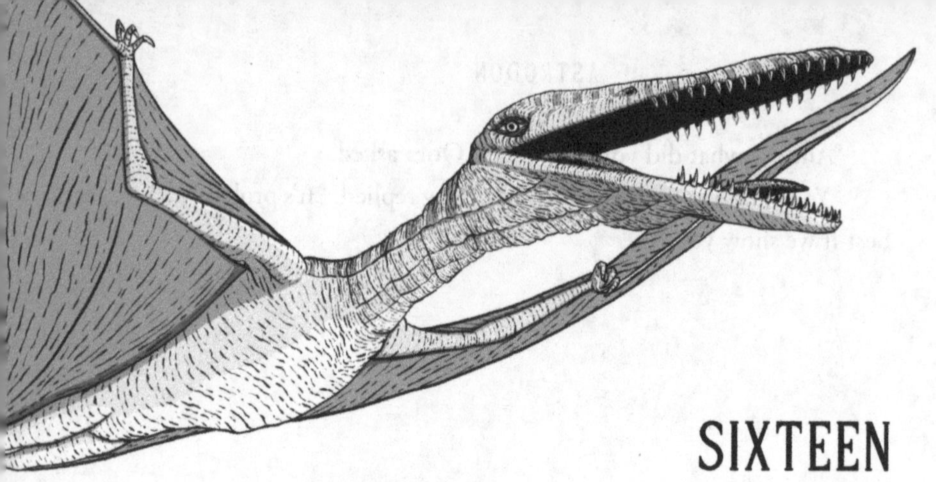

SIXTEEN

A LITTLE OVER TWO HOURS LATER, Qora stood on the nearside of the mountains southwest of Huandoy, along the shoulder of a snowy subpeak overlooking the encampment. Everyone who had been told of this in Allpa stood with her.

Only Kuy and Gorgo didn't gape at the scene, as they had already witnessed it prior to this trip.

Qora shivered, but only in part from the frost around her. The quya had provided the group with appropriate outerwear to handle this climate (everyone in fitted, fur-lined trousers and thick coats) herself wearing a cloak with a hood rimmed in the fur of a deceased smilodon, but nothing could have prepared Qora—or any of the rest of them, for that matter—for what lay below them right now.

At least a thousand pyroraptors lined up in an enclosure, while beastlords wielded the familiar purple crystals and shouted in unison: "Burn!"

Fire spewed from the pyroraptors' mouths in long streams that came within a few inches of reaching the beastlords.

"Burn!" the beastlords said again as the first round of flames dissipated.

They did this in a sort of rhythm, a call and response.

An exercise, Qora thought.

The pyroraptors were training to be fast, precise, to burn on command.

Kondor, Anku, and the elderboughs all stared at the sight with pallid faces (pallid even for them). This was shocking enough for Qora and her friends, who had already encountered similarly mutated dinosaurs, but it must have been so much worse for the Tailfolk—who had probably come here hoping Qora's and Ninan's claims were elaborate lies. Now the Tailfolk could see just how wretched Qhapaq Apo really was, not only with the way he mistreated and controlled the dinosaurs, but with the monsters he had made of them.

A bitter taste formed on Qora's tongue. She squeezed Ninan's hand to ground herself, but she still felt as though the earth were crumbling beneath her feet.

The encampment was situated in a circular fashion, around a high-mounted dominite crystal the size of a megaraptor's skull, while each enclosure took on the shape of a wedge within the greater circle. The dominite crystal had a sort of covering over it, probably to keep the sunlight from degrading its power. All the enclosures had small fire pits scattered throughout, providing warmth for all the different species, and burning a clear liquid that could only be purified sauropod oil (which would burn smokeless flames at a quarter ounce per hour), an efficient fuel source considering the climate and the thousands of dinosaurs here.

"It's so much worse than we thought," said Quya Urpi.

The pyroraptors here didn't appear to be the same as the ones Qora had seen in the Aquchay; these were fully grown, fully developed. That must have been why she hadn't been able to determine their specific purpose then—because those had been juveniles.

"Their ability must not fully develop until they're older," said Wayra, echoing Qora's thought. "Or the beastlords focus on basic commands when the dinosaurs are young, then move on to … this sort of training."

These would have been bred months ago, maybe even a year or two ago, depending on how much the qhapaq had managed to increase their growth rate.

The same went for the scutellosaurs, which the Aquchay base had also had. These, too, were bigger (if only slightly, since even the adults didn't stand higher than a man's knee) except that their special abilities, if they had any, remained unclear.

Another enclosure held what looked like oviraptors, which were covered in silvery scales rather than feathers.

"Those things look like they've got razors on their backs," said Ollan.

One of the handlers stepped over some of the scales that had fallen on the ground, lodged into the mud vertically. He carefully picked them up with a gloved hand and dropped them into a burlap sack.

"You're not far off with that assessment," Kuy told Ollan. "The scales shed easily, and the oviraptors seem to be able to drop them at will. We don't know how sharp they are, just that everyone here handles them *very* carefully … and always avoids stepping on them."

"Looks like the scales are weighted, too," Ninan noted, "so they land upright when they fall."

Gorgo nodded. "A nice little inconvenience for enemies on the battlefield."

"What about those?" Qora asked, pointing to another enclosure full of unusually small therizinosaurs—longer-necked theropods, feathered lightly on the body but thickly at the tail, with claws like tiny swords. While most would tower over their handlers at three times their height, these stood no more than four or five feet tall. "Are they infants? That doesn't make sense considering the others here."

"No," said Wayra. "They can't be infants. Not with claws like that. Therizinosaurs don't start to develop the bigger claws until they've reached puberty. Not to mention the proportions; infants and juveniles have bigger eyes and heads, and shorter necks, relative to the rest of the body. Those have to be a different subspecies. Some kind of *miniature* therizinosaur."

"We think the claws contain a toxin," said Kuy. "Last time we were here, one of the handlers got scratched. She screamed in agony and the others rushed her off to the med tent like she had minutes to live. We're not even sure she made it. Never came back out, at least not before we left."

"How …" said Elderbough Raphi. "How is this possible?" She clung to Kondor's arm like she might collapse otherwise.

"That's what we're trying to figure out," Req replied. "Although we're still a little preoccupied with how to fight them off if and when they get to Allpa—and with how the dominite works. Controlling them is more of a priority than how they were bred."

"It's more than selective breeding, for certain," said Wayra. "It would take hundreds, thousands, and in some cases *millions* of years to get mutations like that. We're not talking about bigger teeth or brighter feathers. Even with whatever the qhapaq is doing to make the dinosaurs mature faster—which means faster reproduction, and new generations for selection—getting them to *breathe fire* is a whole other level."

"If he figured out how to make dominite," said Req, "maybe he also discovered or developed something mutagenic. Although

I can't imagine what sort of mutagen could allow him to choose *specific* mutations—because these are clearly intentional." He gestured emphatically at the encampment.

"Your qhapaq has created a disgrace to nature Itself," Elderbough Mallki said gravely. "We must put an end to this."

"Well it's not really looking good for our side of things," Kondor muttered.

Paqari rolled her eyes. "That's the point, gladewarden. We need reinforcements. That's the whole reason you're here."

"Actually, *I'm* here because I couldn't keep my mouth shut, and the elderboughs saw fit to punish me for it." He glanced pointedly at his leaders, although neither could tear their gaze away from the dinosaurs below to pay him any attention.

"Having you around seems more like a punishment for the *rest* of us," said Paqari.

"It's hardly fair for you to speak for your friends, princess. Surely everyone else is not as easily displeased as you are."

"Well surely *you*—"

"Enough," Qora told them through a sigh. "This isn't the time." She would have thought the group could get some peace from Kondor and Paqari's verbal sparring during such a sullen moment. Putting them in separate gondolas on the way to the mountains had been a good start, but it seemed they were intent on butting cranial domes like two pachycephalosaurs fighting for dominance.

"It's been a long few days for all of us," Ollan added. "Plus another two hours in the air just to land in *this* climate"—he wrapped his arms around himself—"and see *that* down there … it's enough to make anyone scaly. Let's try not to irritate each other."

"We could use a warm meal," the quya said, "before making

the return trip. That at least can sustain us a little longer. There should be a lodge on the other side of the mountain, facing Huandoy."

Req patted his stomach. "Sounds like a plan."

〉〉〉

The two gondola pilots dropped off the passengers a half mile from the lodge, to avoid any close attention on the very obviously highborn transportation, and then flew off to the nearby reservoir below so that the pterobeasts could drink and hunt their own meals.

Qora marveled at the feeling of snow squinching under the soles of her boots as she walked among her group. She had never seen more than a heavy frost during the coldest winters in Qhusi, and even that was rare. The late afternoon sunlight made the white coating sparkle across the ground. It was beautiful, but she was grateful to be protected against it in the fur-lined cloak. The Tailfolk, on the other hand, had already come equipped with woolly accessories from their own land.

As they trekked across the mountainside, Qora tried for the moment to focus on Ninan's warm, gloved hand in hers, rather than the panic building in her chest over the mystical dinosaurs that threatened to advance on Allpa's borders—although the chill on her cheeks and the rumble in her belly should have been distraction enough.

Nearing the lodge, other people came and went, some on foot, others riding in sleighs pulled by teams of feathered dryosaurs. A few came sliding down from the higher peaks on curved wooden boards, somehow maintaining an upright balance on them despite the slippery slope. A few more dragged dinosaur carcasses—cryolophosaurs, from what Qora could tell—on big sleds, toward the hunting lodge's butchering facilities.

From the gondola flight, Qora had seen several cryolophosaurs among the snow-dusted trees, so this must have been a primary hunting zone for them.

On the way over, the gondola had also passed over the summit, the endpoint for the thirteenth quinquennial Venture—the place where Thalu Machaqway had made a name for himself ten years earlier. Qora shuddered at the memory of Qhapaq Apo informing her that she was to consider herself betrothed to the "beloved competitor," and that he would announce the engagement officially at the Revelry taking place after Ninan and Paqari's wedding. The highborn matchmaking event had been intended to ride the wave of a successful match, although Qora knew the qhapaq's only intention had been to keep her in check. What a union that would have been, she thought, trapped in a life with a shameless rake constantly high on pachyrhine. She would have rather faced the swoop of pin-toothed pterodaustro that had guarded the Venture prize during Thalu's competition year.

The lodge was made of thick logs, stacked and laid together to form a main building with a couple of smaller attachments, along with a few outbuildings.

Inside, several dining tables surrounded a central column fireplace of piled stone. The group split up at two of the tables, with the quya sitting among the elderboughs, along with Anku, Wayra, and Paqari. Qora sat with Ninan, Ollan, Kondor, and the other Razorclaws.

A lodge steward came to welcome everyone and provide information on provisions—the mountain fare included a stew of cryolophosaur meat and vegetables, anise bread, fried plantains, and coca tea—and then returned to the kitchen with the group's order.

Everyone waited with hanging heads and weary gazes. For several minutes, no one spoke, still working out the facts about what they'd seen.

Eventually, though, the elderboughs asked the quya about the more recent history of the Terrains, prompting her to explain the political tensions between Sumaq and the others over the past decade or so.

Being well aware of most of this, the Razorclaws at Qora's table started their own conversation on the potential anatomy of a dinosaur's mouth that might allow it to breathe fire.

"Like anything," said Req, "it's just chemistry. They've got to have glands that secrete reactive chemicals. When the chemicals combine, they ignite. The muscles surrounding those glands probably pressurize them, creating a stream that shoots out."

Kondor leaned against the backrest of his chair, sighed, and folded his arms. "I really did not sign up for this."

"It doesn't matter how it works," said Gorgo. "What matters is … What are we going to do about it? How do we protect ourselves against it?"

Ollan glanced over his shoulder to where Wayra sat next to Anku at the other table, subtly lingering on them for a moment. Then he turned back to the group and said, "It *could* matter. Knowing the source of the enemy's power gives us an advantage—and possibly an understanding of how to cut it off."

"Sure," said Kuy, "if we could get those pyroraptors to swallow a bucket of snow, maybe."

"What happens if they attack during a rainstorm?" Kondor mused. "Would that put out their fire?"

"Depends," Req told him. "If it's like a grease fire, then no.

The secretions could be hydrophobic."

Ninan dragged his fingers through his hair. "Honestly, I'm still stuck on the scutellosaurs. What the other dinosaurs can do is bad enough, but at least we know. The *un*known presents a danger we can't prepare for."

"Scutellos are herbivores," Kondor pointed out. "Not to mention they're small. How dangerous could they be?"

Qora shook her head. "That's probably the idea. They don't look threatening, but they'll come out of nowhere with a feature we would never expect. Qhapaq Apo wouldn't breed them for no reason. Ninan's right; not knowing could be very bad for us."

"Well we can't just hang around and wait to see," said Gorgo. "We still need to go look for other encampments, try to figure out the whole scope of what we're up against."

"And what do you suggest we do, then, Gorgo?" Kuy asked. "Go down there and try to provoke one of the little beasts?"

Gorgo leaned forward conspiratorially. "Actually ... I was thinking ... maybe we go down there and *snatch* one."

"Are you insane?" Qora said.

Kondor shrugged. "I'm game."

Qora scowled at him. "Of course you are. You haven't learned to *fear* dinosaurs. Not all of them keep to themselves—and not all of them operate of their own free will. Even with fire breath, I'm sure the ones here don't seem that big or that bad to you. But you haven't seen these kinds of creatures in an attack."

"I don't know," said Kuy. "It's not the *worst* idea Gorgo's ever had."

Wayra scoffed. "Sure, but it's got to be one of the top five, at least."

SEVENTEEN

OLLAN SIPPED THE FOAM off the top of his third ale, feeling a tingle warm his body. He had foregone the coca tea in favor of something with a little more strength to it, and now everything around him dampened nicely. Despite the way his muscles relaxed and his mind fogged over, however, the drink did not erase the ache in his gut as he glanced over at the other table, where Anku told Wayra the entire backstory of each tattoo on his forearms.

Meanwhile, at his own table, Qora was sitting too close to Ninan for Ollan's liking, but he tried to remind himself that all that drama was resolved now. From what Ollan knew of Ninan, the boy had more than proved himself and his loyalty, and even shown a willingness to self-sacrifice, although that didn't fully temper Ollan's instinct to keep Qora from emotional harm. Not that he'd been able to keep her from harm, in general.

He groaned mentally at his pathetic state. The ale was drawing out his insecurities again. While it muted the stimulation from his surroundings, it seemed to let loose the thoughts he'd been trying to suppress, and allow them to run rampant in his mind. He wanted Qora to be happy—obviously—and from what he could see, she was. On the other hand, he had the overarching sense that the coming war would destroy Qora's happiness (along with everyone else's) before she even had the chance to relish it.

"I almost forgot," Ninan said to Req, as he withdrew the dominite crystal that the Razorclaws had given him to take to the Verdant Reach, "I've been meaning to return this to you." He polished it quickly with the hem of his shirt, then handed it to the elementalist. "Any updates on your experiments?"

"None that have yielded enough information to recreate dominite on our own. The quya's laboratorium has made testing much more easy, at least. I'm learning a lot from her elementalists, and we have many resources at our disposal: chemicals, equipment, skyrock powder."

"So you break down the skyrock and filter it to its bare elements?" Qora asked. "And then you just have to create different environments to see what might stimulate … uh … What did you call it before? 'Synthesis'?"

"Yes. Mainly we're suspending the nebulum and saurigon in liquids and experimenting with temperature, pressure, and light. And of course different amounts of agitation. Much more precise than what I was able to do on my own before. But no definitive results so far."

Everyone was winding down as far as meals, but now the group waited for the pilots and the guards to take a quick meal as well, which necessitated a sort of rotation so that each could eat and rest a moment while at least two people remained with the pterobeasts at all times.

At some point, Qora and Ninan had joined the conversation with the quya and the elderboughs, and then Ollan found himself working on a fourth ale, sitting at the bar alongside Gorgo, Kuy, Req, Kondor, and one of the pilots.

"I'm not that eager to get back to Allpa," admitted the pilot, who was a broad-shouldered—and perhaps even more broad-minded—woman of forty or so. Her head was shaved along the sides, but woven into a long, dark plait from the top of her scalp to the nape of her neck and extending at least three feet down her back. She took a gulp of ale and slammed her glass down, wiping her lips with the back of her hand. "I like new places. Can't get enough of the views, not to mention all the interesting things one encounters beyond borders."

"I'd say you ought to come down and see the Tail," Kondor told her, "only we're not exactly keen on foreigners arriving by air."

"No argument there," Ollan muttered, remembering the meganeuras. He watched the bubbles of his ale zip up from the bottom of the glass, then slowly pushed the glass away so that he could stop drinking and allow his head to clear.

"What did you think of those Sauroguard units earlier?" Kuy asked the pilot.

She cracked her neck and took a deep breath. "I think we have to destroy them before they destroy us."

"Except we can't aggress them without consequence," Req reminded her. "Currently, Allpa has time to get itself in order, to prepare, thanks to the pending cession agreement. But acts of aggression on the Sauroguard could result in immediate retaliation—and we aren't ready to face that."

"Right," said the pilot, taking a big swig of ale. When she swallowed, she asked, "So you'll continue with these little scouting missions, then? Espionage? Experiments?"

"Basically," said Req.

Kondor leaned forward so the pilot could see him past the others, who all sat in a line facing the barkeep. "Actually, we were discussing something like 'asset retrieval' a little while ago—capturing one of those little scutellosaurs to try and figure out what they can do."

The pilot paused before her next sip and quirked a brow. "Go on ..."

"We would need to get to the ground level where the encampments are," Kuy explained. "But not too close as to be conspicuous. I suppose, if you're willing, you could help us with that—fly us down there, within a half mile or so, the same way we kept some distance from the lodge to avoid attention. Only we aren't sure how we would get through the enclosures unnoticed."

"Oh that wouldn't be a problem," Ollan offered freely. He knew he shouldn't encourage them, but his mind was too loose for him to hold back. "Those palisades are only for show—for keeping the dinosaurs with their own species, at most."

"What do you mean?" said Kondor.

"He means," said Req thoughtfully, "that there's no *need* for strong barriers. Right?" He ran his finger along the dominite, its soft purple glow shining on his skin. "The dinosaurs will congregate as closely to the central dominite crystal as they can. They exist in a trance as long as they can feel the energy, as long as the dominite is in the open for them—which the beastlords make sure of."

Ollan nodded. "Trained dinosaurs, according to Wayra, can be loyal under good conditions. Dinosaurs trained under dominite, however ..."

"They'd die just to be near it," Req said with a woeful gaze toward the fire, and Ollan recalled what Qora had told him about the crystal Req had lost in the woods (only to find a heap of small, dead dinosaurs in formation around it, having stood there entranced for a week without leaving to eat or drink).

"Anyway," Ollan added, "it wouldn't be that hard to get in.

During my military training, I learned the basics of encampment operations, and I can tell just by looking that those palisades are relatively new—there's hardly any weathering on the wood— and that they aren't staked very deeply—based on their height and thickness, which determines how deep they need to go into the ground to be stable. Not to mention there are gaps between them, and they don't have horizontal stabilizations like beams or packed-in dirt, which means they're not designed for serious or long-term containment."

"So you think we could easily dislodge one and make enough space to slip inside?" Kuy said.

Ollan shrugged, once again not sure why he was entertaining this conversation. It wasn't like he and these guys and the pilot were really going to go down and try to capture one of the scutellosaurs. "Sure. Plus, the encampment barely even has any guards, from what I saw—because they don't need them. Not when those dinosaurs are self-defending weapons on legs, surrounding and protecting the very power that keeps them in place."

Spirits, why do I keep elaborating?

Maybe it was simply a nice change of pace to be able to put his military knowledge to use. After all, before losing his memory and becoming a miner, the military had been his career. And what of that now? Now that he was "dead" to so many of his old comrades? Now that he'd betrayed his country by fleeing with his sister to a foreign land and siding with the enemy in war?

Maybe it was also a nice change of pace to be useful, in general, since Qora could clearly handle herself, and since his brothers and mamáy were safe in Allpa. If he was no longer a breadwinner or a protector, and no longer a miner or a soldier, what was he? At the very least, he could be the one who knew a thing or two about what these people seemed to be interested in—in theory, because, again, they were most definitely *not* going to break into the scutellosaur enclosure.

"We have to do it, then," said Kuy. "This is a rare opportunity. We won't always know where the Sauroguard troops are stationed—and these ones might move on at any moment. We'll likely be here another hour or so while the other guards switch out and get a meal. We have the cover of growing darkness. We have *flight*." He gestured at the pilot, who smirked over the rim of her glass.

Ollan shook his head and glanced at the table where the leaders sat with the rest of the group. "The others won't go for it. Not a chance."

"Who says they have to know about it?" Gorgo said. "It's too many people anyway."

"As it is, there would be six of us," Kuy pointed out.

Ollan, Kuy, Gorgo, Req, Kondor, and the pilot.

"Five," said the pilot. "I'll need to stay with the pterobeast after we land."

Gorgo gave a nod. "Five is a good number."

"But how do we get one of the scutellosaurs to cooperate and come with us?" Ollan said. "They'll all be fixated on the center of the encampment, on the dominite."

"We've got dominite too," Req reminded him. "Sure, one crystal isn't much, but it should be plenty for a small dinosaur at the edge of the enclosure—one who is farthest from the main source and eager to be up close to the energy."

"I don't know ..." Ollan said. But the more they talked about this, the more it started to come together and make sense. Except that couldn't be right. He wasn't in his right mind at the moment, at least not fully. And yet, he was slowly beginning to convince himself that he was *needed* for this. That his knowledge could make or break this mission. That, while otherwise useless, he could finally get off his hindquarters and take action in a way that might help prepare Allpa for an attack. Those dinosaurs were small, but for all anyone knew, they could be lethal under the proper circumstances.

They could be lethal to us right now, he also thought. Although it would be better to find out here than in the heat of battle, wouldn't it? At least the beastlords would be in their tents for the evening and not among the scutellosaurs commanding them to advance.

"We were lucky to even come across this encampment," Kuy said. "We have to take advantage where we can."

As Qora nestled against Ninan's shoulder and laughed softly at something he'd said, Ollan turned back to the bar, where the other young men looked to the pilot for confirmation that she would assist.

Then they all looked at Ollan expectantly.

He dragged his ale back to his lips, taking several huge gulps before setting it back down. He swallowed and, with a grimace, said, "Alright. Let's do it."

⫶⫶⫶

The snow on the ground was sparse at the foot of the mountain, unlike what the group had seen on its peaks. And thank the earth spirits for that, as five men in various shades of gray and brown would have stood out against all that white, even now that the sun was mostly set.

The pilot landed Ollan and his friends a half mile from the encampment as promised, on the west side where the scutellosaur enclosure lay. From there, they hurried toward the wall of palisades, dominite in hand, along with a very dim lantern so that they could remain obscured as much as possible while still being able to see where they were going.

They had a bit of leeway with this, since the fire pits they'd seen in the daylight were still burning—and would have to continue to burn throughout the night to keep the unfeathered oviraptors and cold-blooded scutellosaurs warm and alive—which added more ambient light to the environment.

The group had told the rest of their traveling companions that they were stepping out for different reasons—the pilot to return to the gondola, which wasn't a lie, while Ollan and Kondor went for "fresh air," and the Razorclaw men supposedly left to have a look at the recreational "frostgliders" (as some of the lodge patrons had described the people riding those wooden boards down the snow) who were about to come in from the slopes for the night.

Huffing and wheezing, the men arrived on foot outside the palisades about ten minutes later. Exerting oneself in weather so cold felt like knives in the throat, Ollan thought as the cold turned the air sharp each time he inhaled.

Gazing up at the tops of the palisades—which stood only around six feet high—he couldn't help remarking that the tips were "barely even pointed," yet another indication that the officers in charge of this encampment didn't find defense necessary.

Somewhat sobered by the climate, Ollan shuddered at the meaning behind the lack of defense. In this case, minimal defense implied maximum danger. This was a crazy thing to do … except he could hardly back out of it now. They were already here.

Peering through one of the gaps, Ollan noted that no guards

patrolled the enclosure, just as he'd suspected.

Kuy and Gorgo quickly set to work using large daggers to dig out the base of a single palisade and loosen the hold on it. They pried and scraped and pried and scraped.

Ollan observed the four-inch diameter of the palisade. Another inch separated it from the palisades on either side, enough to contain the scutellosaurs (who would probably require about three inches to slip through any space at a squeeze) were they not already well contained by their obsession with dominite and also their lesser desire to be near a heat source.

Although dark green and otherwise hard to spot without daylight, thousands of scutellosaurs were visible through the gaps as the fire pits' light lapped against the faint sheen of their scutes.

The ones closer to the center congregated in a circular formation, while those on the outer edges only loosely bordered the others as the distance from the dominite energy kept them somewhat lucid.

"They all look normal to me," Kondor said. "Aside from whatever trance they're in."

Ollan gazed up the length of the pole that held the mounted dominite crystal, which emanated a purple glow so powerful it seemed to pulse.

Gorgo grunted as he gripped the palisade and tugged upward. "Maybe they have a keen sense of smell." The palisade wobbled but didn't come out.

"Yes—tracking abilities," Kuy said. "Maybe they scout enemy territory and communicate the information to the other reptiles."

Req, who had been keeping a lookout, crossed his arms and said, "That's hardly severe enough, considering what we've already seen.

"Maybe they spew something toxic," Kondor suggested, joining Gorgo at the palisade and applying additional muscle, "like slime."

A few more grunts and the palisade loosened further.

"Maybe they're just used for their armor," said Ollan. "Maybe they'll converge on fallen Sauroguard soldiers to shield them from additional blows."

"Or maybe—" Gorgo started before the palisade tore out of the cold dirt and nearly smacked him in the forehead.

Kondor and Ollan both came to offer balance, and together they laid the palisade horizontal, resting it on one of the patches of unmelted snow and letting it sink.

"Ruck," said Gorgo. "That could've been bad."

From inside the widened gap, a few of the scutellosaurs glanced over, but none seemed compelled to investigate, still keeping the majority of their focus on that mystical energy.

It did strike Ollan as odd, though, now that he thought about it, how these particular reptiles remained unguarded. If an enemy—like him and his companions—were to choose any enclosure to target, it would most certainly be the one containing the small herbivores. The carnivores with razor-scales and venomous claws and fire breath clearly needed no protection … but these?

He observed the armored dinosaurs, any of which he could easily carry under one arm, and wondered how the guards could be so confident in their safety.

Underneath the fading haze of intoxication, a sick feeling crawled up Ollan's spine.

Gorgo clapped him on the back. "You're looking a little pale, Kanchaya."

"I guess I'm just … not sure about this. It's too easy."

"Unfortunately, we don't have time to deliberate," said Kuy. "Potential threats might not be obvious at the moment, but if we don't grab one of these little monsters and get out of here soon, those threats could become very clear very quickly."

"Right," Ollan agreed. "Sorry."

Req nodded and pulled out his dominite crystal which, while faded after much unintentional sun exposure, still glowed enough to make several scutellosaurs near the palisades jerk their heads in his direction. He went forward and stuck his face into the gap, along with his crystal-wielding hand. "Come on … Come to me now. That's it …"

Slowly the scutellosaurs approached him, snouts in the air, eyes wild.

Backing away, Req held the crystal low for the little reptiles, drawing seven or eight of them out of the enclosure. They fit easily through the six-inch gap, following him in single file until they were a few yards from the edge, then formed a circle around him.

"Alright," Req said. "One of you grab one."

Ollan, as a sense of committed resolve overcame him, reached down and snatched one around the middle, tucking it under his right arm just as he'd imagined he might do a minute ago. Its gaze remained fixed on Req, who then slowly slipped the crystal into his chest pocket.

And then a shrill, ear-busting cry warped the air.

One of the scutellosaurs had its jaws open wide, wailing like some otherworldly soul stripped raw and tormented in the Pits of Tapuy, its fibers stretched beyond the limits of reason. Which was bad enough in and of itself, until the other reptiles layered their own cries on top of it.

Ollan dropped the scutellosaur he'd been holding and collapsed, jamming the heels of his hands against his ears with such force he thought he might crush his own head—but he couldn't let go because then he would feel the full effects of that sound. The others collapsed too, similarly shielding their ears.

Ollan wanted to run, to flee from these demons, and yet somehow his legs would not move. His mind turned to liquid, his consciousness waning. He squinted, eyes barely open wide enough to see Kuy crying out—see, not hear, because certainly nothing else in the world was audible at this moment—mouthing something at Req.

Get ... the ... crystal. Get ... the ... crystal.

It apparently took Req and his own watery mind a moment to gather himself, and then the horror on his face made his thoughts clear to everyone else: He would have to uncover one ear to pull out the dominite.

Wincing fiercely, he withdrew the dominite once more— and instantly the sound cut to silence.

Ollan's heart pounded and his head throbbed and his ears rang. He wasn't sure whether the quiet that followed was real, or only that every sound by comparison seemed mute, or perhaps that his hearing had now been damaged beyond repair.

The men all scrambled to their feet and Kuy shouted— though it came no louder than a whisper—"Go! Go! Go!" and ran back toward where the pterobeast gondola was stationed.

It felt like slow motion, despite their haste, and Ollan fell to the end of the group, struggling to keep pace behind them as he grappled with what had just happened.

Stupid, he thought. *So stupid.*

Qora would be so disappointed to know he had not only come along on this foolish errand but that he had also supplied advice to encourage it. And what had he helped? Nothing. In fact, he may have allowed this unit of the Sauroguard to permanently deafen most of the Razorclaws and one of the Tailfolk in less than ten seconds.

Somewhere in the background, he thought he could make out the sounds of other roaring dinosaurs—others that had been disturbed by the scutellosaur cries—and perhaps the shout of guards emerging to investigate, but it was only after sprinting for a few minutes that Ollan glanced back and found three of the scutellosaurs trailing the group.

Req still held the dominite in his fist, too intent on racing to safety to consider stashing it again. Its glow kept the scutellosaurs close at hand and docile enough not to shriek again.

A distance that had taken ten minutes to cover at a normal pace had become half that at the group's current speed, and before they knew it, they'd arrived back at the gondola, where the pilot had already positioned the pterobeast in a flapping hover that sent chilly gusts of wind across the ground.

With the gondola already a couple of feet up, the men had to take it at a running leap (a move that came with relative ease considering the momentum they'd each been building) and clamber over the rim, making it sway.

Ollan, who was the last to make it, slowed and inclined his body so that he could scoop up one of the scutellosaurs at his heels and fling it into the gondola before he flung himself in too.

He tumbled along the gondola floor and the pilot commanded the pterobeast to rise and flee.

When they'd flown far enough away that the fire pits were mere specks in the distance, Kondor said, "Well, now we know what the scutellosaurs can do."

Gorgo stuck a finger in his ear and wiggled it around before pulling it back out. "Sorry—What did you say?"

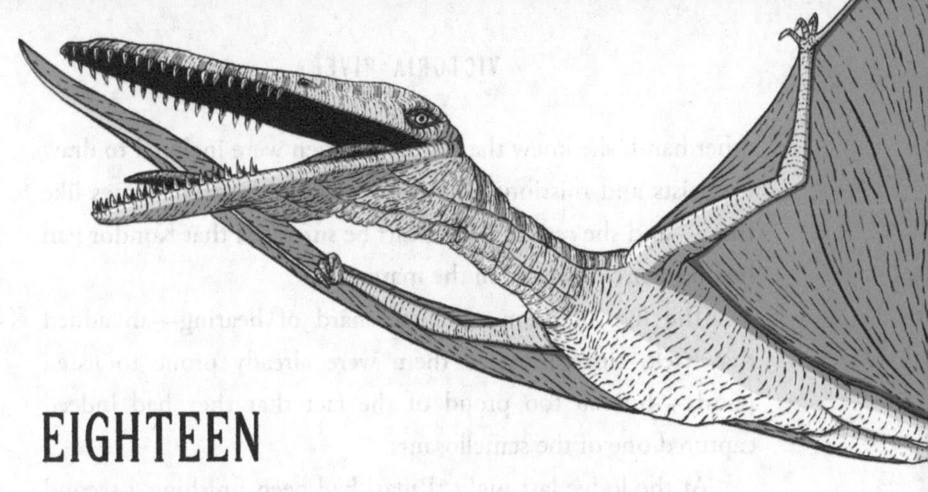

EIGHTEEN

PAQARI HAD BEGUN TO REALIZE, after several days on the mainland, that any place without an ocean view felt stuffy. She'd lived her life in a castle on the coast, and rarely spent more than a day away from it. Pterobeast rides high in the air had somewhat assuaged this feeling, but she continued to long for the edge of the land. For now, however, the best she could do was spend more time outdoors and with her mind occupied by the content of whatever books she could get her hands on.

After returning from Huandoy, she had collapsed into her bed and woken to late-morning light. She wasn't sure how she had slept so well, considering everything she'd seen from the snowy mountain peaks—the stuff of nightmares. The Sumaqi qhapaq was a menace, to say the least, preparing to unleash those monstrous creatures on his enemies. And her own father had helped create them, provided resources and land on which to breed them. She curled her lip in disgust as she strolled toward the quya's gardens with a book under her arm.

Fire-breathing pyroraptors, she thought bitterly. *Screaming scutellosaurs.* And she couldn't believe those idiot men had gone down to the encampment last night to see the reptiles up close. She would have expected more from Qora's brother, who was a bit older and wiser, and didn't seem to seek out trouble. On the other hand, she knew the Razorclaw men were inclined to draw up heists and missions—especially during desperate times like these—and she *certainly* shouldn't be surprised that Kondor had had no sense of shame in the matter.

The five of them were still hard of hearing—an added drawback, since most of them were already prone to listen poorly—but all too proud of the fact that they had indeed captured one of the scutellosaurs.

At the lodge last night, Paqari had been finishing a second coca tea with Quya Urpi when the most desolate wail had sounded in the distance. The lodge patrons had hardly paid it any mind—perhaps it hadn't been the first time they'd heard it, what with the Sauroguard stationed below for many days, even weeks prior, with the possibility of having unintentionally provoked the cry more than once—but everyone in the quya's party had rushed outside and headed for the pterobeast gondolas, only to find one had been missing. The second gondola had appeared in the sky a moment later, and after what its passengers had just done, there had been no time to lose in making a quick escape before the encampment officers could determine the cause of the commotion.

Upon return, the quya's reprimands had quite literally fallen on deaf ears. Mostly deaf, at least. Which would have been funny if it hadn't given Kondor an excuse to be even more obnoxious than usual. When Paqari had told him, "If only the scutellosaurs had had the ability to make you *mute* instead," he'd inclined his head toward her, cupped his hand around his ear, and said, "I beg your pardon?" but she was certain he'd heard her well enough.

Gods, he was such a side thorn.

Paqari found a bench overlooking a mass of pruned hedges

and inqa-lillies in a spectral order (purple, three shades of pink, then red, orange, goldenrod, yellow, and white), and opened her book by its bookmark ribbon and began to read from where she'd left off.

Environmental vibrations exhibit a strong influence over avian brain chemistry, regulating activity cycles critical for migration preparation. Birds can even perceive and react to low-frequency vibrations caused by atmospheric pressure changes and seismic activity.

She read on for several minutes, and then, as if from nowhere, someone said, "Plotting your escape?"

Paqari jerked up her head as Kondor strode across the garden path in front of her, with Anku trailing him.

Kondor nodded at her book, *A Study on Bird Migration Patterns.* Then, likely making note of her scowl, he said, "Sorry, princess. I didn't mean to *ruffle your feathers.*"

Even Anku snickered at that, although he tended not to engage in such banter.

Smiling flatly, Paqari replied in an extra-loud voice, "Although it's above your reading level, to be sure, it wouldn't hurt you to give these pages a glance. With your damaged eardrums"—she tapped on one of her own ears with her index finger—"you may have to begin relying on environmental vibrations for communication from now on."

"Interestingly enough," Anku said with full sincerity, "we were hoping to catch sight of some gallimimus—we don't have any at the Tail—and the quya said we'll be able to feel the ground vibrations a few seconds before they pass. She told us they tend to run by in herds in the late morning each day— just for exercise, which is absolutely fascinating to me—and that these eastern gardens are a perfect place to view them."

"Well," said Paqari, "it comes as no shock to me that your

people think it's recreational to watch reptiles. Please enjoy yourselves. Perhaps later you can watch the trees for sciurumimus hunting those little striped frogs they like to eat."

Kondor raised his thick eyebrows and cupped his hand over his ear again. "What was that?" His grayish eyes gleamed.

Gleamed.

Paqari's stomach dipped—but only with repulsion, she told herself. She pursed her lips and went back to reading, silently cursing her own breath for catching in her throat when Kondor casually brushed a section of golden-brown hair off his forehead.

Another several minutes passed with no ground vibrations to indicate any gallimimus, and then Qora and Ninan approached the gardens too, with Wayra and Ollan, only they all seemed intent on passing through rather than lingering.

"Good morning," Wayra said.

"Good morning," Anku replied. "Where are you all headed?"

"To the laboratorium," Wayra told him. "It's a separate building. We're going to see Req. He's been out there since dawn with the quya's elementalists, working furiously on the dominite experiments after seeing those Sauroguard dinosaurs yesterday."

"Would you three like to join us?" Qora asked.

Kondor and Anku looked at each other and shrugged.

"Sure," said Anku.

Lifting her gaze slowly, Paqari sighed and closed her book. "Why not."

⟩⟩⟩

The grassy fields beyond the gardens could have belonged in the wild for how vast they were. Paqari recalled that the quya had mentioned she didn't like to feel detached from her

180

land—certainly she preferred the luxuries of Qhispina House, to a point, but she had no desire to dwell too far from nature. For that reason, she allowed the grasses to grow waist high, and permitted herds of gallimimus to run freely through them, and kept a smilodon sanctuary. Everything was sectioned and manicured, but still retained a sense of natural, untamed beauty.

Paqari supposed the wild things were beautiful sometimes. Even the reptiles who lived in the filthy woods had a certain graceful quality in their movements, a nice sheen to their scales, a sparkle in their amber eyes that she might appreciate—provided she didn't have to smell the ruck or watch the carnivores tear their prey to bloody shreds.

She stole a glance at Kondor.

That's all it is, she thought. *Admirable qualities in a wild thing.*

The man was most certainly wild, with his wavy hair and bristly jaw and woolly clothes. And while she couldn't deny that his broad shoulders made for a nice silhouette, or that his wicked grin did something not-unpleasant to her insides, he also had a sardonic wit and a crude presence that she didn't care for—nothing like the clean-cut and well-mannered Tisquvian watchman who had once won her affection. Kondor was an absolute beast, and she only need wait for him to act bestial again to temper any positive reaction she might incidentally have to him.

Then he caught her watching him and winked.

She huffed and moved past him to catch up to Qora and Wayra, linking her arms with one of each of theirs and refusing to look back again.

A minute or so later, halfway to the laboratorium, the ground began to vibrate. It was subtle at first, such that Paqari thought she'd imagined it, but it quickly turned heavy and distinct.

The grasses swayed.

A honking chorus washed over the grounds. Several hundred large feet thumped in succession.

The vibrations increased.

Everyone looked toward the source of the sounds.

Gallimimus, Paqari thought.

"Move!" Ollan told them.

Releasing her friends, everyone in the group picked up speed. As they broke into a run, distances formed between them.

With grass whipping at her arms—and now having dropped her book—Paqari slowed without meaning to. In her haste to catch up, she stepped right into a small hole, which temporarily swallowed her foot, twisting her ankle. She fell to her knees.

"Paqari!" Qora called from somewhere ahead.

Grass swished as Qora searched for the princess, but Paqari was no longer visible above the grass for her friends to find her.

A full herd of gallimimus came bounding through. With their long necks, they stood at least twelve feet high, covered in iridescent scales and each with a stripe of feathers down their spines. Their legs propelled them forward swiftly and as if on tiptoe.

Directly at the center of their wide path, Paqari scrambled to her feet with only seconds left to evade them.

She pushed herself harder, thighs burning with the effort, hands cutting the air at her sides.

The herd was almost upon her.

Just a few more strides. She might be able to get in the clear.

Please, she begged the gods.

With an instant to spare, she removed herself from harm, stumbling to a walk as she clutched her chest and gasped for air.

Qora, Ninan, Wayra, Anku, and Kondor received her as the gallimimus swept past.

Then, with the briefest flick of his gaze beyond Paqari, Kondor grabbed the princess around the waist and pulled her to his chest.

The motion was so abrupt that it flung them both to the ground—just as a final, rogue gallimimus thundered over the spot where Paqari had been standing.

Hidden by the tall grass, Paqari stared into Kondor's face, his light eyes tinged with … *concern*?

Her chest rose and fell in a rhythm, her body still buzzing with the aftereffects of the fear that had empowered her to run beyond her normal capacity.

She hadn't noticed before, in her panic, but the grass closer to the soil smelled sweet, like herbs. And Kondor smelled woody, despite his rhino-hair vest, which seemed to have absorbed and maintained many of the more pleasant scents of the forest in which he'd been raised—woodsmoke and tree sap and petrichor.

"Are you alright?" he asked, his voice a bit softer than usual.

His arms were firm and warm around her. In the aftermath of near death, she found the woolly rhino hair an odd comfort against her skin. It was softer with the nap matted flat against her. She nodded.

As the others parted the grass to check on them, Paqari snapped to attention, pushing herself away from Kondor and sitting up.

Qora and Wayra were at her side fast, assessing her for damage.

"I'm fine," she insisted. "My ankle's a bit sore and I've had a severe puncture to my pride, but otherwise, you have no cause to worry."

Dubiously they helped her up and Kondor stood too.

The princess and the gladewarden both took a moment to

brush off their clothes, and Paqari had to look away to hide the warmth spreading over her cheeks, muttering a reluctant "thank you," to which Kondor only nodded once.

"Other than you almost dying ..." Anku remarked breathlessly, "That was incredible!"

🌙🌙🌙

The laboratorium was a smaller, less elaborate version of Qhispina House, made of the same bricks. Paqari imagined its distance from the castle was to avoid any collateral damage from volatile experiments or research.

Inside, elementalists in dark robes tended containers on several long tables in rows. Many of the containers were set over flames fed by sauropod oil, some of their contents bubbling and steaming while others merely simmered. Some of the liquids manifested colors while others remained clear.

Among the elementalists, Req observed his own container and scribbled notes. His mussed hair and weary gaze told of an already-long morning of unsuccessful labor.

"Req," Wayra said. "Have you eaten today? You look awful."

He didn't bother to look up. "As much as I love your compliments, Wayra, I can hardly be thinking of food when there are dinosaurs out there that can spit fire and acid, and shed razorblades."

"You know what I mean. You're not going to get very far with your work if you pass out from a lack of nutrition. Try conducting an experiment when you're unconscious, Req."

He waved her off and added something to the sauropod oil in front of him, probably to make it burn hotter, and then inspected a thin, vertical tube with lines etched in grades along its length as the red substance inside began to rise.

"Is there anything we can do to help?" Qora asked.

Req scoffed. "Make my ears stop ringing?"

"That's on you, my friend," Wayra told him. "You and your little band of thieves." She smacked Kondor with the back of her hand for emphasis, then shot Ollan a side-eyed look of disapproval.

"Speaking of your band of thieves," said Ninan, "I thought Kuy and Gorgo were here with you." He glanced around.

"They're in the war room with the quya and Marshall Hatun and the elderboughs," Req said. "They came by earlier to let me know they would be working on a strategy to capture more Sauroguard 'specimens.'"

Paqari rolled her eyes. "I'd ask if they heard a single word the quya said last night, but I'm sure that was too difficult under the circumstances. Not that they would heed good advice even if their ears were working properly."

"She's actually not opposed to it," Req said. "It was the spontaneous lack of planning she didn't appreciate. Otherwise, she said it's not a bad idea to try and get a hold of as many breeds of enemy dinosaurs as possible, provided we know in advance what they can do and we prepare delicate extraction plans before taking action." He added a bit more chemical to the sauropod oil.

"Well," Wayra said, "I have to admit, I wouldn't mind getting my hands on more of them. The quya's handlers let me have a few minutes with the scutellosaur after we got back from Huandoy, and it was … fascinating."

"How?" Qora asked.

"I examined its snout, mouth, and throat—which was easy with one of the handlers holding the dominite close by to get the thing to cooperate—and they were so different from a typical scutellosaur's. The vocal folds were thick, with unusual nodes and ridges surrounding them. And the nasal cavities were very complex, like special resonating chambers."

"It's incredible what sound alone can do," said Ninan. "The power it has."

"Like the whistlemutes," Qora said.

Paqari thought of the book she'd recently been reading.

Environmental vibrations exhibit a strong influence over avian brain chemistry.

"It wasn't only that the scutellosaur was loud," Ollan commented. "It felt like … it did something … to …"

"To your mind," Kondor supplied.

"Yes," Ollan said.

"Vibrations," Paqari said. "The sound vibrates in your ears. Your mind interprets those vibrations and it means something to you. But not just in terms of helping you identify what that sound belongs to; it can also affect emotions."

"Similar to the way certain notes of music can make you feel sad, or empowered," Qora said.

Wayra perked up. "That's why the whistlemutes persuade the dinosaurs in the Tail to do what the whistler wants. The vibrations at that pitch and frequency must make them feel good."

"No doubt that's how the dominite works too," said Req. "The crystals vibrate. The reptiles can't ignore it."

"Do you think it's something they can hear?" asked Wayra. "Or more something they simply sense? Like the gallimimus on the ground on the way over."

"That's a question for another day," Req told her. "Right now my priority is to figure out what goes *into* the elements to encourage the crystals to grow, not what comes *out* of the crystals. And honestly, I'd appreciate it if those gallimimus didn't keep thundering across the field every day. The vibrations keep agitating my containers and it's—" He froze instantly, fingers curled around a vial. His breathing turned heavy and his eyes darted back and forth like he was trying to make sense of something in front of him no one else could see.

"Req?" said Wayra.

"Is he alright?" Kondor whispered to Ninan.

Ninan shook his head like he wasn't sure but kept watching the elementalist and waiting to see what happened next, as did everyone else.

"That's *it* ..." Req rasped. "Gods and spirits. It's been *so obvious*."

"Obvious?" said Qora. "What is?"

Req seemed to snap back into focus. Then he shouted, "Somebody get me a set of tuning forks!"

꙳꙳꙳

Two hours later, the elementalists had sectioned off a huge area of the field—with assurance from the quya that it was now late enough in the day that there would be no more gallimimus runs—and set up multiple stations with skyrock elements suspended in water as before, but this time each container was manned by a separate elementalist directing sound vibrations close to the glass.

The elementalists began with warmer water, since it would be more likely to precipitate crystals as it cooled, and later, depending on the outcome, might experiment again with different temperatures. They struck tuning forks of different sizes (to produce different sound frequencies) repeatedly at the containers, all spread out so that the vibrations of other stations were less likely to cause interfering effects.

Everyone had come to watch now—the quya, the elderboughs, the other Razorclaws, and many attendants and staff.

Once again, Paqari stole a glance at Kondor, who had finally removed his woolly vest under the heat of midday, revealing a hint of the muscles of his arms beneath the sleeves of his green gladewarden shirt. And dangling at the front of that shirt was his whistlemute, hanging by a strap of pteroleather around his neck.

"Wait!" Paqari said, drawing the attention of those closest to her, including Req. Many of them stopped their sounds for the moment.

The princess approached Kondor, who looked over at her with a furrowed brow. She reached for the whistlemute and, as if instinctively, he ringed his fingers around her wrist, stopping her—sending a shiver up her arm. "Your whistle," she explained, nodding at it. "We should have tried that first."

After a pause, he released her and bowed his head so that she could slip off the strap.

She put it to her lips before it had even occurred to her that his lips must have been on it hundreds of times.

Everyone gathering around her, thankfully, distracted her from that thought, and so she blew into the whistlemute, releasing its sound that was so delicate and high it could almost go unnoticed by human ears.

She held the note until she ran out of breath, then inhaled and blew again. She did this a few times and produced the sound in long stretches for a minute or so, all too aware of Kondor watching her.

Then Kondor bent toward the container, his nose a centimeter from the glass, and said, "Limbs above. It's …"

Req hurried to get a closer look. He covered his mouth, tears welling in his eyes. He gripped the edges of the small table and stared intently at a tiny purple mass forming within the liquid.

As Paqari continued to whistle, the mass grew, collecting invisible particles that formed a crystalline structure and built upon it.

It was slow, but within a few more minutes it was the size of a cacao nib—about a quarter inch thick—with tiny, sparkling protrusions. It sank to the bottom of the container.

Req drained the container and caught the tiny crystal between his fingers. Gleefully, he raised it so that all gathered could (mostly) see it.

They applauded with vigor as he cried, "We've done it!"

Even at the summit,
the clouds may part to reveal
yet a higher summit.

Sumaqi Proverb

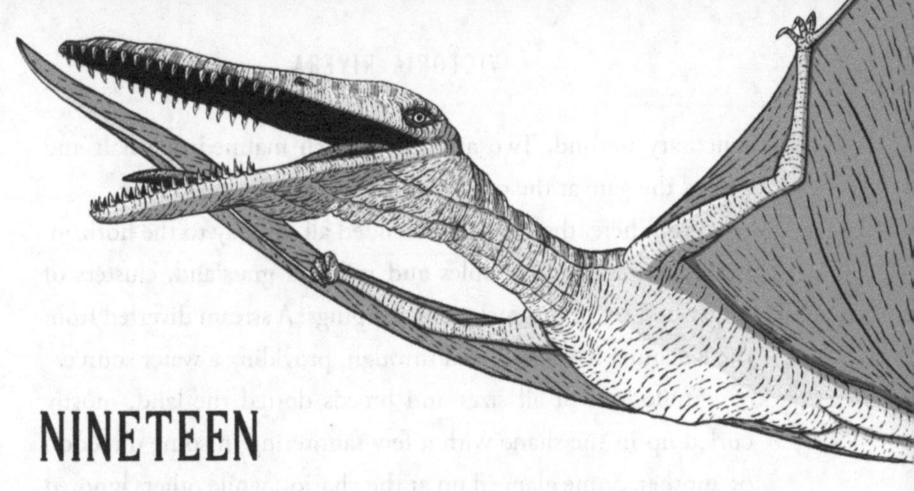

NINETEEN

NINAN SLIPPED AN ARM AROUND Qora's shoulders and drew her close within a four-wheeled, iguanodon-drawn chariot that rolled over the western stretch of land surrounding Qhispina House. They rode with most of the usual crew, wedged in the chariot's third and final row between Paqari (on Qora's side) and Ollan (on Ninan's side), with Wayra, Anku, and Kondor in the center row ahead of them as Quya Urpi rode at the front with the elderboughs. Kuy and Gorgo were visiting Req at the laboratorium again, and the whole castle was abuzz with excitement over the new dominite developments.

The elementalists were working tirelessly to grow—and accelerate the growth of—the crystals, while handlers were testing samples on small reptiles.

Ninan glanced at Ollan, who had been oddly quiet since the trip to Huandoy. Maybe it was only that his ears were still recovering, Ninan thought, but there seemed to be a more pronounced shadow over his being.

Today, the book in Paqari's lap was *Smilodon: The Magnificent Sabertooth*, in preparation for what the quya was about to show them, she had said.

Within a few minutes, the chariot arrived at a large gateway, where gilded metal curled and flourished to section off the sanctuary beyond. Two attendants each manned one half and parted the gate at the center, allowing the chariot passage.

From here, the grounds extended all the way to the horizon, it seemed, containing miles and miles of grassland, clusters of onyxwood trees, and rocky outcroppings. A stream diverted from the Kuchuna River slithered through, providing a water source.

Smilodons of all sizes and breeds dotted the land, mostly curled up in the shade with a few sauntering in some direction or another. Some glanced up at the chariot, while others ignored it entirely.

Wayra gripped the edge of the chariot and gazed out, eyes fixed on them.

Even though it was an artificial wildland, it was rare to see so many mammals out in the open like this. Practically everywhere else on the continent, mammals lived mostly in hiding, or under the careful protection of humankind, to avoid over-predation by reptiles. Not many could hold their own like a smilodon could, Ninan supposed, and he was eager to see a feline-reptilian encounter at some point (provided he could remain at a safe distance from it).

Those fangs must have been somewhere between eight and ten inches long—enough to pierce a man clean through the middle.

"Most of them roam freely," the quya explained, "except for those at the southern reach, where we have separate enclosures: one for training and another to encourage breeding. Once the newly bred cubs are large enough, we release them to the greater sanctuary. As adults, many are released to the wild."

"You breed them to replenish the population lost during The Roaring Thirst." Paqari pointed to a passage in her book.

"That's correct," said the quya.

"It says here that the smilodons' primary food source, the minmi dinosaurs, diminished in the wake of an intraspecies parasite—which coincided with the drought."

The quya nodded. "Many of the smilodons tried to adapt to other food sources, but the drought reduced *all* our animal populations for a time, causing the smilodons' near extinction. But as the smilodons are such a part of who we are here in Allpa, my ancestors took it upon themselves to protect and restore them to whatever extent possible. For the past two hundred years, we have bred them and delivered them back to their habitats throughout the Terrain. And because we love them so, we keep plenty here as well, and utilize them when we can."

When the chariot stopped outside the breeding enclosure, a few free-roaming smilodons approached lazily.

Wayra was already reaching over to stroke their backs, but Paqari flinched as one raised its head near where she sat.

"They know me and my attendants," said the quya, "and tend to trust others who arrive with me. They won't harm you— but you must remain calm, as they have the instinct to pin down anything that moves too quickly."

Everyone stepped out of the chariot and entered the enclosure, where dozens of smilodon cubs napped together in piles under the shade of onyxwood trees planted exclusively for their benefit. Others scampered along the ground, where they had worn down the grass in a few places, and pawed at the shifting shadows of the tree leaves that swayed in the breeze.

One scampering cub came up to Paqari and pounced on her leg, grappling with it like a playful opponent.

Paqari gasped, but Wayra chuckled and came to her rescue, gently prying away the cub and taking it into her own arms like an infant. It squirmed and squeaked for a moment before it calmed at Wayra's fingers massaging behind its ears, and then nestled against her chest and began to purr. Already its baby saberteeth were peeking down from its closed mouth.

Ninan caught sight of Ollan watching Wayra briefly before he turned and pretended to be looking at the rest of the enclosure.

Qora cautiously snatched up a different cub, holding it by the underarms as its fat paws dangled. "Oh my gods, they're so cute …"

"And soft," Wayra remarked. She slid a curled fist down its thick tail.

More cubs tried to climb on Paqari, but she shooed them away and brushed the remnants of their fur off the pants she wore—some fine linen ones the quya had provided her with, apparently, and very "in fashion."

Kondor smirked. "Looks like those silky little hellions recognize one of their own kind."

She shot him a seething glare.

When one of the adult female smilodons approached her with a regal stride, Paqari seemed to gather some resolve and reached out to touch the big cat's nose. The cat then pressed her head into the palm of Paqari's hand. This time, the princess didn't flinch. She held herself firm, then looked up at Kondor with narrowed eyes. "I quite appreciate the comparison to such an elegant creature—particularly one that could bite your face off if you make her angry."

"And that's our cue to keep moving," Qora mused, setting her cub back down.

After a brief tour of the rest of the breeding enclosure, the quya took the group over to the training enclosure.

One trainer, with eight smilodons sitting on wooden platforms in a circle around her, raised a rod, causing all the smilodons to rise up until they were standing upright on their hind legs. She lowered the rod and they all returned to the first position.

Other trainers worked one on one with the smilodons, shouting commands at them, prompting them to swipe with their big paws—*right, left, right, left*—or rise to their hind legs like the first group, or lunge forward, almost like shadowboxing exercises. Ninan remembered those exercises well, pushing his body to learn fighting motions until they came to him as easily as breathing.

"They're honing the cats' agility," said Wayra.

"And their speed," Ninan added. Not that they needed it; they were already lightning fast. But keeping them in shape, he supposed, was vital to their success against the Sauroguard.

Another area featured rows of tall wooden poles. Multiple trainers used hooked rods to place pieces of meat on the top of each one, then gave a command. Smilodons jumped and dug their claws into the poles, climbing until they reached their prizes.

Ninan imagined those cats climbing an irritator the same way, digging their sharp claws into its scales, pulling themselves up onto its back and plunging those saberteeth into its neck until it bled out. He shuddered.

"We have several types of smilodontini here," the quya told the group. "The smallest you'll see are paramachairodus, the mid-sized cats are megantereon, and the longest and largest of course are the smilodons. Each will have their place, depending on our defense requirements. In some cases we may need to employ the more robust cats, in others those which are more stealthy."

Once they had seen all of that, the group returned to the chariot and the quya instructed the driver to take them to a stretch of property far from the castle and the sanctuary.

In this zone, the grass was cleared, leaving the earth bare but for the piles and piles of pale debris of some kind. From the far end, carts pulled up with more of it, unloading it alongside the rest. When the chariot moved closer, Qora covered her mouth. Paqari grimaced. Kondor and Anku leaned over the edge, squinting. Ninan scanned the scene, making out the details—the straight lines with knobbed ends, then rows of curved lines attached to perpendicular pieces, and rounded masses with symmetric holes in them.

The quya turned back to see the reaction of her guests. "The Roaring Thirst left countless mass smilodon graveyards throughout the Allpan lands. I send my workers to collect what they can find and we provide them to craftspeople in order to stimulate the economy. Smilodon bone art and adornments are very popular among the middle classes, and the tourists like them too. However, we keep the teeth."

When the carriage reached the boneyard, the quya hopped down and greeted the man who seemed to be running things. Ninan and the others climbed out as well, observing the piles as workers sorted them into long bones or skulls or ribs, and finally the teeth that the quya had mentioned.

The man produced a large basket full of more teeth, only these appeared to be mounted onto pieces of metal.

"Here's one example," said the quya, "of how we plan to utilize the unmatched sharpness of smilodon teeth." She picked up one of the items and raised it so the group could see.

Ninan stepped close, analyzing the shape of the metal. Brass, perhaps, forged into a short bar on one side from which three mounted fangs stuck out, with four loops underneath fused together. Almost like …

"May I?" he found himself saying as his pulse pounded.

The quya nodded and passed it over to him.

With one hand, he lined up the four rings with his opposite index finger, middle finger, ring finger, and little finger. He slipped those fingers through the rings, the metal already warm from the day's heat. He curled his fingers downward, then wrapped his thumb over them, flexing his fist like he would in preparation for a fight. Except now, his fist was a claw—with the sharpest tips known to humankind.

"My gods ..." he whispered.

The fangs were relatively short; they must have come from one of the smaller cats. But that was logical. Full-sized saberteeth would have been too bulky for something like this. These were ... *perfect*.

One corner of the quya's lips quirked. "You like it, Your Highness?"

Wide-eyed, he nodded.

She gave him another. "We call it a strikefang."

After placing the second strikefang on his other fist, Ninan held both up in a fighting stance. He imagined throwing one of his fists into an uppercut, stabbing those smilodon fangs into anyone who dared come at him with intent to take his life—or Qora's—or hurt anyone he cared about.

Before he could even ask, Quya Urpi said, "Yes, you can keep those. Try not to hurt yourself."

》》》《《《

The chariot driver delivered the group to the castle courtyard.

The quya and the elderboughs went inside to rest. Qora, Paqari, and Wayra were gathered around one of the quya's pet smilodons that had prowled out to see who had arrived. Then Anku and Kondor stepped away to privately discuss some of what they'd seen earlier, leaving Ninan and Ollan alone in awkward silence.

They both seemed to be looking in the girls' direction, while Wayra teased the smilodon with a large flower as Qora and Paqari laughed at the way such a large creature playfully nipped at the red petals.

"I really ... love your sister," Ninan told Ollan. He inclined his head toward Qora, who smiled and stroked the smilodon's furry cheek. "I just want to make sure you know that. I know I hurt her when I couldn't warn her about the engagement to Paqari, and after that when I asked her to wait for me while I figured it all out but ... didn't ... totally ... figure things out very well. I'm guessing she's told you everything."

Ollan kept his gaze focused on Qora. "She did."

"But hurting her is the last thing in the world that I want."

Now Ollan turned to look at him. "My sister is practically a grown woman now, whether I like it or not. And she's smart. I have to trust that her feelings for you are based on something good she sees in you. From what I've seen, you're a decent guy, and you fight for what's important." His jaw twitched for a second. "That doesn't mean I won't break your face if you prove me wrong."

"Of course not." Ninan smiled, although he knew Ollan wasn't joking. "Except Qora might beat you to it."

Ollan huffed a knowing laugh at that.

A moment later, Kuy, Gorgo, and a tired but exhilarated Req appeared and updated them on their progress.

"We've got a hundred good-sized crystals forming as we speak," said Req.

"Also," Kuy said, "the elementalists have received the first import of fool's silver and are testing dosage and duration of the effects."

"That's great news," said Ninan.

Qora filled in their friends on what they'd learned about the smilodons, and Ninan was just beginning to show off his strikefangs when three pteranodons closed in from above.

Each pteranodon had a rope dangling from around the base of its neck in front of the saddle, and each rope ended in a rope net holding what appeared to be a dinosaur.

The riders carefully lowered the dinosaurs to the ground and landed beside them, ropes slack in the grass.

"What are those?" Kondor asked.

Wayra approached and analyzed them through the netting. "Looks like a troodon and a … hypsilophodon."

"The guards at the pteriary said you all were out here," Kunaq explained as he and the others dismounted. "We thought you'd want to see these immediately. We captured them from Camp Kawsay—after bribing a few disgruntled guards with a bit of gold from Kallpa House, and using stolen dominite to get the dinosaurs to cooperate."

"This is … incredible." Wayra stroked the troodon's greenish feathers. "Some of the guys got their hands on a scutellosaur too. What do these do?"

Kunaq motioned for Tika to loosen the rope netting on the troodon while he took out a dominite crystal and held it up.

The troodon scrambled out toward the crystal in a trance.

"Ensnare!" Kunaq commanded.

With an open mouth, the troodon projected a stream of whitish liquid—except that it remained in a sort of long strand that landed several yards away on the grass, and kept its shape.

Ninan cringed.

Kuy crouched beside the excretion and poked it with his

index finger. "It's sticky."

Tika followed and brought a knife, picked up one end of the strand, pinched it into a loop, slid the knife inside, and pulled it tight. She made a show of trying to cut it with a sawing motion, but the strand wouldn't break. It took at least thirty seconds for Tika to cut through it, and after that, it stuck to her fingers with a vengeance.

Ninan remembered when he and Qora had tried to separate the pterodactyl nests along the Amaru River. There was some excretion holding those nests together too, a powerful adhesive. Whatever mutations Ninan's father had bred in this troodon, it seemed to have made something similar, only in projectile form.

"Sort of like a spider's web fibers," said Req.

"More like a silkworm," Paqari said, "since the troodon extruded it from its mouth."

Qora shot Ninan a disturbed look.

"These troodons are meant to blend into the grass," Kunaq explained. "They shoot their fibers at high speed at a running enemy, instantly entangling the feet and legs, and incapacitating them. As Tika demonstrated, it takes a while to cut through it, which could cost victims precious time in the heat of battle."

Everyone took a moment to let this notion sink in.

Finally, Wayra asked, "What about the hypsilophodon? What's the damage there?"

It was only now that Ninan realized how Yaku had been oddly quiet, standing back a ways from the others, and not participating in the conversation.

Tika stalked over to Yaku and dragged him by his shirt. Before she gave any explanation, everyone wrinkled their noses. Paqari covered both her nose and mouth.

"Yaku took a full blast of the odor before we could get the hypso under control," said Tika. "If you think *this* is bad, he's actually had a bath and a change of clothes. We had to burn everything he was wearing before."

Gorgo pinched his nostrils closed. "Okay, so the Sauroguard hypsos can make a stink. That's not so bad. The quya's army could work through that."

"At this level, sure," said Kunaq. "But at full strength, all three of us were doubled over vomiting. It's involuntary."

Ninan felt like vomiting this very minute. Where would these atrocities end?

"The guards we bribed also told us that the beastwardens of each encampment possess a bestiary," Tika added. "A bestiary that contains what we expect to be the extent of the Sauroguard, detailing every dinosaur or reptile and its features—a sort of catalog or guide so that Qhapaq Apo's military leaders can keep track of them. We intend to acquire one of these bestiaries and, if possible, use it to help us capture at least one of every Sauroguard reptile for study."

Everyone exchanged glances.

"If you can really accomplish that," said Wayra, "the information would be invaluable."

Yaku nodded. "We're hoping Quya Urpi will support us."

"She will," Qora said. "There's already talk of a similar plan."

"We'll go with you." Kuy gestured to himself and Gorgo.

"I will too," said Ollan.

"What?" Qora choked.

Ollan avoided his sister's question, as well as her pleading gaze. They all knew Ollan's military experience would be helpful—maybe even vital.

"The rest of us will help in whatever way we can," Ninan

assured them. For the moment, he was certain that he and Qora would have to return to the Tail to work out the migration of the giant theropods, but hoped they might return in time to assist here too.

"I'll work with the elementalists," said Req, "to get you all a solid supply of dominite before you head out again. You're going to need it if you want to handle more of those mutant reptiles."

With these endeavors, and the migration efforts in the Tail, and the preparation of the smilodons, Ninan dared to hope it might be possible to resist his father's attacks. The growing number of mutant reptiles brought him no comfort, of course, nor did the idea that he and all his friends would soon be required to divide and conquer—separating to where each of them was most needed.

But whatever they had to face, they were going to do it with relentless force.

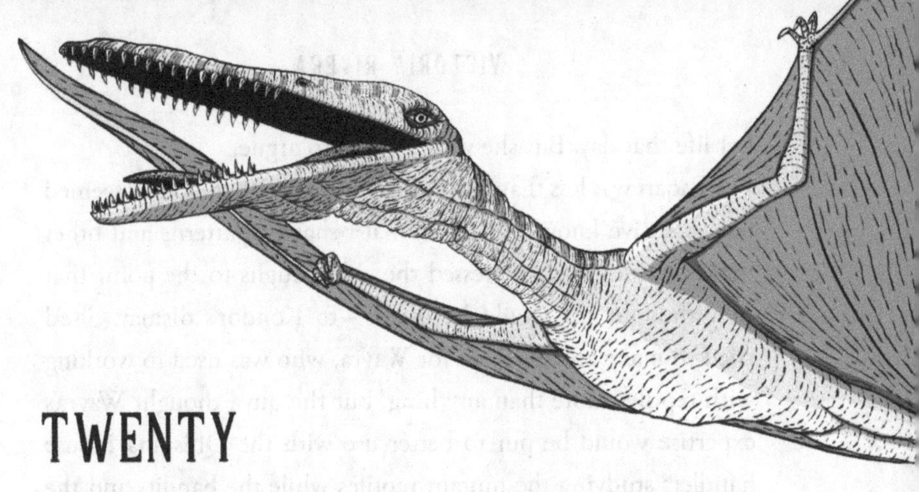

TWENTY

QORA WAS DRESSED in proper flyer-riding gear, for once, with all the aerodynamic leathers and guards, and a set of huge goggles that currently rested on top of her head. She was due at the pteriary in ten minutes to fly with Ollan to Wiñay, to see how their mother and brothers were faring among the quinoa.

Ninan had already visited Wiñay—to see his friends and that all was going well—earlier that morning on his own, so that he could be back in time to help coordinate the pterobeast arks for the Tail. The elderboughs, now having seen the extent of the impending war, were willing to supply a team of their sharpest archers for battle, but would need a form of mass transportation to get them to Allpa's capital. The three arks Ninan had stolen from Kallpa House were an ideal solution.

When Qora and Ollan returned, it would be time for everyone to separate for their own missions.

The elderboughs—as expected—had insisted that Qora and Ninan spearhead the giant theropod migration, since they had both been integral in persuading the Tailfolk to work with them. The spinosaur's acceptance of Qora's request was a sign, too, Elderbough Raphi had said, that Qora had a special connection to reptiles. Qora knew better, that it had been luck—and perhaps her very non-threatening stance—that had allowed her to keep her life that day. But she wasn't going to argue.

Paqari was less than thrilled to be joining them, but it seemed her extensive knowledge of animal behavior patterns and other fields of study had impressed the elderboughs to the point that they thought she would be useful—to Kondor's dismay. She'd tried to make an argument for Wayra, who was used to working with reptiles more than anything, but the quya thought Wayra's expertise would be put to better use with the Qhispina House handlers studying the mutant reptiles while the bandits and the Razorclaws worked to bring back more to complete the collection.

Ollan was dead set on being part of that extraction team. Qora still had hope that she could talk him out of it. As if the other night at Huandoy and the scutellosaur hadn't been a close enough call, Ollan would be actively putting himself in similar danger, repeatedly. Kuy and Gorgo had argued that upcoming missions would be different and that Ollan's military background would once again give them a good advantage, but that didn't change the fact that Qora had already spent years without her oldest brother and only recently gotten him back. How could she let him out of her sight at all, let alone to fly straight into enemy camps full of reptilian mutants?

Wringing her hands at the thought of all that was to come, Qora walked through the corridors of Qhispina House on her way to the pteriary, stopping only when she passed the quya's scriptorium.

The quya was sitting at her desk, poring over what appeared to be a pile of correspondence. She looked up as Qora appeared in the entryway.

"Good morning," said Quya Urpi. "I'm told you're headed off to Wiñay?"

Qora nodded. "What are all those?"

The quya lifted one of the papyrs. "Messages from the people of Allpa who have caught word of Apo's ultimatum."

"They don't want a war," Qora concluded.

Nobody *wanted* a war, of course. Even at the threat of losing independence, at the prospect of being stripped of one's culture and living under the rule of a tyrant. It was better than losing loved ones to battle, seeing one's homeland destroyed, and potentially living in poverty afterward.

"They don't," Urpi confirmed, "but … they're begging me not to cede."

"Really?"

"For days I've been caught between the thought that I ought to fight, and the thought that I ought to give in to Apo's rule so that my people won't have to suffer invasion and casualties. Of course if Apo takes control, he'll do what he's done in Sumaq—taxing everyone for personal gain, seizing the better part of crop yields and mining outputs, changing everything we know and love about Allpa to create a workforce and a network of resources for his own bidding. But is that worse than the destruction of war? Does it even compare?"

"I don't know," Qora admitted. "It depends on the extent of it, I guess—on how much damage the qhapaq can really do, and how well we can hold him back. At the moment, that's hard to say. We still don't know all the reptiles in the Sauroguard, or how much dominite the elementalists will be able to make, or whether we can get the giant theropods here. But … from the look of that pile of letters, I'd say it seems like the people think that if we have a fighting chance, we should at least try."

Urpi set the letter down. "And try we shall."

ꝺꝺꝺ

Ollan was already on the pteriary platform when Qora got there, with a pair of saddled pteranodons. He pulled on his riding gloves and mounted.

Without a word, Qora did the same, and together they took off over the grassland.

Hakan, Rimaq, and their mamáy must have spotted them a mile away, because they all stood waiting to greet Qora and Ollan before the pteranodons had even begun their descent. Once everyone was on land at the same time, the family embraced.

Qora's mamáy clung to her and Ollan with a new ferocity after their absence in the Tail and the risks that had been involved.

The quya had provided messenger service shortly after Qora and Ollan had returned with the elderboughs (and after returning from Huandoy) to update the new community on the unfortunate news of the cession demand, as well as to inform them of the safe return of the Kanchaya siblings and their friends. Thus, the reunion was bittersweet, knowing what was yet to come.

Dozens of other members of the community hurried to greet Qora and Ollan as well, as it was impossible to have missed the large flyers.

"You're the Raptoriva!" a young woman said.

Out of habit, Qora put on her performance smile. Hearing her Venture name drew it out of her. She stood patiently while people introduced themselves and told her how they'd heard the stories of her bravery.

A few of them asked about Ninan—girls, mostly, wanting to know if the romance rumors were true. Others *told* her about Ninan, about his arrival in Thak to get them out, how shocked they were to learn of his true origins but how he'd redeemed himself and become the hero they'd needed.

She even met Ninan's friends, Pidru and Tamya, and their mamáy.

"I can't believe you put up with him," Tamya teased.

Laughing, Qora said, "I know. I'm not sure how Ninan won me over." Except she was exactly sure. It was the fact that he was kind, even having had a life of bitterness; it was his sense of duty to the people he cared about; it was his rare roguish smiles and his soothing voice and his patience with her during her worst moments.

"It's good to finally meet you," Pidru said. "When we saw him this morning, he wouldn't shut up about you."

"He's told me much about you as well. You mean a lot to him; I hope you know that."

More people came, and Qora tried to turn their attention to Ollan, to let them know that it was he who had taught her to shoot, that she would not have survived the Venture without his training, and that he had fought in the battle in the Aquchay.

Finally some of the adults apologized on behalf of their youth and children for the excessive praise and questions, and left the Kanchayas to their private business.

"Come now," said Qora's mamáy. "Let's eat."

Qora had purposely taken no breakfast at Qhispina House today because, while the food there was very fine and decadent, it wasn't her mamáy's cooking.

Inside, while her mamáy finished dividing and dishing up a huge iguanodon egg—scrambled with some peppers, onions, and tomatoes—and several bowls of sweet quinoa with cinnamon and honey, Qora admired the interior of the new house. It had a small stairwell leading to a second level, and there was a fireplace with a chimney. New wooden chairs and tables filled the space, and several pieces of wool-knit fabric were draped over racks in the sitting area. Warming at the idea that her mamáy was keeping busy with her craft, Qora smiled.

Hakan and Rimaq were both dirty from the fields—but had apparently been given special leave in advance of their brother and sister coming—and their mamáy reminded them both to wash before eating.

Rimaq was so tall, Qora thought. Hakan had surpassed her height last year, but in her mind, Rimi was still a baby and his rapid growth induced a pang in her chest. Of course she was happy to see him growing—especially after thinking for a time that he might never have the chance to live, to age, let alone grow—but she hated all that she had missed, all that she was going to miss in the upcoming weeks. She dreamed of coming back here and staying with her mamáy and brothers—all three of them—and living a sweet, mundane little life.

With that in mind, she watched Ollan as he took a seat at the table. While perhaps an argument could be made for the potential dangers of her next trip to the Tail, and the effort of herding giant dinosaurs such a long distance, it wasn't the same as dropping in on enemy encampments and abducting their soldiers. Not to mention those weren't just any soldiers; they had special abilities, some of which could decimate a victim on the spot. Why was he so insistent? What was he trying to prove?

She helped her mamáy put out the food and the boys dished it up for them before filling their own plates. Their mamáy made a brief tribute of thanks to Sky Mother and the earth spirits.

Qora savored the simple flavors that reminded her of childhood. Despite all the fine foods she'd been served on the *Velosaura* tour and more recently at Qhispina House, nothing made her feel the way this did.

"The farmers are optimistic that we'll have a decent harvest," said Hakan. "The quya has been so generous, and given us anything we've asked for. Supplies, equipment …"

"They're letting me train with a sickle," Rimaq informed his siblings.

It wasn't the kind of work the boys were used to, but they seemed to enjoy it well enough.

They spoke also of the community's activities in the evenings and on days of rest. Apparently much of the traditions of Thak continued here with little deviation.

"There are quite a few kids our age," said Rimaq. "Hakan is *always* talking to Tamya—"

Hakan shot him a silencing look.

"Tamya?" Qora said. "Ninan's Tamya?" She suppressed a grin, not wanting to embarrass Hakan more than Rimaq already had.

When Hakan's ears went red, she knew they were past that.

Her mamáy rescued him by changing the subject, asking Qora to recount her experience in the Tail.

To that, Qora responded with a version of the truth, leaving out some of the more gruesome details. Ollan didn't contradict her, probably wanting to preserve a bit of their mamáy's sanity as much as Qora did. The younger boys had many questions, the answers to which by nature revealed more of those details, but their mamáy took it well considering her two oldest children had both been potential victims of a giganotosaur.

Then the topic turned to the cession demand, and what the quya was planning to do about it.

Qora told her mamáy about the dominite developments and the smilodon training, and explained that the migration was set to move forward soon, with herself, Ninan, and Paqari taking charge of it.

Nobody spoke for a long moment.

"I realize it means I'll have to leave again," said Qora, "and I'm sorry …"

"No, no," said her mamáy with a forced smile that did little to hide the worry behind her eyes. "Don't be sorry. We couldn't expect that you would sit by for these things. You've been an important figure in the rebellion, and your relationship with the people of the Tail is vital if everyone is going to work together. I'm grateful, at least, that you will be among allies. Of course I take no comfort in the fact that your task involves interacting with giant dinosaurs, but at least for now you won't be plunging straight into danger."

At that, Qora and Ollan exchanged a glance, in which Qora silently urged her brother to come clean about his assignment.

Their mamáy caught on in an instant. "What? What is it? Ollan …"

Ollan picked at his food, then took a bite, chewed, and swallowed with more aggression than was necessary. When he could no longer ignore his mamáy's cold stare, he blurted, "I'm part of a team that will be locating Sauroguard encampments and capturing a specimen of each species of reptile."

"Sauroguard … encampments?" she repeated. "Meaning that you'll be entering enemy territory …"

"Yes. That's the only way to do it."

"Ollan Kanchaya."

"I know. I haven't been back long, and it's dangerous. But I have valuable Sumaqi military knowledge—and just like Qora, I can't sit by and do nothing if I might be useful somewhere."

Secretly, Qora hoped her mamáy's reaction to this would inspire Ollan to reconsider. If only her mamáy's eyes weren't already brimming with tears, shattering Qora's heart.

"Mamáy …" Qora went to her and knelt beside her chair, clutching her hand.

"I'm fine," her mamáy said. "It's fine. I understand. As much as I want to keep you all with me for as long as possible, I know I can't expect that. You're both needed for this, that much is clear."

Hakan looked like he was chewing the inside of his cheek. Qora wouldn't have been surprised to hear him ask what he could do to help, but he would know as well as the rest of them that that was most definitely out of the question. Besides, for how important it was to resist this war, it was equally important for everyone else to keep performing their usual duties, to keep industries and routines functioning as normal. He was a part of that, and Qora hoped that was enough for him.

The rest of the meal was melancholic, and no one seemed to know what else to say. Qora and her brothers helped their mamáy clean up, and then Ollan stepped out.

Qora found him at the back of the property, staring off into space with his hands in his pockets.

"You're really going to go with the bandits?" she asked.

"What choice do I have?"

She shrugged. "You can come to the Tail with me." It wasn't as thrilling as stealing from the enemy, she thought, but it was an important part of the war preparations. It couldn't hurt to have more help when it came to rounding up giant dinosaurs and herding them through the wilderness.

"You already have Ninan for that."

Qora narrowed her eyes. "Is that why you've been acting like this?"

He shook his head. "No. Yes. Partially …"

"Ninan doesn't change anything," she told him.

"I know. It's not that. It's just that you … grew up … while

I was gone. I came back in the middle of this mess, and you were the Raptoriva, and you were already involved in a rebellion. At first, I tried to go along for the ride, and I felt like my being there made somewhat of a difference. But lately … I don't think it does. For me to follow you, to stay with you, at this point it would only be out of selfishness. Right now, we all need to do what we're best at, to make sure Qhapaq Apo doesn't destroy everything we have left of Runaqa as we know it. They need you in the Tail. They need me to infiltrate the Sauroguard."

Now it was Qora's turn to fight back tears. "But if we go our separate ways and then something happens to you …"

He came up to her and pulled her to his chest. "I'm not going to stand here and tell you everything will be alright. I don't know that it will. But I do know that you're strong, and that I'm ready to fight my way back to you when this is all over. This isn't the time to do what's easy."

"I don't think I remember the last time *anything* was easy," she muttered.

That was a lie. She did remember. It was before Ollan had disappeared. Before her papáy had died. She might also have said before her mamáy had lost the baby that should have been born after Hakan, although that would have taken her back to a time without Rimaq, and she couldn't say she wished not to have him. Sometimes, though, it seemed life was a never-ending strand of sorrows.

⟫⟫

Another tearful goodbye was in order. Qora and Ollan took turns embracing their mamáy and younger brothers, and then it was time to leave again. Before allowing them to step into the gondola, their mamáy kissed their cheeks one last time and said, "Don't forget: If the fire burns too hot, forge your weapons in it."

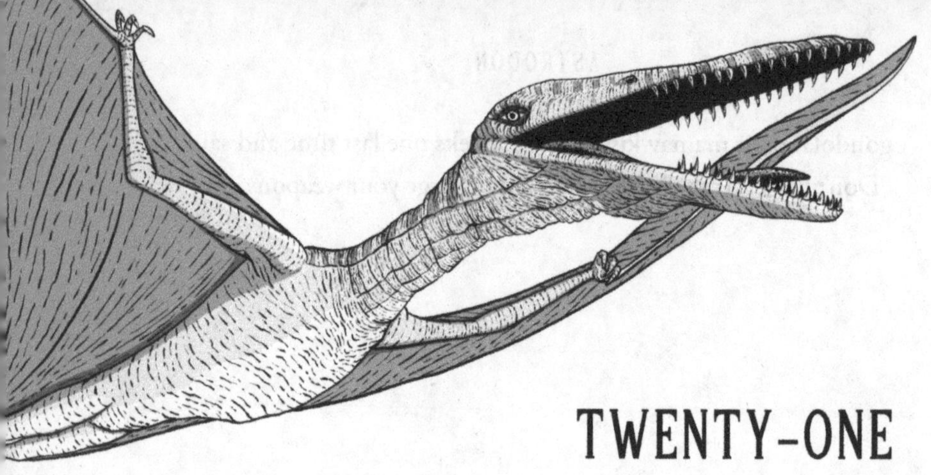

TWENTY-ONE

ENTRY INTO TAIL TERRITORY was much smoother this time. With the people expecting the return of two of their beloved elderboughs, they were lenient in their border security, which allowed the pterobeasts to fly directly to the Verdant Reach. The arks seemed to cause a bit of a stir, but Elderboughs Raphi and Mallki waving down at onlookers was enough to reassure everyone that all was well.

Once all authorities were briefed on upcoming plans, Ninan, Qora, and Paqari met with the rest of the elderboughs and a team of gladewardens to discuss what would come next.

They held council at the Perch, a rounded platform overlooking a habitat of giant dinosaurs. Six bridges spanned the distance between the platform and the surrounding walkways, making the whole thing look like an enormous wheel.

The round table at the center reinforced the image as a sort of hub.

"What we have seen in the Terrains," said Elderbough Raphi, "is an abomination to the sacred dinosaurs and a threat to the safety of everyone on this continent, including our own people. Everything Miss Kanchaya says is true; her qhapaq has used some diabolical means to mutate several species of dinosaurs and other reptiles into monstrous creatures with unnatural abilities."

She described some of the mutant dinosaurs in detail. "While I would not otherwise agree to send our own dinosaurs to a place with such horrors, I now believe it is a call to action we must heed with haste. Here, we send traitors and menaces to the waiting jaws of our tyrannosaurs and our giganotosaurs; in this case, we must deliver the reptilian gods swiftly into the midst of the monsters to deal with them justly."

It was no surprise the others had a lot of questions, which Ninan and his friends did their best to answer. But soon, everyone was in agreement that the giant theropods would go to Allpa's capital—it was just a matter of how to get them there.

"In anticipation of this news," said Elderbough Lluta, "our people have conducted several examinations in your absence and compiled that information with what we already knew about the dinosaurs here. We have managed to induce hyperphagia, as the princess suggested, by harnessing etherpine compounds. I must say, I did not have complete faith in the method, but I should not have doubted it. The giants have been consuming at three times their usual rate."

Paqari made a face that hinted at a smile, although Ninan knew she was suppressing any outward joy in favor of appearing regal and stoic.

"We've also created new whistles to test different sounds on them more closely," said a young woman named Suri, who made whistlemutes for the gladewardens. "It's been a challenge. One whistle made them race off in a big mass. I'd never seen them move so fast, especially not together; it must have tapped into some deep-seated stampeding instinct."

"Well let's just use that one," said Kondor. "We *want* them to move fast, don't we?"

Suri shook her head. "It would only work in short bursts.

They'd burn up energy too quickly. Anyway, after more tests, we finally figured out one that works." She gestured to several wood-carved whistles attached to straps around her neck, then put one to her lips and blew into it. Many of the dinosaurs below stopped what they were doing and stood at attention. "We think we'll be able to keep them coordinated this way, to encourage them to move ahead or to stop when necessary."

"As for a reasonable speed," said a man who worked as a forager and always spent plenty of time on the ground among land reptiles, "we've determined that they can comfortably cover long distances at around five miles per hour. Oddly enough, they don't seem to tire at that pace, even for extended periods of time."

"That's because they have unidirectional airflow in their respiratory systems," said Paqari. Everyone looked at her with confusion. "They're not like humans, who breathe like the tide. As I've said before, they're like birds; they share the same type of system, where each breath passes through the lungs and then into special air sacs that allow them to use the air more efficiently."

"I don't know …" said Kondor, who had been forced to join this council as well. "Some humans are pretty efficient that way too. You, for example, seem to get the most out of every breath—cramming in as many words as possible. How many air sacs do you have, exactly?"

Paqari scowled at him. "We can't all grunt like Neanderthals. It's very difficult to have an intelligent discussion that way. Which explains why it's such a chore to speak to you."

"The distance," Ninan cut in, "from here to Allpa's capital is approximately two hundred miles."

"Right," said the forager. "So the journey, nonstop, would take about forty hours. If we break that into reasonable eight-hour days, then it should take us five days minimum. That's on flat, even ground, however, and without breaks. As there will be multiple elevation changes, and the need to stop several times for water and eventually food as well, I would estimate closer to eight days if we're being optimistic, and up to ten if we're being conservative."

"Daily, these large dinos require around three hundred pounds of meat," said Elderbough K'ullu. "So I'm told. But with consistent energy expenditure for this migration, it could be as many as *five* hundred pounds daily to keep up their strength."

"What about Qora's idea to bring a herd of woolly rhinos as a food source?" Ninan asked.

"That was an excellent idea," Elderbough Lluta told him, "but they're not fast enough. They wouldn't be able to keep up. We decided it would be best to take mammoths. They're bulkier, but they already know how to travel long distances at a good speed. They're comfortable at five, even six miles per hour."

"How much does a woolly mammoth weigh?" asked Qora.

"Between seven and ten thousand pounds," said a woman who worked as a mammoth-riding courier. "Some of that weight is in the bones and the tusks, though. Each one's probably only got about five thousand pounds of actual meat on it."

"So one mammoth is basically ten days' worth of meat," Qora reasoned. "Except obviously we can't preserve it, so it would make more sense for ten gigas, for example, to share it."

"Hypothetically, yes," said the courier.

Qora said, "Alright, so then, roughly, we'll need one mammoth per day for every ten giant theropods we move."

"And we were hoping to get three hundred giants total," said Ninan.

"Three hundred?" Elderbough K'ullu repeated.

Ninan nodded. "We don't know how many Sauroguard reptiles we're going to be dealing with. Our people are working to get some better numbers, as well as to learn to combat the strange new features, but for the time being, we'll need a small army of giants, and the quya has determined three hundred to be the ideal minimum."

"Alright," said the forager. "Divided into groups of ten … That would require thirty mammoths' worth of meat per day. For a week, with a three-day buffer supply in case of delays, that's three hundred mammoths. So we're going to be migrating three hundred giant dinosaurs, plus three hundred woolly mammoths, for two hundred miles."

"Yes," Qora and Ninan said in unison.

"The mammoths can graze along the way, as we discussed previously," Ninan reminded them. "There are plenty of pastures. And of course … there will be fewer mammoths to feed with each day that passes."

"What about water?" Paqari asked.

"There's a creek that comes out of the Pirqas and flows most of the way to the Tail," Ninan offered. "I imagine travel routes are structured around it, for the same reason—travelers requiring a water source. Even the mountain pass follows the meander fairly closely, based on what I saw from the air."

Paqari raised a brow. "Is the water level adequate?"

"If the streams and rivers within our borders are any indication," said Kondor, "then there's nothing to worry about. Water levels are at a seasonal peak."

"Perfect," Ninan said.

"With the numbers we've just discussed," said Elderbough Mallki, "we should be able to move the giants with some thirty herders to handle them—and ensure they are treated with utmost respect—along with the mammoths, and a few surveyors to keep ahead of any problems on the route. Food and supplies for the herders and surveyors can be packed on the backs of the mammoths. Herders can ride some of the mammoths as well, since we likely won't need all of them; some are just a contingency. We'll have to bring in specialists from the flatlands, of course, who have experience handling them, as mammoths can be aggressive until they've adapted to a routine with humans. We'll also need to round up enough saddles for the herders to ride them."

"I imagine you'll want us to act as surveyors." Ninan motioned to himself, Qora, and Paqari.

"Yes. You've seen the terrain from the air several times now, and you know the mainland better than any of us. Although we would prefer to at least have one of our gladewardens accompany you."

"That's fine," said Qora.

"Gladewarden Sacha," said Elderbough Mallki, clapping Kondor on the back, "since you've already spent a good deal of time getting to know the foreigners and their ways, I think you're ideal for the job."

Paqari's cheeks went red. "But … Anku has also been with us for some time. Would he not be suitable?"

"He and another unit of gladewardens are working to coordinate the archers and the arks, so unfortunately he won't be available."

The princess shot a sideways look at Kondor, but didn't argue further.

"With all that said," said Elderbough Raphi, "I think we're in a good position to put this plan in motion. We've already begun preparations. Now we can proceed with a bit more confidence."

The plan was shaping up, Ninan thought, and they would address new issues as they arose, although his heart palpitated as he mentally went over the calculations again, wondering if it would really be enough. Would the mammoths really be enough to supply the dinosaurs' energy? Would the three hundred dinosaurs really be enough to fend off the Sauroguard? Would the herders and surveyors really be enough to control such a wild force across such a vast distance of land?

And then he found himself clenching his fist and his jaw when he imagined them all on the battlefield—these gargantuan beasts in the midst of several thousand smaller dinosaurs with ungodly abilities. Would ten-times-thicker skin be enough to resist the fire of the pyroraptors?

All this to protect Runaqa from dinosaurs that never should have existed. Qhapaq Apo thought himself so divinely imbued with power that he had the right to alter the very fabric of nature. And worse, even the brightest minds of Allpa and Unu still couldn't figure out how the man had done it.

No science of which anyone else was aware had the power to produce such specific features. With knowledge like that, Ninan's father probably could have changed the world for the better somehow—to remove the parts of nature that were harmful, rather than insert the parts he was now using to weaponize creatures against their will.

Ninan wondered how, if gods and nature spirits truly existed, they could allow this atrocity to occur. As it was, it seemed both sides of this war could only harness what was in front of them, and fight with everything they had.

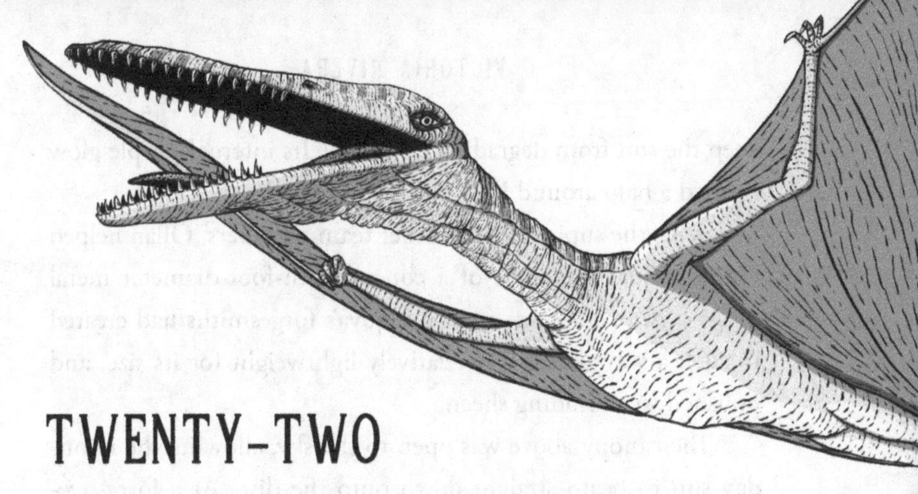

TWENTY-TWO

TO OLLAN'S DISAPPOINTMENT, there would be no hushdust this time. The knockout powder that the Razorclaws had used for previous heists would be a dead giveaway that the rebels were involved.

Qhapaq Apo had stated very clearly in his ultimatum that any attacks on his bases, encampments, or landmarks would be met with immediate retaliation. Thus, it was vital that any efforts to extract "soldiers" or intel remain untraceable.

The bandits had accomplished this before by luring away individual dinosaurs at the outer perimeters of the camps—similar to what Ollan and the Razorclaws had done with the scutellosaur, except that the bandits had been sober enough to plan better and not put themselves in a position to get a full blast of whatever each dinosaur might spew at them.

Currently, Ollan, Kuy, Gorgo, and the bandits (who had called in another four members of their ranks) were stationed some hundred yards away from the encampment, up on a hillside, and ensconced in the trees. There was, however, a direct visual path—albeit a narrow one—to the dominite crystal mounted at the center of all the enclosures.

The crystal was once again massive, up on the same sort of pole as the one near Huandoy, and with a similar shade on top to keep the sun from degrading its energy. Its internal purple glow formed a halo around it.

With the support of the other team members, Ollan helped Gorgo adjust the angle of a concave, ten-foot-diameter metal disc—a *parabolic* disc—that the quya's forgesmiths had created in such a way that it was relatively lightweight for its size, and polished to a blinding sheen.

The canopy above was open to the sky, allowing the noon-day sun to beam straight down onto the disc. At a forty-five-degree angle, it bounced the light forward, while the two young men worked to focus it as precisely as they could on the dominite.

The team had had to assemble a wooden frame to support and secure the disc, but in pieces it had been transportable in nets dangling from the pteranodons' harnesses, as had the disc itself (which miraculously weighed less than two hundred pounds and wasn't an unreasonable thing to lift into position with all ten team members sharing the load).

Ollan had to squint to spot the light beam, only catching it in glimpses in the faint swirls of dust that swept across the open path whenever the wind kicked up.

"That should do it," said Kuy. "Now, we wait."

In the distance, the crystal's internal glow disguised any evidence of additional light that might have shone through or around it, making this method just about as subtle as it could possibly be.

With direct sunlight concentrated on the crystal, it would only be a matter of a few hours before all the energy degraded. Without the dominite to keep the dinosaurs entranced, all hell would break loose.

By midafternoon, the dinosaurs on the far sides of the enclosures were beginning to stir. They crowded around the crystal, shoving past each other to get within range of its dwindling energy.

Ollan used a spyglass to check the crystal's color, which was now almost fully white. A crack had begun to spread vertically down its length, as the heat forced it to expand. "Get ready to move in!"

He pulled on a set of military fatigues that one of Quya Urpi's spies had retrieved from Sumaq a few days earlier. It was of a higher rank than what he'd worn during his own time as part of the Sumaqi Guard—similar, but embroidered with symbols of beastlord leadership.

Everyone slipped supply packs onto their shoulders, filled with hooks, ropes, a few small tools and weapons, and dominite provided by the quya's elementalists.

Ollan, Kuy, Gorgo, Kunaq, Yaku, Tika, and an additional bandit raced down the hill toward the camp, while the last three bandits stayed behind to disassemble the disc setup.

There were three enclosures to separate the dinosaurs, which were one of three types: more of the razor-scaled oviraptors like the ones in Huandoy, red-footed velociraptors (which fit the description Ninan had given for those that had climbed the Unuvian citadel walls), and mononykus that could retract and rapidly extend an extra-long single claw on each forelimb.

Everyone but Ollan would split into three pairs to each focus on capturing one dinosaur species. Meanwhile, Ollan had to get into the beastwarden's tent to find the bestiary.

Having been stationed at such an encampment once before (with human units, of course, rather than reptilian ones) Ollan was familiar with the arrangement and could easily locate the tent in question. No surprise a warden's tent was always the biggest, and usually had a few pieces of furniture for sitting and writing reports or reviewing orders. Other documents or instructional tomes would be kept within a secured trunk.

He extended the spyglass again, although now he was close enough that he almost didn't need it, and focused on the crystal. The crack suddenly widened into a deep fissure as the crystal went completely dark of its remnant purple glow.

The reptiles went wild.

They screeched and squealed and bucked and roared, clambering over one another, clawing at the dead crystal.

Guards emerged, wielding smaller crystals and running into the midst of the reptiles to try and calm them.

Ollan's companions waited at the treeline and, sure enough, dinosaurs of all three species—no longer contained by the special force—chewed through the flimsy palisades and fled in every direction.

The other team members split off to catch any of several oviraptors, mononykus, and velociraptors while Ollan prepared to make his move.

Lesser officers sounded horns to rally all the human military on the premises.

As everyone at the encampment worked to control the chaos, Ollan made his way around the palisades and toward the tents. It was surprisingly easy to get into the beastwarden's tent, as the beastwarden himself was busy shouting commands at everyone.

Inside, Ollan observed a desk cluttered with papyr documents—supply requests, reports on the day-to-day activities at camp, personal correspondence—and then set his sights on a large trunk with a thick padlock.

Having come prepared, Ollan withdrew his lock-picking device, which the Allpan forgesmiths had created for this purpose based on his description of the types of locks used by the Sumaqi Guard. Within a few seconds, he heard a click, and the lock popped open. The trunk was full of books and piles of additional documents. He found the bestiary at the very bottom underneath everything else, removed it, then tucked everything back in just so, so as not to make it obvious that anything was missing. It wouldn't be a book the general was likely to need regularly—just for occasional reference—and by now the man had surely memorized any parts that pertained to his current stewardship here. Ollan hoped the beastwarden wouldn't look for it again unless he were assigned new units of dinosaurs with which he was not yet familiar.

He shoved the bestiary under the front of his uniform jacket, which was slightly oversized to accommodate this, and slipped out of the tent.

The guards were in the process of mounting a new crystal, one that had apparently been buried in the ground, as evidenced by the shovels and piles of dirt surrounding a rectangular hole and an empty, lead-lined crate.

Too much dominite, of course, would draw wild dinosaurs from miles around, so it made sense to keep backup crystals of this size inaccessible most of the time.

Beastlords and handlers were out trying to round up the fleeing dinosaurs, drawing them back with individual crystals in small herds.

Ollan kept to the perimeter again until he returned to the treeline, then raced back to his friends. The concave reflective disc was already loaded up, and now they were securing one of each dinosaur in the nets.

Kuy paused and removed a dominite crystal from between his teeth. "Did you get it?"

"Yes." Ollan let the bestiary fall out from under his jacket.

With everything ready to go, all ten of them mounted, flying as low as possible until they were out of easy view of the encampment, then rose high into the air toward Allpa.

⁍⁍⁍

When the team arrived back at Qhispina House, they went straight to Quya Urpi's scriptorium and laid the bestiary in front of her.

"Well done," she told them after they'd regaled her with the details of the mission, including mention of the three new species they'd brought with them. "It's good you did it on the first try. It would be much too risky to attempt something like that again."

Ollan could only imagine the suspicion it would raise for Qhapaq Apo to find out that not one but two of his encampments' core crystals had mysteriously degraded and sent all dinosaurs into madness. As it was, there was going to be a thorough investigation of the most recent event, and a report back to the capital. "We'll need to move quickly to do the other extractions. I'm sure what we did today will be enough to warrant higher security measures and better contingencies from now on. Maybe we can get the rest of the specimens before word spreads and new orders are executed at the other camps."

"Good thinking," said the quya as she opened the bestiary and flipped through the pages.

The extraction team watched from across the desk. Ollan caught glimpses of familiar reptiles—the color-shifting megaraptors from the base in the Aquchay, the scutellosaur from Huandoy, the mononykus from where he'd just been.

All the reptiles had special names that aligned with their

abilities: "firebreath" for the pyroraptors, "clingfoot" for the velociraptors, "destroyer" for the ankylosaurs, and so on.

When the quya neared the end, she said, "We've done very well. You've already gathered a scutellosaur, a hypsilophodon, a troodon, and now a velociraptor, oviraptor, and mononykus. I think it's safe to say we won't be able to reasonably capture one of the ankylosaurs with the enlarged club-tails—although that one seems fairly straightforward and not in need of much study. The acid-spitting pteranodons will prove difficult as well, due to their size, but at least they fly on their own, so it would only be a matter of getting on one's back with some dominite. Then there are the irritators, which are also quite large. And of course there are the megaraptors that can camouflage."

"Maybe that camouflage could be to our benefit when we sneak it out," Kuy offered.

"True," said the quya. "Aside from that, we only need a dracorex, a pyroraptor, one of the small therizinosaurs, and ..." She turned to the last page and her jaw went slack.

Everyone else leaned in to see what was wrong.

A rough edge of torn papyr ran along the gutter where the pages met.

"It seems," the quya said through a rough swallow, "that this bestiary ... is incomplete."

The apprentice frowned. "It is but one fraying thread. What is one thread to the whole of the tapestry?"

"Pull that thread," said the weaver, "and you will see how it can unravel *everything*."

Excerpt from "The Fray" from *Asiri's Apologues*

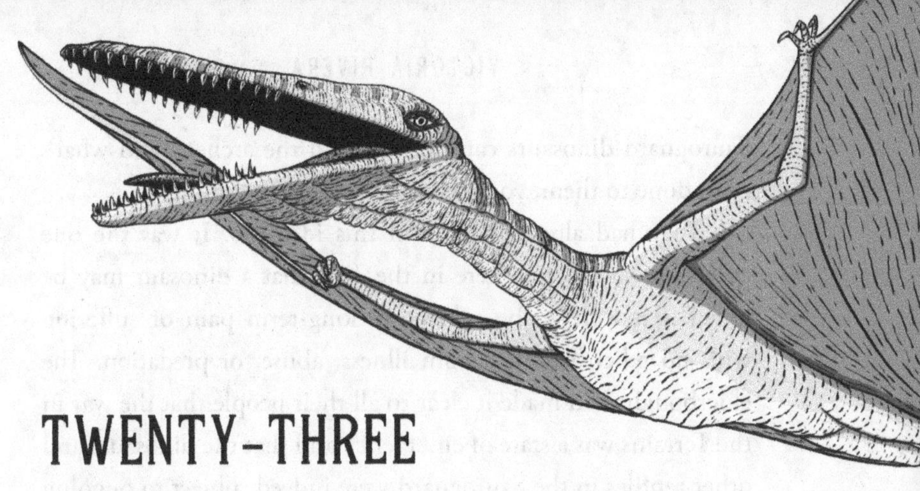

TWENTY-THREE

QORA WATCHED A TEAM OF ARCHERS with their wooden recurve bows, each slinging an arrow per second. Log targets dotted the range—vertical logs for height, and shorter logs fixed perpendicularly to the vertical ones. The horizontal logs had angular cuts at the front to mimic a dinosaur's open mouth, stained red inside with berry juices. With all the special features the Sauroguard possessed, anyone who hoped to combat those dinosaurs would need to aim for their most vulnerable areas, and to hit them with speed and precision.

Qora had requested this type of training specifically. It was either the mouth or the eyes, and she shuddered as she thought about the latter—when the memory of the blinded spinosaurus from the Venture crossed her mind. While she had hunted and killed plenty of dinosaurs, it was a process that was supposed to be quick and humane. For the people of the Tail, however, the act of killing dinosaurs in *general* was not humane, which made this exercise all the more difficult.

"I don't know if I can shoot a dinosaur," admitted one of the archers, a young woman just a few years older than Qora.

Kondor, who had just unsuccessfully tried to persuade Anku to take his place as a migration leader and surveyor, stood with his arms folded and a scowl on his face. "When you see what the

Sauroguard dinosaurs can do," he told the archer, "and what's been done to them, you'll consider it a mercy killing."

They had already discussed this idea too. It was the one exception to the rule here in the Tail, that a dinosaur may be killed if it were to be subject to long-term pain or suffering with no relief, whether from illness, abuse, or predation. The elderboughs had made it clear to all their people that the war in the Terrains was a state of emergency and that the dinosaurs and other reptiles in the Sauroguard were indeed subject to ongoing abuse. Although that abuse was, in large part, psychological rather than physical, their physical wellbeing was questionable, considering the fact that the influence of the dominite rendered them unable to express physical needs at any time. Allowing them to live would mean continued generations of enslaved reptiles, and the spread of a regime that would eventually overtake all lands of Runaqa, including the Tail, where the practice of respecting dinosaurs would be all but wiped out.

A few of the other archers paused to reflect on the reminder. Of course, knowing this didn't make it easier for them to go against their better instincts, or to ignore the spiritual connection to the dinosaurs they'd shared their entire lives. But they continued to practice, putting aside their reservations for now.

That's what everyone was doing, in fact.

Despite how it might affect the local ecosystem, herders were gathering mammoths from the far regions of the Tail—trying to take a few from several areas, rather than all from one—and rounding up the giant dinosaurs after ensuring those selected had no hatchlings and were in good health to travel. It was a grand effort that required much patience and coordination, and an active choice to believe the consequences would be worth it in the end.

Qora glanced at Kondor's folded arms, with special attention on his bracer-mounted weapon. "You're going to give me one of those. I don't care if they're 'only for gladewardens.' Your people almost killed me; I think you owe me that much."

He turned his wrist toward himself like he'd forgotten he was wearing the thing, then rolled his eyes and sighed. "Fine."

After speaking to the chief gladewarden and procuring an extra wristbow, Kondor set about showing Qora how to put it on.

It was a narrow pteroleather cuff with three straps on the underside to adjust to the wearer's size. The dark brown pteroleather was supple and almost rubbery, and tanned to be water and sweat resistant. Kondor tightened the straps around Qora's forearm, then fixed them with their buckles.

Qora, however, was more focused on the details of the wristbow attached to the bracer's topside: the main body made of oiled wood, the forged-metal bow, the little mechanisms that connected the trigger to a thin pull-bar across her palm.

She couldn't believe how small it was. With the way the traders at the Underground had teased her about the compact style of the crossbow she usually carried, they would have mocked her endlessly for this. But she liked the idea of having a crossbow attached to her, something she could operate mostly with one hand while riding a pteranodon perhaps, or carry with no effort as she ran.

It would go on her left arm so that she could use her dominant hand for other tasks.

Kondor provided her with a small bolt. She spanned the bowstring—which drew back the bow limbs and tightened the rod against her palm—before slipping the bolt into its flight groove.

"You have to develop an instinct for wrist control," Kondor

told her, "otherwise it's really easy to fire the bolt"—he flinched and jumped out of the way as Qora's bolt landed next to his feet, spewing dirt and lodging itself several inches deep—"by accident." He frowned.

"Sorry."

"If you can *control yourself*," he went on, "you can carry it loaded, if necessary, so that it's ready to go without you having to stop and load in the heat of a fight. Although, as you can see, loading is a pretty quick process and doesn't require a lot of energy. Not like a real crossbow that you have to brace against your chest and use a strong arm to span. That said, however, it's a bit harder to aim when you don't have your whole chest to stabilize it."

He then showed her a workaround, in which she could use one hand to stabilize the other—her right elbow braced against her body, her left wrist resting in the curved palm of her right hand.

"Eventually your arm muscles will adapt and you'll be able to keep it straight without help, but it will take some practice," he explained.

Qora nodded. "Great. I'll get started right now."

Kondor raised an eyebrow, but handed over a fistful of bolts. Qora slipped all but one into a pocket on her green jacket. She patted the pocket, pleased with how nicely the bolts fit there.

"Careful with those," he told her.

She pulled a face, shoving the tip of her tongue to one corner of her mouth, then turned her attention to a rhamphorhynchus that flew above the trees. She aimed and pulled the trigger.

The rhampho dropped to the ground with the bolt clean through its midsection.

Qora would have preferred a head shot, and worse, the bolt

had struck off center, but for her first try with the wristbow she couldn't complain. She looked back up at Kondor and smiled. "Lunch?"

꒰꒰꒰

After working on her wristbow technique until her arm was sore, Qora mingled with some of the people helping to coordinate the migration, and one of them mentioned a place for quiet contemplation called a "verdanza," which was also where a great many of the Tailfolk went to make offerings to the dinosaurs and pray to the nature spirits.

With the heavy tasks that lay ahead, Qora found herself yearning for spiritual consolation, and soon made her way to this place.

She followed another wood-planked path that led away from the bustling center of Murkroot, and came upon a place where the tree branches curved inward and created a tunnel overhead. The tunnel opened into a dome of trees whose branches— perhaps when they had been younger and more flexible—had been guided to grow together in a twisted, woven manner, and perhaps grafted or pruned as well, to create the effect of an enormous, upside-down basket with leaves sprouting from both the warp and weft. A few larger gaps had been left along the dome, as if for the express purpose of viewing the dinosaurs below, although at the moment there were no dinosaurs in sight as so many had been rounded up in advance of the migration.

The planks that made up the floor of the verdanza had a circular opening cut in the center, and a rounded platform on ropes that seemed to be capable of lowering down into the dinosaurs' midst. *For offerings*, Qora realized when she noticed the stains of cut flower stems and dried meat juices.

Woven mats were strewn about with worn spots on their middles.

Alone in the verdanza, Qora took one of the mats and set it where she liked, and knelt upon it facing an opening in the woven branches that looked northeast. *Toward Qhusi*, she thought, because she longed for her homeland. She wished she had a little bundle of holy wood or some chakapa leaves to beckon the spirits she most trusted to carry her pleas to Sky Mother, although she didn't know whether it was entirely appropriate to pray to her own gods in a place dedicated to different ones. But all in all, she didn't think it mattered much, because all things in nature were connected, weren't they?

While the people of the Tail worshiped the dinosaurs, the dinosaurs were really just an extension of other natural things; the dinosaurs fed upon other creatures, who fed upon the plants, who fed upon the sun's light and the nutrients in the soil, all of which belonged to earth and sky and the life that flowed through them. All belief systems must have once stemmed from the same source, but had simply become subject to different interpretations, names, and explanations, Qora imagined. The gods, whomever they really were and whatever form they took, would surely respond to whatever names they were given and communicate through whatever conduits were provided, so long as both were done in earnest and with respect.

And so, Qora rested her hands on her lap and inhaled the scent of tree sap and of diffused "ether" of the etherpines that the people had used to induce hyperphagia in the giant theropods.

She wanted to believe that the ability to use those pines had been a gift from Sky Mother, a provision of nature to aid in the good cause. Of course, to what extent humans could harness nature for their own needs before becoming corrupt, Qora wasn't sure. The qhapaq had also used nature, and adapted it to his purposes. She supposed it was intent that mattered; survival and protection was one thing, controlling a continent was another. Then again, knowing the qhapaq, Qora was certain he considered the Sauroguard a matter of survival, a way to protect what he considered the reestablishment of a "divine empire."

Closing her eyes, Qora silently thanked Sky Mother for keeping her and her friends safe over the past week, and for reuniting them. She expressed gratitude for Ninan, in particular, and then for all the progress the Allpans had made with the dominite and other weapons. Then she allowed her deepest desires to come to the forefront of her mind, imagining how the coming battles would play out, pleading for the migration's success, for the extraction team's success in obtaining Sauroguard reptiles, for the quya's success against Qhapaq Apo's inevitable aggression. After a few minutes of sitting in a somewhat meditative state, the wood of the floor creaked behind her.

She turned toward the sound.

"Sorry." Ninan paused. "Kondor told me you might be here."

Qora stood and brushed the mat's fibers from her knees. "I heard about the verdanza from some of the locals. I felt like it might be nice to commune with Sky Mother."

Ninan moved further into the dome of branches, gazing up at them, then observing the opening at the center and the gaps around the interior for looking out. His mouth formed a flat line. There was a visible tightness to his jaw, a tension in his shoulders. He'd been like that for the past couple of days, Qora realized, but everyone had been so busy preparing for the migration and the delivery of the archers that there hadn't been much time to talk.

With a careful approach, Qora took one of his hands in hers. "Is everything okay?"

He sighed slowly. "I'm fine. I just … have a lot on my mind."

"Anything besides the obvious?"

"I've been thinking a lot about how one man has caused so much destruction. How we've had to involve so many people, and upend all of our lives, and how we're going to alter an entire landscape and move huge reptiles from their natural habitat, how Quya Urpi is gathering thousands of soldiers and smilodons and pooling all her resources to produce countless weapons, all to try and stop *my father*. And how it's … not fair."

Qora squeezed his hand. "I know. I know it's not."

"And to be honest, it seems a little … pointless … for you to come here and try to reason with gods who clearly don't care about any of us."

A weight tugged at Qora's stomach. She remembered Ninan's nonchalance during the Venture when she'd expressed gratitude over small victories, and also how he'd only passively gone along with her offering to Sky Mother before slaying the spinosaur. "I know you've never put much stock in religion, but you don't have to say things like that."

"Before the *Velosaura* tour," Ninan said, "when my father was holding my friends hostage in Thak, when I was weeks away from being forced to marry Paqari, while I was risking my life to get information to Qhapaq Izhi so he could locate the Sauroguard breeding grounds … I went to the Kallpa House sanctum *every week*. I knelt at the altar and let the High Shaman chant at me, so that he might bless me with 'clarity of mind,' and 'purity of heart,' and 'serenity of the soul.' I begged the gods to help me—to help Runaqa—even though I didn't think they could hear me. Even though I didn't think there was anyone *to* hear me. The High Shaman told me once that dedication to gods and rituals could build my confidence in them, and that I would eventually feel a spiritual presence in my life." He raked his fingers through his hair, which was sweaty and scraggly after a long day of helping with the dinosaurs. "But here I am. Here we are. The war has started despite all of that … and I can't say we actually have a chance of winning."

"But your friends are safe now, at least. You survived your father's attempts to kill you. You helped find the Aquchay base. You didn't have to go through with the arranged marriage. You found me—and saved me—here at the Tail. Weren't those a reply to your begging?"

He drew his hand away from her. "Why should I have ever had to beg in the first place? If the gods care for us like parents care for their children, how could they have allowed the very situation that put us all in harm's way?"

"I don't know," Qora admitted. It wasn't anything she hadn't wondered herself from time to time. There were those who would scoff at such questions and reduce them to the ramblings of "those of little faith," but she knew it was valid. Frankly, it was something she didn't allow herself to think about very deeply, because when she did—when she thought about her own existence, and the existence of all things, and whether she would die and disappear or whether her soul might live on somehow in perpetuity—it made her mind spin and her stomach sour. Trying to imagine the origins of the universe put her in a thought spiral, with no explanation she could come up with that made full sense.

A priest might say, "The gods created this world for us," but none could answer how the gods and spirits came to be. A shaman might say, "All spirits are eternal. They do not experience time the way we do. Time is a construct of the human mind, a necessary perception of our surroundings between the High World and the Grave World, and only upon our deaths shall we be enlightened."

The concept of nonlinear time seemed more logical to Qora than trying to determine whether the gods had been created by some other gods before them, and those gods by gods before *them*, and so on backward without end. But still, nothing really satisfied the question.

For Qora, however, there wasn't much to do but cling to what brought her comfort, to the idea that something bigger than her had set life in motion. Maybe she was pathetic for that, she thought, but in moments like this, it felt like all she had.

"If the gods were capable of interfering," said Ninan, "wouldn't they have done so a long time ago? And don't say they're testing us, or that this is all for our development; that's just a convenient way to make room for a concept that has never had a leg to stand on."

"Maybe it's energy, then," Qora reasoned. "A soul—the mind, everything we are and all that we feel—if nothing else, is energy. So everything alive has it, and it's not that crazy to think it vibrates, probably at levels we aren't aware we can perceive, like whistlemutes or dominite. So maybe I can direct my mental energy, and maybe somewhere, some way, it can affect something else."

"If you ask me, laws of nature aside, everything is just a gamble, and we can either strategize to the best of our ability around the uncertainty, or wait and hope for the best outcome. Maybe a combination of both."

"I already believe in strategizing to the best of our ability. That's why I came down here, why I risked so much to persuade the people of the Tail to work with us. That's why I entered the Venture—because I wasn't going to ask for a miracle for Rimaq and then not do my part to make it come true."

"Right. That was *you*. Your effort, your success. You answered your own prayers. I answered mine. We answered each other's. Our friends played a large part too. We've controlled what we could control, and the rest … it's chaos."

"I don't have all the answers, but I still think there's value in spirituality."

"Not when it's used to control people. 'Spirituality' is the source of my father's power. You realize that, don't you? It's what he uses to justify trying to reunite the Old Empire—*and* trying to expand the new version of it he's been working on. Because he and plenty of other people think the gods have sanctioned the office of qhapaq, and particularly *him* as a descendant of the original qhapaqal lineage."

"Any source of power can be abused. People have been doing that since the beginning of time. That doesn't mean the power itself is corrupt," Qora argued.

"Sure, if it's power at all. But like the gods, it's more illusion than anything. It's lies."

"Why are you acting like this?"

"Because I'm angry. Aren't *you*?"

"Of course I'm angry."

"But you're praying to gods that—if they're even real—either don't listen, or they listen and don't care. Gods on whose 'authority' my father operates."

"*Claims* to operate," Qora corrected.

"What's the difference if they don't stop him?"

"They might."

"They haven't yet. What, exactly, is the delay?"

Qora's heart pinched at his tone. It wasn't that he was saying anything that was wrong, or that this wasn't something on which they'd always had differing perspectives, but the intensity of his argument seemed to have come to a boil so suddenly. And because rather than being angry about the situation, it felt like he was angry at ... *her*.

Worse, he'd physically pulled away from her.

"What do you want me to do?" she asked. "Abandon everything I've ever believed? Bend to your cynicism?" She didn't mean that; she knew he was only being realistic, but she'd said it anyway.

"That's what you think of me? That I'm just a cynic?" He scoffed. "Well I'm sorry if it's a little hard for me to look on the bright side right now—considering there isn't one."

Qora's eyes welled. "There's not? You really can't think of *anything* good in your life right now?" She wasn't naive enough to think an exercise in gratitude would simply wash away all the despair, but she also had long since learned that living in constant anger and acting rashly because of it often caused its own problems. *Be precise or do it twice*, her mamáy had always said. And it was very difficult to be precise in one's actions, in one's defenses, while blinded by rage. She knew that all too well. Since then, she'd learned to latch onto whatever slivers of hope and goodness were available, because after everything she'd already been through, it would be an even greater tragedy to let it all slip away at such a pivotal time.

But Ninan didn't seem to feel the same. His throat flexed. "It's not that simple ... and you know it. Being with you is all I've wanted for a very long time, but it's a cruel thing to get what you want only for it to be under constant threat. Every day, I wonder if that day will be my last, or yours, or the last for someone else we care about."

"So you're just going to act like that's already happened? To dwell on your anger, and shame me for trying to have faith in the unseen, because of things you haven't lost yet and might not lose at all?" Qora shook her head and pushed past him toward the tunnel of branches that led away from the verdanza.

He snatched her wrist. "If you want to make the most of what we have, then taking offense isn't going to help anything."

"Hurt isn't the same thing as offense," she said. "It's not like I'm mad about some thoughtless comment you made at the Underground. I came here because I ache for the life we could have someday, because I ache for the happiness and prosperity of everyone in Runaqa. I don't know how we came to be, or what controls the natural world, but I will fight as hard as I can to keep us all alive—and in between, I will plead with whatever forces might hear me, until my voice is raw. And if that offends *you*, then … I don't know that we have anything to say to each other right now."

Ninan stared at her, lips parted just enough to release a short breath, but couldn't seem to think of how to reply.

Swallowing her tears, Qora tugged out of his grasp and left him there, alone in the verdanza.

TWENTY-FOUR

OLLAN HOVERED ON HIS PTERANODON until the miniature therizinosaur stopped thrashing inside the dangling net below, then gently set the net down and landed beside it.

Wayra was the only one on the paddock at the moment, surrounded by the array of Sauroguard dinosaurs that meandered across the grass, and wearing a vibrant dominite crystal on a string around her neck.

When Ollan dismounted, she hugged him tightly. "Gods I *hate* it when you guys go on extractions."

Her breath was warm against his shoulder, and the feel of her body so close to his made him feel things he wasn't ready to address. Currently, he smelled of woodsmoke, sweat, and pteranodon, his hair was matted, and he hadn't slept at all.

The extraction had been fairly uncomplicated, initially, as the team had developed a routine for these things now. With the exception of stealing the bestiary, they worked at night to take advantage of the darkness as a cover. And so each mission could be more or less the same: keeping a distance from the encampment until well after dusk or a while before dawn (when most personnel on the encampment would be slumbering deeply), approaching with a supply of dominite, and luring one of the dinosaurs close to the flimsy palisades that divided the different species from one another. The team carried all the necessary tools to be quick and avoid problems. The trips, however, were often long, and some of the dinosaurs were dangerous if not handled correctly.

In this case, Ollan and the team had had to bind and cover the therizinosaur's claws in layers of burlap—after one gentle swipe (not an act of aggression, just a simple accident) had left a bandit in dire condition. For that reason everyone else had accompanied the poor girl to the quya's infirmary while Ollan delivered the monster alone. Now it stood at full height, with the net slack over its body, staring at Wayra's necklace.

Wayra released Ollan and went to the net, tugging it open to set the therizinosaur free. The therizinosaur was almost as tall as she was, and coated with short gray-and-white feathers (neutral in color, like so many of the Sauroguard dinosaurs were). Ollan quickly related the story of what had happened to the bandit, complete with a grave warning for her safety.

"Spirits," she whispered. "I thought these missions were going well—except for the inherent risk of getting near Qhapaq Apo's guards, of course." She reached up to stroke under the therizinosaur's chin with her knuckles. It stared at her with giant, greenish eyes, its throat vibrating as though it were content with the touch. Then she examined the claws and their bindings.

"Seriously, though," said Ollan. "Those things could cut through at any moment. The burlap was all we had on hand, but I doubt it will hold long."

It was eerie, he thought, the way she could be so gentle with something so monstrous. Despite the rough skin and severe features—the slimy buccal flaps and jagged teeth and slits for nostrils—Wayra managed to appeal to the soul of each reptile she met. The dominite helped, sure, but he'd also seen her do it without any mystical forces.

"I'll ask someone to contact one of the quya's leatherworkers," Wayra told him. "Maybe they can fashion something out of thick dinoleather that will cover each of the claws. A glove, of sorts."

Ollan tried to imagine the therizinosaur—with its ridiculously long claws—wearing gloves. But dinoleather wasn't a bad idea; it should work to shield the handlers from the venom. He pushed aside the grim thought of a creature wearing the skin of its own kind.

Wayra called for the other handlers to come take the therizinosaur for examination, then handed it off with the same warning Ollan had given her. Once the handlers were gone, however, Ollan saw her attention fall to a patch of dried blood on his shirt.

He quickly pressed his hand over the spot a few inches to one side of his navel.

"What's that?" She set her hands on her hips. "If you say, 'it's nothing,' I'll let the scutellosaur scream at you again."

Sighing, Ollan removed his hand and raised the hem of his shirt to reveal a short gash. "We had to scale a rocky outcrop to get a good view of the encampment and plan our approach. I got caught on a sharp little jut on the way up."

She stepped forward to get a better look, then brushed her fingertips over the skin around the wound. Ollan suppressed a shiver. When he met her eyes, he suddenly felt a lot like how he imagined the therizinosaur must have felt: like a strange creature that didn't know quite what it was, trying to make sense of being transplanted in a new place, and somewhat lost to this woman's spell. While Ollan was no biological hybrid, he still struggled to unite the disjointed parts of his life and his memories—a hybrid of the different identities he'd once possessed. And while dominite had no influence over him that he knew of, he was beginning to feel less and less in control of himself whenever he went near Wayra. Why did it feel like she could see into his hidden depths?

Heart pounding, he stopped the movement of her fingers with his own, but she didn't take her eyes off of him. If he inclined his head forward just a bit, there would be little to no gap between them, and suddenly he had the urge to close the distance.

But her touch, her proximity, was no indication of her feelings. This was her way, to be tender and caring, to show affection to her friends—and to animals. She wasn't one to shy away from physical contact. That didn't mean she wanted anything to do with him beyond their work together. Knowing that, he couldn't allow thoughts of anything more to take root in his mind, and especially not at a time like this. Not when it could have been him in the infirmary instead of the bandit girl; not when he and Wayra both still had dangerous assignments to complete; not with war at their doorstep.

"I'm sure you're going to tell me I should go to the Qhispina House physician," he said. "So I'll save you the trouble. I'll head over right now." With a soft smile, he released her, and she him, and he mounted his pteranodon and kicked off into the air, thinking how leaving her behind stung so much more than his wound did.

TWENTY-FIVE

ON PTERANODONBACK, Qora and Paqari flew loops above the enormous herd of dinosaurs that sprawled below. Half the herders rode mammoths sporadically between dinosaurs while the other half of the herders and the rest of the mammoths migrated together a quarter mile ahead. Qora pulled the reins on her pteranodon to ease into another curve while Paqari mirrored her motion across the way.

Qora felt a flutter in her belly at the prospect of what they had just set out to do, although she'd been eager to leave for days now. She hoped the fresh air would clear her mind and help her focus, despite having barely spoken to Ninan since their conversation in the verdanza—no words but for polite exchanges for the benefit of those watching them, and any necessary communications related to preparation for the trip.

She took a deep breath now as she surveyed the magnitude of the sight, the hundred spinosaurs and hundred tyrannosaurs and hundred giganotosaurs that moved in clusters among their own kind but pressed onward in the larger group. A few on the edges would start to stray now and then, but the herders lured them back with their wooden whistles.

It had been decided that the mammoths (except for the herders' mounts) would always keep a distance ahead, so as not to distract the dinosaurs too much, and when the time came to eat, the mammoth herders would leave behind the right number for the dinosaurs to hunt for the day, and move ahead with the rest of them to avoid depleting the food supply too quickly. It was only the fact that the dinosaurs would outnumber the daily thirty-mammoth allotment by ten times that they would be able to overpower them easily; a one-on-one showdown between a giant theropod and a mammoth was actually a pretty fair fight, according to the Tailfolk, considering how large the mammoths were and the way they utilized their long tusks.

Regardless, Qora wasn't looking forward to the first meal (which would take place an hour before dusk) and the slaughter she would have to witness.

In the meantime, however, she marveled at the way the dinosaurs seemed to fall into formation, each walking behind the one before like they might be trying to reduce wind resistance—even though they were traveling on land rather than through the air. She supposed the principle might still apply, to some degree, and that it could be useful because it would encourage the dinosaurs at the forefront to trample the grasses and brush and help clear the way for the rest of the herd. All together, they made deep trenches in the earth, and of course left a trail of ruck behind them. Their footfalls seemed to synchronize too, and it was then that Qora began to feel as though she were helping to lead an army. That's what these dinosaurs were, after all: a unit of their own to combat the Sauroguard.

On the backs of several dozen mammoths were packs full of supplies required for the journey: tents, lanterns, dried foods, fire starters, medical kits, tools, weapons, and caged messenger flyers from Allpa that would home back to the quya to deliver updates as needed. It seemed a little grotesque to make the mammoths carry everything, Qora thought, when their fates were doomed, but at least the relatively few of them performing this labor would be the *last* to feed the dinosaurs.

It was grim any way she looked at it, though.

Paqari looked equally nauseated. Qora knew the princess didn't like riding pteranodons; the girl preferred to be carried around like the royalborn she was; and yet, she'd flown like that all the way from Tisqu's capital to find Ninan in Unu. It was hard to understand her motives sometimes—but Qora certainly wouldn't complain about having a girl like that on her side, or having a friend up here in the air with her.

Ninan and Kondor, riding mammoths as the herders did, headed up the group on the ground. Ninan would take his turn surveying later, but Kondor would remain on mammothback since he wasn't trained for flying.

With two pteranodons along for the journey, someone would always have to be riding them, even when they weren't performing a survey, which would sometimes require the surveyors to ride them on the ground. The pteranodons weren't quite as fast as the dinosaurs, but they were fast enough not to cause any issue. With their wings folded at the wrist joint and tucked back, their forelimbs were as good as any other quadrupedal reptile's as far as propelling themselves forward in a diagonal gait. And should they ever fall behind walking pace, it would likely be about time to survey again, and then they would outpace everyone by flight.

Qora hadn't expected Paqari to volunteer to be the first to join her in the air, but she suspected that Paqari just didn't want to be down there with the men (or didn't want to be with a particular one of them, at least), an idea with which Qora sympathized. Flying up next to Paqari, Qora let her pteranodon glide for a moment, then raised her voice. "Ready to head back?"

The princess glanced down, twisting her lips.

"He's not *that* bad, is he?" Qora nodded in Kondor's direction.

Sure, the gladewarden always gave Paqari a hard time about her pampered upbringing, but Paqari was equally antagonistic about his "backcountry" roots.

Then again, the princess might be taking it harder than she pretended to, Qora realized as she made note of what Paqari was wearing—no longer the fine clothing from Qhispina House, but a pair of fitted brown riding trousers, boots, and a hooded tunic-dress (in a drab material) whose skirt hem fell just past her hips. The only accessories she wore that might hint at her sense of fashion were a pair of dinoleather gloves and a corseted vest. She had her long, wavy hair tied back in a low tail, similar to Qora's, and no cosmetics on her face.

"No," said Paqari. "He's not *that* bad. If a mosquito buzzing in your ear isn't *that* bad. If stepping in a pile of ruck isn't *that* bad. If a spell of theropox isn't *that* bad."

"Well, say what you will, but I think it's worth mentioning that I used to 'hate' Ninan. Until I didn't." Qora kept to herself the part about how her love for Ninan hadn't entirely made things less complicated.

"That's not the same thing."

Qora shrugged. "Maybe not. But sometimes there's more to people than what they're willing to show—or, if you're like I was, more than what you're willing to see."

Paqari turned up her nose. "Good thing I'm not like you."

We forget our kind were once wild too, before we tamed
ourselves. When we go where the wild things are, we may yet
remember.

Llariku Qumir, Qolqese poet

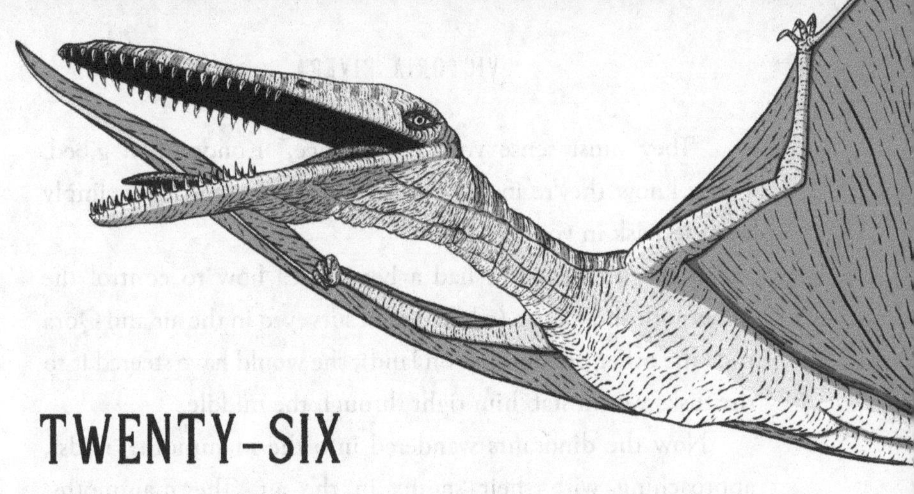

TWENTY-SIX

AT FEEDING TIME, all the herders made sure to remain safely on the sidelines as the giant dinosaurs approached the thirty mammoths left to graze before them. Paqari didn't intend to watch, but some part of her couldn't manage to look away. She slipped her hand into a small pouch on the belt around her waist, where she kept a handful of dominite crystals—just in case. The Tailfolk had no desire to use dominite on the dinosaurs, but Paqari, Ninan, and Qora had each kept a small stash hidden away among their supplies, should anything go wrong. Qora had insisted on it, and Paqari supposed she couldn't blame her after what she'd experienced during the Venture, and after having gone head to head with the giganotosaur that the Tailfolk so lovingly called "Grimjaw."

Paqari had had no inclination to protest the precaution. Lately she seemed to draw the dinosaurs like a slab of raw meat. Back in Murkroot (without dominite), little ones had clustered around her whenever she'd stood in once place for more than a minute, and the entire time she'd been traveling on the ground here with the herds, the large theropods seemed to constantly sniff in her direction—and only hers. "What do they want with me?" she'd asked Qora in a pleading wail, as though Qora would have any idea.

"They must sense your importance," Kondor had gibed. "They know they're in the presence of royalty and they simply want to bask in your splendor."

If the princess had had a better idea how to control the mammoth she was on (while Ninan surveyed in the air and Qora rode the other pteranodon on land), she would have steered it so the tusks would stab him right through the middle.

Now the dinosaurs wandered into the mammoths' midst, approaching with their snouts in the air. The mammoths, apparently used to this sort of predation, began to stir, some of them stamping their feet and trumpeting to warn the others. Soon the mammoths were scattered far and wide across the meadow, and they went quickly, Paqari noted, although their bulky figures made them seem capable only of lumbering. In comparison to the dinosaurs, however, they were similar in size and strength. It was only the position and arrangement of the dinosaurs' frames and limbs and muscles that gave them the look of something that could leap or sprint, while the poor mammoths seemed more suited to meandering along the riverside munching on grass.

Still, the dinosaurs were quick too. They cooperated with one another, with several groups working to each converge on a single mammoth, approaching from the back and sides to avoid its tusks. Then they sank their teeth into the mammoths' necks and flanks and shoulders.

The mammoths' warning trumpets then turned to trumpets of anguish as blood trickled down their dark wool. It was impressive how the tyrannosaurs, in particular, with practically no forelimbs, were so much more menacing than the hefty, quadrupedal mammoths.

Paqari cringed as the dinosaurs tore into the mammoths

and toppled them and tore into them again, ripping away the woolly hide to get to the meat underneath. She had to remind herself this was somewhat natural. While the dinosaurs didn't *usually* benefit from a banquet of mammoths specifically set out for them by humans hoping to harness their brute strength in the near future, dinosaurs did hunt mammoths in the wild. She wondered, briefly, if this was just the way of *all* things, that brutish creatures everywhere—even those like Qhapaq Apo— would always have the upper hand. With the right intelligence, perhaps, and the right coordination, it might be possible for mammoths to survive an attack like this, but as it was, they were prey. She hoped all she and her friends had done to prepare for the impending war would be enough to subvert Qhapaq Apo, and that the battlefield of slain mammoths before her wasn't a harbinger of her own future.

When no living mammoth remained but for the dino herders' mounts (kept safely ensconced under nearby tree cover although not free from the traumatic cries of their friends), the herders allowed the dinosaurs time to feast on their bounty— with the intention that the meal would induce sleep, as large meals often did for dinosaurs, and then allow everyone a respite for the night. The rest of the mammoths and their herders would remain a quarter mile up ahead and camp there, while the surveyors, dinosaurs, and dinoherders would make camp just beyond the feeding grounds, leaving the mess behind.

The mammoth bones and tusks and wool remained, and no one here would be able to utilize those parts. The princess knew it must be difficult for the Tailfolk to waste what would normally be considered valuable resources. But of course the hide would have had to be removed carefully, then scraped and tanned, a process that would take many people with proper tools working for at least a week. Several of them did remove tusks, although it was not possible to bring all of them along, considering the size and weight (as some tusks weighed as much as a grown man). Quya Urpi had promised she would try to provide a means for the Tailfolk to go back later and collect what they could, so long as the outcome of the war allowed it. Everyone seemed to understand, though, that this was how it had to be for now, a temporary sacrifice of their principles so they could get where they needed to go.

It was in the hustle and bustle of unfurling tents and withdrawing equipment that Paqari took the opportunity to sneak away, clenching her bladder muscles to stave off the feeling that she was about to burst.

She suddenly regretted waiting so long, although the idea had been to avoid relieving herself until she could take advantage of the privacy of nighttime. While it seemed that every other person involved in the migration had no qualms about urinating outdoors like animals—even Ninan, a former prince, because he'd apparently spent enough time trying to survive in the wilderness to adapt to it—she still couldn't stomach the idea. She'd avoided water for most of the day, until the heat of the afternoon sun had gotten the better of her and she'd sucked down a full waterskin. Gods, why had she been so weak? She could have sipped, at least. Just enough that her body would absorb the water into her flesh and she might perspire it away. Not that she had any wish to perspire, but baring herself in a crouch while surrounded by insects and woodland creatures did not appeal to her either.

Keeping her lantern dim so as not to attract said insects and woodland creatures, Paqari wandered into a cluster of nearby trees. She cast a glance over her shoulder, seeing that all her traveling companions were well behind her, then moved ahead with the urgency her body demanded. That urgency, however, didn't keep her from halting on the spot when a sciurumimus skittered past her feet, and again when a couple of those rounded-wing pterosaurs—what were they called? vespers?—flew between the branches beneath the canopy and their bulbous eyes bounced her lantern light back to her. Finally she found a place where several trees stood close together, as much of a barrier as she might find (from other *people*, at least) and set the lantern down so she could raise her short dress hem and unlace her trousers.

She winced as she started, not ready for what was to come, and it was then that a crunch of twigs on the ground forced her alert. Without thinking, she drew a dagger from her boot with one hand and dominite from her pouch with the other.

"Calm down, princess," came Kondor's voice from the darkness that lay beyond Paqari's lantern glow. "It's just me."

"Just *you*?" Paqari scoffed, not lowering her dagger. She had half a mind to put it to the gladewarden's throat if he came any closer. The dominite, however, she put away as vespers sensed its energy and fluttered down from the higher branches. "What are you doing out here with no light?"

"Same as you, I'm guessing. Drank a lot of water earlier. Only I didn't want to bother with a lantern. The moon's bright enough my eyes adjusted fine without it. Anyway, I was finished." He paused, then stepped into the light. "Are you … alright?"

"I will be once you leave me alone," she snapped.

"No, I mean … you genuinely look like you're in pain."

"That's because I am! I've delayed this *horrible* act for quite some time and I'm afraid it was longer than what the human body was meant to withstand. But you're making it much worse by standing there like an idiot so please … just *leave*."

He put up both hands. "Alright, alright. I'm going. But don't act like it's my fault you're in this position. You could've stopped any time along the way. There's no reason for you to wait." He paused again. "Unless …"

Paqari squeezed her thighs together and wished for death.

A smirk twisted his lips. "You've never done this before."

"What a ridiculous thing to say." Her voice grew strained and desperate. "*Everyone* has done this before."

"I mean outside. On a random patch of dirt. You've never had to …"

"Maybe I haven't."

"Wait—Didn't Qora say you flew all the way from Tisqu to the quya's castle? That's got to be, what, ten hours? You had to have done it at least once."

"No, thankfully, there were plenty of cities and towns along the way, and I was dressed casually enough to avoid attention on the rare occasion that I stopped to relieve myself in one of the less-than-ideal privies next to pubs and district buildings."

"Wow. This is …" he chuckled. "This is just … incredible. You've held it *all day*?"

"I wouldn't have to hold it anymore if you'd go!"

The light revealed the hint of a dimple on one of his cheeks—he was still smiling because of *course* he would be at a time like this—and then he said, "Do you think you can wait one more minute?"

"What?" One more *second* would be agony.

"One more minute," he repeated. "I'll be right back."

"'Right back'? Oh gods—no!" she called after him as he strode back toward the camp. "Do *not* come back!"

But he did come back, at which point the princess was

squirming on the spot, still brandishing her knife but in a much less menacing way under the circumstances.

Kondor approached with oilskin tarps tucked under his arms. He unfurled one and raised a corner to a low branch a few feet from where Paqari stood, and secured it with a metal clip. He did the same for the adjacent corner and quickly repeated this with the other tarps, sheltering the princess from the open air among the trees.

"Is this a joke?" she practically wheezed at his silhouette against the oilskin.

"No, but it will be *hysterical* if you soak your trousers despite the fact that I've set up such a nice facility for you." He poked his head inside for a moment. "Thoughts and prayers during this difficult time."

Unable to summon the energy to roll her eyes, Paqari waited until Kondor's footsteps faded in the distance before she succumbed to her own need. The trousers made the whole thing even more awkward because she certainly wasn't going to remove them completely, but also they were in the way. In any case, she figured out the logistics just in time for her body to lose all control, and the relief was, oddly, the most blissful thing she'd felt in a good long while.

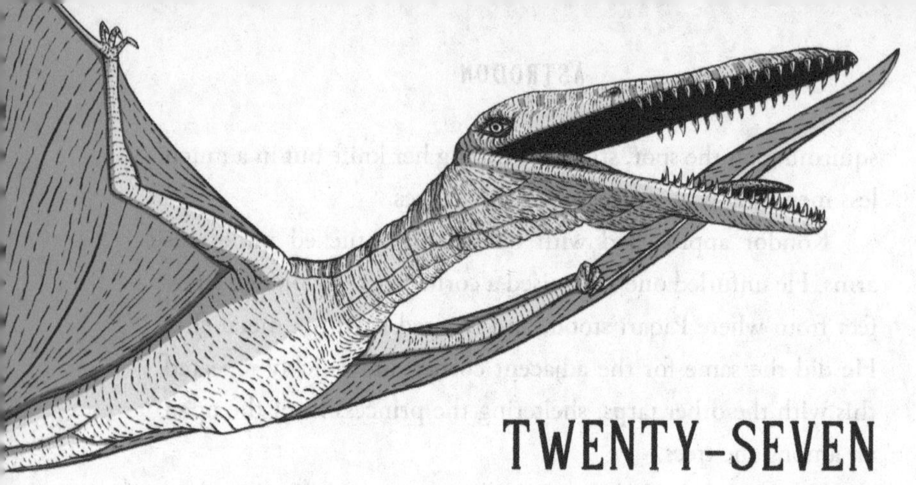

TWENTY-SEVEN

BY THE START OF THE THIRD DAY into the migration, the scenery was already blending together. It was only the sight of Mount Wiru on the horizon that gave Ninan any hope for a break in the monotony.

His legs ached from straddling the width of the mammoth saddle, and the constant rocking motion was beginning to make him queasy. He preferred the pteranodons, but had to take them in rotation with Qora and Paqari.

Even though the walking pace of the group was relatively fast, he couldn't ignore the fact that this same journey only took a few hours in the air. They hadn't even made it halfway—and that was assuming they could meet their eight-day goal.

Both herds—dinosaurs and mammoths—had slept during the nights, but with some stipulations. The mammoths had woken after just four hours of sleep, which had forced the mammoth herders to take shifts for the remaining hours to keep watch over them. Luckily the mammoths didn't tend to wander from their kind (safety in numbers) so the herders' night shifts required minimal attention. The dinosaurs, on the other hand, were naturally prone to taking naps throughout the day, which had resulted in some aggression during the first couple of afternoons when they were not yet allowed to rest. Little by little, though, the dinosaurs were beginning to adopt a sleep-wake cycle that resembled what humans would consider "normal," due to being so tired from walking all day that they couldn't help but extend their resting hours. Still, it wasn't perfect, and the dino herders had had to work around many issues.

When the dinosaurs did sleep, they took on a variety of positions. The tyrannosaurs lay on their sides with limp limbs, as though they had fallen dead. What a sight it was to find them strewn across the fields like that, like victims of some silent widespread disease. The giganotosaurs lay similarly, but tucked their limbs up against their bodies and curled their tails up to almost touch their own noses. The spinosaurs found it more comfortable to lie on their bellies, tall sails sticking straight up, limbs folded underneath, heads flat with chins to the ground. This reminded Ninan of Qoraptor—the megaraptor he and Qora had adopted during the Venture—and how she'd slept in that same sort of position.

Ninan looked to his left now, where Kondor was nodding off, slumped forward (not unlike the spinosaurs) with his head resting on the mammoth's woolly crown while the mammoth maintained a perfect gait. It had been an extra early morning wrangling dinosaurs that hadn't wanted to sleep any longer, and now the gladewarden was paying for it.

On Ninan's right, and slightly to the rear, Qora and Paqari rode the pteranodons on the ground, and spoke in low tones that Ninan could barely make out.

Qora shrugged. "I think it's nice."

"Sure, that's what he wants everyone to think," Paqari told Qora, casting a sideways glare in Kondor's direction. "But he's *mocking* me."

Ninan could only assume this had to do with Kondor's

handiwork in constructing a very small, rectangular sort of tent from oilskin tarps and wooden poles—a "privacy tent," so that the princess didn't have to relieve herself in the open woods or meadows. Apparently she'd had quite a traumatic time the first night they'd made camp.

"You assume," Qora said, "that he wants everyone else to think he's being nice even though he's actually being obnoxious, but I think it's much more likely that he wants *you* to think he's being *obnoxious* when he's actually being nice."

The princess frowned. "What?"

"Think about it. If he wanted to make fun of you, he'd just do that. He wouldn't go to all the trouble of gathering materials, measuring them, cutting them, putting together a whole portable and collapsible structure for you ... as a joke. He knows you'll assume it's sarcasm, which protects him from you realizing how he really feels."

"No." Paqari scoffed. "That's ridiculous."

"I agree. He's got to be at least four years older than you and should really act his age."

Paqari groaned at what she surely perceived to be Qora's lack of understanding over the matter.

By noon, the group reached the pass that ran along the east side of Mount Wiru, skirting the base of the hard-packed, mineral-rich peaks. All the herders gaped at the colors, some even stopping to stare, which caused the entire group to slow. It was such a problem that Ninan and Qora finally agreed on a break in hopes that permission to admire the place would get it out of everyone's systems so they could move on.

Qora didn't seem to mind the break. Ninan had to admit, at least silently to himself, that despite having seen the rainbow mountain from the air, it was another thing to stand on it.

Thinking of the legends that explained the site, however, loosened all the feelings he'd tamped down about faith. The symbol of harmony and peace that the gods had supposedly created here was all but irrelevant when trampled upon by a herd of dinosaurs on their way to battle. Especially when the colors were just different minerals. People might argue that the gods operated within the laws of science, which was a study of the natural world and its laws, which were established by the gods to begin with, but if that were the case, Ninan didn't see why anyone should ever expect miracles, which so often sought to defy such laws.

Knowing the logic behind something beautiful, on the other hand, didn't make it any less stunning. And yet, why was the human mind stunned by bands of color, or specific shapes and patterns? Why did appreciation of natural beauty feel somehow spiritual? Like when he looked at the stars. Ninan hated that he couldn't explain that. Maybe it was just the perfect combination of elements to stimulate the senses, and then people would turn into soothed and happy creatures—similar to the reptiles who responded to the sound of whistlemutes or to the vibrations of dominite crystals. Maybe it was emotional manipulation.

He looked at Qora, with strands of her hair blown loose from its tie and caressing her cheeks in the wind. To him, she was stunning. The sight of her manipulated him in ways that scared him. It didn't seem fair.

If anything, he related more to the Tailfolk's explanation for the mountain—the story of the girl Chayaynin, going on her long and arduous quest to reach the end of the rainbow, only to discover that what she was after had in fact been completely intangible. It was only after her death that the gods saw fit to grant her desires. Only when it no longer mattered. Had Ninan and Qora finally come together at a time when it would soon no longer matter? Had the miracle of their reunion occurred right before war would tear them apart by killing one or both of them? He took no comfort in the thought of an afterlife, because that simply wasn't guaranteed.

Ninan knew, though, despite his reservations, that he ought to resolve things with Qora, to set his anger aside. Not knowing how much time they had together, they should take advantage of every minute. And yet, he resented that. Like by choosing not to engage in end-of-the-world panic behavior he could somehow negate the possibility of separation and death.

When she caught him staring at her, he looked away.

The dinosaurs paused to sniff the ground, probably able to interpret the mineral content by scent alone. They moved the dust and loose gravel around with their snouts.

A few of the herders ran up one of the shorter peaks, turning all around to take in the view. Some of them knelt in prayer.

Beyond Mount Wiru, Ninan took a turn surveying from the air. This next stretch was going to be tricky.

He soared past the mammoths and out to where hordes of pilgrims came southward. Many had already stopped short of their destination, gaping at the mammoth herd that turned the landscape dark with its combined mass.

"Don't be alarmed!" Ninan called as he made his descent. Landing before them, he continued to raise his voice so that as many as possible could hear. "What you are about to see will be unusual, but I'm here to tell you that you are not in any danger!"

"What's going on?" a woman called back.

"Qhapaq Apo Kallpa of Sumaq is waging war on Runaqa," Ninan said. "Have you heard about his Sauroguard?"

The woman shook her head, but a man behind her declared,

"I have!"

Several others chimed in. The pilgrims murmured amongst themselves for a moment to determine who knew what before Ninan continued.

"A battalion of specially bred and trained dinosaurs will advance on Allpa's capital in ten days," he explained. "We come from the Tail with our own recruits, so that those not already under Qhapaq Apo's rule might have a fighting chance."

"Your own recruits?" asked a teenage boy. "You mean those mammoths?"

"No. Not mammoths," said Ninan.

A collective gasp spread throughout the horde as the first of the dinosaurs crested the hill in the distance.

Ninan spared a glance at his friends, who rode on like commanders of this strange military operation. "And that's only the beginning."

Pilgrims gathered along the sides of the procession of animals, watching in awe as several hundred mammoths—and then several hundred dinosaurs with a few mammoths sprinkled among them—marched across the landscape. Ninan didn't like having an audience for this; if some of these people had heard of the Sauroguard, then it was possible that word about the giant dinosaurs could get back to his father. Right now, this was the only potential upper hand the rebellion might have: dinosaurs that substantially outweighed the enemy's, and the element of *surprise*. He asked everyone he came across not to spread the information, warning them what it would mean if Qhapaq Apo succeeded in taking Allpa, and hoping they would take that warning seriously.

After that, the route avoided the direct trail of pilgrim traffic, to Ninan's relief.

It did not, however, avoid the gangs of wild theropods that ran rampant in the area that followed. All other creatures that the herds had encountered thus far had fled in the face of such large theropods, but here they were better matched in size.

Even tyrannosaurs two-thirds the size of what had come from the Tail did not back down so easily. Gigas here were about half the size of the herd's. No spinosaurs roamed this area— perhaps some lived closer to the shores where there was more water. But there were other large theropods like mapusaurs and tarbosaurs.

Many of them approached the herds, sniffing around the mammoths that trumpeted and reared their heads to show off their tusks in warning, or trying to challenge the giant dinosaurs. Herders had to nudge them away with spears. Ninan and Qora tried to get a sense of how many there were from the air. Qora shot a few bolts, knowing they would barely break the skin but might cause enough discomfort to deter them.

It was difficult to keep the herds in formation, especially when a few dinosaurs broke loose to fight their aggressors, which ended in a small bloody battle and uproar among both herds.

Most of the wild dinosaurs scattered during and after that interaction. The sounds of anguish would surely warn others nearby not to try their luck.

Beyond this zone, wild dinosaurs were less abundant, and also smaller. Ninan hoped the rest of the journey would be less eventful.

☽☽☽

The days were warm and the nights were chilly. Ninan shared a tent with Kondor while Qora often stayed up late talking to

Paqari in another shared tent. It had been important to take as little equipment as possible, which meant two or sometimes three people would have to share certain items.

The added time apart seemed to increase the rift between Ninan and Qora, but he still didn't know how to navigate any conversation they might have to repair it. He took comfort in the fact that Qora and Paqari had become such good friends—his ex-fiancee and the love of his life, of all people—especially after all the events that had occurred aboard the *Velosaura* and on the islands the ship had toured.

For most of the morning on the fourth day, the herds were lucky enough to encounter no major trouble. With the skies mostly clear later on, though, a man flying on pteranodonback against the direction of the herd caught Ninan's eye instantaneously. He flinched at first, ready to draw a weapon until he recognized the Qhispina House uniform, then relaxed his shoulders. Quya Urpi probably just wanted an update, since all four surveyors had yet to utilize the messenger flyers provided for this exact purpose.

Qora and Paqari were riding the pteranodons on the ground and had fallen back a bit.

The messenger flew past Ninan and Kondor, then circled back to position himself for landing. Ninan directed the herders to create a wide berth for the new pteranodon, which soon descended. It landed smoothly within the allotted space and quickly fell into step with Ninan's mammoth.

"Your Highness," said the messenger, pushing up his riding goggles. "I have news."

"I imagined you would," Ninan told him.

"It's Izhi."

Ninan furrowed his brow, remembering the last time he'd seen the Unuvian Qhapaq. It had been just after the arrival of the Sauroguard pteranodons, as they'd spewed acid on Izhi's guards. The qhapaq had beckoned Ninan to follow him, to use the citadel's tunnel system to escape, but Ninan hadn't listened; he'd been caught up in the battle, and then Izhi had grown impatient and left him there. As far as Ninan had been aware, his father still hadn't managed to capture Izhi, but there'd been no telling where Izhi had gone or whether he'd still been alive.

"He's resurfaced," the messenger went on. "In Allpa."

It was hard for Ninan to resist the urge to slow his mammoth so that he could focus on processing that information. "Allpa," he repeated. "So … he's with Quya Urpi?"

The messenger nodded. "They're combining resources, although the qhapaq of course now has limited access to most of what he once had."

"Well, I guess anything he can do would be useful. He'll know about weapons stores, maybe secret military reserves. With his knowledge he'd probably be able to infiltrate his old reserves discreetly, with the quya's help."

"Yes, yes, but that's not why I'm here. While it pleases me to ease your mind by informing you of another ally, I've also been instructed to summon you back."

"Summon me back? Why?"

"You and the Raptoriva both."

"Izhi wants to speak with us," Ninan concluded. What terrible timing. There was nothing Ninan and Qora could tell the qhapaq that he wouldn't have already heard from Quya Urpi, and he didn't imagine there was anything the qhapaq could say that would necessitate pulling them away from the migration.

"No," the messenger replied. "He has another mission for you. And he expects to brief you on it—immediately."

Subjects do not simply perceive it; they reorient themselves, compelled by something beyond conscious understanding. It is not unlike a call—specific and irresistible to those tuned to hear it.

"Preliminary Observations on Dominite Response"
The Sumaqi Elemental Institute

TWENTY-EIGHT

QORA AND NINAN LANDED IN ALLPA just before nightfall, following the quya's messenger. They had only taken one pteranodon and left the other for Paqari so that she could continue surveying in their absence, which meant that Qora had been subject to riding directly behind Ninan for nearly two hours. She rode behind because two riders was a lot for a pteranodon, but the lighter person at the rear was better for its spine. Thankfully the migration had progressed them northward far enough that the ride back was shorter than it would have been from Murkroot, but that didn't make the forced proximity any better.

They found Izhi in the grand salon, where he stood stroking the head of one of the indoor smilodons while he admired a kantuta-flower tapestry on the wall.

He turned slowly at their approach. "Your Highnesses."

"Your Majesty," Ninan said tightly.

Qora dipped her head for an instant. "We weren't sure you were still alive."

"Alive" seemed relative in this moment, however. The man was noticeably thinner than he'd been the last time Qora had seen him. His red-rimmed eyes and sallow skin told of a difficult few weeks.

"I have multiple havens," he explained, "although several of them were discovered and destroyed by my fearsome rival. I had to resort to the most secluded of them all, which, unfortunately, is little better than my citadel's underkeep. But I was able to communicate with a few of my spies and, upon learning some crucial information relating to one of my previous investigations, I departed—at great personal risk—for Allpa in hopes that I might recruit the two of you to help me."

"How did you even know we'd been here?" Qora asked.

"I may not be as powerful as Qhapaq Apo," Izhi said, "but I do have a strong network of those who are loyal to me."

Ninan shook his head. "If you expect either of us to go back to Sumaq, to feign loyalty to my father or try to glean intelligence from—"

"Oh it's nothing like that," Izhi told him, taking a seat on one of the lush, red-velvet arm chairs that adorned the room.

The smilodon meandered over to Qora now and nudged her dangling hand with its nose. She scratched under its chin, careful to avoid the saberteeth that protruded downward from its mouth. "It must be nice to have others do your bidding all the time. Which fire do you want us to dash into next?"

"A volcano," Izhi said.

Qora jerked her gaze up at him. She hadn't meant *actual* fire—but apparently Izhi had. Memories of the rift at Kañay flooded her mind so forcefully she could practically feel the lava's heat. The skin of her forearm had remained raised and pigmented even so many months after her fight with Ruyan.

"Why?" Ninan clenched his jaw.

"I've been looking for the source," Izhi told him, "of your father's ability to cause such ungodly mutations in the creatures he now employs. It has become clear that whatever methods he's used to breed them are … unconventional."

"To say the least," said Ninan.

"And you've …" Qora swallowed. "You've *discovered* that source? At a volcano?"

"A small, overgrown, inactive volcano along the border between Sumaq and Unu, to be precise. Its name is known only to remote villagers who fear it for its monsters. It's called Pakasqa."

"Monsters …" Qora repeated.

Izhi nodded. "A team of my spies tracked Sumaqi pterobeast movement to the area. The Sumaqis appeared to be retrieving eggs."

"So it's another breeding ground," Ninan concluded. "Like the Aquchay base." He scoffed. "We can't do anything about that. You know what happened last time—and surely the quya has told you that any aggression from our end will cause my father to deploy the Sauroguard on Allpa, effective immediately."

"It's not just a breeding ground. It's *the* breeding ground. Don't you understand?" Izhi stood. "The base in the Aquchay was just a place to perpetuate the species Apo had already created. Pakasqa is where he developed them at the start. It's the source of the wickedness that makes them all possible—the fire breathers and the acid spitters and the poison-claws and the little demons that can scale military-grade walls."

Qora raised a brow. "How do you know?"

"When my people investigated the flanks of that volcano, they discovered horrors unlike anything anyone has ever seen," the qhapaq said. "Mutant dinosaurs running wild—but not just any mutant dinosaurs. Not species that simply look like those we know that merely carry some enhancement by design, but *true* mutants." Izhi began to gesture wildly. "Dinosaurs with bulging growths, with extra limbs, with missing eyes! The backplates of a stegosaur jutting from the belly of a protoceratops, and patches of velociraptor scales on the wings of a rhamphorhynchus, and double-headed troodons, and atrociraptors with three rows of teeth! Horrors from folklore that no sane person would ever believe were real."

Now Qora took a seat because she couldn't quite find the strength to stand anymore, but leaned forward in Izhi's direction as she tried to better understand. "So you're saying that Qhapaq Apo found this place, where he saw these mutant dinosaurs in the wild, and then he somehow figured out how to exploit whatever has been causing them to change?"

Izhi sat back down. "Exactly."

Still standing, and with his arms folded, Ninan said, "How does it work, then? What exactly is it that he's exploited?"

"Pakasqa has a special sort of … microclimate," Izhi replied. "It's hard to explain, but basically the environment covers one side of the dormant volcano for approximately ten square miles—four miles or so up the volcano's slope and a little more than two and a half miles laterally. Some combination of the sulfur vents on that side, a bubble of humidity due to geothermal heat that traps the mists, and the soil content from past eruptions, has allowed for a number of unique plants to thrive there, a few of which in turn produce some very important organic compounds."

Volatile organic compounds. Qora remembered from Paqari's explanation of the role certain plants could play in alerting animals to the seasons and thus promoting hyperphagia to prepare for winter.

"These compounds," Izhi continued, "have allowed for the evolution of a species of mosquito whose bite can transmit bits of one living creature to another."

Finally Ninan sat down too, paling. His throat bobbed. He looked at Qora, as though he wanted to see that she'd heard the same unbelievable thing.

Qora's pulse thrummed. Some people of intelligence described the concept of a "blood cipher," saying that all living things carried a unique cipher not only in their blood but perhaps in every fiber of their being. They believed that selective breeding allowed a breeder to focus on certain figures in this "cipher" and emphasize or de-emphasize them as desired.

It was all guesswork, of course, as it was impossible to see whatever figures said ciphers might contain, let alone try to make sense of them. But if that were true, then the blood ingested by a parasite like the one Izhi described could infect anything else it stung, potentially altering its victims' physical appearance.

Ninan would know the theories, probably better than Qora did, with all the scholarly tutors he must have had. Paqari could probably explain it in thorough detail, if she were with them.

"But why does my father need to breed new reptiles there? Why not capture the mosquitoes—even breed more of *those* at sites closer to him?"

"It seems the mosquitoes don't survive beyond the boundaries of Pakasqa," said the qhapaq. "My own people tried it. The mosquitoes fell dead in their containers within an hour of separation from their environment. They thrive on those compounds—from flora that won't grow in any other climate or soil—and the specific gases in the air, and the exact heat and humidity that that side of the volcano provides."

Qora wasn't sure whether to be fascinated or horrified that something like that could exist. It was the perfect setup for evil to breed, which made her suddenly feel that Ninan's arguments against the gods rang more true. Except, for all the horrors of nature that had allowed such a thing to occur, it also came with a limitation. Was it better to be angry that this place came to be, or grateful that it was somewhat contained? Was there room for both emotions to exist?

Izhi took a deep breath. "Apo could recreate the environment, if given enough time. He would have to put the greatest minds to the task, to measure every detail of the soil and air and plant growth and mosquito breeding patterns. Currently he's more focused on churning out his special reptiles in droves, but there is no doubt in my mind he will soon seek a way to more efficiently harness this power away from its origins. With that in mind, we have limited time to destroy Pakasqa."

"You expect us to destroy the whole area?" Qora asked. "You just told us it was ten square miles. How could we possibly—"

But it only took her a few seconds to realize exactly how.

Which fire do you want us to dash into next?

She fixed her gaze on him, narrowing her eyes.

Izhi smiled. "There's really only one way, isn't there? One surefire method for permanent destruction of everything that keeps that power alive, and it's *right there* beside it ..."

Qora swallowed, not wanting to say it out loud. How many near-impossible tasks would she be expected to perform in her lifetime?

Extract a gilded tooth from a living spinosaur. Find a hidden military base on a chain of islands from a ship on which she was never supposed to be a passenger. Migrate several hundred giant theropods that didn't naturally engage in migration behaviors. And now ... "You want us to trigger an eruption."

She and Ninan exchanged a weary glance.

"It's like one of those old scriptures the Kastillans loved to recite," said Izhi. "'Only in the fire can we be truly cleansed.'"

TWENTY-NINE

AN HOUR BEFORE DAWN, Ollan rode bareback on a gray and white "spitter" pteranodon, hurrying it along on its all-fours on the ground through a stretch of trees. He wore seven dominite crystals around his neck—plenty to lure away a beast this size and keep it calm. How he wished he could have flown it from the encampment rather than taken it out at this pace, but at least he wouldn't have to try to get a net around it and attach it to another flyer. As soon as they reached the rendezvous point, he'd be able to take the pteranodon up and fly the rest of the way back to Allpa.

Extracting the smaller Sauroguard dinosaurs hadn't been so bad, but now all that were left were the bigger ones. Getting one of those camouflaging megaraptors had damn near gotten him and the extraction team caught. One of the guards on night patrol had heard them rustling around in the bushes and had come out to have a look.

Thankfully, Ollan had remembered the command to encourage the megaraptor to shift its skin pattern to match the leaves; he and the team had huddled behind the megaraptor then, and even with a lantern the guard hadn't spotted them.

Needless to say, the trek back to where the rest of the team was waiting to net the megaraptor and harness it to a pterobeast (because a pteranodon wouldn't have been able to lift anything that large) had been a stressful one.

Keeping his lantern dim, Ollan soon reached an open field where Kuy and the bandits met him on their own pteranodons. From there, they would fly in darkness and arrive in Allpa after daybreak.

"Excellent." Kuy rubbed his hands together when he saw the pteranodon. "No problems, then?"

"No problems," Ollan confirmed. This encampment hadn't even bothered with palisades, considering the pteranodons could move vertically as well as they could horizontally. The team had seen this from their scouting missions and, despite the fact that this was one of the more menacing of the Sauroguard reptile breeds, they'd been very optimistic about their ability to get it.

Ollan dismounted for a moment and picked up his waterskin. He drank eagerly.

"We're getting close," said Kuy. "We've almost captured all of them now."

"All except the last one." Ollan thought about the bestiary with its final page torn out. While other pages detailed the size and features of each reptile, the missing page left the resistance without a single clue. That last reptile could be a flyer, or it could be a ground-ridden biped; it could be tiny and vicious or enormous and destructive; it could have indestructible scales or venomous teeth. And not knowing was the worst part. How could they prepare for it?

"Well, let's just focus on what we can do." Kuy clapped Ollan on the back.

"Wayra will at least be pleased, I think," Ollan said before taking another swig. "She's especially good with flyers. Although I don't love the idea of her trying to reason with one that spews acid from its throat."

Kuy folded his arms. "Yeah, I'll bet you don't."

Ollan narrowed his eyes. "What's that supposed to mean?"

"I think you know."

"I definitely do not." In all the back and forth, Ollan had barely had a combined thirty minutes with Wayra over the past week. Between travel time, following leads to find new encampments, scouting those encampments, and moving reptiles around, it was a wonder he was even functioning right now. Of course it probably didn't help that he sometimes avoided Wayra on purpose, too.

"If you like her, you should tell her," said Kuy.

"*If*," Ollan emphasized, but without additional comment on the possibility. "Anyway … To what end? We're never in the same place for long, and when we are, there's so much to do. Everyone has to be where they're needed most right now, and unfortunately she and I possess very different skill sets. Besides, I doubt she looks at me in any special sort of way."

"That's a lot of reasoning for a hypothetical."

Ollan shot his companion a stony glare. "Come on, you know how she is. She's so sweet with everyone; it's impossible to know who's a friend and who's … more. Meanwhile, I'm still trying to figure out where I fit into my own life. I've been 'gone' for four years, and the second I resurfaced, it's been nothing but chaos. How am I supposed to even *think* about anything else, let alone talk about it?"

"I've known Wayra for a long time," Kuy told him as he picked up a new saddle and hefted it over the pteranodon's upper back, "and, although I can't speak for her, I do think there's a chance she would respond … positively … if you were to broach the subject." When Ollan huffed, Kuy added, "We could die *tomorrow*, Kanchaya."

"Another great point! No sense spilling my guts when the very next day I might end up going off to … well, to spill my guts." Ollan had to will away the bloody visuals that came to mind. Arrows sticking out of his abdomen with blood soaking his clothes, or dinosaurs feeding on his corpse.

"Okay, but would you rather die not having said anything? Or die knowing she's thinking of you?"

"Die not having said anything."

Kuy shook his head. "You're an idiot."

With a sigh, Ollan replied, "I know."

〉〉〉

They flew into Amachakuna a couple of hours later and, after a brief check-in at the pteriary while Ollan gazed out toward the paddocks thinking about what Kuy had said in the clearing, Kuy asked, "I don't suppose you want to do the honors?" He patted the Sauroguard pteranodon's beak meaningfully.

Wayra was always out on the paddock early and would surely be there now.

But what could Ollan possibly say? "I've admired you since I met you, and although we don't know each other well, I'd like you to know that I see you as …"

Ugh. Anything he could come up with just sounded pathetic.

He imagined himself gutted in an entirely different way—not by arrows or sharp teeth—as he tried to explain the jumble of thoughts in his head.

But Kuy was right: Tomorrow wasn't promised. And while on one hand that made Ollan not want to bother, it also triggered a deep sense of desperation, especially when he considered how meaningless the last few years of his life had been. Just as he'd told Wayra, he'd spent most of his days working in the mines, rarely socialized, and his few brief romantic attachments had come and gone without emotion. He couldn't remember the first time he'd actually *felt* something the way he did around Wayra—and it certainly must be something because otherwise it wouldn't keep niggling at the back of his mind, would it?

Suddenly the thought of losing his life exactly as it was in this moment seemed so much more pathetic than whatever he might say to embarrass himself.

With one last grimace at Kuy, he climbed back onto the pteranodon and headed down to the paddock.

Kuy grinned and waved him off.

Ollan landed somewhat gracelessly among the other handlers and dismounted in a similar manner. Panting, and feeling like his heart might beat right out of his chest, he asked, "Is Wayra around?"

One handler approached and began to unfasten the pteranodon's saddle buckles. "Afraid not."

"Oh. Is … she alright?"

"As far as I know," said the handler. "But she left first thing this morning."

Ollan's shoulders sank. "Where to?"

"That's right, I guess you wouldn't have heard. Qhapaq Izhi came out of hiding. He managed to get here to Allpa to join his remaining forces with the quya, but he also brought news of a place where mutant dinosaurs have been found in nature—something Qhapaq Apo was able to exploit to create the Sauroguard—and he pulled Prince Apo-Kimsa and the Raptoriva off the migration mission to go help destroy the whole place. When Wayra heard about it, she asked to go with them. Your friend Req went too."

"Wait—what?"

Qora wasn't helping with the migration anymore? And Izhi had somehow dragged both girls, along with Req and Ninan into … probably some kind of suicide mission?

Ruck.

"I'm sorry," said the handler. "I don't know when they'll be back. I only know as many details as I do because everyone's talking about it. The Unuvian qhapaq is still at Qhispina House, though. Maybe he can give you more information."

Ollan clenched his fists. "He better."

"Why do we so admire the sun and the moon? Because they always rise again, without exception."

Shaman Sisa Achirana

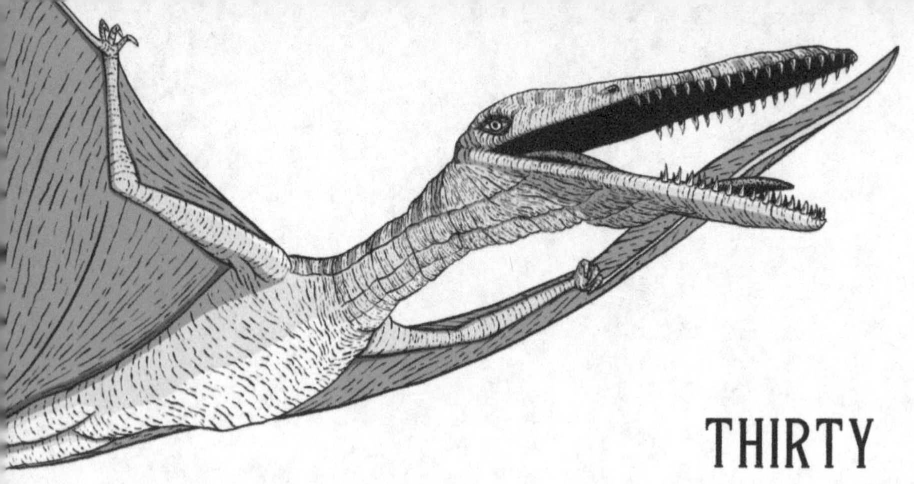

THIRTY

PAQARI GROANED from the back of her walking pteranodon. How she longed to fly the remaining distance to Amachakuna, rather than trudge along at this pace. Even surveying didn't help, because she always had to circle back and land again, which made the brief sensation of speed nothing more than indulging in a fantasy.

Thanks to delays at Mount Wiru and encountering all those pilgrims, and then all that trouble with the wild dinosaurs, the group had fallen behind substantially. By now, the group should have migrated past the Pirqas, and instead they were barely approaching them. The mountains stood boldly some half-dozen miles ahead.

A full week in and they weren't even three-quarters of the way through the trip. *Ten days my hindquarters*, Paqari thought.

Kondor had insisted they would pick up speed and make up for lost time, but the princess had her doubts. At least there was still time to make it before the cession deadline. Paqari didn't imagine it would take the eight remaining days to arrive, although the march across the extensive valley made it feel that way sometimes.

She couldn't believe Qora and Ninan had left her like this. Sure, she had her own tent now, but the past few days had only grown more strenuous physically, not to mention there was no one to talk to but Kondor and a group of equally backwoodsian herders.

She'd tried to be friendly to some of the female herders—even cracked a smile to prove she wasn't as scaly as they probably thought she was—but they seemed to find her disingenuous (she couldn't imagine why).

It wasn't that she refused to associate with foreigners; she could be open minded, even if they did live in trees and worship dinosaurs and consider coarse mammoth wool to be a good material for clothing; it was that she simply didn't belong among them. Although, to be more realistic, she didn't belong anywhere at the moment.

Qhispina House was a lovely place, and the best of accommodations she could hope for outside the place she'd been raised, but it wasn't home. And while her intelligence made her useful at times on missions such as these, she constantly found herself falling behind in terms of survival skills. She would never admit it out loud, but she feared she was too soft in too many ways. Too soft for this sort of life, and too bold for the life she once led as Tisquvian royalty.

Every hour or so, she wondered again what she was doing here. Was she any help at all? All her former strength and power had come from her position within the Huapaya household, in the authority she commanded and in her connections to be able to get what she wanted or needed (mostly). Now she was no one.

As far as she'd heard from Quya Urpi's information sources before the migration, however, Paqari's father had given no indication to the public that she was missing. He didn't seem to have told anyone that she'd run away, hadn't denounced her as a traitor or disinherited her like she deserved. While

Ninan's father had elaborated on the lie of the prince's death, Qhapaq Achik had apparently explained Paqari's lack of public appearances by telling everyone that she was mourning the loss of her "beloved Apo-Kimsa Kallpa." Anything to save himself the embarrassment of the truth. That was, after all, why he'd pawned her off on Ninan, to staunch the rumors of her disgrace with her former watchman, because few other "worthy" men would take such a wife; she and Ninan had both been damaged goods in their own ways, and therefore had made a perfect pairing.

Joke's on them, she thought in relation to both qhapaqs and their conspiratorial arrangement. *Look at us now.*

She didn't bother to try and keep up with Kondor. Instead, she rode somewhere in the midst of the dinosaurs who, as they had since Murkroot, continued to creep close to her. At one point, she caught the one called Grimjaw trying to nuzzle her shoulder.

"*Excuse* me," she said, as though he could be reasoned with.

"Don't be rude," Kondor called back at her. "He likes you. Go on … give him a pat on the snout."

Looking up at the looming dinosaur, with its green-striped scales and enormous head, Paqari reached out with a grimace. To her surprise, Grimjaw bent forward and met her fingertips. She flinched at first, processing the rough texture, then slowly moved her hand along the scales between his nostrils and his eyes. He blinked as a low vibration sounded in his throat.

Then a spinosaur crept forward, a female called Terrora, and snorted a gust of air at Paqari's neck. Paqari reached back to swat at her, and she nipped at Paqari's hand although never actually tried to bite into it. Almost as though she were … playing?

Paqari's pteranodon squawked at its reptilian cousins and

sped up to get out of range, but the theropods caught up with no effort as though this were a game.

"You foul beasts …" the princess muttered.

Kondor watched her and laughed.

Eventually they settled back into a rhythm, and then it was time for the day's first water break. Each time they did this, the herders and surveyors went first to fill their waterskins, then urged the dinosaurs toward the creek. The dinosaurs would spread all along the banks—some would cross the creek itself (in just a few strides) to utilize the space on the opposite side—and dip their snouts in, lapping the water with their enormous tongues. Despite going up and down the creek's length, however, there was always another row of dinosaurs waiting their turn behind the others, due to the sheer number of them.

As Paqari drank from her own waterskin, Kondor said, "Careful not to drink too much, princess. You know what happens when—"

She spat water at him but he jumped back in time to miss the brunt of it.

He grinned. "I guess that's one way to keep it out of your system."

After a few minutes, some of the dinosaurs began to growl and nudge one another. They crowded the banks and swung their tails and reared their heads. One of them opened its mouth wide and roared. Then others did the same. This continued in a chain reaction spreading down the herd.

Paqari and Kondor exchanged a glance, then hurried to the creek bank.

When they arrived, the creek was teeming with dinosaurs—not just along the banks but throughout the bed. Except, at their feet, there were only rocks and mud.

"Limbs above," said one of the herders who had followed to investigate the commotion. "Where's all the water?"

It had only been a few minutes. Maybe ten. The water had been flowing in what had appeared to be abundance when they'd first stopped. And yet …

"In their bellies." Paqari nodded at a tyrannosaur who let out a wail as it dug into the mud with its toe-claws. She squinted at the blazing sun above, a solitary object in the wide blue sky. Today was hotter than any they'd seen since leaving Murkroot, now that she paid attention. The increase in temperature had been gradual, but it was most certainly getting worse.

"How could they have drunk the whole of it?" said the herder.

"The heat's made them need more," Paqari told him. "But something else I hadn't considered before is that we're much closer to the headwaters now. Ninan said that back in Murkroot if I recall correctly; this creek begins in the Pirqas."

"What does that matter?" Kondor asked.

"Headwaters are more shallow and narrow. They start with mountain springs, melted snow, and rainfall that adds to and enhances the flow. But they don't become full rushing creeks and rivers until further down the line, when other water sources contribute to them. So while the creek might have initially been delivering several thousands of gallons of water per second, here we might be looking at only a few hundred. And with the magnitude of these beasts drinking it all at once …"

"They've drained it faster than it can refill," Kondor concluded.

The princess nodded.

Between the dinosaurs and the mammoths, this creek hadn't stood a chance.

Water came trickling through, but only enough to keep the creek bed a wet, rocky mess. All the animals lapped at what little they could get until Kondor instructed the herders to get them back into formation so they could figure out what to do about this.

As Paqari and Kondor discussed their options—stay here and wait until the creek refilled itself, keep moving while the creek refilled (making the animals thirstier in the meantime), fly out and look for alternate water sources even if it took them off the route—one of the herders came up to them in a huff.

"Princess," he said, "I'm sorry to bother you, but we're having some trouble over there trying to keep the dinosaurs together. A few of them keep wandering off and they're ignoring the whistlemutes."

Paqari sighed. She supposed it made sense. The whistles might have made the dinosaurs want to cooperate when they were well rested, well fed, and well hydrated, but conditions were not ideal right now. They were much less likely to want to follow each other around.

"While I understand that I'm apparently the authority on this"—Paqari brushed a few strands of hair off her forehead—"I'm not sure what you expect me to do about it. You all are the ones who have studied their communication and developed the whistles."

"Yes, but—"

"Should I go among them and have a little chat? Maybe give them a good reprimand?"

"Actually," said the herder, "that *is* what we were thinking."

The princess cocked a brow. "I beg your pardon?"

"They do like you," Kondor reminded her. "Perhaps with a strong argument, you can make them see reason."

She pursed her lips at his sarcasm.

"It's mainly Grimjaw." The herder nodded toward five dinosaurs that had broken from the group—Grimjaw, Terrora, and three others, whose names Paqari was annoyed she'd memorized by now. A tyrannosaur called Rumble, and two more gigas, Spike and Echo.

Grimjaw had progressed partway up a slope with his snout to the ground, pushing little rocks around and snorting his frustration at the lack of water. Terrora, Rumble, Spike, and Echo trailed him doing the same. Some of the other dinosaurs at the edge of the group were watching them and starting to break off too.

"Good gods," Paqari muttered as she went off to have a better look.

When she approached, Grimjaw looked up for a second, sniffed in her direction, then returned to his task.

Kondor came right behind and observed with his hands in his pockets.

"Alright you heathens." Paqari clapped twice. "Come now. Let's get back into formation. I don't know what we'll do about water just yet, but we won't accomplish anything with our noses in the dirt now, will we?"

Terrora groaned, then clawed at the ground.

"Maybe if you say it with a little more authority," Kondor suggested. He grunted when the toe of Paqari's riding boots came up against his shin.

"I didn't ask to be the leader of this little ... expedition." Paqari gestured at the wandering dinosaurs. "Alright? I would have much preferred to remain in Amachakuna. Now without Qora and Ninan here, I have to try and round up these beasts like they have any good sense at all? I mean, just look at them."

All five were snorting at the sparse grass, and blowing up little puffs of dust with their breath. They'd done it at Mount Wiru too, Paqari recalled, enticed by the mineral stripes.

The ground between the brownish blades of grass was pale here, with a thin dust layer on top of hard-packed and cracking dirt. The princess crouched and put her fingers to it, feeling the crusty texture that was somewhat cooler than the surrounding air. She brought her fingers an inch from her nose and inhaled carefully, but caught no scent.

Grimjaw nudged her ear with his snout.

"Yes, yes." She gave him a gentle push away from her. "I'm trying to understand. But there doesn't seem to be anything here. Just solid ground." In demonstration, she pounded a fist on the dirt, causing little cracks to form from the point of impact, which loosened the surface into several distinct pieces. She picked one up—a thin, flat, jagged, whitish piece of earth. Like a layer of rock flaking off. It crumbled when she closed her fist around it.

"Does that … mean something?" Kondor asked.

Standing abruptly, Paqari stomped her heel against the ground. It gave a sort of brittle noise, cracking again in new places. She pushed the pieces around but only uncovered a new crusty layer beneath. She stomped again, and made more cracks, then knelt again to observe.

Kondor crouched beside her and pulled the flakes away.

It seemed to be layered like this repeatedly. And as each underlayer was revealed, it was more and more cool to the touch.

As Grimjaw and the other dinosaurs continued to explore, Paqari watched the ground under their feet, which she hadn't noticed before—or thought to consider—and spotted the cracks that formed in response to the weight of them against it.

"I think there's water here," she told Kondor.

He frowned. "How?"

"Groundwater can be trapped under a crust of built-up minerals. You can see how the ground here isn't just soil. This is pale, and it's in layers like sedimentary rock. And the temperature …"

"Groundwater," he repeated. "Like what can be reached with a well."

"I think it's closer than that. The dinosaurs wouldn't be able to sense it if it was too deep."

"Okay," said Kondor, "but at any depth, unless it's just a few inches, we don't have tools to get to it."

"No, we don't. But it's cracking under pressure. So maybe all we need is more pressure."

They both gazed up at the dinosaurs, who seemed to be watching them with great intent.

The gladewarden gave Paqari a crooked smile. "Well, *that* we do have."

⫸⫷

Paqari hardly had a second to catch her breath before Kondor commanded a team of herders to move the main group of animals out of the way, creating an open space as he organized a double-file line of ten dinosaurs and drew them into a circular path. He raised his hands above his head and clapped out a hard, steady beat to which a smaller team of herders blew their whistles.

The dinosaurs tromped in time, cracking the surface of the ground as they went, then turned into a curve that led them back over the same area again. With each round, the cracks deepened,

290

new layers came loose, and the material crumbled.

The princess stood at the center of the circle, fists tight and gaze fixed on the scene.

Soon, a damp scent wafted out.

On the fifteenth round, a dark hue emerged over one spot and began to spread. Paqari gasped and covered her mouth.

Kondor shot her a wide-eyed look. He grinned as he kept the beat, leading the dinosaurs like the drum major of a band of military musicians on parade. His own feet passed over the same cracks and the trickle that emerged, and he kicked up his pace so that the dinosaurs did too.

The gladewarden could certainly rally a troop; Paqari had to give him that, even if his sense of humor was insufferable. It would have been much more difficult to do this without him.

Come on, Paqari thought, willing the ground to fully break.

The spreading water was a beacon of hope, sure, but there was no telling how much—or how little—water was trapped below. It could be next to nothing, and then this whole thing would have been an unnecessary expenditure of energy.

But they were standing on a transitional landscape, on wide open terrain approaching the mountain range. The mountain runoff would have mainly gone to the creek, but surely some of it had infiltrated the ground through loose soil or porous rocks. It would have been blocked from going deeper by impermeable rock layers underneath, allowing it to accumulate. Paqari remembered some of these details from books she'd read on waterways—she'd gone through a phase in which she'd wanted to understand how the rivers met the sea, how currents formed, how tides went high and low—and although it had been a few years now, some of it came back to her.

A more audible crack set her at attention again, and even

forced Kondor to pause for a moment. He stopped the beat and the herders took their lips off their whistles. Water spurted a few inches into the air from within the crack, muddy and full of debris.

Everyone waited.

Paqari held her breath.

Slowly, the water cleared, riffling out with white edges.

It spilled onto the trampled ground, soaking back into the broken mineral crust.

Limestone, Paqari thought.

And as the water only continued to squirt in a steady but very thin stream, her heart sank.

It had been too good to be true. Even the dinosaurs, with all their baser instincts, hadn't been able to sniff out a significant water source. They'd caught the scent of what little lay beneath, and nothing more.

The princess moved numbly toward the water until she was only a yard or so from where Grimjaw stood beside it. Kondor came up next to her and stared at their failure with a dumbfounded look on his face.

Apparently as distraught as the humans were, Grimjaw threw his head back and roared over the tiny spring. He flailed his tail, to the chagrin of his dinosaur companions, then stomped on the spring like he wanted to force its disgraceful trickle back to where it had come from. He stomped and roared and cracked the ground again, and then—

The crack split wide and spewed water several feet high in a violent gush.

Paqari only felt the first spray before something blocked her from the force. Brown wool came up against her cheek. Strong arms came around her shoulders. Kondor's chin, rough and unshaven after a week in the wild, came up against her forehead. In her surprise, she didn't fight him. Instead, she wrapped her arms around his waist and sank into his hold. Despite his attempt to shield her, the water soaked them both within seconds, and she caught herself beaming up at him.

He squinted at the water raining over them, but smiled.

All around them the dinosaurs roared out their gratitude, snapping their jaws at the water. But soon the slope of the ground carried the water down to the creek bed, where it flowed downstream and joined the slow-forming pools that the mountain water had not yet fully replaced.

Mammoths and dinosaurs alike followed the water down and began to drink. The herders, for now, abandoned the usual watering routine and accepted the chaos, too tired to try and enforce a sense of order. At least the creek was filling fast.

It was only after what must have been a full minute of standing together, soaking wet, chests colliding with exhilaration, that Paqari realized she ought to let go of Kondor. They were too close. And she probably looked like a drowned rat. This was horrific …

Eventually the force of the water died down, no longer a geyser shooting up.

Paqari stepped back and wiped her face, although her hands weren't particularly dry either. "Thank you."

Kondor scoffed. "For what?"

"For being a leader. For helping to make this happen." She glanced at the creek, scanning the variety of dinosaurs that drank among the mammoths.

He narrowed his eyes, then wiggled his finger in his ear canal like he was trying to dislodge trapped water. "Wait—did I hear that right? Did the princess just *thank* me?"

"She did." Paqari pursed her lips again, daring him to get cocky about it.

"Well," Kondor said, rubbing the back of his head, "I guess I can't take all the credit. The herders helped too. Dinosaurs did all the hard work. And you ..." He paused, looking at her like he was searching her face for something.

When he trailed for an absurdly long amount of time, she said, "I ... what?"

Kondor panned his gaze to the cracked earth, to the flowing water—which a couple of the herders were now trying to divert more directly by digging a shallow trench using camping tools—then to the dinosaurs, then back to Paqari. "You ... are something else."

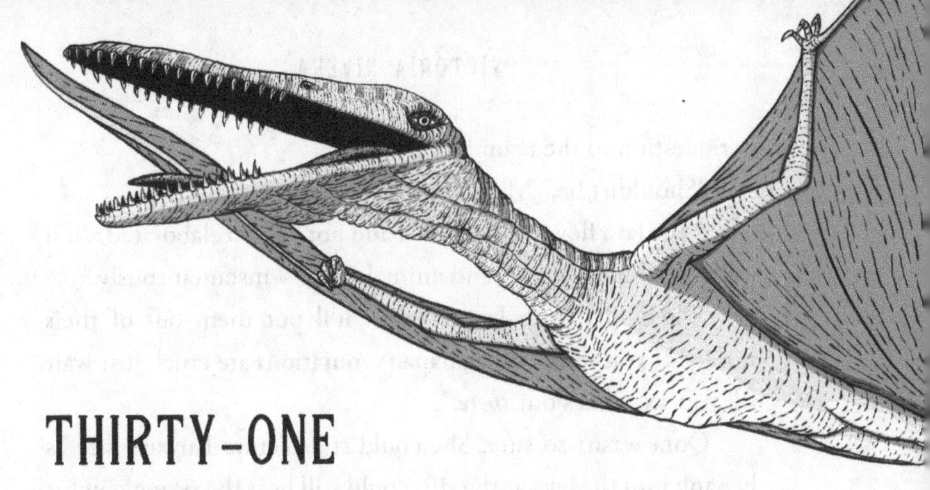

THIRTY-ONE

NO SOONER HAD QORA TOLD WAYRA about the mission than Wayra had insisted she was going too. While her work with the handlers had been fascinating, Wayra wanted to see these natural mutants and help ensure that no more could be made.

Req felt he had done all he could with the elementalists, who were now making dominite easily and didn't really need more help, so he'd decided to tag along.

Now, Qora and her friends were nearing Pakasqa. Qhapaq Izhi had sent them first to a hidden fort where a small unit of his operatives watched the volcano from a distance. There, Qora and her friends met Miyil, who would lead the destruction effort, and Ruka, a "volcanist" who had studied the domes in the volcanic region for years. Miyil was a military man with a shaved head, dressed in gray fatigues. Ruka was a tall woman with her hair pulled back into a tight knot at the nape of her neck, and she wore a sleeveless shirt and loose-fitting trousers.

The ethical hunter in Qora made her clench her fingers around the rim of the pterobeast gondola as she thought about where she was headed. She imagined thousands of wild, mutated dinosaurs crying out in anguish as fiery lava swept them down the volcano and broiled their flesh.

"Will it be cruel?" Wayra echoed Qora's thought, directing

her question to the team leader.

"Shouldn't be," Miyil replied.

"The lava flow will be so fast and hot," Ruka elaborated, "it'll kill everything—plants and animals alike—instantaneously."

"Plus," the team leader said, "it'll put them out of their misery. If you think your qhapaq's mutations are cruel, just wait till you see what's out *there*."

Qora wasn't so sure. She could still picture Ruyan's face as he sank into the lava at the rift, could still hear the strangle in his cry. But of course the lava bubbling in the rift had been exposed to the open air longer, and might have been substantially cooler (by comparison) than lava fresh from the chamber would be.

A bright, citrusy smell on her clothing brought her back to the present. When she and her friends had gathered at the fort, Miyil had doused them all in something called kukuella—pumped out of what looked similar to a perfume bottle, with a squeeze bulb attached to a tiny hose attached to a glass container—that would repel the mosquitoes in Pakasqa. It hadn't even occurred to her that those mosquitoes might sting a human. But why wouldn't they? Blood was blood, and they would feed on anything that had it. And all it would take was a single, infinitesimal transfusion and she could easily find herself developing a row of scales on the back of her hand, or scutes on her cheek.

Ninan had asked how the mosquitoes were able to break through the dinosaurs' thick skin, and Miyil had replied, "The bulkiest of beasts still have their soft spots—around the eyes, along the underbelly. That's where you'll see most of the mutations. But a lot of times the mosquitoes will sting juveniles or hatchlings whose scales and scutes are still thickening up. That's most likely how your father made his works of art, exploiting the sting while they were young. Then, once a new feature develops, the victim passes it on to their offspring."

It seemed the cruelty was never ending. Where nature went awry, humankind had the ability to set it right, and yet, so often they did not. Izhi was right; a cleansing was in order.

Now the gondola came within a mile of the volcano, although for all Qora could see, it was a small overgrown mountain with a subtly flattened top. Izhi had said the volcano's full surface area was roughly thirty-five square miles. Its foliage was thick like a jungle, but with different kinds of trees, particularly to one side where everything took on a different hue from the rest—on that ten or so square miles where the environment fostered the monstrosities.

"That must be the place," Req remarked. "Spirits, those boundaries are stark."

"A stark signal to alert my father to its wonders," Ninan said bitterly.

"Well it explains how he discovered it," said Wayra. "After that, I'm sure it was a quick jump to how useful it might be."

They all looked at the view in pensive silence as the gondola dipped down and flew low on the approach—as always, to avoid being spotted by any of Qhapaq Apo's personnel. There had to be a team of elementalists there, Qora thought, and maybe some handlers too, probably a small military unit with beastlords in case any of the reptiles got violent, but they probably also had plenty of dominite.

Nearing the fields that extended from the base of the volcano, Qora peered over the rim at several long, snaking trails that marred the landscape, some of them overlapping, some more prominent and others more faint, although none seemed to lead anywhere in particular.

Ninan tensed visibly. "Please tell me those aren't what I think they are."

Miyil glanced down. "Not much else they could be."

Qora thought about what could make shapes like that. Certainly not the wind. Likely not a shifting water source that had dried up, since that would have left sediment and rocks behind. It had to be a creature, but … there was only one type of creature that moved that way—and made tracks that large.

"Serpentosaurid," Qora whispered in a strained voice.

Yet another horrific memory was summoned to the forefront of her mind. Forty-five feet of muscle wrapped around an undulating spine, shimmering scales that rubbed together to produce a rasping noise that still haunted Qora to this day. It had been bad enough to witness it in person, but to *feel* those muscles clenching around her shoulders, to be woken from sleep by their death grip …

"Qhapaq Izhi told me they don't typically move west of the volcanic region," said Ninan.

They'd never discussed it, but Qora suspected that someone— maybe even Izhi—had made certain that a serpentosaurid was slithering through the jungle that night during the Venture. Izhi's apparent knowledge of serpentosaurid behavior didn't make Qora any less doubtful of his involvement. It made her wonder what she and Ninan had been thinking, agreeing to this. They'd done too much to help Izhi as it was, given his sometimes-questionable methods. But of course this wasn't for *him*; as always, it was for the "greater good." The qhapaq seemed to have a way of convincing them both that that's what most of his missions were, pandering to Qora's and Ninan's desire to protect the land and the people they loved. Now he pandered to their desire for vengeance, too; the thought of obliterating all of

Qhapaq Apo's resources in one shot was irresistible.

"Well," said Miyil, "this is a hot-spot volcano. Even in a dormant state, it still gives off heat, affects the environment to some extent. But there's no need to be alarmed; serpentosaurids steer clear of the volcano's flanks because they don't like the sulfuric gases. Those creatures are very scent-motivated and scent-repelled. They'll be all over anything with dryosaurid musk, but get them near too much sulfur and they run like mad."

"That must be why they don't invade Amachakuna," said Wayra. "I'm told there's a collection of them about six miles out, but the hot springs keep them contained over there."

"There are serpentosaurids in Allpa?" Qora asked.

Wayra nodded. "Huge ones. I think it's only one species, though. Megaboa. Probably displaced thousands of years ago and adapted to the climate. One of the quya's handlers was telling me about them. It's a small population because local hunters keep it down. That skin goes for a rexload."

Qora shuddered. She would have slept much less soundly at Qhispina House had she known there were serpentosaurids only six miles from the capital.

"Although, interestingly enough," Wayra added, "it's the megaboas' favorite prey that really dominates the Allpan markets. Dryosaurid glandular oils make a strong salve that's very popular—even though it apparently stinks as badly as the musk."

"They'll be all over anything with dryosaurid musk."

"Remind me never to use that salve," said Qora.

The gondola maxed out with seven people: Qora, Ninan, Req, Wayra, the volcanist, the team leader, and a pilot from the fort who would leave after dropping them off. The team would disembark at the dropoff point, and Miyil, who knew his way around, would guide them on a trek to another hideout—a bunker—where they would meet with a retired bioelementalist who had once worked for Qhapaq Apo. The bioelementalist apparently had much to explain before helping them prepare to trigger the volcano.

Even before descending below the canopy, the air grew noticeably warmer. It was as though the mountain was releasing a constant, slow exhale, with the same sickly heat that a dinosaur's breath always seemed to carry. It reminded Qora of the jungle, only somehow more wild, making her jacket feel thick on her arms. But like the jungle, it most definitely carried things that Qora did not want on her bare skin.

The kukuella, whose scent was lost among everything attacking her senses here, didn't comfort her as much as she wished it did. The tang of sulfur with traces of mineral-rich soil and damp stone filtered into her nose. Insects chirped and small flyers trilled and a distant gurgle of water came at her ears. She jerked her head at a sudden hissing sound, but Miyil told her, "It's just a steam vent. Pressure builds, and then it releases at certain intervals."

"Those are the kinds of things we'll want to keep in mind," said Ruka. "Trapped heat, building pressure, methods of release." Using a stick of charcoal, she jotted a few things onto a page in a book of bound papyr. She had made it clear before leaving Allpa that this was terribly unsafe, that tampering with volcanic forces was incredibly stupid, and that they were probably all going to die, but Qhapaq Izhi had paid her a lot of money to help give them their best chance at success.

Apparently, Izhi's operatives had also given Ruka some samples of the volcano's rocks, whose composition and porosity revealed that past eruptions had been explosive (rather than calm and oozing), so in that regard at least, she was optimistic.

A few seconds later, the gondola touched down. Everyone gathered their gear—knives and machetes, dominite, extra kukuella for when they would inevitably sweat off the first application, dried foods, fire starters, and thick canvas packs to hold everything that could fit inside.

Qora had left her crossbow back at the castle and instead brought her new wristbow, which she fixed to her forearm with trembling fingers. She'd opted to carry it loaded, despite the risk of shooting the bolt unintentionally; she'd practiced with Kondor for an hour each night at camp during her time on the migration and felt confident enough now in her ability to control her wrist, but she also felt that a rogue bolt to the ground was trivial when compared to the risk of not being able to load in time to defend herself against a threat.

As she fumbled with the buckles, Ninan stepped forward and held the bracer firm for her, not meeting her eyes. Thanks to his help, she secured all the pieces and murmured her gratitude as he slipped his own fingers through the rings of the strikefangs he'd received from Quya Urpi. When he clenched his fists, he looked as menacing as a therizinosaur.

"Alright, gang," said Miyil. "Brace yourselves. We're about to walk into a nightmare."

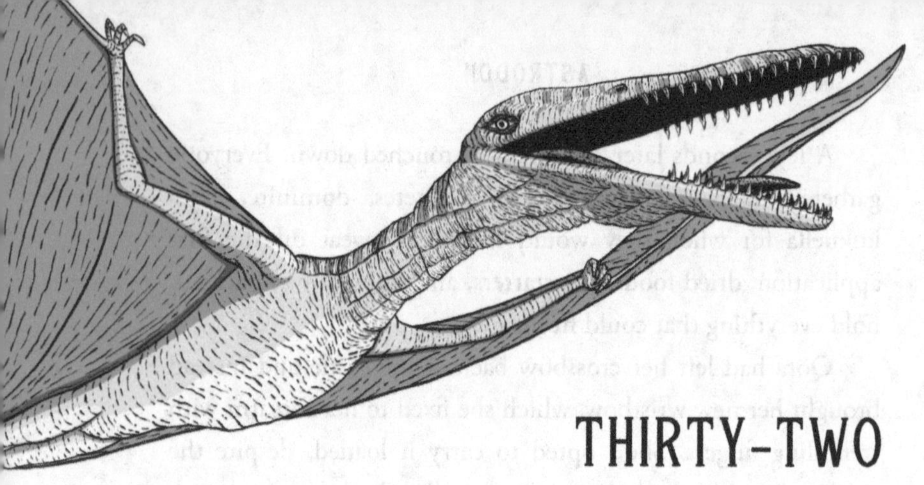

THIRTY-TWO

STEPPING INTO PAKASQA was like stepping into another world. Whatever eerie scents and sounds had emanated from the perimeter were barely a whisper of what lay within.

The trees seemed to block out the sun, leaves dark and branches twisted and contorted like fingers of giant demons reaching up from the Grave World. And yet, it wasn't too dark to see the way ahead—only too dark to make full sense of the scene right away.

A mist hovered at Ninan's ankles, swirling slowly. Small creatures flitted and scurried and snapped twigs under their feet, but they were so fast that Ninan couldn't make out anything specific. The team moved as if in slow motion, with even the team leader afraid to take too sudden a step.

It wasn't until a few minutes later that Ninan's eyes began to adjust. As they did, new figures took shape.

The bark on most of the trees grew in overlapping layers like scales—a species of lepidodendron, maybe—except for that of a few sporadic, grayish trees whose trunks were plated with scute-like bumps. But as Ninan glanced up the length of one of those trees, he found that it sprouted no branches, and instead tapered off just below the canopy.

"Those aren't trees," Miyil said, probably in response to what was sure to have been a strange look on Ninan's face. "They're mushrooms."

"Mushrooms?" Wayra grimaced.

A far cry from the little glowing fungus Qora had brought to the Venture, Ninan thought.

The actual trees each had multiple holes with globules of amber sap forming within them. Ninan recalled some of Paqari's ramblings from their time together at the Tail on the way to find Qora—the princess had been fascinated by the grafted orchards and the syrup production—something about trees oozing sap in response to what she'd said was a "freeze-thaw" cycle, where the contrast of cold nights and warmer days affected the pressure on the trees' internal fluids. However, Ninan could not imagine cold nights here, and determined that this sap must be a different sort of thing. Many of the globules had trapped flies or mosquitoes, and one even encased a rather large beetle.

The team leader nodded at Wayra's question. "Just ... try not to touch anything. Try not to *step* on anything. And don't look too closely at anything, because, trust me, you probably don't want to know." He went on to explain that Izhi's operatives had cleared a narrow trail, although it was subtle; it couldn't be anything too obvious since Apo occasionally had his own operatives coming and going from the volcano, even if it was far on the other side of the flank. Activity had slowed now that Apo already had plenty of new breeds to focus on, but that didn't mean he didn't still have "boots on the ground" for future projects. It would ruin the whole mission if he discovered enemies sniffing around the area. "I should also add, for your own safety, that half these plants are raptorial."

Raptorial. Ninan knew that word. Where had he heard it before?

In a rush, entire phrases came to mind.

These plants have evolved to extract nutrients from unlikely sources.

They rely on digestive enzymes to break down their prey.

Although typically evolving as a result of nutrient-poor soil, carnivorous flora may thrive under changing conditions.

"You mean they're carnivorous," Ninan clarified.

"But," said Wayra, "by that you mean they might consume *insects*, right?"

The volcanist looked up from her notes. "Or, at worst, very small animals …"

When Miyil didn't respond, the hairs on the back of Ninan's arms prickled.

Qora panned her gaze across the forest, then raised her weaponed arm slightly.

As Ninan made his own observations, what he'd initially taken for a cluster of ferns now glimmered in the low light, revealing its curled "fronds" to be lined with fibers that each held a clear bead of liquid as big as an eyeball. He recognized those details from that book Paqari had brought on the way to the Tail. It was a type of sundew plant. Except that the sundews described in *Raptorial Green* were said to have leaves no longer than a few inches—these were several *feet* in length—and liquid excretions the size of dew drops (hence "sundew").

What had appeared to be a patch of large flowers, he now realized as he tracked their shapes downward, were all part of the same base plant, and the mauve spathes—yes, he knew the word "spathe" now from that blasted book—were in fact the tips of funnels into longer, tubular structures that, if *Raptorial Green* had anything to say about it, were probably full of fluid meant to drown and digest anything that fell into them. The way the color faded to green gave the illusion, from a distance, of a stem separate from the blossom.

And then, he focused on a couple of plants with large, semicircular fronds only to see, upon more keen inspection, that they were not fronds at all, but the lobes of a sort of snap trap, and that the palmate tips were actually cilia—fibrous teeth that could interlock to form a tight seal as the pair of lobes came together in a snaring motion.

"I'm not saying they'll eat you," said the team leader. "But I'm told the curly ones can trap a velociraptor."

Mentally, Ninan conjured the approximate size of a velociraptor: two feet tall, three feet long (not including the tail), thirty to forty pounds. He imagined green plant tentacles curling around the head and spine and hindlimbs, secreting viscous juices that would slowly dissolve the scales. Not so different from the Sauroguard pteranodons' acids that could corrode solid tile. Depending on the strength of the secretions, it wasn't farfetched to think a grown man might at least suffer damage to an arm or a leg that way, provided he wasn't able to free himself in time.

The team leader motioned for everyone to follow. "Let's not dwell on the horrors. We have somewhere to be, and the sooner we get going, the sooner we can get to safety."

Ninan stepped ahead of Qora and Wayra, preferring to remain up front with Miyil, should anything jump out unexpectedly. Req and the volcanist kept up the rear. For the most part, all remained in single file, machetes or other weapons at the ready.

The trail was long and winding, taking them up an incline that was just subtle enough to escape attention, but steep enough to make them winded—although the air seemed to be somehow both thinner and thicker at the same time. Thick with moisture, perhaps, but stripped of essential gases to healthfully sustain life. Would they suffocate here before anything even had a chance to attack them?

Moving deeper into the woods, Ninan spotted a few compsognathus—one with two tails, another with a spare limb growing out of its back, another with a patch of feathers along half of its chest although its companions had bare scales all over. A sciurumimus leapt between tree branches across the group's path, its left eye pinched off in the folds of an abnormal facial growth.

Wayra whimpered and covered her mouth.

A dozen protoceratops startled as the team came through the place where they had been feeding on moss, staghorn ferns, and even the "trunks" of the tree-like mushrooms that stood among the actual trees. The protoceratops had fled too quickly to reveal the extent of their mutations, but one had had distinct sections of discoloration along its ribcage and another had had at least five nostrils. Ninan was sure he'd also seen one with fur growing on part of its frill.

When the air and the incline finally necessitated a break, the group stopped to sip from their waterskins and loosened their formation as Wayra stepped off the trail to approach a rhamphorhynchus nest and Req pushed ahead of the team leader to peer into a pitcher plant that seemed to be in the process of chemically digesting a compy. Then the volcanist said she'd be right back; she wanted to have a look at the soil because it would be indicative of the extent of this volcano's potential lava flow. The team leader said he had to "take a piss." Which left Qora and Ninan to themselves, with the silence between them as thick and suffocating as the air here.

"How are you holding up?" he asked in a tone that didn't

quite convey his actual concern for her. He knew everything they'd seen since the gondola's descent must have been a shock.

She took another swig of water and wiped her mouth with the back of her hand. "I'm as fine as I can be, under the circumstances." Her tone was bland—neutral. "You?"

"Still trying to process all this." He swept his gaze across the twisting undergrowth and the sickly light that filtered in through the tight canopy. "I don't think I would believe any of it was possible, were I not seeing it with my own eyes."

"Yes. I guess it *is* hard to believe what you can't see ..."

His brows pulled together. The words settled between them like an accusation. Was she implying what he thought she was? After some ten days now since she'd walked out of the verdanza, and all the quiet tension between them, was she finally going to bring it up?

The visible tightness of her lips told him she already had.

He laughed bitterly. "If I were meant to believe what I can't see—or what I can't hear or touch—then the *gods* shouldn't have given me senses."

Qora glared at him. "Your senses can't always help you determine what's real and what's not."

"They haven't failed me yet."

"Haven't they, though? You've never 'seen' dark figures in the shadows of a swaying pine, or mistaken the cry of one reptile for another's? You've never woken from a nightmare with your heart racing like the threat was still in the room with you?" She shook her head. "My eyes reading that quipu in the jungle told me you'd left me behind ... but then you came riding up on that megaraptor and snatched me from those pterodactyls and swore to me it had all been lies and that you would never leave."

"That's different."

"And the way I perceived you when we first met was nothing like the way you are. Relying on my senses kept me from really *seeing you* for a long time."

"And that's supposed to convince me to get down on my knees and beg invisible forces to make *this*"—he gestured at their surroundings—"better?"

"I'm not trying to convince you of anything. I don't care what you believe or don't believe. I just want you to stop pretending like you're better or smarter than those of us who still have hope."

"You don't think I *want* to have hope? You don't think I would love for magic to rain from the sky and fix all our problems? But instead of magic we get meteorites whose elements can rearrange to control reptilian monsters, and we get pteranodon-spewed acid that corrodes anything it touches."

"But here on the ground," Qora argued, "we have resources to help us. We have friends and allies. We have the giant theropods on our side, and great minds that have replicated the dominite. *Under* the ground, we have the fire from the center of the earth that we can harness to destroy this place and put things right. That's magic in itself—gifts we can't take for granted."

"Gifts." He scoffed.

"You don't think it's a gift that you and I met? That in all this bitterness, all the violence of the Venture, all the dangers on the *Velosaura*, we've at least had each other?"

"Everything good in this life only becomes another weakness. Something to lose. Leverage for villains. Maybe with that in mind, you can understand why I find it difficult to give thanks. 'Blessings' shouldn't cut both ways."

"Well, then," Qora said, clenching her waterskin with

unnecessary force, "I'm sorry to be another ... *weakness* ... for you."

She turned back onto the path and strode a ways onward without looking back. Ninan opened his mouth to call after her but he couldn't seem to summon his own voice. She needed a bit of space, that was all, he told himself, and she wouldn't wander far. There was no use going after her, or asking her to return to this spot just for them to continue arguing.

As she stepped past a vine that had spread across the ground, the underbrush twitched. Qora leapt away from the sound, raising her wristbow.

Ninan rushed over to her as her shoulder grazed a tall, narrow plant with a bulbous top that curled over itself like a cobra's head, sprouting a split red leaf that hung down like a tongue.

Cobra lilies, a type of pitcher plant, are composed of tubular leaves that lure prey into the "mouth" (an opening at the head) with an enticing scent. A host of bacteria within its leaves allow it to break down anything that enters the trap.

Again, what Ninan was looking at was significantly larger than what he'd read about. What should have been a two- or three-foot-high plant stood taller than he did, with a stalk at least four inches thick. But this didn't seem to be the source of the movement.

Qora turned to see the cobra lily and gasped. She unintentionally bent her wrist at the perfect angle to launch her loaded bolt at the ground.

The bolt pierced the thick vine at her feet.

The vine hissed, whipping out its thick tendrils and wrapping them around Qora's ankle. In one swift motion, it wrenched her down.

"Qora!" Ninan cried.

Flat on her back, Qora screamed and tried to turn so she could grab hold of nearby ferns, but her fingers slipped as the vine dragged her away.

Everyone that had been off exploring their own interests now converged on the vine with Ninan, drawing blades.

"What in the Grave World's pits is that?" Req asked.

They hacked at foliage and chased Qora, no longer hesitant over what they might encounter off the beaten path.

Clawing and thrashing, Qora did all she could while the vine drew her forcefully toward its base.

Ninan used his strikefangs to slice plants out of his way.

Gods, this is all my fault, he thought. *If I hadn't been so harsh with her, she wouldn't have gone off like that ...*

Miyil pushed ahead of Ninan and swung his machete at the vine; once again the vine hissed as though it were sentient, but the blade only dented its sinewy shoots. "What the—" He paused to stare at his ineffective blade.

By the time the team got through the trees and plants that separated them from Qora, they found her with her whole body tangled up.

Suddenly Ninan couldn't breathe.

Qora bit into a tendril that had begun to curl around her chin, and wriggled against others that kept her arms pressed to her sides.

Req hacked at the thick of the vine with another machete, with the same lack of success as the team leader had had. Wayra plunged a dagger into the lateral shoots over and over, managing to get through with this puncture technique where the broad strokes of a large blade had failed, but only served to anger the vine into wrapping her wrists.

"Ruck," said Miyil as Wayra went down too.

The volcanist and the team leader both struggled against tendrils that snatched at their arms and legs, while Req proceeded with his machete even if only to spite the monstrous plant.

Ninan leapt onto a sprawl of shoots and punched them with the saberteeth barred to his knuckles. He stabbed and he sliced, spilling a viscous purple juice that kept the plant supple. He worked his way closer to Qora and stabbed again to weaken the tendrils that wrapped her. The hissing grew louder and soon turned to a squeal, but Ninan didn't stop until he'd decimated the majority of the vine so much that the even undamaged tendrils relaxed and came loose.

The other team members wriggled out of the vine's hold.

With Ninan's help, Qora pushed the tendrils off and broke free too, and he caught her in his arms, panting. He felt like he must be holding her tighter than the vine had been, but he didn't care. He swore he'd never let anyone or anything touch her ever again.

"Oh my gods," he muttered into her hair. "I'm sorry. I'm so sorry."

Tears streaked her dirty cheeks. She pressed her cheek against his shoulder and her breath hitched as she observed the botanical wreckage at their feet.

Suddenly she tore herself from his grasp and drew a bolt from her jacket pocket, which she loaded into her weapon with two clicks, then raised her wrist and fired.

Ninan spun to see a tendril behind him—pinned to the nearest tree by Qora's bolt. Another tendril hovered like a snake ready to strike, but before Ninan could react, Qora had already loaded and fired again. She didn't miss.

He swallowed.

She looked up at him with glossy, red-rimmed eyes. "I'm starting to think you're right. Nothing's watching over us. We're on our own out here."

Although the kantuta may look vulnerable, its high-altitude habitat produces thin air, cold winds, heavy sunlight, and low-nutrient soil, which the flower must withstand consistently. Its stems and leaves are sturdy but flexible, with a waxy coating that reduces water loss; its intense pigment protects against the harsh rays of the sun; its roots grow deep and spread wide like an anchor on the mountainside. The kantuta flower is hardy, as a matter of survival.

Field Guide to the Floral Wonders of Sumaq

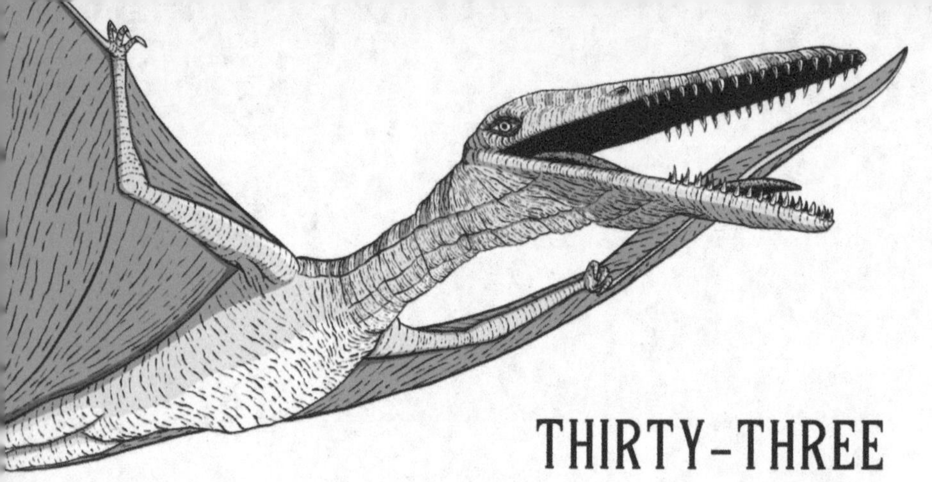

THIRTY-THREE

QORA FOUGHT THE URGE to curl her fists. With the wristbow's trigger bar across her palm, she had to remind herself not to move without purpose—although she certainly wasn't going to keep her weapon loaded anymore—but after what had happened with the raptorial vine, her muscles didn't seem to know how to relax.

Every twitch in the woods had her reaching for another bolt, and she hardly took a step without scanning a five-foot radius first. It had been bad enough during the Venture when she'd had to fear human enemies *and* wild reptiles; now she had to worry about plants too?

She nearly jumped out of her skin when a female dromaeosaur—with a patch of teal scales along her otherwise purple flank, and a brood of seven trailing behind her with a similar mutation—crossed the group's path.

Ninan stuck annoyingly close to her, such that if she were to stop suddenly, he'd probably trample her. She gritted her teeth at the thought, knowing he only did it out of paranoia. Because of his *weakness* for her.

Was he her weakness too? Surely. A threat to him was a threat to the part of her he had become. His sorrow was her sorrow. His pain was her pain. But did she wish it weren't?

Never. She would choose him every time, no matter what gaps he made in her armor.

It hadn't been fair of her to make the comment that had set that whole argument in motion; she knew that. It had been a spiteful thing to say, and something she'd only said in frustration after days of him barely speaking to her. If it hadn't been for that, she might not have gone off and encountered the wrath of that vine, and the rest of this trek might be that much less tense.

Now Ninan apparently felt the need to remain on high alert, for her sake, and she wondered how much he resented her for it.

A buzz at her ear drew her attention to the dusky sky. It had already been so dim in the forest, she'd practically forgotten about daylight, but over the last half hour or so she'd begun to squint, and the sweat under her arms inside her jacket had cooled. Instinctively, she swatted at the mosquito, and although she missed, it flew wide and displayed its large wings and prominent antennae. She swallowed a lump in her throat.

"Spirits," muttered Wayra as it hovered her way. Her shoulders came up against her neck. "That thing's *huge* ..."

Like everything else here, it was a monstrosity of nature—with a two-inch wingspan.

A few other mosquitoes came near, but none made the attempt to land on any member of the group. The kukuella seemed to confuse them, mingling repellent odor with the scent of blood that otherwise enticed them.

Even with this invisible shield, Qora couldn't help but flinch. There was something unsettling about the fact that the shield against these things was invisible, and very thin, and that any breach could result in some gross reptilian growth on her body.

Thankfully before the darkness blinded the group completely (since lighting a lantern would only draw more insects), they pushed through the last section of the trail and stepped into the small clearing they'd been seeking.

The citrusy scent of kukuella overwhelmed them. Dozens of mosquitoes whined in swarms around the clearing's edge as though they'd come up against an invisible wall.

A man came forward, tall and bespectacled, wearing a worn and dirty tunic with the top buttons open to his chest. A large patch of reddish scales covered his collarbone and half of his neck.

Qora couldn't help but stare.

"I am Uturunku Waman," he told them. "Yes, I know my appearance can be quite jarring. Perhaps it provides some insight into my lack of loyalty to Qhapaq Apo."

The strange fusion of skin and scales made Qora want to *bathe* in kukuella. She was sure the bioelementalist was one of the lucky ones; he must have had colleagues with even more severe conditions, to which the qhapaq would not have been sympathetic.

"Uturunku has seen the inner workings of Qhapaq Apo's laboratorium," Miyil said. "He'll brief us on all the details about this place, the mutants, and so forth."

Uturunku shook each of his guests' hands in turn until he reached Ninan, then stopped to bow instead. "Your Highness. It's an honor."

"Thank you," Ninan said tightly, "but there's no need. I'm sure my father no longer considers me a prince. He's stripped that title from me before, for much less than the crimes I've committed in the past few weeks."

"Then the honor is only more fitting," Uturunku replied.

For a moment, Ninan looked like he might smile at that, but seemed too emotionally exhausted to even blink.

"Please," said Uturunku, gesturing to a rimmed hole in the

ground, through which the top of a ladder protruded, "join me below."

The ladder led the team members into a surprisingly large, open space that was damp but cool. Qora fastened the toggles on her jacket, although she couldn't decide whether it was in response to the drop in temperature or if she somehow felt safer that way. Whatever she was about to learn would only make things worse.

Cinder bricks sealed off the underground space, and shelves took up most of one wall. The shelves were lined with survival gear and glass jars of food. Lanterns flickered in each corner and on a long table at the center.

The bioelementalist invited everyone to take a seat at the table and provided them all with a jar of beans and an eating utensil.

Qora was hungry enough that the bland beans brought her an odd sense of comfort. None of the others seemed to mind either, silently devouring the food straight from the jar without complaint. While she and her companions ate, Uturunku sat at the table's head and cleared his throat.

"You're probably wondering why I'm here," he began. "After years of working for Qhapaq Apo, it must seem strange that I would betray him … that I would be willing to make a deal with his greatest rival, and agree to meet with a team of rebels to destroy the very place that has been my livelihood for so long. Well …" The bioelementalist took a deep breath. "Let's just say that I, like so many others, was coerced into a situation from which I could not flee." He glanced pointedly at Ninan, and Qora thought perhaps Izhi had mentioned the Venture, or the arranged marriage, to explain why the son of the qhapaq would dare to be a part of a mission against his own father. "I was forced to use my intellect to manipulate nature, to help create things that should not ever exist. Now, I must atone for what I've done."

"How did you manage to get away from my father?" Ninan asked.

"He has already killed everyone I care about," Uturunku said. "And also … he believes I am dead."

Morbidly, Qora thought that the bioelementalist should have *led* with that information, because vengeance seemed a much stronger motivation for betrayal than guilt, but she digressed in silence.

As she watched Ninan tense in his chair, suddenly repulsed by his food, it occurred to her what he might be thinking: caring was weakness. *Leverage for villains.* Who was it that had kept Uturunku from walking away from the qhapaq sooner? A parent? A lover? His children? Her nausea came on more forcefully.

"I'm sorry," Ninan said with a terse sense of finality.

"Don't be," Uturunku told him. "I intend to make him pay. I'm grateful that you're here to help with that."

Ruka set down her utensil and straightened up. "First, though, I think we would all like to know a little more about Pakasqa—about the mutants, and what exactly makes them, uh … possible."

"Yes," Wayra agreed. "I've been working with reptiles for a long time, and I understand plenty about how to breed them to get a new kind of offspring, but what we've seen today, and also among the Sauroguard dinosaurs, is …" Her expression pinched.

"Unreal?" said the bioelementalist.

Wayra nodded.

"There is still much to understand," Uturunku told the team, "but I'll begin by discussing the factors that are passed from one generation to another in any living thing. We know there are factors that each species shares—fibers of being, if you will, that make up the threads of the living fabric; tiny particles, imperceptible to the human eye, over which we typically have little control.

"We encourage mating and we select the individuals that participate, which can help produce new breeds that are more robust or have tougher scales or exhibit a bolder color or a better temperament. Changes to the individual *after birth*, however, were unheard of—until Qhapaq Apo discovered that the mosquitoes at Pakasqa had developed the ability to not only extract the 'fibers' of a living thing but also to transplant them onto another, in a morphogenic way. This affects the flesh of the host organism for a small radius around the bite, usually up to a few inches across and up to a few inches in depth, although it varies depending on the amount of blood extracted by the mosquito as well as the saliva left behind."

"You mean if the mosquito has more time to feed," Qora said, "the reaction will be more intense."

"Correct," said Uturunku.

"I understand how the transfer works randomly," said Ninan, "but I don't understand how it's possible to target it. My father hasn't made an army of reptiles with *random* features. He's given them entirely new glands, special skin, enhanced vocal folds ..."

Pressing his hands to the table, Uturunku said, "All he had to do was find those features elsewhere in nature. Surely you can think of several sources."

Ninan pursed his lips. His jaw flexed.

Qora knew he must be thinking of the reptiles he'd seen in Unu. The climbing velociraptors came to mind first.

"Frogs," she said quietly. "They can grip with their feet.

Also, velosaurs can alter the color and texture of their skin to match their surroundings. And lots of animals spray foul odors as a defense."

"Plenty have venom glands," Wayra added. "Spiders produce adhesive silk."

"So then," Uturunku told them, "all that is necessary is to force a mosquito to extract from the desired source, then deposit where it will be most useful."

"How does the mosquito deposit 'fibers' from only one source at a time?" asked Req. "Wouldn't it have collected from several? And wouldn't it gather new material from its current host *as* it deposits?"

"All very good questions. The mosquito extracts source material from the blood, but deposits through saliva. Typically, it seems that the material of one host only remains inside the mosquito for a single feeding cycle. We believe it moves from blood to saliva during digestion, and is then released on the *next* host and thereby leaves the mosquito's body once and for all—just as a new, separate cycle begins. Occasionally there is some overlap if feedings occur too closely together, but in a controlled laboratorium environment, it's quite predictable. And the mosquitoes are easy to manipulate; they're drawn to certain scents, colors, and temperatures. It's only a matter of marking what we want them to bite."

"You're saying whatever these mosquitoes transmit," said the volcanist, "sort of … unravels and reweaves an individual's tapestry? At least for the 'threads' it touches?"

"Essentially. The qhapaq has utilized a variety of methods to get the results he wants. Selective breeding, of course, with some chemical growth modifiers, and then methodical application of this 'reweaving' technique. So not all Sauroguard reptiles have been subject to the mosquitoes, although most have. Those that have, well, they've undergone many experiments, plenty of which have caused horrific defects and conditions."

Wayra clenched her jaw. "I'm guessing the qhapaq just … disposes of them?"

"More than you could imagine," said Uturunku. "Although those that still function may be let loose into the forests of Pakasqa. It takes many trials and many failures. Thankfully once a modified species is finished, the laboratorium has a clear and repeatable production plan to produce mates, who will then pass the new traits to their offspring without further human intervention. I say 'thankfully' in that the trials on those species can then end, although I acknowledge that producing mutants so quickly through reproduction—as opposed to the months or years it initially takes to develop them with the mosquitoes— will devastate our world."

He let the information sink in for a moment. Members of the group exchanged looks of hopelessness, concern, and disgust.

Eventually, Req said, "So if we cover this mountain in lava … we destroy the sources of the gas or compounds or whatever it is that lets the mosquitoes thrive, effectively making them extinct?"

"Yes," said Uturunku.

"Along with the laboratorium and breeding grounds," said Ninan, "leaving behind no evidence of this phenomenon so that no one in future generations can ever get the idea to breed animals like this again."

"More importantly," said Miyil, "destruction by lava leaves no ties to the resistance, no ties to Allpa, no ties to this team. It'll look like a natural disaster."

"Except first we have to figure out how to trigger a volcano that hasn't erupted for more than a hundred years," Qora reminded them.

The volcanist nodded along. "That's where I come in. I understand that the bioelementalist is aware of an entry point via one of the volcano's old flank vents—is that correct?—and that Qhapaq Izhi's operatives have already done a bit of exploring to map out some tunnels that branch off to see what's inside. It should be as simple as placing some explosives to stimulate trapped magma, and if the pressure has built up enough, we'll be well on our way to an eruption."

"But will we be able to get ourselves off the mountain before it's too late for *us*?" Wayra asked.

"The operatives will have a pterobeast at the ready," said Uturunku. "The qhapaq has also supplied us with gearbombs. Their wind-up mechanisms will delay explosion for a brief period to allow us time to move out of range."

"Only three minutes, though." Qora remembered that clearly from the attack on the Aquchay base. "That's barely enough time in an *open* setting. But we're talking about a network of tunnels inside a volcano."

"If we plan it well," Ruka argued, "then it shouldn't be a problem. I'm told that the vent tunnel gives us access along the upper third of the volcano, where the flanks taper and the distance between the outside and the center is less than a half mile. Somewhere between a half and a third. We'll have to sprint but it won't be impossible. And even after the gearbombs go off, eruption won't happen immediately. First the rocks will fracture, then the gas pressure will release, then we'll get some steam jets. It could take up to a minute for the first magma breach. Then it'll be an ash plume, which at this altitude will probably shoot straight up and cool as the ash falls. Then the lava will have to move up the vent before it can spill over. Unless we get a pyroclastic surge first …" She glanced down at her notes, where a charcoal sketch of the volcano took up the center of the papyr in front of her.

"What's a 'pyroclastic surge'?" Wayra asked.

The volcanist bit her lip. "It's an ash-and-gas cloud that spreads down the sides of the volcano—fast as a pteranodon at full speed, hot as lava itself."

"Great," Req muttered.

"But we can explore the tunnels carefully in advance," said the volcanist, "find the quickest route from bomb placement zones back to the outside. We'll make sure the timing makes sense."

"What if we don't produce *enough* lava?" Qora asked. If the lava flow were to bypass any part of that forest of nightmares, the whole team would all be risking their lives for nothing.

"With the history of this volcano—at least what I was able to find in old records," the volcanist told her, "it shouldn't be a problem. Past flows have been significant in proportion to its size."

"And," Miyil said, "Qhapaq Izhi promised he would send in another team within a week to look for remnants of the mutagenic zone and burn them by hand, if necessary, once his spies give him the all-clear that Apo's people are gone—which they should be, having either evacuated or been burned alive by then. There might be a delay, depending on what happens in Allpa, but rest assured we won't leave anything to chance."

"Speaking of 'burned alive,'" Wayra said, "aren't there villages down below? Small ones, but still."

The team leader nodded. "The qhapaq has warned villagers that it won't be safe to remain in their homes. Quya Urpi will provide them with the means to relocate."

Ninan raked his fingers through his hair and sighed. "It seems the qhapaq has thought of everything."

"We can do this with a clear conscience, at least." Req folded his arms and leaned back in his chair.

Qora couldn't say this act wouldn't weigh on her conscience to some degree, but that seemed to always come with the territory in these sorts of things. *Necessary evils.*

Obliterating a habitat. Forcing villagers from their homes. Killing hundreds of animals in one shot.

"One way or another," Uturunku said, "we must destroy this place—and I, for one, am prepared to die doing it."

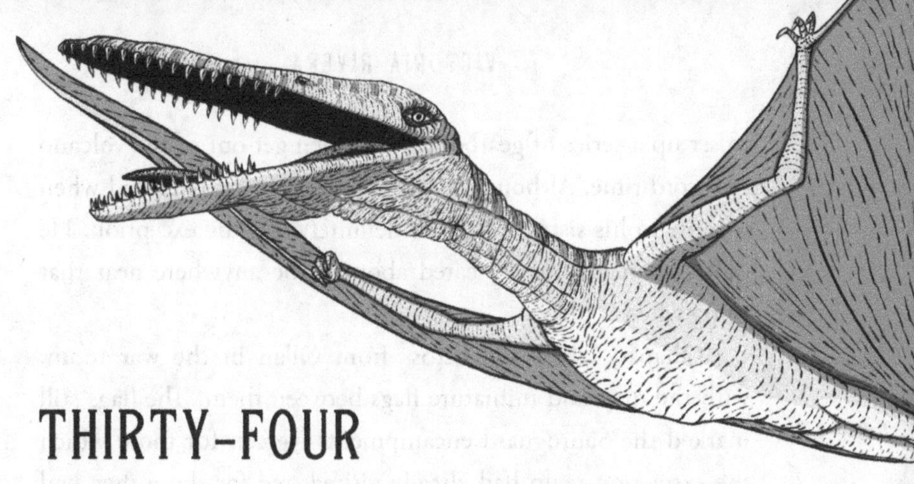

THIRTY-FOUR

"**WOULD YOU CARE TO EXPLAIN** to me what my sister and friends are doing at the base of a volcano?" Ollan demanded.

The Unuvian qhapaq did not look like a qhapaq at this moment, with his hollow cheeks and tired eyes. He wore a simple highborn's robes rather than the more elaborate robes and cloak of a royalborn, and held no scepter, and bore no crown upon his head. The gilded likeness of a triceratops skull, however, would not have helped the shame he carried in his shoulders at having lost command of his Terrain.

Ollan knew he ought to have more respect for the man, but right now he could only think of Qora and Wayra, and of course also Req and Ninan. It had taken a full day to get an audience with Qhapaq Izhi, who had apparently been detained by meetings with the quya to cover military strategy and perform inventory on their combined resources.

In the meantime, Ollan had had to gather what other bits of information he could about the mission at the place called Pakasqa, which apparently involved the destruction team *entering the volcano itself* through a vent that led to the main shaft. While anyone who knew anything had assured him the volcano was dormant, he'd also learned that the very idea was to wake it with a fiery blast, which meant that the team would need to set up a series of gearbombs and then get out of the volcano in record time. Although he was prone to being paranoid when it came to his sister, this most definitely was the exception. He didn't want anyone he cared about to be anywhere near that thing when it blew.

Qhapaq Izhi stood across from Ollan in the war room, with the map and miniature flags between them. The flags still marked the Sauroguard encampments—green for those which the extraction team had already visited, red for those they had yet to visit, and yellow for any locations believed to be hosting mutant dinosaurs and which required scouting—and wooden blocks marked areas along the border where security breaches might occur whenever Qhapaq Apo might choose to advance.

"If you've gathered that much," said Izhi, "then I think your question must be rhetorical."

"You could have sent anyone. Why send two teenagers and a couple of self-appointed saboteurs who have important things to do here as we prepare for war?"

"Your sister and the prince are young adults, both of whom have faced and conquered many formidable foes already, not to mention they both have deeply rooted motivations to ensure that not a single blade of grass remains unscorched at Pakasqa. I did not send them by force; I simply provided the opportunity and they accepted. As for your Razorclaw friends, I didn't even offer; they volunteered."

"You didn't have to tell them about the mission to begin with. You *knew* they would want to go. You can't just dangle a docodon in front of a velociraptor and expect it not to bite."

"And a velociraptor is not a house pet. It is designed to kill with stealth and speed. Likewise, your sister and her friends were designed to put right the wrongs of their world, not perform menial tasks. From what I understand, the migration has plenty of herders, the Qhispina House reptile handlers are already well staffed, and dominite production is now a repetitive process that any elementalist's assistant can perform. There's a reason these young people are prominent figures in the resistance—because they were not meant to sit and watch while others accomplish magnificent feats. Neither were you, in fact. If you and the other Razorclaws had not been on an extraction mission when your friends and sister left, I expect you would be with them now."

"My work here isn't done," Ollan argued. "We still have five reptiles to capture."

"I suppose that's the difference. Your talents are being utilized—for now."

Ollan gritted his teeth. It was no use arguing, of course. The destruction team was already gone, and they wouldn't come back until that volcano erupted. He could go after them, but … should he? Was this another one of those times when he was supposed to ignore his instinct to protect his sister? She was smart and, like Izhi had pointed out, she'd already faced worse things; she wasn't an innocent thirteen-year-old still learning how to shoot. Then again, a volcano was much bigger and much more destructive than a giant dinosaur, and it couldn't be controlled with whistles or dominite. "How long until they're finished?"

"The plan is to force an eruption tomorrow morning. Today the team should be exploring the vent and fine-tuning all the details of the plan. I have spies watching the site at a distance, who will send word should anything go … awry."

"Awry?" Ollan said sharply.

Izhi shrugged. "Anything is possible. But there is little cause for concern. The timing mechanisms on the gearbombs will allow a few minutes for escape, and I've provided a flyer to get the team out of range swiftly when the lava breaks loose."

"You really need *all* of them in there?"

"We want to set several gearbombs in motion at once. One or two people would waste precious seconds winding additional bombs while the first set is already ticking. Instead, each person can handle an individual bomb simultaneously—and then simultaneously flee. It's more efficient that way."

Ollan didn't want to admit that this made sense. But a full team didn't necessarily require his sister, and the woman he now wanted to confess all his feelings to, and his other friends. This could have been handled with a small military unit and no one here would have needed to hear about it until after the fact. He understood the importance of obliterating whatever freaks of nature Qhapaq Apo had used to create his army, he just didn't understand why Qora couldn't leave it to someone else.

Qhapaq Izhi picked up an extra flag and placed it on a small mound within Sumaq's borders. Then he moved toward the warroom doors and gripped a handle. "I apologize for the way you had to discover your sister's absence. It must have been a shock. Regardless, I have complete faith in her and in Apo-Kimsa. I believe they will survive this as they have survived their trials thus far. Should you decide to join them, please inform me and I will see to it that you are delivered to Pakasqa promptly."

With that, he left Ollan to stare at the topographical map.

Ollan focused the new flag. If he had to guess, the distance between that flag and Amachakuna in the real world would take about five hours by pteranodon. Unfortunately, he was already due for a three-hour flight to one of the yellow flags, where the extraction team expected to pick up a dracorex and an irritator. For a moment, he wrestled with the thought of flying to Pakasqa as Izhi had mentioned, but he reasoned that the only purpose in such a thing would be to oversee Qora and to assuage his feelings for Wayra, both of which were selfish indulgences during a time when he was especially vulnerable to them.

Finally he toppled the flag with a flick of his finger and strode out of the room.

"It is only from the outlook of the winged ones that we may find the hidden valleys and observe the scars upon the land—and it is only when we take the high view with our fellow man that we may find his hidden sorrows and obverse the peaks and valleys of his soul."

The High Shaman of Qhispina House

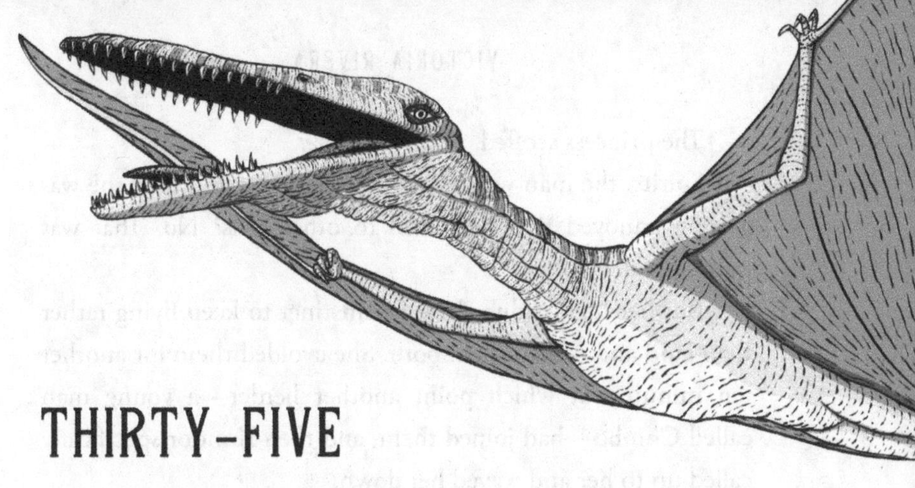

THIRTY-FIVE

"YOU'RE SOMETHING ELSE."

Paqari kept thinking the phrase in her mind. She hadn't known whether to be offended or not. Something in Kondor's tone the previous day had suggested sincerity, curiosity perhaps. Not his usual mockery. But one of the herders had called Kondor away to help widen the trench to keep water flowing to the creek, taking them both out of the moment.

On her pteranodon, she soared back and forth over both the dinosaurs and the mammoth herd, and a bit ahead on the landscape, making note of potential issues: a spinosaur at the rear appeared to be favoring one leg and might need to be assessed for injury, some of the mammoths had started shedding because of the heat, and the ground was about to get rocky over the next mile or so. They were into the Pirqas now, making their way through the pass, which forced them to narrow their formation.

As Paqari flew back toward the dino herd, she spotted Kondor talking to Suri—for the second time this morning. Suri was the young woman who had helped create and test all the whistlemutes; she'd come along on the migration as a herder and seemed somewhat fond of Kondor, often making her way to the front to socialize with him, but usually only when Paqari was on a survey.

The princess scoffed. *What do I care?*

Spirits, the man was nice to her one time and now she was getting annoyed that he talked to other girls? No. That was nonsensical.

But her logic didn't abate her instinct to keep flying rather than land and talk to them both. She avoided them for another ten minutes, at which point another herder—a young man called Chinbo—had joined them, and then Kondor specifically called up to her and waved her down.

The pteranodon staggered a bit before falling into step with Kondor's and the herders' mammoths.

"Everything looking good from up there?" Kondor asked.

She told him about what she'd seen from the air. Then: "If we veer west—slightly—we can avoid the rockier side of the pass, which might help us improve our pace, and it will be better for any dinosaurs that have injuries. We should also consider giving the mammoths more time to drink during water breaks; the heat is tougher on them with all that wool."

After the incident with the creek, Paqari, Kondor, and the herders had arranged a new watering schedule that would require more frequent stops so that the animals would drink less each time and not affect the water level so drastically, but the mammoths especially were going to require more with the change in climate. The inclines were getting steeper too.

"I guess we can see how it goes at the next stop," said Kondor. "As long as we're not getting down to bare creek-bed again, I agree that the mammoths could use more water." He nodded at the way ahead where the mammoth herd had already gone, where tufts of brown wool specked the ground.

"I'll bet that view is lovely." Suri gazed up at the sky.

The princess forced a smile. "Sure, if you like looking at

an endless trail of ruck, or at the bloody mammoth bones left behind every morning."

"You know," said Chinbo, who scraped at a piece of wood with a small knife as he rode, "Kondor and I were actually just talking about how it must be a lot for you to have to survey so often, seeing as you're the only one who can."

The princess observed the man's craft. He was always whittling away at something; all his items had intricate details and seemed to take him no time at all. This one looked like a sauropelta—similar to an ankylosaur, with pebbled armor and spikes coming off its neck and shoulders, but no club-tail.

"I don't mind surveying often," Paqari told him. At least when she was flying, she didn't have to ride next to anyone in awkward silence, or try to come up with polite things to say. At least when the pteranodon was in the air with its wings spread wide, it didn't look like some huge, lumbering insect the way it did when it walked.

Chinbo raised a brow. "Well, anyway, I told Kondor he ought to do something about it."

"Why should Gladewarden Sacha do something?" asked Paqari. *What a suggestion.* "He doesn't know how to fly a pteranodon. I know it looks easy, but it takes a lot of practice to keep one's balance. Not to mention it's murder on the thighs."

"Sure, but you could train him." Chinbo blew a few wood shavings off his little sauropelta.

Kondor shot him a tense look.

"What?" the man said. "You were just saying how you thought it was 'too much' for the princess to always be—"

"The princess isn't an instructor," Kondor argued.

Too much? Paqari thought. Why did it matter to Kondor if she wore herself out on her surveys? And no, she wasn't an instructor, although she was probably capable of teaching someone else how to fly, if they were interested (which Kondor seemed not to be).

"If you say so." Chinbo shrugged.

"It would take him away from leading the migration," Suri reasoned. "He and the princess would have to go off alone somewhere to train, leaving us without both of our leaders. Also, I imagine there wouldn't be enough time during breaks to learn much."

Paqari tried to parse those sentences for meaning. Was the girl just being logical? Nothing she'd said was incorrect. But if Suri wanted Kondor to herself, this whole business about flight training would surely ruin that.

"The rest of us would be fine on our own for a stretch now and then," said Chinbo. "You both could fly ahead in tandem, do some surveying while you're out there, and Kondor could pick up a few flying skills. I mean … I think it would be good to know we have a backup surveyor in case we need it. What if you get injured, princess? It's unwise to rely on you alone."

Hmm. The idea was sound, Paqari had to admit that, but … did Chinbo think she wasn't capable? Is that why he wanted Kondor to survey too? Maybe he thought the information she brought back was insufficient, or that her assessment of the terrain was faulty. The fact that they were still so far behind probably didn't reflect well on her.

The princess looked to Kondor for his input but he seemed to be avoiding her gaze. Did he *agree* with Chinbo? After all, Chinbo had said he and Kondor had been talking about her right before she'd landed.

"You prefer Gladewarden Sacha's supervision," Paqari concluded.

"That's not what I said," Chinbo told her.

She turned on Kondor. "You want my assignment?"

"What? Gods no. I just thought it might be tiring, being up there all the time. But if you're going to get *offended*—"

"Actually, you know what?" said Paqari, "I *will* train you. I'll take you up right now—and you won't last five minutes. Get on." She slapped the back of her saddle.

Kondor rolled his eyes. "Princess, please. Don't be dramatic. Besides, you already went out twice this morning and I'm sure you don't want to go again so soon."

"Oh, I do. If everyone here is so worried that I can't handle this job, then maybe you need to see what kind of stamina I have."

The two of them locked eyes for a moment. Chinbo and Suri watched warily.

Then Chinbo leaned closer to Kondor and stage whispered: "Maybe you should just let her take you."

"You'd like that, wouldn't you," Paqari snapped at the herder.

"You just offered ..." Chinbo said.

Okay. She needed to calm down. She knew that. But she didn't like the man's interference when she was trying to prove a point, even though he was the one who had brought up the subject to begin with.

"Fine," Kondor said. "Let's go."

꩜꩜꩜

Paqari and Kondor had only been airborne for a few seconds and already Kondor was clinging to her like a drowning man to driftwood. She hadn't thought it through, how close he would be to her when they rode together. But his arms were tight around her waist, his chin hovering over her shoulder, her back to his chest. It was very difficult to concentrate on directing the pteranodon. If she didn't think too hard about who it was behind her, she could almost relax into his hold, and forget where she was and what she was supposed to be doing.

He made a strange sputtering noise from his mouth and then he let go with one arm to brush his hand down the back of her head. "Gods—could you possibly have any more hair?"

And ... the spell was broken.

With her hair loose from a tie right now, the wind whipped her long waves all around, something that usually felt sort of freeing when she was alone. The princess gave her head a little shake so that Kondor might get another mouthful, and smiled to herself.

"You smell like some kind of orchid, by the way," he told her as though this were borderline offensive.

"Night-lady orchid," she clarified. It was silly to have brought the scent with her, but it was the only thing that gave her some sense of refinement while she was forced to endure these rugged conditions.

They flew up over the mountain now, where bits of snow coated the rock. A few trees grew along the ridges, and wild flyers came and went from clusters of nests on cliffs. The creek snaked through the hollows.

Kondor inhaled deeply several times, releasing his warm breath close to Paqari's ear. She recognized the technique; her first time flying had unsettled her stomach the same way.

"We're ..." Kondor practically choked as he tightened his hold on her. "We're up so high."

"Isn't the view 'lovely' though?" She echoed Suri's earlier sentiment. It *was* a lovely view, but flying was more than admiring everything below. It required a sense of confidence, a connection with the pteranodon, steady breathing, and a muscular strength to stay upright and firm.

"I don't know. Maybe if I could manage to keep looking, I'd be able to tell you."

Locating a jutting ledge, Paqari steered the pteranodon and turned into a descent. She came to a skittering halt and heard Kondor gasp. The gladewarden jumped down from the saddle, fell to his knees, and immediately vomited over the side of the ledge.

This altitude was bad enough on the ground, but flying up to a thousand feet above that would make anyone sick. Paqari's flight training had been done at sea level—with Tisqu being a small island and its capital located near the shoreline—and it had been quite an adjustment when she'd had to travel by air on the mainland over mountain ranges. Luckily she'd been on several gondola flights abroad with her parents, and her recent flights across the continent had allowed her to adapt gradually. But even now, she often felt lightheaded in the air, with a fog descending on her brain if she stayed up too long.

She slid down and knelt beside Kondor, hesitating before she put a gentle hand on his back.

He coughed out the last of it, then wiped his mouth and sighed, relaxing onto his haunches. "For the record ... I never thought you weren't capable of this."

"Oh really?" she said tightly. "So you weren't telling Chinbo that you thought it was 'too much' for me?"

"I was." He coughed again. "Because I feel bad that you have no one to relieve you. Not because I think you're doing a poor job."

"But Chinbo thinks I could do better ..."

Kondor shrugged. "He might. But ... who cares what he

thinks? And since when do you care what *I* think, either?"

"I don't."

She didn't.

Did she?

A gust of cold air grazed Paqari's cheek and she shivered, realizing that the chill of the altitude had begun to seep into her. When she was moving on pteranodonback, blood rushing, leaning in and using her muscles to steer and clench the saddle with her legs, it wasn't as noticeable. Here, though, sitting still, was a different story. She tugged down the sleeves of her tunic dress after having had them pushed up to her elbows, and wished that the dress had more length to it; the riding trousers she wore underneath helped some.

One glimpse of her sleeves, though, and Kondor pulled off his mammoth-wool vest, draping it around her shoulders.

"Oh," she said, "you really don't have to—"

"Take it," he insisted.

It was good he had it with him. Usually by midday he took it off, but it was still early enough that he hadn't overheated yet.

"Thank you."

"I'm used to the cold, remember? Not like you, island princess." He changed positions so that he was sitting cross-legged now, and pushed his hair off his forehead. "Do you miss it?"

"What—the islands?" When he nodded, she said, "Sort of. I miss the sea. It … unsettles me when the land goes on for too long without a large body of water visible."

He chuckled.

"You think that's strange?" she asked.

"I want to say yes just to spite you, but"—he shook his head—"I understand. I've felt the same, but with all the open spaces where there aren't any trees. I don't quite know how to function without a border of woods around me. Where you feel contained, I feel … exposed, I guess."

"Oh. So the gladewarden *does* have feelings." Paqari half-smiled.

"You caught me."

She was quiet for a minute. Then she said, "So you don't blame me for our delay? You don't think it's my fault we're behind?"

"Of course not. Honestly, you've surprised me every step of the way, with everything you know, with the way you solve problems …"

"Because you thought so little of me when we set out?"

Kondor scoffed. "Look, I won't deny my first impression was that you expected everyone to fall at your feet and do your bidding, and that you had no desire to set foot outside your usual comforts—whatever those might have been. But if that was right, I don't think you'd be here. You never would have gone to the Tail, and you would've abandoned this mission within the first few hours."

"Well, my 'usual comforts' are not available to me anyway, for starters, although 'comfort' is relative. I can't say I was always comfortable in Tisqu, even if I did have all my favorite material possessions."

"You're a 'poor little rich girl' kind of princess?"

"You joke, but wealth isn't everything. My mother liked to dress me up and parade me around like a show raptor to be judged against my half-siblings, to prove she was more worthy than my father's other wives. And to a man of my father's status, a daughter is just an item for trading, which he must keep in good condition until an opportunity arises for her. I was required to take an acerbic tincture every month to prevent any 'unfortunate circumstances' should I 'fall prey to defilement.'

Except that it takes very little for royalborns to consider a young woman 'defiled,' even if it was her own choice to engage in certain behaviors. But I was lucky, my father said, that Qhapaq Apo had a son in need of redemption, which allowed him to offer me up as Ninan's bride and thus trade me for Qhapaq Apo's favor. If I'd had to go through with it, I would have at least had a kind husband; other young noblewomen become the property of much older, more disagreeable men very early in life."

"Gods," he said. "I'm sorry. I never thought …"

"You never thought I was human?"

"Of course I did. But you came to my land like you owned the place—and it still wasn't good enough for you."

"That's because your border patrol tried to take down my gondola at first sight, and then I found out you fed my friend to a giganotosaur."

"*I* didn't do anything. In fact, I *saved* Qora. You're welcome."

"Yes, well, I do give you some credit for that."

"How gracious of you."

Paqari sighed as she watched a swoop of yellow sordes flying northward in a V formation. "Tell me about your life, then. What are *your* parents like? Did you grow up in Murkroot, or …"

The dino and mammoth herds progressed closer in the distance, mere spots of color but they were growing larger in Paqari's view, which reminded her that she was supposed to be teaching Kondor something about riding pteranodons but instead had only made him sick and taken his wool. Still, she struggled to summon the guilt she ought to bear; the air up here was crisp and didn't smell of ruck, and for once she was sitting on something other than an animal even though the rock under her was rigid.

Her pteranodon sat too, probably also grateful for a rest, and stuck close to her.

"I grew up in Thistlebriar, actually," said Kondor. "My father's a miller and makes a very good living. My mother works in textiles. They're both simple, kind people who work hard."

"Why did you go to Murkroot?" Paqari asked.

"I wanted a fresh start. I heard the people out west were different than those who lived in the eastern cities—more tolerant."

"Tolerant?" she said. "Tolerant of what?"

Kondor gestured to his face. "Of this. Of my ... blended heritage."

Of course, she thought. What had seemed to her an odd but intriguing set of traits obviously implied a history that would not have left his culture without emotional scars. Most of what she'd read about the wars with the Kastillans had focused on what had happened in the Old Empire, but there had always been a few paragraphs in each book about the foreigners' occupation of the Tail. It wasn't as though she didn't know why the gladewarden— and many other Tailfolk—had lighter hair, skin, and eyes than most people on the rest of the continent. But she had assumed that by now, everyone was accustomed to the differences.

"Thistlebriar is a tight-knit community of people who, historically, resisted Kastillan occupation, where other regions embraced it as a means of progress and diversity—but obviously embracing conquistadors didn't end well."

"But you drove them out eventually."

"At great cost to everyone who was left standing."

Paqari pulled Kondor's vest more snugly around her arms, although her shoulders peeked through the armholes.

"Where Murkroot has plenty of people who look similar to me," he added, "Thistlebriar does not. There, they look at mixed blood like a disease. They don't even have grafted orchards because it's a symbol of 'integrating foreigners.'"

"But you have no control over your heritage." The princess imagined a younger Kondor coming out of a tree-mounted schoolhouse, getting kicked by other boys.

"Does a rabid hyaenodon have control over its disease? No, but that doesn't mean anyone wants it around."

"So you left."

"So I left. My parents didn't come with me; Thistlebriar was their home and they had no intention of leaving. When I ran out of money, I saw a recruitment poster for local gladewarden units and I joined. I've lived in Murkroot ever since."

Now it made sense, Paqari thought, that he would be sensitive to anyone who appeared to think themselves superior for whatever reason. Her not-so-subtle opinion of the Tailfolk must have struck him in a way she never could have guessed.

"That must be difficult, being away from your family," she said.

While the princess couldn't relate directly to the idea of *missing* her own family members, she understood the sentiment well enough.

"I try to visit often," he told her. "But yes, it's difficult. I wish it didn't have to be that way."

"You too are … more human than I expected."

"I thought you would have figured that out right after I hurled my insides down the face of this rock."

She huffed a laugh. "That did give me a clue. Speaking of, though, you're going to have to have something to show for all the time we've spent out here. I don't those the spots on your tunic are going to cut it."

The gladewarden glanced down at his chest where a few

specks of vomit blemished the fabric. He frowned.

They both stood, and then Paqari instructed him to climb onto the pteranodon's saddle by himself. They discussed how to use the reins to make turns, as well as a few riding positions and commands.

Paqari commanded the pteranodon to flap a few feet off the ground while Kondor did his best to maintain balance, although it was only a minute or so before he went pale again.

"We should probably try this again at a lower altitude. Tonight at camp, maybe, before it gets completely dark."

"Sounds good," Kondor said through a weary breath, clutching his stomach. His brows drew together as she climbed onto the saddle behind him. "Wait—what are you doing?"

"You're going to fly us back to the herds," she told him. "First because it will show everyone that I've taught you something, but more importantly because, if you're going to be sick again, I'll be well out of the way."

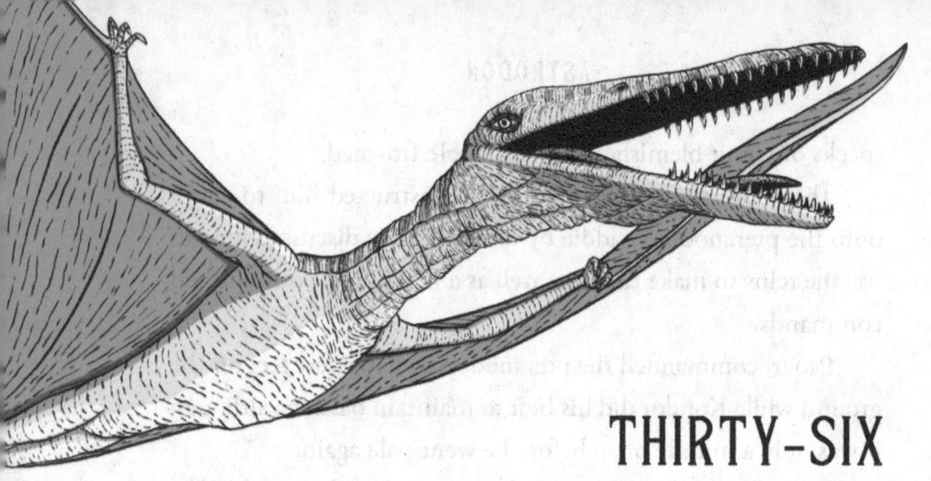

THIRTY-SIX

GETTING TO THE LAVA-VENT ENTRANCE required another trek through the eerie woods of Pakasqa. Ninan tried to keep close to Qora, but she seemed to put distance between them whenever she had the chance. And could he blame her? He'd only turned protective after the vine. Before that, he'd been keeping his own kind of distance. But this was exactly the reason he struggled with having any sort of hope for the future. They were always one misstep away from tragedy, and the pressure only built with each passing day.

Ten minutes into the trek along the still-narrow trail, a large figure appeared in the distance, stopping everyone in their tracks.

Uturunku put a finger to his lips.

Ninan held up his strikefangs. Qora spanned her wristbow and loaded it. Wayra and Req reached for the dominite in their pockets while Miyil and Ruka drew their machetes.

The creature was the size of an irritator—no—Ninan squinted—it *was* an irritator. Or at least it used to be. From his and Qora's secret excursions on Tisqu Isle, he knew what he was looking at. He recognized the mottle of yellow and brown on its skin, and the conical spikes along its back that raised its full height to around twelve feet. What should have been a finely tapered snout, however, was gnarled and engorged. Its eyes bulged. Several other growths disfigured its body.

"Those that still function may be let loose into the forests of Pakasqa."

It must have been a version of the Sauroguard irritator breed that had come close to the final "product." This only served to remind Ninan that he still didn't know what these irritators could do, what special and terrifying features they might possess. Hopefully the rebels back in Allpa had figured it out by now.

Eventually the irritator passed without taking note of the team, and with sighs of relief, they moved on. But scares like these only served to drain Ninan's energy faster, and he was tired enough as it was.

The night in the hideout had been a long one, trying to get comfortable in the cramped space, feeling like he'd been too big for his sleep sack. Breakfast had been another jar of beans. He was starting to think he and Qora should have stayed with Paqari on the migration. At least there would be open air, and dried meat to eat. It was only the thought of destroying all his father's work in a lava flow that made Ninan put one foot in front of the other, again and again and again.

Finally, as they reached the upper third of the volcano and the ground became practically too steep to walk on, Uturunku said, "This is it."

Ninan stared at the upward slope of land, covered in ferns and vines, and blinked away the humidity that had gathered on his lashes. *Here?*

Miyil and Uturunku went to either side of some apparently designated spot, and dug their fingers into the dirt. A piece of the ground lifted, revealing a hidden entrance tall enough for everyone to stand without slouching. It was six to eight feet across in all directions, not a perfectly rounded or straight tunnel but it would make for a decent passageway.

"We keep it disguised," Uturunku explained as he stepped inside the vent.

The walls within were a marble of blackened rock and veins of white. A layer of ash and rocky debris coated the ground and any protruding ledges.

"Lava once flowed through this tunnel," Ruka informed them. "Or, more accurately, lava *created* this tunnel."

"And lava could potentially flow through here again," Req concluded.

The volcanist nodded. "Yes, a new eruption could push lava into any of its former vents, depending on the flow and pressure. We definitely don't want to be in here at the last minute."

Qora stopped to touch one of the walls where the blackened rock took on a glassy sheen.

It occurred to Ninan that this was actually the second time he'd been inside a lava pathway with her. At the Volcano Kañay, they'd slept in the opening of a lava tube, although it had been closed off by fully cooled lava so that it didn't tunnel deep.

He'd been closed off too, much like he was now, although for very different reasons. It had been *starting* something with Qora that Ninan had thought to be so terrifying, what with his secret identity looming over him, and the Venture's prize making the two of them unwilling rivals.

He wanted to believe that higher powers had brought them together, but that was difficult when those same powers seemed just as likely to let war tear them apart.

"Uh oh," said the volcanist as she looked up at the ceiling.

Everyone followed her gaze to a crack that ran parallel to the tunnel, almost dead center above them.

"That doesn't bode well," said Req.

Having already made a note about the lava vent on her diagram, the volcanist now seemed less enthusiastic about the team's success. "Vents like these can be unstable, especially considering the age. Thermal contraction, along with erosion, will have weakened it some, and the rock will be brittle."

"Unfortunately, this is the only entry point we've found on this side of the volcano," said Uturunku. "It would be too risky to try and find one on the opposite side, where Qhapaq Apo's operatives may come and go. We also have no time to scour the flanks looking for anything else, and we need to be up high where the mountain tapers, so that our distance from the flank to the main shaft will be shorter. This is the most ideal vent, and we're lucky we found it."

"I'm sure it would be the same either way." Ruka chewed her lip. "Lava *tubes* would be more stable than old vents like this one, but they won't go deep inside like the vents do. And it's not like we can go down from the top of the main shaft; it could be up to a thousand-foot drop, and it's probably choked with debris anyway."

"We'll be careful," said Miyil. "But we don't really have a lot of options."

"It would require some pressure to cause a collapse," admitted the volcanist. "That means, of course, that we'll need to be fully in the clear before the gearbombs go off, though. As soon as the mountain starts rumbling, this vent is done for."

Req wiped beads of sweat off his forehead. "Great."

This information didn't motivate Ninan to want to go any deeper into the vent. The team leader was right, though; options were limited, and if they wanted to destroy Pakasqa, it was a risk they'd have to take.

They all seemed to tread more carefully after that, as though their footsteps would be the thing to cause the crack to lengthen and expand.

The rock underfoot was rough but not sharp, and the vent snaked slightly in a jagged way.

Further in, the vent branched off into smaller tunnels (Ruka described them as "conduits" or "secondary vents") coming the opposite direction (outward from the center of the volcano) sometimes into small pockets that ended after a few feet and other times into other long but more narrow tunnels. Ninan actually found it to be a fairly comfortable walk (aside from the threat of dying inside of it somehow) compared to the wildland outside where he might step on an angry vine or fall onto a snap-trap or encounter a mutated monster.

Ignoring the branching conduits, the vent was fairly direct, with some subtle turns, and Uturunku and Miyil knew where they were going.

The temperature rose every several yards inward, as did the humidity. The ground sloped down, from long-ago lava breaking through weak points that branched off of the main vent to spew out and *up* before oozing down the flanks aboveground, the volcanist told everyone. The walls seemed to sweat, and also bore the scars of old eruptions, streaked with obsidian and flows hardened like black waterfalls.

"This is perfect," said the volcanist. "The heat … the steam. That means there's not only magma down here, but water too. If we can release both at once, water and magma will unite, and the rapid steam expansion will blow the whole thing like a fiery geyser."

A strong, sulfuric scent overpowered the vent. Ninan's throat stung whenever he inhaled too sharply, which was getting difficult not to do as the air seemed less breathable the deeper they went. He stole a glance at Qora, whose cheeks were red in the minimal lantern light Uturunku had brought for them to see by.

At a decent pace, the walk took about ten minutes before Uturunku said, "Here we are."

Uturunku stepped aside so that everyone could see where this particular tunnel ended, but held out his arm so no one could actually pass him. Ninan and Qora somehow ended up side by side, with Uturunku keeping them back, and as Ninan looked down, he understood the reason for the barrier.

The whole world seemed to drop away. Illuminated by Uturunku's lantern, a vertical shaft plunged downward.

Peering in, a wave of heat blew up against Ninan's face.

Then Uturunku extinguished the lantern. In the depths below, magma flickered like a distant red star. High above, a sliver of the sky peeked through what must have been much overgrowth across the crater and a clog of solidified old lava and debris in the mountain's throat.

"I thought it was dormant," said Wayra once she'd had a turn to see the glow at the bottom.

"Dormant enough," said the volcanist, "that no one around here worries about an eruption. According to record, it's been more than a century since it last spewed, but in the meantime it seems our friend here has been pressurizing."

"Is it just me," asked Req, "or is the ground vibrating too?"

Ninan glanced at his feet, taking a moment to consider. If he focused, he could feel a subtle tremor.

Ruka said, "It is. This volcano is in perfect condition for our purposes."

"Do we even *need* to put gearbombs down here?" Qora fanned herself with a flat hand.

"Yes," the volcanist told her. "It probably wouldn't blow on its own for another few years at least. It's only getting ready."

For how long it had taken to reach the shaft, though, Ninan was not optimistic about planting the gearbombs and getting out in time. Especially with this heat, with the strangling air, and with the slope of the ground—which would be uphill on the way out. Perhaps at a sprint, and with no hesitation as to which tunnel to take, it might be possible, but that was something the team would have to rehearse to be sure of.

Wayra expressed Ninan's thought with near exactness.

"We have an empty gearbomb," Uturunku explained. "It will act as a timer so we can run some drills and get a sense of the actual event, down to the second. I know it looks unpromising, but I believe success is possible."

They went on to discuss a few of the places where it would be best to place gearbombs.

Ruka pointed out a fissure where the ground was especially wet, which implied that there could be a good amount of water collected behind the rock there. She also located a few fractures similar to the one on the ceiling at the entrance. "Blasting these could make new paths for lava to flow, and release pressure rapidly to get that flow built up fast. It's too bad we can't get a gearbomb right into the magma chamber though; the rapid gas expansion would be devastating."

There was some talk of dropping a gearbomb down the shaft and making a run for it, but the idea was immediately dismissed. Even for how deep the chamber sat, the bomb would strike the magma in a matter of seconds, and the heat alone—even before touching magma at all—would instantly detonate the bomb regardless of its timing mechanisms.

"We could dangle it inside from a rope," Qora suggested.

"We would only be able to drop and suspend it a few yards down, but at least it would explode close to the center."

Everyone agreed this might be a viable option.

Then Uturunku said it might be good for everyone to get some fresh air before resuming their work here for the day. After that, it would be time to use the empty gearbomb to rehearse an escape.

Most of the way back to the entrance, however, a roaring squeal set everyone at attention.

Instinctively, Ninan stepped in front of Qora.

The sound came again and echoed through the vent.

Ninan found his dominite, but Qora frantically searched through her jacket pockets—her jacket now tied around her waist—before looking up at him with wide eyes. "I think I … I think I must have dropped mine."

"It's alright." Uturunku drew a blade and a crystal of his own, motioning for everyone to follow him. "Probably just a mutant dinosaur that discovered the entrance."

Approaching the entrance now, the silhouette of a large spiked reptile thrashed against the light that spilled onto the tunnel's ground from the outside.

A few feet beyond the edge of the light on the inner side, a purple glow caught Ninan's eye.

The irritator from before, who stood twice as tall as the entrance, bent forward and shoved its head at the dominite, but couldn't push in past its own shoulders. It roared and flailed, snapping its jaws.

With such a small crystal, and at this distance, the dominite was just powerful enough to entice the irritator, but not enough to lull it to a calm, entranced state.

"Don't worry," Uturunku told her. "We'll give the mutant

what it wants, and then it will let us be." He prepared to throw his own crystal—presumably to within the irritator's reach—but as he pulled back his arm, the irritator thrashed against the opening. A sudden, sharp noise made the man freeze.

Everyone looked up at the ceiling.

The crack had doubled in length.

The irritator slammed its shoulders forward twice more, forcing the crack to lengthen inches at a time.

Uturunku launched his crystal at the irritator, but the ceiling fractured into several pieces that fell between him and his target, trapping the crystal in the rubble.

"Ruck!" The volcanist crouched and covered her head as smaller debris rained down.

Ninan and Req pulled Qora and Wayra a few steps back into the tunnel's depth while Miyil tried to shield them all.

Within seconds, the entire entrance had fully collapsed on itself, cutting them off from the outside.

THIRTY-SEVEN

"Some walls are built intentionally; some walls are made of the matter that falls between where we stand and our way onward; and some walls are figments of our imagination."

Tupaq Kanchaya

THIRTY-SEVEN

OLLAN GUIDED THE PTEROBEAST that carried a netted irritator dangling from its harness. He landed his pteranodon and called up to the pterobeast, commanding it to lower itself, then to hover until the irritator was settled firmly on the paddock. A minute later, Kuy swept in with a dracorex.

It was odd to come back from an extraction and not see Wayra. Ollan had been used to seeing her for at least a few minutes each time he brought a new reptile for study.

Sometime today, Wayra would be going into a volcano and setting up a deadly explosion she might not outrun. He thought of Qora there too, and his stomach churned. Worse, he wouldn't get word about whether they'd succeeded until much later in the day, when they either returned safely, or when microraptors arrived with a message.

A five-hour pteranodon flight, he reminded himself. Or just under four if they came by pterobeast.

To distract from his anxious thoughts, Ollan asked if he might have a look at the growing collection of Sauroguard reptiles. Kuy decided to join him, and together they walked past the enclosures where each reptile wandered somewhat freely.

This menagerie of creatures included the scutellosaur whose scream still had Ollan's ears ringing sometimes; the hypsilophodon that had left Yaku smelling like a pile of fresh ruck; the troodon with its sticky extrusions; the mononykus with the punch-claws; the razor-scaled oviraptor; the wall-climbing velociraptor; the acid-spitting pteranodon; the camouflaging megaraptor; the miniature therizinosaur with venomous claws; the fire-breathing pyroraptor.

Now the handlers worked to prepare the irritator (which could rumble its diaphragm in such a way that the sound vibrations would severely disorient anyone nearby) and the dracorex (which could generate electric charges from its horns) for containment. All that remained was the ankylosaur with the enlarged club-tail—which, according to Ninan and Qhapaq Izhi, had no other special features and did not require study—along with whatever had been on the missing bestiary page.

In a way, the extraction team's work here was done, at least as far as they were able to progress. Still, Ollan shuddered to think that there were hundreds more of each of these reptiles ready to invade Allpa.

Ollan focused on the therizinosaur for a moment, remembering the day he'd brought it to Wayra, how careful she'd been with it. She'd stood face to face with that thing and never so much as flinched. No doubt she wouldn't flinch at the heat of a volcano, or whatever mutants she might encounter at Pakasqa.

And then there was Qora, who might tremble in the face of danger, but damn it if she wouldn't hold her ground just to prove a point—or to get what she needed.

"She'll be fine," Kuy told Ollan like he knew what he was thinking.

"Which 'she' are you referring to?" Ollan said.

Kuy shrugged. "Both."

"Should we have gone to the volcano?"

"No. I think we did what we were supposed to do. This was where we were needed most."

"*Were*," Ollan emphasized. "Unless we get a lead on the mystery reptile, there's nothing left to extract. What's next for us?"

"I suppose we should ask the quya."

The Sauroguard sampling was complete (or, as complete as could be). Allpa's dominite supply was growing. Urpi's military, including the smilodons, was training (along with the small Unuvian units Izhi had maintained). The giant theropods were on their way. And any minute now, the volcano whose flanks supported mutant life and research would be incinerated. And there were still six days left before the cession deadline.

Circumstances were not perfect, but the resistance was well prepared. Ollan said a silent prayer to Sky Mother that this piecemeal defense would be enough.

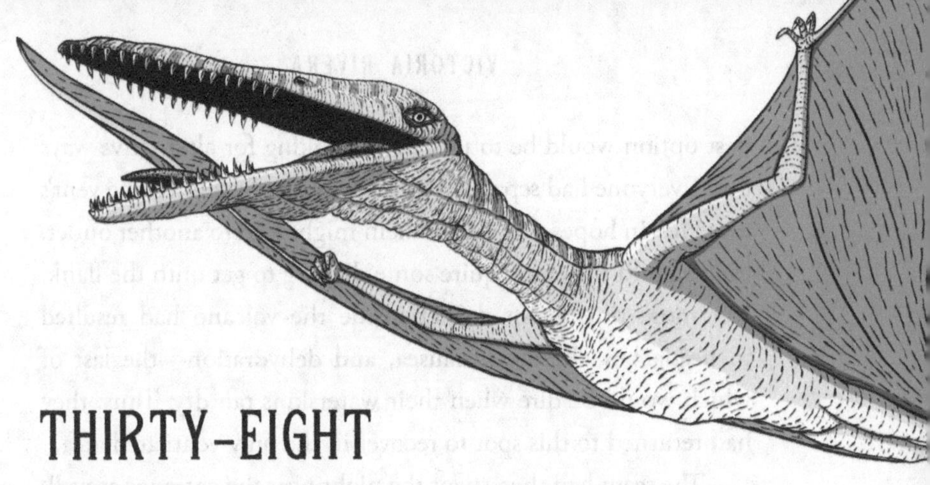

THIRTY-EIGHT

QORA SAT BACK AGAINST THE WALL of the lava vent and inhaled slowly. Sweat tracked down her forehead and into the corners of her eyes. "Nothing up that way." She'd finally made use of the special feature of her green jacket, particularly the lace-up seams that joined her sleeves to the main panels, removing the sleeves completely so she could wear the rest of it like a vest. Even though there were no monsters or enemies here, she wanted to keep her bolts handy, and likewise wore her wristbow.

The volcanist drew a charcoaled X over a diagram of the lava vent and its branches in her notes, crossing out the branch from which Qora and Ninan had just returned.

After the collapse at the entrance the previous day, the team had spent nearly an hour trying to clear the debris, but some of the rock slabs had been too heavy to lift, and so they had succeeded only in letting in a bit more fresh air through the gaps, along with a bit more light.

With both dominite crystals buried in the rubble, the irritator had lost interest in its pursuit and disappeared somewhere into the woods, leaving the team to deal with the consequences of its destruction.

When it had become clear that the effort at this entrance was futile, Uturunku and Miyil had determined that the next best option would be to take turns looking for alternative ways out. Everyone had separated into groups and explored the vent's branches in hopes that one of them might lead to another outlet, even should the end require some digging to get onto the flank. But more time spent deeper inside the volcano had resulted in headaches, dizziness, nausea, and dehydration—the last of which would be dire when their waterskins ran dry. Thus, they had returned to this spot to recover in the only ventilated area.

The team had then spent the night near the entrance as well, to avoid death by prolonged exposure to noxious fumes. Qora, Ninan, Req, and Wayra had all slept huddled together while the others had spread out on the ground within the vent, and when morning winked through the rubble gaps, they had set to work once again on their exit route.

By this time, they should have been setting up the gearbombs and hightailing their way off this volcano. Instead, they were exhausted, dripping with sweat, and ravenous, and they still hadn't found a way out.

Loosening the collar lace on her brown roughspun shirt that she wore under her jacket-vest, Qora swallowed to wet her throat. This was all her fault. If she hadn't dropped that crystal, the irritator never would have come and destroyed the entrance trying to get to it. Her eyes stung as she suppressed the flow of her tears.

A few minutes later, Wayra and Req returned from their own investigation.

Wayra plopped down beside Qora. "We keep finding water *everywhere*. In little puddles, or trickling through a crack in one of the walls."

"Don't let it tempt you," the volcanist told her without looking up from her notes.

They had already had this discussion last night: Any water

inside the vent would be toxic to drink. It would be packed with dissolved minerals—sulfur, iron, arsenic—and maybe even acid from gases interacting with it. Or it could carry toxic metals like lead or mercury, not to mention potentially harmful thermophilic bacteria fostered by the warm environment.

Qora tried to keep all the names and terminology straight, and then realized it didn't matter. Everything in here was little better than poison; that was all she needed to know.

After a rest, Uturunku and the volcanist worked on a strategy to explore additional zones.

"This one seems to branch off into even smaller branches," Ruka said, pointing to her diagram, "so we should split up again to see where those end. It might be a tunnel that's so small we have to crawl through it, but if it leads to the outside, I'm all for it."

This time, Qora and Wayra went together, while Req went with Ninan, and Uturunku went with Miyil and Ruka. The volcanist gave everyone another rough-sketched map of where they were going and how to get back.

Going back into the haze of heat and gases turned Qora's stomach. She had to calculate her breaths. Wayra suggested they slow down; even if it meant more time spent in the haze, it also wouldn't do to pass out from pushing themselves too hard.

All the tunnels came outward and upward from the main shaft, where lava had once broken through weak points in the shaft wall and flowed to try and reach the surface. Its heat and pressure had carved full pathways, and broken through new weak points within *those* pathways, creating all the branches. Thus, many of the branches came off the vent horizontally at an upward angle, while others came off through the vent's "ceiling." All the branches were jagged with unpredictable turns, and they narrowed the deeper anyone walked into them. But not all of them led to the outside, because there were plenty of spots that had held up against the old lava, where the pressure must have petered out and the lava had drained back down.

Qora stopped to catch her breath and gaze up at an overhead offshoot. If someone were to hoist her up there, she might be able to crawl into it, but it was already narrow to begin with and she doubted she would still fit once she'd made it a few yards in.

She and Wayra found their assigned tunnel and made their way through it. They both clung to the walls for balance, staggering along, faces glistening with sweat.

"I couldn't help but notice," Wayra said in a raspy voice, "that you and Ninan seem to be ... having trouble."

With a weary gaze, Qora simply said, "Yeah."

"Wanna talk about it? We're going to be in here a while. Nothing else to do."

"It's complicated."

"It always is. Especially now."

Qora brushed sweaty hair off her forehead. Even with all her hair tied back, some of it still stuck to her skin. "I don't really know how it happened. Sometime during all the migration planning, he started acting ... strange."

"It was wearing on him," Wayra guessed.

"It must have been. Although he didn't say much about it. We were so busy, we didn't really have the chance to talk. Not until I went to the verdanza—a spiritual sanctuary in the trees. I wanted to send up a few prayers before we left. Then Ninan found me there and he just ..." Qora shook her head. "All the sudden he was so angry. At his father, at the gods ..."

"At you?"

"That's what it felt like."

Wayra took a sip from her waterskin, which must have been

close to empty by now.

"It just doesn't make sense," Qora added. "He tells me he loves me, and then he … pushes me away?"

"Maybe it's not that he's pushing you away," Wayra told her, "but that you've reached a point where he feels safe enough to tell you what he really thinks—safe to tell you he's scared, and that he's struggling to find the meaning in everything."

"But I'm struggling too. I'm just struggling *differently*, so he thinks I don't understand."

"Do you really understand, though?"

"Of course I do."

Wayra cocked her head.

"I want to believe that Sky Mother will provide us with what we need to survive," said Qora. "But he thinks every good thing is 'a blade that cuts both ways.'"

"It does feel that way sometimes," Wayra admitted. "Every loved one, every prized possession, every bit of gold or silver … it's just another thing you might end up losing."

"Is it better to have it a while and lose it, or always be alone and lacking?"

"Maybe that's not the point. I don't think anyone disagrees. I think it's more about being frustrated by the fact that everything is mortal and temporary. Ironically, that should be an idea we can accept, considering we've never known anything else. Nothing lasts forever, so why does it hurt so much when the lives of those around us run short, or when resources run out? Nobody can answer that question. It's just something we feel. People try to explain it with religion or faith, to say it has a purpose, or to console each other by promising there's more to come—a place where 'forever' is real and where wealth doesn't matter and where all families and lovers are reunited after death.

But when all we can see is right now, when the rest is unknown, how are we supposed to believe that? Sure, a lot of us can do it on a normal day, but when death is at our doorstep, it's hard to have faith that things will be alright."

Qora sighed. "Yes, but obviously there are things far beyond our understanding, and we have to make room for that too. Not everything can be based on what we see. There's still so much we don't know. Even so, I don't expect Ninan to think like I do, but it's like he's angry that I have faith in *anything*."

"You have to remember that his relationship with faith is complicated. He comes from a long family line that has exploited other people's faith to stay in power. Plenty of people still believe that Qhapaq Apo is a man of the gods, even after all he's done, because 'the gods may work through imperfect beings' or because the efficiency with which he accomplishes his goals makes him seem almighty. For Ninan to have grown up so close to that, to be taught a type of faith and then watch his father use it like a weapon … that's going to cause some issues."

Qora stumbled a little. "I know, but that's different. That's not what faith is for me—all the rituals and 'rules' that everyone's always arguing about, or prophecies. For me, it's believing there's meaning in our existence, and trying to figure out what that is."

"Under these circumstances, I'm guessing it might take Ninan a while to separate one kind of faith from another."

"Well, besides that, he basically said I'm a weakness—and not in the way that he can't eat or sleep because he's thinking about me, or because he loves me so much he could deny me nothing. More like a loose thread in a cloth. Something that will unravel everything and lead to his downfall."

"I'm sure he doesn't mean it like that. Men are ruck at explaining what they feel sometimes. To be fair, they don't get a lot of practice. It's basically not allowed when they're growing. They're supposed to keep it all contained, act like it doesn't matter."

Qora thought of her brothers, how they sometimes fumbled over their self-expression. Their papáy had been a man of good principles but few words, and like so many of his generation had rarely been a good example of expressive behaviors.

"However," said Wayra, "that doesn't mean his words hurt you any less."

The tunnel took a sharp turn, and Qora quietly replied, "Thank you."

Here there was barely enough room for Qora and Wayra to stand side by side, but the scent in the air lost some of its sulfuric tinge in favor of a more organic quality.

"Dirt!" Qora said.

Wayra pressed her fingers into the wall where the rock layer was thin and crumbling, revealing dirt, silt, possibly compacted volcanic ash from long ago. The rock here was pale, with many fractures, a feature the volcanist had told the girls to look for. And then …

"Roots!" Wayra pulled away the loose layers to get to a few twisting, whitish growths.

Together they clawed into the dirt behind the rock to start a small excavation, finding the soil somewhat damp.

Panting and coated with dust, they looked at each other and smiled.

ↄↄↄ

The volcanist tore off a piece of the exposed root and put it in her mouth.

Qora grimaced.

The whole group crowded in the tunnel, practically in a single file line.

Shaking her head, Ruka said, "It's yuca."

"So?" said Req.

"Yuca roots go six to ten feet deep in environments like this," the volcanist explained. "The plant has to work harder to anchor itself in loose volcanic soils, and on steep terrain. I'm sorry. This is a dead end too. It's close, but not close enough."

Six to ten feet, Qora thought. That was like a grave. Deeper, even. And she and her friends were buried in it.

Upon their return to the blocked entrance, Qora noted that the light coming through the rubble had dimmed. But it wasn't that late yet—at least, she didn't *think* it was. She paused to listen to a soft patter coming from outside.

"Is it …" She crouched beside the rock slabs and strained her ears. "Raining?"

"Sounds like it," said Uturunku. "We get a rainstorm out here every few days."

A rumble vibrated the air.

The patter turned to a downpour, forcing water into the exposed vent. Tiny streams raced down the incline and wet the entire surface.

The volcanist picked up a big rock with a point on one side, then knelt in the water's path.

"What are you doing?" asked Ninan.

"Making a ditch," she told him. "If we're quick, we can catch some clean water."

Everyone else looked for similar rocks and joined her, hacking away at the ground to loosen the layers.

While the ditch was still shallow, the flowing rain rinsed

away excess dust, and then the water ran clear and pooled up.

Between the seven of them, they'd managed to create a six-inch-deep ditch that ran about three feet wide and maybe ten inches across. It wasn't huge, but it was enough for them to take turns dipping their cupped hands into it to drink. It was also enough to submerge a waterskin and allow it to fill.

The water burned going down Qora's throat, and then her stomach gurgled in response. Her body seemed to absorb the water in minutes, eager to restore its normal levels.

In no time at all, they exhausted the water and had to wait for it to collect again.

The rain also cooled the air substantially, easing the symptoms brought on by the heat emanating from the lava's core. Now if only they could get some food.

As if in reply to her unvoiced prayer, a wild compsognathus eventually poked its head through the spaces between slabs of rock—perhaps to escape the rain—then inched the rest of the way inside. Then came another, and another, and another, a whole scrabble of them. All had various growths all over their scaly bodies, but otherwise appeared healthy.

Everyone exchanged glances and Qora put a finger to her lips, then carefully withdrew a bolt from her pocket and loaded it into her wristbow.

She hated to do this, remembering how the compies back home had been reliable egg-layers and—against her better judgment—pets. They didn't have much flesh on them either. Still, meat was meat.

With a click, she struck one through its middle. The others scattered briefly, then returned with caution to investigate their friend, and at that moment Qora struck again—but the compies wouldn't come back twice, and so she had to load and shoot with lightning speed to snag another two as they fled. The last one fell dead between the slabs and required some strain to get to. The others darted out of the vent completely and disappeared back into the rain.

"I'd complain about having to eat them raw," said Req, "but … I think I'm hungry enough that I don't care."

The volcanist frowned at him and snatched up the dead compies by their feet. "Raw? You forget, sir, that we are at the threshold of a great earthen oven." She consulted her diagram for a moment, then looked at Qora. "You're a huntress, I'm guessing?"

Qora's aim had been a dead giveaway. She nodded.

"Then you'll know how to prepare these."

"Yes."

"Great. Follow me." Ruka turned down the tunnel.

Using the diagram, Qora and the volcanist went to the volcano's inner depths and followed a branch, which led to a sweltering pocket where a few rock slabs appeared to have collapsed from the ceiling like the ones at the entrance. The thermal stress in this area would be more severe, so Qora wasn't surprised.

The air was thick again, but Qora found herself more able to tolerate it now that she had rehydrated.

"Here." The volcanist pointed to a big flat slab.

Qora held her palm above its surface, testing the intensity of the heat. It was perfect, like a stone grill. She withdrew a knife from one of her vest pockets and began her work on the compies— gutting and decapitating them—while the volcanist managed the process of frying them on the hot rock as Qora finished and handed them over one by one.

They saved the final cutting for when they reached the rest

of the team, where they could divide the meat in the comfort of the rain-cooled breeze. In silence, Ninan helped Qora rinse off all the blood (because the relentless rain had now fully replenished the water supply), cupping handfuls of water and pouring them over her hands and forearms away from the ditch to avoid contaminating it.

Everyone ate with groans and grunts, devouring the meat.

It wasn't enough, but it was something.

Qora mentally thanked Sky Mother. Maybe the goddess wasn't real, but the team had managed to survive another day, and Qora didn't take that for granted.

Even stone can be softened
by a steady stream of water.

Tisquvian proverb

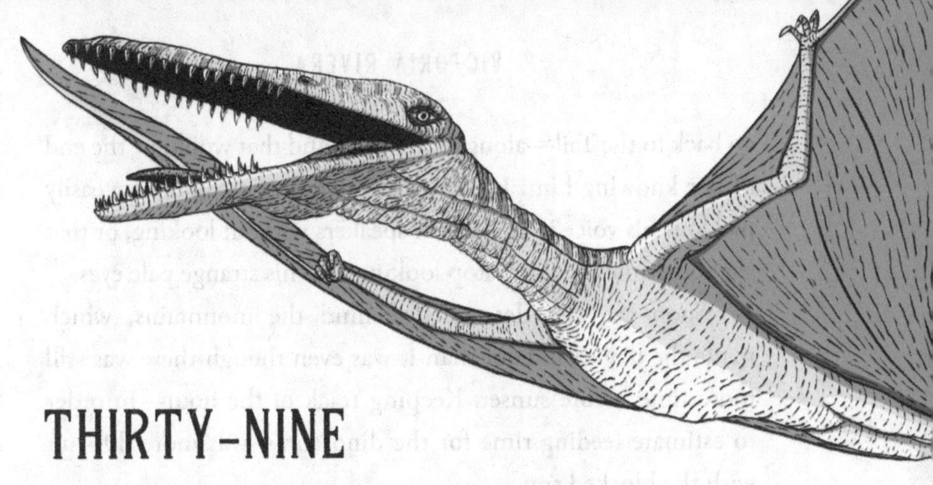

THIRTY-NINE

THE HERDS WERE WELL INTO the mountain pass now, and the rocky juts felt like enormous walls closing in on them. If not being able to see the sea was suffocating, Paqari thought, not seeing a scrap of open land was even worse.

"Where you feel contained, I feel ... exposed."

Paqari wondered if Kondor appreciated the sense of protection these mountains might offer—at least to someone like him, who hadn't lived the entirety of his life with the ability to see countless miles in any direction. And there were some trees, too. A few conifers here and there.

She took the gladewarden out twice more for flying lessons, and this time he managed to control his stomach. They kept to lower altitudes and flew in short bursts. By late afternoon, Kondor was able to fly the length of the herd and back on his own, albeit much more closely to the ground than Paqari would have flown, with several of the dinosaurs playfully snapping their teeth at him as he passed. But the herders—particularly Chinbo—seemed pleased that there were two aerial surveyors now.

Suri still rode next to Kondor whenever Paqari took a turn to go up solo again. The princess did her best not to think about it because, again, what did she care? As soon as this migration was over, she'd probably never see the gladewarden again. He would go back to the Tail—along with Suri—and that would be the end of her knowing him. It didn't matter that she could now easily pick out his voice in a group of speakers without looking, or that she sometimes couldn't stop looking into his strange pale eyes.

Soon the sun descended behind the mountains, which made the day seem later than it was even though there was still more time before sunset. Keeping track of the hour—in order to estimate feeding time for the dinosaurs—was more difficult with the blocked sun.

Feeding time, however, went much more quickly here, where there were fewer places for the mammoths to run. The hills and dips kept them contained, and the dinosaurs snatched them up in seconds.

Paqari caught sight of Kondor looking over the wreckage when it was over, with a tick in his jaw that told her this was getting more difficult for him each time. How many people in the Tail could have benefited from this wasted wool? How many tools and weapons could have been made from those ivory tusks? At least the meat fed the sacred dinosaurs and sustained them for another day so that they might fight against the Sauroguard. But the sheer volume of wasted matter here was overwhelming regardless of the tradeoff.

Making camp within the Pirqas was a much different experience than it had been out on the plains. Where most of both herds had been visible at a glance, the rugged terrain with its ups and downs now kept many mammoths and dinosaurs obscured. Paqari had, however, spotted a waterfall during one of her surveys, and suggested pushing the dinosaurs an extra mile so that they might camp close to it and enjoy the pool of water at the bottom. This had won her some favor with the female herders, all of whom were dying to wash away the grime of travel in something deeper than the creek.

Water sources, at least, were much better in this area, with more springs and runoff, much of which fed into the Kuchuna River that the migration would follow coming out the other side of the Pirqas.

A series of caves surrounded the waterfall, and a few of the herders quickly discovered that an entire cavern was also filled with water, like a private pool. As soon as everyone finished setting up tents and building fires and had eaten, many wandered off to swim and bathe and socialize.

Paqari kept to her own small tent for a while, which she was very proud to say she had learned to set up by herself, even though Kondor had tried to do it for her several times at the start of the journey, but she'd refused to let him treat her like a dullard and had shooed him away. The gladewarden did continue to set up her temporary privy every night whether she liked it or not, but she had tolerated it.

Tonight, she'd retrieved her ration of dried fruit, dried salted potatoes, and pterosaur jerky, refilled her waterskin, and eaten in the tent while she read by lantern light. She was dying for a bath—a real one, now that there was enough water to fully submerge herself, rather than just enough to splash her face and limbs—but the cavern pool and waterfall would be crowded for a while with the herders, most of whom were men she'd barely spoken to.

So, for the moment, she read a few passages of *Layers of Earth: A Geological Guide to Runaqa* from a small collection of books the quya had given her.

Basalt is an igneous rock formed when lava cools rapidly near the surface of the earth. It is one of the most common rocks.

When she'd had enough of that, she resumed reading *Upon*

the Moors of Scalebane, which followed the life and romance of a young woman called K'acha who was forced to flee her life of wealth to avoid the dangers of a killer seeking vengeance against her family, and while in hiding met a man with a dark past who soon proved to be more than she expected.

As the sounds of social activity died down, Paqari slipped out of her tent. Dinosaurs lay all around, a few of them stirring, but most were already deep in slumber, scattered about like great scaly mounds. She stepped in front of a spinosaurus, whose upright spinal sail was almost three times as tall as she was, even with the spinosaur's legs tucked up to subtract from its height. When she came close to its snout, the nostrils widened. The spinosaur slowly cracked its eyelids, watching her, and sniffed. She stepped back, palms out. "No, no. Go back to sleep."

The princess was eager to get her bath, in hopes that she could wash off the strength of whatever natural odors she gave off that the dinosaurs seemed to like so much.

Taking her lantern with her, she moved along the rocks. The cavern was located across the water, but a narrow strip of rock ran behind the waterfall, allowing quick and easy passage.

The waterfall's white noise filled Paqari's ears, blocking out everything else. A fine mist fell on her skin. She crept up to the main cavern and peeked inside. Several herders were drying off and putting their clothes back on. One woman wrung out her hair. It was clear, though, that everyone had been fully bare and not the least bit shy about it.

With the last of them making their way out, Paqari went in. Thanks to the dim space, and all the honey wine the Tailfolk had brought from Murkroot making them tipsy, they didn't seem to notice her.

First she removed her boots and only put her feet into the

water. It was cold, but the feel of it cleansing the sweat and the dust made her yearn to get all the way in. She waited a few minutes more but eventually stripped down completely and lowered herself from the rock ledge into the watery depths.

It was a shock to her body at first, and she cringed at the temperature. She clenched her fists and waited for her senses to adjust.

Her feet touched the bottom easily. Standing at full height, the water level covered her chest, but she bent her knees to let the water come up over the rest of her, gathered more water in her cupped hands to wash her face, and then lay back to wet her long hair.

She sighed at the feeling of the water holding her, buoying her up, and felt the stress of the day begin to lift away. Several minutes passed while she soaked and floated, her thoughts percolating on everything that might happen in the coming days.

It had been nine days now since leaving Murkroot. Too long. Paqari had not sent a microraptor messenger to Quya Urpi to update her on their progress in *three* of those nine days because, to be honest, she was ashamed to admit how their pace had slowed. It was probably about time to send another message— with the truth—although she hoped the upcoming descent from the Pirqas would give them new speed (due to downhill terrain, a more powerful water source, and miles of open grassland for the last stretch). With Qora and Ninan off on another mission now, Paqari felt responsible for both herds, and the weight of that pressed on her.

Then, somewhere in the middle of her mental wanderings, the sound of footsteps on stone snapped her alert.

Not far off. Approaching fast.

The rush of the waterfall had masked any sounds that would

have given the princess more warning. At this point, she was certain she wouldn't have time to get out without being seen.

"Anyone in there?" asked a masculine voice.

It was muffled, again by the waterfall, but she knew its cadence at once.

Of all people.

Paqari bitterly mused that she was surprised the gladewarden would bother to bathe at all.

Without thinking, Paqari extinguished her lantern and ducked into a crevice, the echo of her splash fading just as Kondor entered.

He'd brought his own lantern, but kept the flame low.

The princess wondered if it was dim enough for her to sneak out later, but one glance at the pile of her clothes several yards away and she knew it wasn't possible. It would make too much noise just to get to them—sloshing through the water, clambering out of the pool—let alone trying to put them on in a rush and run out. There was no privacy outside the cavern if she were to make a break for it with the clothes under her arm and the intention of putting them on after.

This was ridiculous. She should just say something. Every passing second that she didn't only made it worse.

But then the gladewarden slipped his shirt up over his head, his back muscles flexing.

Paqari's heart pounded. She bit her lip.

Oh gods. What had she gotten herself into?

Then he unbuttoned his trousers.

At this point he stepped into the shadows just enough that Paqari couldn't see any of what was about to come next, and anyway she shouldn't be looking—she'd have been furious if their positions were reversed—so she ducked deeper into the crevice. A protrusion of the cavern wall kept her concealed.

Maybe she could wait here until he left. Yes, that would be the best solution. In a few seconds, he'd be in the water, then he would take a quick dip, and that would be it. He would leave, and she would be free to come out, and he would be none the wiser.

She took a deep breath and waited for the slosh that told her he had entered the pool.

Kondor sighed as he moved around.

Paqari imagined that the cool water must have felt nice on his sore muscles, as it had on hers.

Feeling safe to look again, she inched forward to see him with the water up to his shoulders while he ran his fingers through his soaked hair.

She only bothered to look so she could keep track of whether he was still there, she told herself. She wanted to know the instant he left, to know when she could breathe easily.

His flickering lantern light lapped against the water, which lapped against the cavern walls. The flicker highlighted the ripples that surrounded Kondor, and filled the space with a soft glow. Flecks of metal glittered in the minerals of the rock.

Metallic flecking often forms when hydrothermal fluids rise through porous rocks or rock fractures. Cooled fluids allow their metals to precipitate. This may be evidence of ancient rivers, where mineral-rich waters once flowed.

Yes, that was it. *Think about rocks.* Her books had given her plenty to mull over. She could think about the layers of sedimentary rock that formed to create line patterns on the plateaus in Qaqakuna. Or how some such patterns appeared to be diagonal, as the earth shifted over millions of years and entire mountains sank and tilted.

Except then passages of the *other* book surfaced in her mind.

"I ... don't understand why you'd want anything to do with me." Asiru's hand curled into a fist at his side, and he clenched it as though he were trying to will himself not to move.

K'acha took that hand, urged Asiru to relax it, and brought it to the side of her own face and whispered, *"I want* everything *to do with you."*

Paqari shook her head. She would have to put that book away for a while.

Alternating bands of limestone, sandstone, and shale ... Ancient seabeds ...

Suddenly Kondor went still, looking in her direction. No—not *quite* her direction, just near it. Off to the side.

Where her clothes lay.

The gladewarden furrowed his brow and swam over to the side of the pool near the pile.

Easing backward, Paqari held her breath, but then—

"Princess?" Kondor panned his gaze until it fell to where she hid in the crevice. He squinted.

She lowered herself so that her shoulders barely came above the water's surface.

"I know it's you," he said. "The night-lady orchid scent is still on your clothes. I didn't even have to touch them to smell it. What are you doing back there?"

"I was hoping to bathe alone." Paqari crossed her arms under the water, even though the lighting situation kept it fairly murky. But just in case.

"You and me both."

When he focused on her and held her gaze too long, her cheeks began to warm. She dug deep to find her resolve and firmly said, "I was here first. You can come back later."

"Hang on ... It was completely dark when I came in." His

eyes darted to the extinguished lantern beside her clothes. "You heard me coming. You could have said something before I took my clothes off, but *instead* you just—"

"I panicked, alright? I wasn't thinking. And then you got in and it was too late to—"

He raised an eyebrow. "How much did you see, exactly?"

"Nothing," she insisted. "I looked away."

"Are you sure?"

"Of course I'm sure!"

Kondor grinned. "Okay."

She scoffed. "You think no woman could look away from your exposed body? Well I assure you I am fully capable of it."

Mostly capable.

"No, I don't think that. But I do think you're acting very frazzled, and it's a little suspicious."

"It's not. I've already explained myself. And if you don't go, I will scream until someone comes to see what all the commotion is about."

"You want *more* people in here with you?"

Paqari gritted her teeth and made a guttural noise. "You are so—"

"I'm going." He held up his hands, then turned and reached for the pool's edge.

At that moment, something swept past Paqari's leg. She shrieked.

"Good gods, woman—I already told you I'm—"

"Wait! Don't go!" Paqari cried.

Kondor looked over his shoulder, his jaw slack. "Are you serious? You *just* said ..."

She felt it again, something swimming right in front of her.

"I know, but"—she backed against the rocks—"there's

something in the water!"

"Yes, there is: a shrill young woman who can't seem to make up her mind."

Had Paqari been by herself, she would have climbed out at once, but with Kondor here, there was no way she could bear to do that. "No, I'm serious! It just touched me!"

He chuckled. "I guess you weren't alone to begin with, even before I got here."

"It's not funny. You have to find it and kill it!"

"Kill it? With what? My bare hands? It's probably just a fish. Although I guess it could be an eel. Didn't you grow up on the seashore? You're not *really* intimidated by whatever's in here …"

Paqari folded in on herself, putting her hands out under the water to try and keep back anything that might come at her again. "Yes, I grew up on the seashore. I know all about the kinds of horrific things that live in water, especially in *dark* water. Which is fine, except I'm not usually *naked* in that water. And since every herder we have was in here at some point tonight and no one complained, I assumed it was clear. Now I know I was wrong."

Warily, Kondor came toward her, with a look that said he was more fearful of her next reaction to him than to whatever might be swimming around their legs.

When the thing fluttered against her knee again, she didn't think, she instinctively drew up next to the gladewarden.

"Whoa, whoa, whoa …" Kondor put both hands up in the air again.

She knew she was too close to him, but all she could think was that they could be dealing with a water snake, like what lived in the coastal caves of Aleta. Of all her dabbling in random studies, she couldn't remember whether those snakes were partial to saltwater environments or if they might also inhabit freshwater caves. It hadn't occurred to her until now, and worse, those kinds of snakes were venomous.

Not knowing where the thing was, it took her a second to get her wits about her, and then—

"Oh my *gods*." What she felt against her hip was less of a mystery. She glanced up at Kondor and instantly sloshed away. "Tell me that's not—"

"Ruck." Kondor looked down at himself as though he could see through the water. "Not on purpose! You're … We're both …" He gestured at his exposed upper half.

Ugh, Paqari thought. Why were men like this? And what was wrong with her that she'd turned to *him* for help—in the dark, in the water, in a state of undress?

"Never mind. Just … just go!"

"I was *trying* to go, remember?" He pressed down on the rock and pushed himself up and out of the pool.

The princess turned away again, but otherwise tried to be as still as possible so as not to upset the water and attract the creature underneath.

Kondor picked up his clothes without even putting them on, and left the cavern.

Paqari waited a beat, then sloshed gracelessly to the water's edge, looked at the entrance to ensure Kondor had really gone, then scrambled out and reached for her clothes. She got the undergarments on first, then put her dress over her head.

The fabric stuck to her wet skin, but she forced her arms through the sleeves. She didn't bother with the boots, or the riding trousers (even though the skirt of her tunic dress barely covered what needed to be covered). But it was plenty dark outside and she would run to her tent before anyone saw her anyway.

This had been a horrible idea, and nothing like what she'd hoped for.

With a huff, she picked up her lantern, then Kondor's, which he had left—on purpose? Or in haste? Either way, she took that one too; she'd give it to him later.

As she hurried out of the cavern, she only made it three strides before she stumbled right into the gladewarden. He stood leaning against the rock, fully dressed now but with wet splotches all over his shirt, the waterfall gushing behind him.

"What are you still doing here?" Paqari said.

"I wanted to make sure you were okay."

Paqari drew back.

Her stomach fluttered.

Kondor was proving to be a very confusing man, and she hated that he was seeing her like this. She hated that this migration was a task she so often wasn't up to—because while she prided herself on her ability to do whatever she decided she could do, she just wasn't built for this.

"*Are* you okay?" he asked.

Her eyes welled against her will, and she choked on a sob. "No. I'm not."

He took a step toward her, concern in his eyes.

"I've spent more than a week," she said, "on the backs of foul-smelling animals, surrounded by people who think I'm some scaly, high-crested dracovenatress. I've eaten nothing but the shriveled remains of food that I'm quite certain was substandard to begin with. I've slept on the ground, wrapped in mammoth furs, with the grumble of enormous dinosaurs mere yards from where I lay. My body aches and my mind is weary, and I want to go home—except that I *can't* go home, because I no longer have one. I have nothing. I can't ever return to my

old life … and I'm not saying that I want to, but … this …"
She gestured around. "This is … an endless torment. And all
I desired tonight were a few minutes alone, to wash away the
filth that has become my daily cloak, to feel like myself instead
of some hopeless vagrant. But then *you* had to be there. So I got
scared … because whenever you're around, I feel so … so …"

Kondor took another step closer. "So … what?"

Paqari stared up at his gray eyes.

Aphanitic basalt. That was the color. Dark gray but warm,
with flecks of lighter gray like feldspar. In the lantern's glow she
could just make out the details.

Spirits—even rocks couldn't distract her from what she felt
when she looked at him.

What was wrong with her? It was foolish to linger like this,
to let him see how she was barely holding herself together.

"Nothing." Paqari handed him his lantern. "I have to go."

She pushed past him and hurried to the path behind the
waterfall with no way to light her own lantern and nothing but
moonglow to see by.

"Wait!" Kondor said.

But she kept going, trousers and boots tucked under her
arm, a cool mist clinging to her bare legs and feet.

"Come on, princess. Talk to me …"

No, no, no. Do not stop for him.

Directly under the waterfall now, his voice barely audible
through the white noise, he said, "Paqari."

The princess stopped dead.

She spun around.

The gladewarden strode over to her.

Her lips parted, voice caught in her throat. "I … You …"

"What's wrong?" he said through a breath.

"My name. On your lips. It's ..." Paqari searched for a word but couldn't think of anything that fully captured the description she was looking for. He'd only ever called her "princess," and not in an honorific way. Regardless, she wasn't a princess now. No matter how he'd said it, it didn't fit. Finally, she settled on, "It's ... nice."

He set down his lantern and eased up to her until only inches separated them from one another.

"You know what else would be nice on my lips?" He reached out and let his hand come against her cheek.

Her pulse pounded but she didn't dare move.

Gently, his thumb brushed over her skin.

His gaze fell to her mouth, then turned up to meet her eyes like a silent question, lashes glittering with waterfall mist.

Paqari could hardly breathe, afraid that the slightest shift in her composure would ruin this. At the same time, it felt like a dare, as though the gladewarden were testing her to see whether she would face him or back down.

Well she would not back down. She would hold her ground. This man did not scare her.

That was right, he didn't *scare* her—he absolutely terrified her.

But his touch somehow calmed her too.

When she gave no indication that she wanted him to stop, he leaned in.

His lips pressed to hers.

She dropped everything she was holding. Her unlit lantern shattered. She slid her fingers into Kondor's damp hair to bring him closer even though it wasn't possible.

The chill of the water rushing past and the feel of his arm around her waist made her shiver, but she shivered *with* him.

Kondor kept kissing her, and she kissed back with a fury.

There was no denying it now: She wanted him.

But more surprising was that he seemed to want her too. Even in her disheveled state, even when she hadn't been brave in the cavern, even though she was a shell of what she used to be.

He pinned her up against the rock wall like he was afraid she might try to run away again, and she relished the security of his body.

When he kissed her neck, she thought she might fall apart. And she wanted to.

She was ready to be undone.

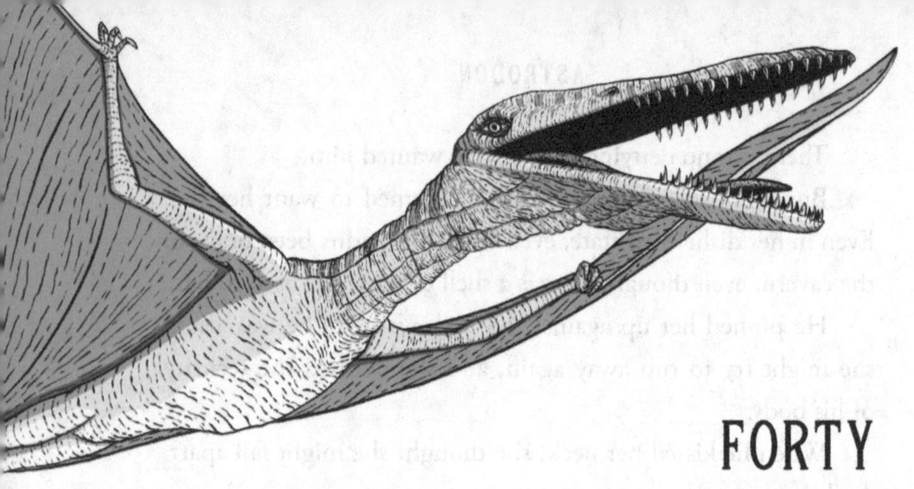

FORTY

OLLAN TUGGED AT THE COLLAR of his new uniform. "Still no updates?" With no further extractions to perform, Quya Urpi had offered him an Allpan military position—a rank above the one he'd served under in the Sumaqi Guard. He wasn't sure how he felt about it yet, after so many years having no memory of his service and now having essentially deserted once he'd regained those memories. His former participation had only been for financial security and benefits after his papáy's death (to help his mamáy take care of Qora, Hakan, and Rimaq) and so he couldn't say that it was because he was a patriot, or that he'd ever had a strong sense of loyalty to Qhapaq Apo; it was difficult, though, not to feel like a traitor to his Terrain as he sided with an opposing force.

But he hadn't had time to really think on it, not with the lack of information on his sister and his friends. Messengers had sent word yesterday afternoon via microraptor to state that the volcano had not yet erupted. If the team had managed to cause an eruption later on, the messengers might not have sent out the microraptors until closer to sundown, which would have caused a delay since the diurnal flyers always stopped to roost for the night and wouldn't have resumed flight until daybreak.

Quya Urpi shook her head. "I'm afraid not. It could be a

simple thing, however; a logistical problem with the gearbombs, or they might be working to secure a quicker escape route. They'll want to be careful with every detail. After all, they really only have one opportunity to get it right."

"Or they were attacked by wild mutant dinosaurs," Ollan said. "Or discovered by Qhapaq Apo's operatives and captured. Or—"

The quya took his hand and held it in a firm grasp. "You must not think like that, do you understand? I know this has been difficult for you. After weeks of extractions, and being separated from your family, and under the threat of attack, it's natural to be on edge, but thinking of the worst possible scenario will only make it worse."

He took a deep breath, although it didn't seem to satiate his lungs. Not when his sister was hours away, and on a potential death mission. Although, the quya had a point; letting his mind run wild could do no good. "You're right."

"Give it a few more hours. I'm sure we'll hear something soon. In the meantime, it's best you acquaint yourself with your new squad. We're five days away from the cession deadline; we'll need everyone to be ready."

Quya Urpi had given Ollan command over a squad of spanners (crossbow shooters). While his position in Sumaq had been that of an entry-level "boltling" who occasionally performed guard duties, he now had the opportunity to support the newly trained Allpan Bolt Corps recruits.

Boltmaster Kanchaya.

The thought of preparing for a real battle, however, made his skin prickle. For his brief time in the service, he'd only faced real opponents once. Six months in, extracontinental forces had breached the naval blockade along the South Coast. Sumaq and Unu had worked together (as the attack had threatened the Unuvian coastline in equal measure) and sent armed ships into the Anqas Ocean. But the sheer numbers of both Terrains' militaries had been enough to intimidate the enemy, such that the battle had lasted less than an hour before enemy ships retreated. Ollan had fired dozens of times on his squad leader's orders during coordinated volley fire—intended to saturate an area with bolts—with no idea whom or what he and the squad might have hit. *"Ten paces above the hull! Span! Load! Fire!"* None of the return fire had so much as grazed his copperskin mail armor. And then the whole thing had ended, the ships had returned home, and he'd spent the rest of his service (up until the sailbeast had dragged him off and cost him his memory) patrolling city streets or guarding community buildings from airborne offenders. Now *he* would be the one to shout "Span! Load! Fire!" at a group of boltlings—except that these ones might not get away unscathed.

"Yes, Your Majesty," said Ollan. But something deep inside of him screamed *"No."*

ↄↄↄ

"What do we know so far?" Ollan asked the handlers on the paddock. Before he could work with his squad, he wanted a full rundown of the Sauroguard to exploit weaknesses wherever possible. While volley fire wasn't meant to employ precision, there may be other opportunities to do so depending on how battles played out.

"We've determined some level of weakness for each of the reptiles," said the handler. "Considering the length of the list of reptiles we've collected, however, it's probably best if instead we provide you with a document detailing each one."

Ollan nodded. "Fine by me." When the handlers gave him the document, he scanned it with keen eyes.

Ankylosaur (Destroyer)
Feature: enlarged club-tail, augmented dermal plate structure
Vulnerability: gaps between bony plates (inferred similarity consistent with most ankylosaur breeds)

Dracorex (Stormhorn)
Feature: emits electric pulses from cranial horns
Defense Method: rubber-lined armor

Hypsilophodon (Repulsor)
Feature: noxious gas emission
Defense Method: airway filter-masks for defenders

Irritator (Growler)
Feature: bodily vibrations disorient victims
Defense Method: muter bombs to dampen vibration waves

Megaraptor (Morph)
Feature: skin pigment and texture shift for camouflage
Vulnerability: shifting takes up to five seconds to match environment, unstable environmental visuals such as rapid movement or bright light may reveal subject to viewers
Defense Method: powder to reveal subject's form

Mononykus (Punchclaw)
Feature: extra-long monoclaw, rapid claw protraction
Vulnerability: small stature, requires close range
Defense Method: fortified greaves/shin guards

Oviraptor (Bladescale)
Feature: razor-scale shedding
Vulnerability: will shed when threatened, may be baited to shed wastefully (rather than in a targeted effort)

Pteranodon (Spitter)
Feature: oral acid expulsion
Vulnerability: requires pressure buildup between expulsions, a puncture to throat pouch could permanently disrupt attack

Pyroraptor (Firebreath)
Feature: firestream exhale
Vulnerability: too many firestreams in rapid succession likely to cause internal combustion

Scutellosaur (Screamer)
Feature: sonic scream
Defense Method: military-grade earplugs, muter bombs to dampen sound waves

Therizinosaur Brevis (Slasher)
Feature: compact stature, venomous claws
Vulnerability: sauropod oil impedes effects of venom

Troodon (Webber)
Feature: rapid sticky-silk expulsion
Defense Method: greased armor

Velociraptor (Clingfoot)
Feature: adhesive foot pads
Vulnerability: sand interferes with adherence

Unknown Reptile
Feature: to be determined
Vulnerability: to be determined
Defense Method: to be determined

The "unknown" reptile of course gave him the same sinking feeling he'd had when he'd seen the page torn out of the bestiary. His mind went wild with what it could be, similar to the reasons he continued to fabricate for whatever was going on at the volcano right now. He tried to take the quya's advice, to not allow himself to think that way.

"Basically," said the handler, "we have most of the information we need to put up a good fight. Quya Urpi has teams working on gathering weapons and supplies to focus on the reptiles' vulnerabilities."

Ollan nodded. "Thank you for the information."

Now he tried to keep his mind on the vulnerabilities that might be affected by well-aimed bolts. Any of the reptiles whose special abilities were expulsion based—shooting acid, gas, flames, or sticky-silk—could be deterred with a puncture to the proper gland. Even for the scutellosaurs, an injury to the neck might damage the vocal folds that allowed them to produce those horrific sounds.

And then there were the gaps in ankylosaur armor—although it would have been nice to have a Sauroguard ankylo specimen for the handlers to observe in person.

"Do you happen to have diagrams of each species that detail the parts of the body where these functions come from?"

"We do, in fact." The handler disappeared, then returned with another set of documents.

Ollan looked them over for several minutes, noting points

on the reptiles' bodies to aim for. "Excellent. Please have the scribes duplicate these five times and deliver them to the war room. I want to distribute them to the other boltmasters this afternoon, and I would like one for myself as well."

"Yes sir."

"Also … based on your observations, how do you think a bolt to the skin would affect the megaraptors' ability to camouflage?"

"I think it depends on where the bolt strikes. Likely, the area immediately surrounding the wound site would malfunction in its ability to shift color and texture. For a deeper, more severe wound, it could activate the megaraptor's alarm response, which—we've learned while trying to wrangle it without dominite—will cause it to shift to an 'alarm color,' which tends to be a bright yellowish green. In nature, the intention is to make predators believe their prey is poisonous to feed on, although it doesn't really apply to these."

"Well, they're not exactly *natural.*"

"Right. Anyway, the point is … if you land a bolt, you'll probably at least see a spot of the original color; at most, you may reveal the whole megaraptor at once."

That would, of course, involve causing great pain and harm to the megaraptor in question, Ollan realized, which was not ideal. He'd been the one to teach Qora the principles of hunting, that it was an exercise in merciful killing. That was something he'd also learned from their papáy long before learning to shoot a crossbow. Unfortunately this would not be a hunt; it would be a battle; and he'd also learned from his military commanders that war was more often than not an exercise in priorities.

"Seldom are there good choices and bad choices," his squad leader had said once. "Just better choices—smarter choices, to be more specific—and worse choices."

Before Ollan could reply to the handler, someone called his name from across the grounds leading up to the paddock.

"Kanchaya!"

Ollan turned to see Kuy and Gorgo, riding together on the back of a—

"What in the Five Terrains …" Ollan whispered.

The bulky club-tail swung behind them as Kuy waved his arms from his place at the front of the saddle—a triceratops saddle, technically, although it had been adjusted to fit the ankylosaur.

"Kanchaya! Look what we got!"

Excusing himself from his discussion with the handler, Ollan hurried out to meet them part way.

When he was within a conversational range, he said, "How did you—"

"It was a long ride." Gorgo dismounted and patted the ankylo's side.

Kuy came down next, wearing dominite around his neck, and gripped the reins, panting. "Snuck her out of her encampment before dawn—the usual—and rode her all the way here. We stayed in the woods as much as we could because obviously this little lady would turn some heads."

"'Little lady …'" Ollan repeated as he observed the dark, female ankylosaur and her extra-thick armor. She blinked her large yellow eyes and opened her beak just enough to emit a docile rumble from her throat. He stroked one of her cheek-horns. "This is incredible. I can't believe you guys did this."

Gorgo shrugged. "We didn't feel the job was done until we'd captured them all."

"All the ones we know about, that is," said Kuy.

Ollan sighed. "Yeah. Well, does she do anything besides

smash walls with that club-tail?"

Her body basically tapered to a cluster of rocks—and in this case, much bigger ones than normal.

"Not really," Kuy told him.

"If anything," Gorgo said, "her features have some drawbacks. She almost lost balance whenever we went up an incline, and she had a hard time if the ground was uneven."

Mentally Ollan filled in the information.

Ankylosaur (Destroyer)
Feature: enlarged club-tail, augmented dermal plate structure
Vulnerability: club-tail size prone to cause balance issues and disorientation on rough terrain

"But Qhapaq Apo doesn't care about that," Kuy said. "He only cares about the destruction her breed can cause."

Ollan continued to stroke the ankylo's horn as she blinked innocently back at him. He imagined what Wayra would think if she were here, seeing this poor creature that was never meant to exist, whose own body—when not in use by the qhapaq for nefarious purposes—would be her downfall. It wasn't fair. It wasn't right. It made him sick.

He looked at his friends with a fire in his chest. "We'll just have to make sure we destroy him first."

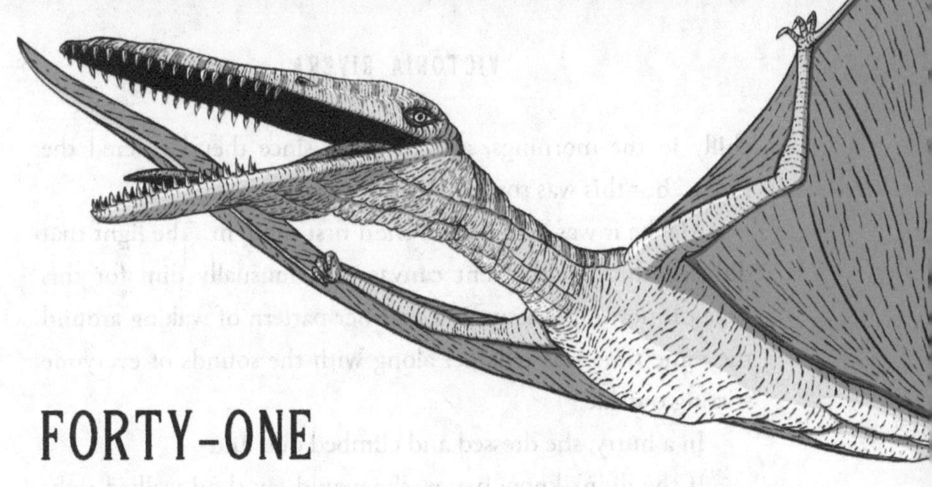

FORTY-ONE

PAQARI WOKE IN KONDOR'S TENT, wrapped in mammoth wool blankets. Kondor was gone. She put her fingers to her lips and smiled.

Had she lost her mind? Perhaps. But did she regret it? Not in the slightest.

She felt the ghosts of his hands on her skin, his mouth on her mouth. Of all the men she'd ever met, she never would have guessed that she would have allowed herself to feel anything for Kondor Sacha.

Did he really feel for her too? Even with what she ought to consider evidence, the thought still baffled her. She'd been wanted her whole life because she'd been a princess, but Kondor had never seemed to care for that; if anything, that had been a point against her. Her beauty was, more than anything, the effects of her title, her refined clothes and accessories, her excessive grooming, and the way she'd always carried herself; without those, she couldn't claim to be much more exquisite than most other young women, a fact she didn't like to admit. But the gladewarden had made her feel beautiful and wanted in entirely new ways.

When the edge of the blanket slid off her shoulder, she suddenly became aware of a new chill in the air. It was always chilly in the mornings, and more so since they'd entered the Pirqas, but this was something else.

Maybe it was earlier than she'd first thought. The light that diffused through the tent canvas was unusually dim for this time of morning—assuming that her pattern of waking around the same time was reliable, along with the sounds of everyone stirring outside.

In a hurry, she dressed and climbed out, and—

If she didn't know better, she would say she'd walked right into a wall of smoke.

But of course it wasn't smoke.

It was cool and moist and it carried the scent of fresh mountain air. The thickness of it, though, caught Paqari off guard.

Her eyes slowly adjusted to the shapes and figures moving through it. The fog clung to everything like dinosaurs to dominite.

And the dinosaurs …

They grunted, crowding one another as half-dressed herders tried to keep them under control while also stumbling into things. Heads or arms or snouts would appear for an instant among the white mist, then disappear again.

Kondor was talking to Chinbo and Suri a few yards away, but Paqari only knew this by sound, not by sight. The princess pushed through the fog to get to him.

He squinted at first until the fog immediately around her wafted slightly at her motion, then one corner of his mouth quirked up, but he seemed to remember that he was still part of a serious conversation and cleared his throat before he continued.

"I'm sure it'll burn off within an hour or so," he told the herders.

"And what are we supposed to do in the meantime?" Chinbo

waved his arms around like he might be able to chase the fog away from him.

"The dinosaurs have no clue what's happening," Suri reasoned. "I don't think we can keep them calm for an hour, assuming the fog doesn't last *longer* than that. They're getting more restless by the minute."

"There's not much we can do," said Kondor. "We just have to wait. Unless you want to take off when we can't see more than two feet in front of us."

Suri huffed. "No ..."

The gladewarden took a deep breath. "We just need to work as a team. We'll gather the herders and divvy up responsibilities. Half of you will focus on keeping the dinosaurs under control, the other half will focus on packing up the equipment. That way we won't have more of a delay than necessary; we'll be ready to go when the fog lifts. While you're all doing that, the princess and I will go check on the mammoth herders and see if they're having the same issue with the mammoths, and afterward we'll fly out and see what the landscape looks like for the next few miles. Maybe it's something we can push out of, if the air doesn't warm up enough before we absolutely need to leave."

"Fine," Chinbo said.

Both herders went to gather their companions.

Kondor turned to Paqari and pulled her up against him, brushing hair away from her eyes and staring into her face with a weary grin. "Good morning."

Paqari felt a flutter in her core. "*Is* it good?" The princess had been optimistic after waking the way she had, but the cloudy sky and seemingly cloudier mountain pass said otherwise.

"It is now." He put a finger to her chin and drew her mouth to his and kissed her slowly, deeply, sending chills down her arms that the weather only made more severe.

Under other circumstances, the princess might have felt self-conscious of a display like this with so many people nearby, but the fog was like a veil around her and Kondor, and anyway, everyone was well occupied.

Touching his forehead to hers, he sighed and said, "Is that all I had to do to get you to stop being so scaly? Kiss you?"

Kiss me till I couldn't see straight, she mentally corrected him. *And a few other things.* Out loud, she said, "I think it had more to do with your behavioral improvements. You've become much more … sufferable."

"Oh, now I'm *sufferable*?"

She scoffed. "Barely."

"Hmmm." He brushed his fingertips along her jaw, making her blush. "That rose color on your cheeks tells a different story, princess."

"It's cold this morning," she told him, "and your body is warm."

"Whatever you say," he murmured against her lips before kissing her again.

ⅅⅅⅅ

After getting the dino herders set up to handle the dinosaurs, and seeing to the mammoth herd (which was somewhat unsettled but not in full upheaval thanks to their dwindling numbers), Paqari flew herself and Kondor out to see the extent of the fog.

She had to land the pteranodon on a very high peak to see above the low clouds, which made the mountaintops look like little islands in a vaporous sea.

"Spirits, it's heavy," Paqari remarked.

They both dismounted and scanned the remainder of the pass, then beyond.

"Well we definitely won't be getting through it any time soon," said Kondor. "It goes clear out to the valley."

Once they could get out of the mountains, it would only be fifty miles to Amachakuna, which seemed such a pitiful distance and yet …

Under perfect conditions, and with a strong push, they might have been able to make it by nightfall. Now, though, who could say? They were supposed to have arrived two days ago, but here they were, still trudging along. They only had thirty mammoths left— one meal's worth of food—aside from the herders' mammoths, and if they didn't arrive at least before meal time tomorrow, they were going to have some very hungry dinosaurs.

The princess wondered if the Tailfolk would be able to abandon their principles when it came to not riding the dinosaurs, because if they could, that was another thirty mammoths and could buy them one more day of travel if need be.

"So we have to try to navigate it." Paqari pursed her lips.

There was no other option. It could take hours to clear, and the herders were going crazy down there. Better to deal with it on the move, and at least let the animals expend their pent-up energy.

"Looks like it."

"It still might burn off, right? By midday, maybe?"

"I should think so," said Kondor.

They would have to wait for the temperature to rise, and in the meantime, they'd try to get a few miles in.

))))

It took three times as long as usual to get everything

packed up and to put the animals in order for departure. The mammoths were more cooperative, but the dinosaurs crowded one another and groaned and moved listlessly. Even the whistles didn't motivate the dinosaurs, but only served to encourage them to coordinate briefly before they settled back into their erratic behaviors.

The herds moved forward inches at a time, it seemed. Every few minutes, something would cause one of the animals to stumble, which would cause a pileup, whose delay would ripple all the way to the back.

Whenever one of the dinosaurs got especially frustrated, it would let out a strange roar—a short burst of sound that didn't vibrate or resonate in the chest cavity so much as it pushed through the nasal passages. Then others would echo the first, and it would become a horrible cacophony. Each type of dinosaur sounded slightly different, but they all expressed themselves similarly, with jaws barely parted and snouts in the air.

"Do they do that back in Murkroot?" Paqari asked Kondor.

"Sometimes. Not this much. But we do get a light fog in the woods now and then, and that's usually what causes them to honk that way. I'm guessing they don't like it. If a little fog in Murkroot distresses them, this must be agony."

A while later, Kondor went up to check on the mammoth herd again, and then one of the dino herders asked Paqari to come back and deal with Grimjaw, who was being "especially difficult."

She wasn't sure what she could do other than let him sniff her and then give him a good scolding that he would most certainly ignore, but she agreed anyway, and steered her walking pteranodon into the fray.

Finding him was the hard part; the herder herself couldn't

get back to him without approaching the wrong dinosaur twice, and forcefully squeezing through because apparently none of the dinosaurs felt safe to resume their usual spacing. But there Grimjaw was on the fringes of the herd, honking and moaning.

Paqari stuck out her arm for him to smell, but he only looked at her and honked again. It was such an odd sound for a creature of his size. If it weren't so loud, it could almost belong to a wild goose. She didn't imagine why the dinosaurs were so averse to fog; this kind, sure, but little forest mists in Murkroot?

What a temperamental oaf.

"What, you don't like me anymore?" she said.

HONK.

The princess frowned up at him. "You know, the herders are just trying to help you. Sure it's not like we're taking you anyplace you might enjoy much, but we've done our best to secure your comfort along the way—and we've let you feast on mammoth meat day after day. You should at least be grateful for that."

HONK.

"Well you don't have to agree with me, but you also don't have to be so—"

"The princess …"

A voice through the fog made her pause and turn her ear. Of course she couldn't see who was talking, and it was several yards back, but she caught a few words between other dinosaur honks.

"… and spent the night in his tent."

Paqari's stomach dropped.

"Which means you owe me forty silvers when we get back to the Tail."

In places where the fog thinned a bit, Paqari saw a flash of Suri's face, and Chinbo's and two other herders' too, but the fog kept wafting back and forth and keeping them mostly obscured—which was a benefit, because it kept her obscured from them as well.

"It was only a matter of time," Suri said.

"Why do you say that?" asked another female herder called Naya.

"That's just how he operates. He loves a challenge—and the princess is definitely a challenge. I heard him say she's like a wild dilophosaur, 'pretty with a frill but vicious and ready to bite.'"

The other herders snickered.

"You mean he likes to 'tame a beast,'" said the male herder riding next to Chinbo.

"Oh yeah," said Chinbo. "Suri, remember that girl from Bramblewood?"

"Yes …"

"She was so scaly. I thought there was no way in the umber underbrush he'd be able to 'tame' that one, but … you saw what happened."

Kondor's words this morning echoed in Paqari's mind. *"Is that all I had to do to get you to stop being so scaly?"*

Was she just some beast of a girl he'd aspired to tame?

No. That was ridiculous. For all his roguish behavior, he'd also been softhearted at times. She shouldn't pay any mind to what the herders said.

Except they'd known him much longer than she had. They'd seen him in Murkroot, knew his reputation and his social history. What did she really know about him?

HONK!

Grimjaw blinked at her as though he'd been trying to make a point, but Paqari couldn't determine what it was, not on a good day and certainly not at this moment when she was beginning to think she'd made a horrible decision under that waterfall.

The herders' conversation soon turned to reminiscing about some previous summer when the apple orchards had been so fruitful there had been a jolly festival and everyone had been drunk on apple wine, and that's when Paqari told Grimjaw she'd had enough and took the pteranodon up for another flight.

Beware of cracks in the facade;
you may not like what lies behind them.

From *The Sky Temple of Punuq*

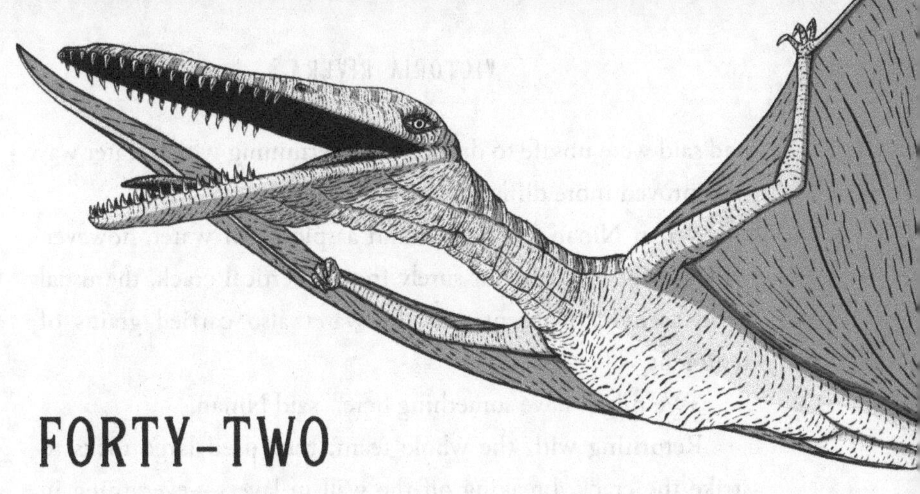

FORTY-TWO

THE SUBSTANTIAL RAINFALL had lasted throughout the night, which had provided a cool, fresh environment for the volcanic destruction team as they'd slept once again near the semi-blocked entrance. Ninan thought Qora would probably consider that a gift from Sky Mother—quite literally, with the sky pouting itself out—but in his mind, there was still the issue of being trapped *inside a volcano vent* that had him stuck in a sour mood.

What kind of game was this, for the goddess to let him and his friends fall into peril, just to taunt them with short stretches of relief when it suited her? More likely it seemed a game of chance, and the odds had not been in their favor this week.

Sometime in the morning, the volcanist had suggested they use rainwater seepage as a clue to find new ways to get out to the flank. Having had hours of rain, the likelihood was high that water would have gotten in through other areas by now, where the volcano's outer layer was weak and thin and easy to break through.

Seepage was, in theory, much easier to locate than *dry* potential weak spots, considering the way the water darkened the rock and gave it a sheen. Except that there had already been plenty of watery trickles and leaks before—the kind the volcanist had said were unsafe to drink—so determining which water was new proved more difficult.

When Ninan and Req found a splotch of water, however, which dripped lazily but surely from a vertical crack, the usual acrid scent was absent and the water also carried grains of sediment.

"We might have something here," said Ninan.

Returning with the whole team, they used large rocks to strike the crack, breaking off the wall in layers—everything in here was layers, it seemed—and slowly releasing more water.

It had been tempting to want to use the strikefangs too, but Ninan also hadn't wanted to dull them, so he'd left them with the team's few supplies at the entrance.

"The water's clean," Ruka confirmed after putting her face next to the trickle and giving it a sniff. Not clean of sediment, of course, but at least it wasn't toxic water suffused with volcanic gases. This was newer, and suffused with opportunity.

"Thank the gods," Wayra breathed.

They wore away several inches of the rock surface thanks to its brittle, flaky composition, and went surprisingly deep in a short amount of time. The crack became a gap and streamed water like a faucet, wetting the wall, the floor, and everyone close to it.

Uturunku pulled back and then struck with great force, causing a new crack to scribble up from the strike point in a curve that continued around until it made a full loop and touched its own tail. The wall creaked and groaned.

Everyone stood back.

And then the water gushed out like the sea through a broken dike.

Water spilled into the vent branch and rose ankle high,

knocking several members off balance.

The hole was now a good two feet in diameter, and only somewhat uneven, gushing as though it had been built up and desperately longing for release.

Ninan crawled against the flow, scrambling for purchase on the jagged rock walls and trying to see where Qora had fallen. Like the rest of the vent, this floor was sloped, forcing the water downward and the team along with it.

Req got a foothold where the branch narrowed, forming a wide stance with one foot tight against each side, and caught the volcanist before she slid past. Wayra, Uturunku, and Miyil forced their way in the opposite direction beyond the gushing hole to slightly higher ground, so that even as the pressure pushed some of the water upward, it wasn't enough to take any of them with it when it flowed back down.

Qora was barely holding on by her fingers. Even the rough texture of the rock wasn't enough to keep a solid grip when it was wet. Her wristbow, which she was still wearing—because of course she was—didn't seem to allow her full movement of her wrist. The hem of her green jacket (now vest) fluttered in the moving water. She gritted her teeth as she dug her fingers into the crumbling rock, fingernails beginning to bleed.

Ninan's heart pounded as he tried to reach out to her while also trying to stop himself from sliding further. In his attempt to angle himself toward her, he got right into the brunt of the flow and shot straight out the vent branch into the main vent.

"Ruck," he said through a pant.

No. He had to remain calm. If he panicked, he was only going to make hasty moves and then he'd really be in trouble.

Thinking quickly, he flipped onto his belly and spread his limbs to give himself more area to snag on the textured rock floor—except that the ground was suddenly slick. Loads of powdery particles—old ash and dust—washed out into the water, forming a slurry. When he tried to grab hold of a rocky protrusion where the wall met the floor, he slipped and went tumbling into the other wall at a diagonal, and met the rock with a crack to the skull.

"Ninan!" Qora called.

He twisted his neck just enough to see through the dizzying blur as she came sliding down behind him.

Spirits, he thought. Had she let go on purpose?

With the ground coated and water running down the incline, it was bad enough, but after multiple nights of poor sleep, and the weariness that came with extreme hunger and thirst—and now with a throbbing pain across the back of his head—there was no getting his wits about him.

It was hard to say how long they had both been sliding, as every second felt like a minute, and every turn in the vent a new opportunity to try and fail at getting a grip on anything. He knew, though, that eventually this vent would end, and when it did—

Oh gods.

The water sloshed up onto the walls, hitting pockets of geothermal heat with a hiss and a sizzle that pushed out small clouds of steam.

Ninan covered his face with his forearm to keep the steam from his eyes.

"Hang on," Qora muttered.

If he'd had any energy for a quip, he would have said, "That's quite literally what I'm trying to do!" but he didn't, and it wasn't the time anyway.

What she wanted him to wait for, he didn't know.

Any chance he'd had to flick his gaze in her direction had been fleeting. The next chance he got, he saw her on her back, making a futile effort to plant the soles of her feet in the slurry, and digging in her vest pocket for—

"Qora—What are you doing?" he demanded.

She snapped a bolt into her wristbow, then aimed at the ceiling—not directly overhead but further along down the vent. Her bolt struck crumbling layers of rock and knocked them down in a shower of flat, jagged fragments. Somehow in her unstable state, she managed to strike again, and again.

She was trying to collapse the damn vent, Ninan realized.

If she hit the right spot, she might make it work, but would it fall before or *after* they reached the breaking point? Or during?

Ninan swallowed.

A successful shot might save them, but it also could compromise the mission. It would be difficult to plant gearbombs near the main shaft if Qora blocked it. On the other hand, that only mattered if they survived this *and* found a way outside.

One problem at a time.

Qora kept shooting, but to no avail. Some shots had no effect at all; others peppered the slurry with more rock; none brought down the ceiling in its entirety, or even in any large part. It was useless.

That was, until Ninan felt the grit against his body. He'd slid right into the small debris, but it seemed to slow him.

Qora shot again, sending down another mess, creating more friction.

With it, Ninan was able to angle himself anew, reach out, and get his hands around a rocky jut.

Then Qora caught onto something too, and clung to it behind him, her feet just inches from his head.

"Now *really* hold on!" she said.

They held on and they waited.

Little by little the rest of the water washed through and beyond as more slurry oozed after it.

From here, they could see down to the main shaft. It was distant and small, but almost a straight shot with hardly a bend in the vent.

Ninan imagined that drop and the heat that could burn him alive before he even reached the bottom—the heat that was already teasing them now, some fifty yards away.

Suddenly he looked up at Qora, who looked back down at him. There was no doubt in his mind they were sharing a thought.

The water would react with that heat. It wasn't a lot, when compared with the full shaft and the volcano's monstrous flanks, but it could expand and create enough pressure to destabilize *something*, couldn't it?

The ground was still slippery with leftover sludge. Ninan and Qora were far down the vent at this point, and on an incline, with all their strength exhausted. There was no way they could sprint up to the entrance—which was still blocked anyway— before disaster struck.

With all his remaining energy, Ninan clambered his way up to Qora. She grasped at him as they both sat up and warily eyed the shaft.

It was yet another moment when Ninan would have to brace himself for death—just in case. He was so tired of it, he didn't even tense; he just laid his head against Qora's, closed his eyes, held his breath, and waited.

A second later, the hiss of steam startled him alert.

Pale clouds billowed up from inside the shaft and seeped into the far end of the vent, wafting slowly through and dissipating as they emerged.

Now that Ninan thought about it, the water had probably never gotten more than halfway down before the heat turned it to vapor. His understanding of the water's volume against that deep, yawning space must have been rather pathetic.

Still, it could have been *him* feeling that direct heat halfway down, and all his internal fluids boiling, so … he considered himself lucky.

He and Qora collapsed against each other, soaked and filthy and half alive, and stayed that way for what felt like a long time.

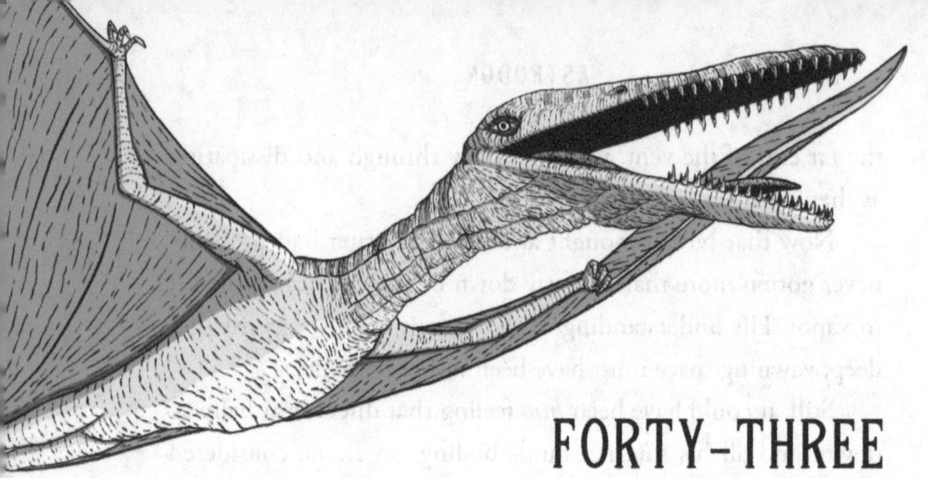

FORTY-THREE

WELL PAST MIDDAY, the sky over the Pirqas remained overcast, and Paqari's most recent survey showed no sign of relief up ahead on the ground. There was no hope to arrive within their original timeframe now, and Paqari had to tell the quya. She sent out a microraptor with her apologies, and said she hoped to arrive soon. In case of other setbacks, she said not to expect them for at least two more days. It was hard to admit, but worst-case scenario they would still arrive with a few days to spare before the cession deadline.

Currently, with the sky blanketed against the full force of the sun, and insufficient heat to burn off the fog, the herds had traveled only a handful of miles from their previous campsite. Hesitant footsteps, clumsy missteps, and continuous pileups kept them slow and only mildly steady.

The next time Paqari landed, Kondor steered his mammoth up to her and said, "Hey, princess. I haven't seen you much today. Everything alright?"

"Everything's fine," she told him. "I've just been trying to keep an eye on any changes in the weather, and I've had to deal with a couple of dinosaurs."

"Grimjaw still giving them trouble back there?"

"Always," Paqari said flatly.

He quirked an eyebrow, but didn't question her further.

She knew her tone was unfriendly, but she couldn't muster the energy to pretend she wasn't feeling that way. Logically, she should just ask Kondor about what she'd overheard, but she needed more time to think, to decide whether it was even worth the trouble to bring it up. What could he possibly say, anyway? If he was the manipulative womanizer the herders had made him out to be, he would likely only deny it. If it wasn't true and he did care about her, he might think her insane for her emotional investment when they'd barely crossed the line into something beyond mutual tolerance *yesterday*.

It was all a muddle in her mind—a stubborn fog, not unlike the one in front of her. And in keeping with that line of thought, she would continue to press on in silence for both, ignoring the pit in her stomach, and despite the fact that everything ahead was painfully unclear.

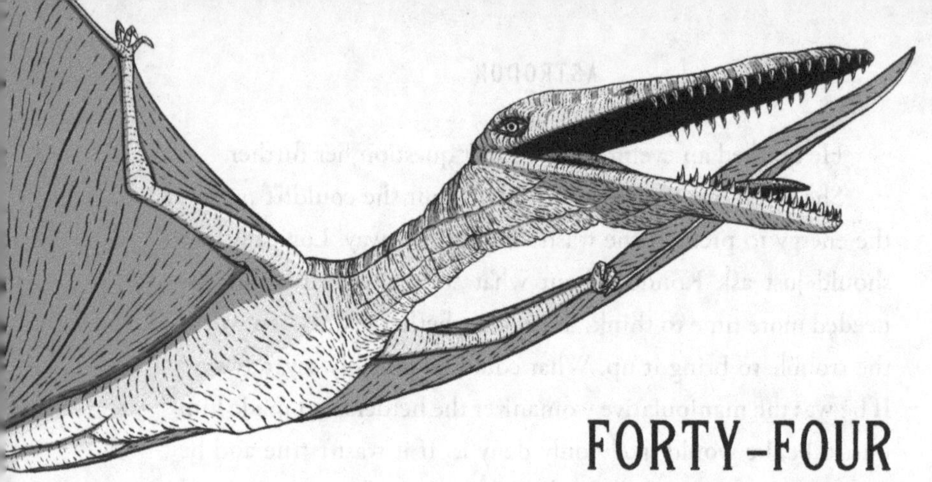

FORTY-FOUR

WHEN THE MESSENGERS ARRIVED, Ollan was ready and waiting. The missives master kept telling him she would be sure to deliver any news of Qora in person once it was received, but Ollan had no patience for that.

A microraptor flew into the loft and landed on its perch with a papyr note rolled up and attached to its leg-wing.

Not bothering to read it herself, the missives master handed it straight to Ollan.

Ollan unfurled it.

The mountain sleeps.

He crumpled the papyr tight in his fist.

"Apologies," said the missives master.

Not knowing what to do with himself for the moment, Ollan took a seat and unfolded the note on one of the tables, flattening out the crinkles he'd made, reading the words over and over. They were supposed to be in code, although he thought it a little too obvious, had it been intercepted by the enemy.

How could it still be "sleeping"? What could the team possibly be waiting on?

Ollan wasn't sure how long he sat there, not ready to put this out of his mind just yet, and knowing he should, but eventually a courier arrived on pteranodonback, after having been approved at the pteriary.

"News from Sumaq," the courier told the missives master. "It's a tough read." He handed over several copies of a Sumaqi chronicle, along with some miscellaneous parcels and a stack of letters tied together.

Perhaps reading about his homeland would take his mind off Qora and the volcano. Once he got his hands on the papyr, though, he instantly regretted it.

THIRD QUYA CAPTURED, UNU ATTEMPTS TO FORCE WITHDRAWAL OF SUMAQI TROOPS

In light of recent events, Quya Illari Kallpa, third quya to Qhapaq Apo, was sent by advisors to the countryside to seek respite from the stresses of the capital. "After the capture and execution of her son, Prince Apo-Kimsa Kallpa, her health has waned," said Mullu Quispe, chief attendant to the qhapaq. During the quya's visit to one of the family's more remote estates, some hundred and fifty miles from Qhusi and less than a hundred miles from the border of Unu, the quya was captured by Unuvian rebels under the direction of Qhapaq Izhi, and is now held hostage at the Ñiqay Arena.

Ollan numbly held the papyr.

Ninan's mother was in danger. But which "Unuvian rebels" were these? Was Qhapaq Izhi involved somehow from this distance—or was it some kind of ruse to implicate the Unuvians and have cause for another attack? Qhapaq Apo had told the public that Izhi had captured and killed Ninan, but of course that wasn't true. Maybe this wasn't either.

And … the Ñiqay Arena? Of all places to set up a holdout, these "rebels" had selected a torofighting venue? It was a place for bloodsport, in which a "fighter" dressed in bright colors would bait a raging torosaurus in some stylized manner, dodging its attacks for the better part of an hour, and attempt to kill it dramatically to entertain the spectators. Fallen torosaurs were then butchered and sold as meat, while the fighter received the horns as a prize.

Rebel leaders have issued their demands: Sumaqi forces have until this Fourthday at noon to withdraw from the Unuvian citadel or Quya Illari will be released into the arena with a torosaurus—to fight to the death.

Swallowing the lump that had formed in his throat, Ollan read that again.

Was this for real?

It didn't make sense that Qhapaq Apo would be behind it if it were. All qhapaqs took a blood oath to protect their wives. Any direct hand Apo might have in his wife's death would mean eternal torment in the afterlife. But how seriously did this qhapaq take that oath? What loopholes might he be able to exploit? Or maybe it was pure lies to incite the people's rage against anyone who opposed the New Empire.

Either way, Ollan had to talk to Izhi about this.

⟫⟫⟫

Bursting in on a meeting between Qhapaq Izhi and Quya Urpi as they spoke in the scriptorium, Ollan uttered a rushed and thoroughly insincere apology, then thrust the chronicle forward. "I need to know how much of this is true."

Ollan had become much too comfortable around royalborns over the past few weeks. While most common citizens held them in high regard and considered them exemplary and wise, Ollan was beginning to understand how very human they were—fallible, fearful, and sometimes quite fragile. He had no issue with the quya, but all he'd learned of Izhi since joining the Razorclaws during the *Velosaura* tour had not impressed him.

Quya Urpi took the chronicle, read it with darting eyes, then handed it to Qhapaq Izhi and clutched the gem around her neck.

The qhapaq took his time to absorb the information. When he finally looked up at Ollan, he said, "I believe it is true—that Quya Illari has been taken to the arena. But it was not done by my hand, nor by any hand that I control. This is Qhapaq Apo's method of punishment for his third wife and son."

"What do you mean?"

Izhi took a deep, shuddering breath. "Apo-Kimsa's mother has been feeding my spy network for years. I suspected it long ago, when all my insiders were too good, too accurate with the information they provided. There had to be someone powerful on the inside helping them, someone closer to the source than others could get. Rumors implied it might be one of Apo's quyas. Many times I feared my operatives were walking into a trap, but each time, they found everything exactly as promised, and I got what I needed. It's how we learned about the beginnings of the Sauroguard, how we were able to locate dominite shipment destinations, and I believe how we learned about the volcano."

"Alright …" said Ollan. "What does that have to do with the abduction? You think Qhapaq Apo discovered the quya's work against him?"

"He must have. High treason is grounds for breaking a blood oath."

"Then why not execute her himself?"

"Qhapaq Apo would not bring such shame upon his household," said Izhi. "Especially not when he could use the quya's treason as an opportunity to rally hatred against me and my Terrain. Don't you see? This way he *does* perform the execution, in a most brutal and degrading manner, while keeping his own hands 'clean' and at the same time making everyone believe he is more justified than ever in uniting our lands under his rule. He'll make a martyr of his wife in the name of Sumaq—and in the process, he will draw out his son."

Ollan clenched his jaw. "You think he's using this as a way to get Ninan to go to him? To …"

"There's no doubt he wants that boy dead." Izhi set the chronicle on Quya Urpi's desk.

"The question now is," Quya Urpi said, "Do we tell him? He'll want to know. He'll want the chance to ensure his mother's safety, but …"

"But once he finds out, he will go to her." Ollan wouldn't try to stop Ninan when the time came, but he also knew what it would mean for Qora to watch Ninan leave for almost certain death. "Not that it matters at the moment. We still haven't had any news of what's happening in Pakasqa. They all should have been back by now."

Keeping his own mind off that subject had been grueling, every minute nagging at his mind. What could have gone wrong? Even without an eruption, there were plenty of other risks and dangers. Or had the team finally completed their task late and departed, and they would arrive at the pteriary any time now?

It had taken all his mental effort to ignore his instinct to get on a pteranodon and fly to Pakasqa. He'd reasoned with himself that he was being paranoid and overprotective, that he needed to let go and trust that Qora would be alright. She was the Raptoriva, for gods' sakes. And yet, he couldn't shake the feeling that something was wrong.

This update from Sumaq only made it worse.

Ninan would want to know about the limited time he had to potentially decide his mother's fate. Qora would need to process the threat as well, and perhaps say her goodbyes.

That was *if* both Qora and Ninan were still alive and unharmed, and if anyone could access them.

The quya came forward and squeezed Ollan's arm. "I think you know what you want to do, Boltmaster Kanchaya."

He did know. He knew it with everything in him.

Maybe it was wrong to run to his sister's side at every hint of trouble, but he didn't care anymore; it wasn't worth the risk to her. She might be fine whether he was there or not, but on the chance that she wasn't … well, he was no longer willing to *take* that chance.

"How soon can I fly out?"

FORTY-FIVE

BEDRAGGLED, QORA AND NINAN EASED back up the vent, where their friends were emerging from the branch.

Ninan only lost his hold because he was reaching out to me, Qora thought.

Because he had thought she was in danger.

Another weakness.

He walked with one hand on the wall for support, and the other on the small of Qora's back.

"Thank the gods you're alright," Wayra said.

Uturunku, Req, Miyil, and Ruka trailed her, splotched with water all over.

Qora hugged Wayra, who then also drew in Ninan.

Req flipped a tuft of wet hair off his face. "Well *that* was horrific …"

They all wearily recounted what had happened, how they had each managed to keep from being washed down, with Ninan's and Qora's story of course being the most eventful, and lamented that the leak had not led to the outside as they'd hoped.

"Good news though," said the volcanist. "Now that the water's drained out, it seems there's a *new* potential outlet."

"What do you mean?" Qora asked.

"We'll show you." Ruka went to get a couple of lanterns

from the supplies at the entrance area, then met back up with everyone in the branch where the water had broken through.

The rough hole gaped before them. Uturunku took one of the lanterns and held it just inside, illuminating an empty chamber with wet, earthen walls and a jet of water streaming down from a rocky ledge above.

"What we thought was a leak coming through just a few feet of earth from the surface," Uturunku explained, "was apparently a large pocket of accumulated groundwater. Probably fed constantly with the regular rains we get, and overfilled enough with the most recent storm to leak through the crack we found earlier. In short, that obviously wasn't the breakthrough we were looking for, but all the water came into this pocket from somewhere, and I think *that* is our way out." He climbed inside, his feet making small splashes in the few inches of water on the ground.

Qora and Ninan both peered in after him.

Uturunku held the lantern higher, up next to the water jet.

"You think *that's* the spot that'll lead to the flank?" said Ninan.

"There's a good chance," said the man. "Seems like yet another collection of water, which must be what filled this one. It's got to be mostly drained by now. I imagine if we wait a while, it'll empty completely."

Everyone else climbed in too. The entry hole was large enough for one person at a time; it required some ducking to fit through, but wasn't too tight a squeeze. Inside, all seven of them could stand upright easily, and even spread out a ways from one another. It was basically the size of a tiny room.

The dark space was damp and stuffy, and it smelled of wet earth and minerals. The walls were a fusion of soil and rock and what looked like the tips of tree roots—which the volcanist said wouldn't likely have spread more than a few feet deep, so this was good news—and formed a sort of rough dome overhead.

"Do you really think the upper chamber is going to finish draining any time soon?" Req eyed the water pouring down.

"There's no way to know for sure," Ruka replied, "but I don't think we should go poking around leaks after what happened last time. We can wait."

Even though Qora wanted nothing more than to break through that rocky soil and get out of here, she knew the volcanist was right. It would be better to spend a few more hours in here, if necessary, and take precautions. Although she wondered if releasing another gush would be so bad from here, as long as they were to stay away from the hole and let all the water flow out of the chamber and down to the main shaft.

She sighed, watching as the jet streamed down and frothed against the water that soaked her boots. The noise was almost soothing, like a cascade—until the slabs above her began to creak and groan.

Qora gazed up at the ledge, then slowly stepped back. "Do you all hear that?"

"Hear what?" said Wayra.

"It sounds almost like …" Qora focused her ears. "Like the rock is …"

"Straining." Ninan took Qora by the arm and pulled her back another step.

Req scanned the entire wall from which the ledge protruded. "If this chamber was full before, then the water itself would have been pushing back on all the walls from the inside—supporting them, in a sense, against any pressure coming from *other* sides."

A fragment of rock broke loose at that moment, from

around the jet, and plopped into the water below. It was a flat piece like others that had broken off in layers throughout the vent. So much of the materials in the lava vent were brittle, Qora thought; if only they were brittle in more convenient places.

"Req is right," said Miyil. "We shouldn't be in here."

"We can wait outside," Uturunku agreed.

A few cracks appeared along the ledge, lengthening in seconds, seeping water.

Two more fragments fell and splashed.

The groan seemed to grow louder, but so did the water as its flow rate increased and as new jets appeared in other places.

Everyone hurried for the exit hole, but as Req approached it, Wayra grabbed the back of his shirt and dragged him aside. Rock spewed with a burst of water—in chunks large enough to have knocked Req unconscious.

Five jets now gushed into the chamber. In seconds, the water level on the ground was up to everyone's knees, and, at first, much of the excess water spilled out into the vent branch. But the original jet broke wide, bringing with it a slew of gritty mud and more chunks of rock from the upper chamber, which began to clog the hole.

Qora's heart seized.

Without a word, the team set to work on moving the rocks to clear the way again—until a jagged slab split from the ledge and sent them all sloshing out of its path before it slammed down.

It wasn't as big as the slabs that had fallen near the vent's entrance, but once again the team was cut off. Once again, there was a sliver of an opening, but not enough to fit a whole body. Another slab broke off somewhere in the middle, although it made no difference except to startle Uturunku and extinguish his lantern. Another lantern remained aflame outside the hole, providing minimal light but keeping them from total darkness.

Despite these large breaks, the water thankfully did not come any faster than what the five rough jets released. The upper "chamber" it seemed was more of a series of channels. Except there was no telling how long those channels ran, or how much water remained in them.

The water could be draining through nearby lava tubes, Qora realized, remembering something the volcanist had been saying on the trek to the vent. Lava from past eruptions would have flowed down the flanks, and then more lava would have flowed over the first flows. The lava on top would have cooled and hardened, while the lava beneath would have remained liquid and carved tubes inside. It wasn't a stretch that some of those tubes might have filled with water and somehow leaked into this area. From what Qora understood, those tubes could be hundreds of feet to miles long. On a volcano this small, it was likely closer to the lower range, but the volume of water contained in the tubes could still be enough to refill this chamber.

Ninan and Qora worked on the slab that blocked the hole, but it was slippery and difficult to get a hold on. The water level rose and flowed over the slab, and the turbulent flow stirred sediment into every crevice.

The others joined in the effort to move the slab but any time their strength was enough to make it budge, it slipped out of someone's grasp and slammed back down.

"Ruck, ruck, *ruck*," Req muttered.

Water continued to spill above the slab and out the exposed area of the hole, but it wasn't pouring out faster than the new water was pouring in. The lantern sat at a high point out in the branch, just out of reach of the water, but the light dimmed significantly with water pushing through the same crevices that had been allowing that light into the chamber.

Eventually the water level rose high enough that any other attempts at dislodging the slab required the team to go fully under water to grasp it, and then it became not only a matter of strength and grip, but also holding one's breath and staying down against the buoyant force. The team members had to take turns, coming up for air in between, but by the time the water was up to their shoulders, it was even more difficult to get down to the slab, everyone was exhausted, and the volcanist said it was probably time to consider other options.

"Like what?" Ninan shouted over the jet noise.

"The outer wall of this chamber already broke once," she offered. "Maybe we can get it to fracture again. In another spot."

Qora and Wayra paddled to stay above water, which now had begun to sweep them off their feet. The volcanist and then the men, who were slightly taller, were still standing as the water rose to their necks, but would soon be in the same position.

Wayra panted. "Say we do manage to break out that way. We'll be washed down the sloped vent again—and this time we might not all be so lucky to survive it."

"It's either that or drown in here, though, isn't it?" said Req. "I'll take my chances."

"We don't have to make a big opening," Qora said. "Just enough to get the water to drain. We can try to avoid being right next to any new holes."

"That's the only option now," said Miyil. "Especially since we're damn near blind."

They all dove to the bottom to find something jagged for striking, and then swam to the wall that separated them from the vent branch. For several minutes, their strikes echoed sharply amid the rushing water, but little by little began to dampen as the walls endured and as the chamber filled and as the air diminished along with Qora's hope of ever seeing the light of day again.

When the water pooled around her neck and she sensed even in darkness that very little open space remained above her head, she felt around for Ninan and laced her fingers through his, and prayed for a miracle.

It was then that Chayaynin came to see that the bands of color—
much like the promise of a better life—had all been an illusion.

Excerpt from "Chayaynin and the Rainbow on the Mountain"

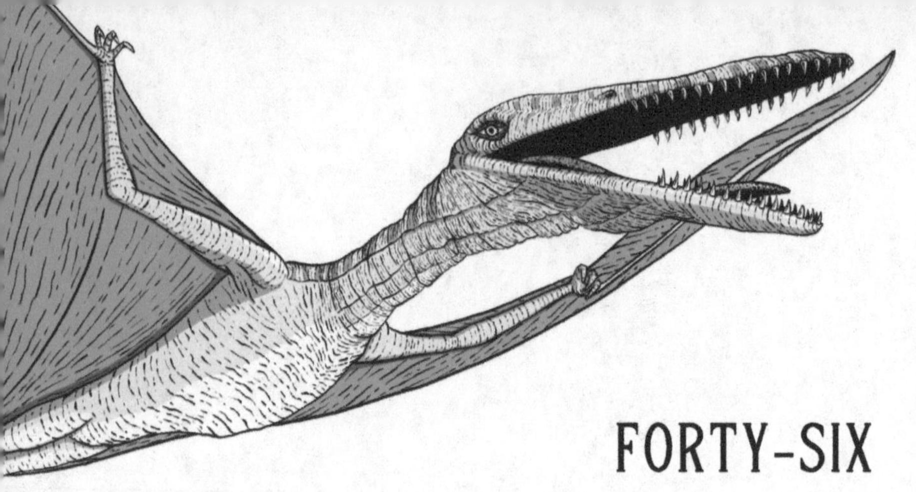

FORTY-SIX

THE WIND COULDN'T CARRY OLLAN and his pteranodon fast enough. He'd temporarily traded his uniform for layman's clothes again (suede riding trousers, steel-toed boots, and a roughspun shirt) and loaded up the pteranodon with all the same equipment he'd used on extraction missions (ropes, grappling hooks, nets, harnesses, tools like sledgehammers and pickaxes, and blades of all sizes from daggers to machetes), along with a few survival supplies (waterskins, dried foods, firestarters, a couple of location-signal firesticks, and a lantern). He wasn't sure what to expect out here and he didn't want to take any chances.

For the last dozen or so miles, the sky had been dark with clouds and drizzling like mad, with rain that only seemed to worsen as Ollan went on. Maybe the mission delay had been weather related, he thought. Not that even the wildest of rainstorms could stop a volcanic eruption, but surely the whole thing might be less effective if the environment were to cool the lava more quickly. Or it could simply be more difficult to coordinate the escape plan in this, while the trees and underbrush whipped in the wind. Were it not for his goggles, the rain would have stung his eyes. It was no time to be moving equipment around on the ground, wrangling pterobeasts, or trying to keep gearbombs from getting wet.

He leaned forward against the pteranodon's neck as they cut through the air. Somehow he'd flown fast enough to make it in only four and a half hours, which was fortunate since sundown would soon be looming. Not that the sun was much help behind the rain clouds, but at least it wasn't pitch black outside.

Izhi had been unable to join him in person for this, as it was unwise to risk his capture by crossing the border with Unu and then into Sumaq. If Unu ever hoped to stand again, it was important to ensure that its leader didn't end up in the hands of the enemy.

The quya had also offered to send a pair of guards in Izhi's stead, but Ollan had insisted that all military operatives remain in Allpa to continue preparations. Even though Ollan no longer cared whether following Qora was irrational, he wasn't going to drag needed defenders along with him.

Ollan followed Izhi's directions to a hideout about two miles from the small volcano, where he met the intelligence team and spent mere seconds on introductions (handing over a document with Izhi's seal to show he wasn't a threat) before launching into a tirade about the lack of communication from their end.

"Apologies, Boltmaster Kanchaya, but we prefer not to send messengers without cause," a female operative explained as she ushered him into the shelter. "For safety reasons."

"'Without cause'?" Ollan pushed up his riding goggles. "Is a full day's delay on a mission like this not cause for concern? And what about the *destruction team's* safety?"

One of the male officers came forward. "We were told that we would receive a message from the team one hour before they went in to place the gearbombs. From there, we were to dispatch a pterobeast for their escape, and prepare for eruption. If the team were to force eruption successfully and escape, there would be no need to send word back to Allpa, as the team would return and deliver the news in person. If, after a successful eruption, none were to make it out alive, then we were to send word to Allpa. Or if we were to see no eruption *after* receiving word ourselves from the team that they had entered, we were to send word that perhaps something had gone wrong in detonating the gearbombs. But since we received no message that the team was preparing to enter, we waited, as instructed."

"They have a guide who can warn them against dangers in the area," the first operative reminded him. "They also have dominite to protect against wild reptiles, and they have a volcanist with them to make sure they can navigate the interior of the volcano with few issues. Knowing all that, and with the rainstorm, we had no reason to think anything was amiss."

"Besides," said the second operative, "it's risky to send out microraptors from here, in case any of Qhapaq Apo's personnel spots them. Surely you understand that."

Ollan was familiar with messenger flyer risks. If any of the Sumaqis working at Pakasqa saw a microraptor flying out, and it hadn't come from their own missives master, it would arouse suspicion of spies in the area. It was difficult to know who might be watching and when. Still, when it came to his loved ones, those risks seemed minimal.

"Yes, I understand." Ollan exhaled sharply. "Anyway, that's not important right now, I guess. What I really need is for you to tell me how to get to the vent."

A third operative produced a crude map and handed it over. "You'll need to fly low and stop here." He put his finger to a point on the lower third of a drawing of the volcano's flanks. "Follow this path on foot until you reach the bunker, here. Miyil is already at the bunker, so I'm afraid you won't have anyone to lead you through the forest, but if you stick to the trail and don't touch anything, you should be fine. Our contact, Uturunku, will guide you the rest of the way."

Shaking his head, Ollan said, "That will take too long. I want to go straight to the vent."

"Again," said the second operative, "it's risky to have flyers in the open out here. It's best to go on foot. It takes less than two hours."

Two hours …

That was all Ollan heard. And while two hours was short compared to the four and a half hours he'd just flown, and the two days he'd waited to find out whether his sister and his friends were alright, he couldn't fathom spending another minute not knowing what was going on.

"I appreciate your concern but I can't do that." Ollan took the map and stormed back out into the rain to mount his pteranodon.

"Boltmaster, I would strongly discourage you from—"

But Ollan was already up and gone.

He flew as low as he could, to the point that his pteranodon tried to resist for fear of skidding over the treetops, but he pushed on, following the map as the corners of the papyr fluttered in the wind and threatened to disintegrate in the rainwater. It only took a couple of minutes to reach the upper flank where the vent was marked, and the second he landed, he understood why there had been no message to the spies.

Sliding down from the saddle, Ollan nearly fell to his knees looking at the pile of rubble collapsed in the entrance. His pulse pounded in his ears.

"Gods above ..." he rasped as he stumbled forward. "Qora?! Qora!"

He waited a few beats.

No reply.

Don't panic, he thought. The team might have found another way out, or they might have even just been sheltering a bit deeper inside.

Except something told him it couldn't be that easy.

He tried calling his sister's name a few more times, but his gut pushed him to take action instead.

One glance at the equipment on his pteranodon's back and he knew what to do.

The broken vent slabs had jagged ends that stuck out from the pile in a few places. With a setup of ropes and hooks, he got the ropes around both ends of the biggest slab and tightened them. Then he harnessed that to the pteranodon and commanded it to fly out.

Of course it met resistance after just a few flaps of its wings, but already the slab began to budge.

"Come on," he encouraged the flyer.

It tried to fly again but again the weight held it back. The pteranodon screeched its frustration.

"I know, I know ..." said Ollan. "Just a little more. Please. You can do it."

When the pteranodon refused to keep up what must have seemed like a futile effort or perhaps a torturous exercise, Ollan pulled out his dominite and held it in front of the pteranodon's beak. Instantly the pteranodon fixated on the purple crystal. Ollan flung it high and the pteranodon followed it up, up, out, and—

Rock ground against rock as the slab slid out and everything on top tumbled down in its place, some of the smaller slabs breaking in half. The motion and sound startled both Ollan and the pteranodon and the crystal plopped into the wet grass. Smaller flyers and land reptiles scurried toward it, but Ollan snatched it up and tucked it away.

He and the pteranodon had created enough of an opening for him to crawl inside the vent now. Not knowing what else he might encounter, or if anything else would fall and he'd need to break his way back out, he took a full pack of tools and supplies with him. There would hopefully be time to clear the rest of the rubble later, but for now, he had to make sure the team was still alive.

Past the rubble, the entryway was littered with miscellaneous items: a couple of empty waterskins, a notebook and charcoal, Ninan's strikefangs, Qora's jacket sleeves, and the bones of small reptiles with the meat picked clean off.

With lantern alight, Ollan crept into the vent, peering into the deep throat of the sleeping giant. Only maybe ten yards in, the color of the ground darkened significantly. Although the rain had already streaked the ground in tiny streams—a lot of which collected in a carved-out trough, it was minimal compared to the large amounts of water that swirled down the tunnels' slope from a gap in the wall up ahead.

No—not a gap. It was an offshoot. The whole system seemed to branch out from the center like veins.

At the far end of the section of the vent that he could see before the split, faint vapors floated through. He wasn't completely sure how things worked in here, but he knew this tunnel must lead to the center, and that the center of a volcano might be hot even before it erupted. Water and heat would produce steam, which meant that this water was flowing toward that heat. And if water could end up down there ... then so could the people he cared about.

His chest rose and fell in a persistent rhythm he couldn't control. His skin felt clammy, and he didn't know whether it was the temperature that seemed to get more severe the deeper he went, or the fact that he was imagining Qora, Wayra, Req, and Ninan in those depths, facing heat no human was ever meant to withstand.

It was only as he veered into the branch that the pressure in his chest lessened—when he spotted a lantern flickering weakly above the source of the water. He ran to it, feet splattering the stream that washed down. Aside from this, there were no other signs of human activity ... until a weak thud came from the wall of rock.

A few seconds later he heard it again.

The water poured out from a two-foot-wide hole in the wall, most of which was blocked with another rock slab, several other large rocks, and thick clay riddled with gravel. Small cracks had formed in various places on the wall as well, with water trickling through in slow motion.

He didn't understand how it was possible, or by what logic this had happened, but he knew he had to break this thing open.

Ollan dropped his pack of supplies and rifled through until he found his pickaxe, along with a grappling hook and rope.

Lest any sudden gush of water try to wash him down the slope—because the risk of this was all too obvious by the water's current path—he tied one end of the rope around his waist, then tossed the end with the grappling hook deeper into the branch, where the open space curved around a corner and the rock stuck out. The hook caught on and he pulled the rope snug to test its hold. He set both lanterns on protruding ledges up out of the way. Then he positioned himself in front of the biggest crack he could find ... and swung.

FORTY-SEVEN

QORA HAD TO TILT HER FACE UP so she could breathe. Water filled her ears and crawled up her cheeks. Her nose grazed the ceiling.

"I love you, Qora," Ninan choked out in the darkness.

"I love you." Tears swam down against the rising water around her eyes.

Her words felt like they had come from somewhere else, somewhere outside her body.

For all the times she'd already faced death, none had felt as certain as this. Before, there had always at least been somewhere to run, or hide. She'd usually had a weapon, if nothing other than her flimsy fists. This time, though, her wristbow would do no good. The rocky walls that contained her would only bloody her fists should she try to employ them against it. She could not hide from the water because it had already filled most of the empty space in this chamber and would soon fill every cavity of her body, most notably her lungs. It was an entirely different kind of monster, which could not be distracted or manipulated or harmed to keep it at bay. She couldn't run because her legs would not touch the ground, and she couldn't swim away because eventually she would have to come up for air and in a few seconds there would be none.

She had finally run out of ideas—out of resources and options. There was no silver lining in the clouds that thundered outside and dumped the rain that had overwhelmed this place. Her mamáy had taught her that there was always a way.

Even grass has a blade.

A cutting edge could be found anywhere, if only she would look around.

Glowing mushrooms could light the way when she had nothing to burn for light. A pterodactyl nest could carry her down the river like a raft. The sinking sand that had almost swallowed Ninan could also swallow a monstrous spinosaur's feet to keep it from pursuing her. Compies seeking shelter could feed her and her friends when they were suffering from hunger inside an old lava vent. Rain could bring clean water for drinking, and brittle rock could be easily chiseled into a trough to hold it.

But what did she have now?

At least the water keeps me afloat, she thought.

She sobbed at those words as she turned them over in her mind. *"At least the water keeps me afloat"?* Suddenly she caught a glimpse of what Ninan must have felt whenever she spoke of Sky Mother's gifts. What a ridiculous way to look at a dire situation. Of course it was lucky that a human body could float in water—and yes the team had remained alive longer than if they had each been so dense as to sink to the bottom of the cavern instead of rising to the top as the water did. But what good was that extra time if they were only going to die in the end? What good was that wonder of nature if circumstances prevented it from helping?

Ninan was right. Life, at least in this moment, felt like a cruel joke. How ironic that she had been allowed to survive so many things—public execution at the Tail, terminonatators at sea, a battle in the Aquchay, everything during the Venture, and multiple setbacks here in this lava vent—only to die in dark waters having accomplished nothing.

Without the eruption, Qhapaq Apo would continue to breed new and more horrifying reptile species. No matter the outcome of the pending battle, the qhapaq would strike again, and eventually he would be unstoppable.

What was the purpose of it all? Why had she been made to endure for all these years if it only amounted to a sad, pathetic death?

She shivered and gasped and continued to strike the wall with her jagged rock, her strength waning. She imagined water trickling through the cracks on the other side—cracks that she and her friends had made by striking again and again even though it was hopeless. That's all it had ever been, hadn't it? Cracks. Tiny fractures. Leaks that gently striped the rocky outer layer on the way down but ultimately made no difference. Meanwhile the qhapaq was flooding Runaqa and drowning anyone who got in his way.

Qora understood now.

Just before the water came up over her mouth, she sucked in what she assumed would be her last breath and held it tight in her lungs. Her thundering heart was already depleting that breath, using it to keep her resistant muscles rigid, to power her arm when she struck the wall yet again—because if nothing else she wouldn't simply submit to this death.

Another strike.

Another.

Another.

When she pulled back her arm once more, she faltered mid-strike, as panic prompted her to inhale even though she knew she couldn't. She let go of the rock.

Preparing for the pain that would come when she could no longer control her body's impulses, a *crack* rippled through the water.

Her eyes flew open, despite the fact that the water would sting and the darkness wouldn't allow her to see. But somehow she *did* see.

Because it had been so dark, the only thing visible was the faint glow that split down the wall like lightning.

Hands grabbed at her, and she grabbed back, not knowing whether it was Wayra or Req or Ninan, but wanting to cling to all of them, and to Ninan the most.

The crack widened and pieces of rock broke loose in the water's force.

Qora tilted her face up again, and just when she thought her lungs might drag in a breathful of water no matter how she resisted, a rush swept past her legs. She managed to endure for a few more seconds, and then she found the thinnest slice of air above the water level.

She gasped, practically kissing the ceiling, then coughed and sputtered.

Had someone on the team finally been able to break through? Or could it have been someone on the outside? Izhi's operatives might have found the delayed eruption suspicious and come to investigate. But finding Qora and her friends among all the branches of the vent would have been difficult.

Over the next minute, the water continued to flow out and away, draining from below. The water level fell below Qora's ears and she heard others taking huge gulps of air. Somehow she was able to identify Ninan by his gasp alone, and reached out to him. He pulled her to him. His cold, wet cheek met hers, and she grasped his shirt to keep him close.

"Wayra?" she said when she found the strength. "Req? Uturunku?"

A new hole burst open a few feet from the original, about half the size but it seemed to drain dozens of gallons of water every second.

That most definitely could not have been the result of anything she or the other team members had done.

Qora looked around, finding only Ninan, Req, Uturunku, and Miyil.

"Where's Wayra?" she asked. "And Ruka?"

The others swam around trying to find them, diving back down, feeling their way through the water. More light leaked in through the new breaks.

Water continued to flow in from the upper ledge, although it appeared to have slowed.

"Work on draining the water faster," Uturunku told Qora and Ninan. "The rest of us will look for the others."

Nodding, Qora swam with Ninan to get close to the wall. They kicked the edges of the openings, pried away brittle rock layers with their bare hands, exerted any force possible to weaken the barrier.

The water drained faster and faster, overcoming the inflow.

"I've got her!" Req called. "I found Wayra!"

"Is she alright?" Qora asked.

In partial darkness, Req panted and swam with uncoordinated splashing movements. "I'm not sure yet."

"Ruka's here too." Uturunku held up the volcanist from behind, supporting her by her underarms.

"I'll grab her legs," Miyil offered.

The water level was low enough now to swim toward the new opening. With desperate strokes the men approached it.

Someone on the outside continued to work. Metal rang out against the rock.

Ninan urged Qora through the opening first, then Uturunku and the team leader with the volcanist and Wayra.

Delirious, Qora stumbled out to see her savior.

She'd scarcely caught a glimpse of him before he violently threw his arms around her and tightened his grip.

"Oh gods, Qora …" he breathed. "Gods in the High World. I almost … I almost didn't …"

Her brother was warm and strong, and she leaned on him to keep her balance. Tears poured from her eyes like the water that poured from the chamber. "Ollan …"

She couldn't believe he had come for her. How had he known? Of course Izhi must have told him where she'd gone, but Ollan had said he wouldn't follow her anymore. Whatever had made him change his mind, she was eternally grateful.

He'd brought dozens of tools, and he'd anchored himself somehow. It seemed he'd thought of everything.

"I should have come sooner." He dropped his pickaxe and pulled back to look at her face, framing it with his hands. "I'm sorry. I'm so sorry. I was in my head, thinking about how you've survived without me all these years, who you're becoming, all that you've accomplished. I just thought you didn't need me anymore, and—"

Qora curled her hands around his wrists. "Ollan. I will always … need you. *Always*."

His jaw flexed and his eyes welled and he pulled her into another tight embrace. "I'll never not be there again. I swear it."

By now Uturunku and the team leader had hoisted the volcanist out, and then came Req and Ninan with Wayra. Neither of the women were conscious.

Qora's heart sank. She looked at her brother, who now seemed to be clinging to *her* for balance, as he stared at Wayra's lifeless form.

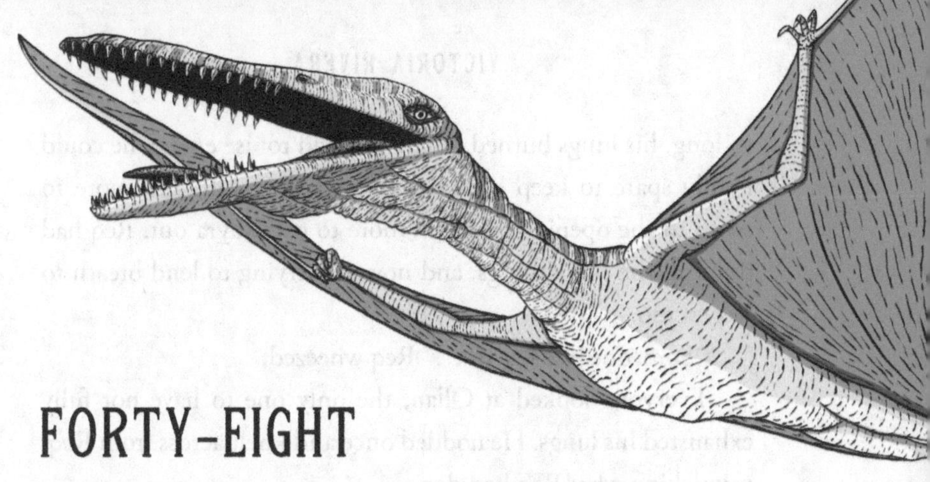

FORTY-EIGHT

NINAN HELPED SET WAYRA DOWN on the part of the slope that was relatively dry, above where all the breaks were leaking.

The volcanist abruptly sat and coughed out a lungful of fluid, while Uturunku and the team leader supported her and patted her back.

Wayra, however, remained still, her complexion bluish.

Ollan approached her and swallowed hard. "Is she …"

Req shook his head to indicate that he didn't know, but immediately knelt beside her and put his ear to her chest. "Heart's still beating. Slow, but it's there." Then he pinched her nose closed and put his lips to her mouth.

It was a technique Ninan had only seen once before in person, something called "lending breath" that was documented in some of the old texts as a time-tested practice. He figured that blowing air into someone's body was a logical way to displace fluids that had gone to the wrong place.

Wayra's chest rose when Req exhaled, then fell when he paused to take a breath and repeat the action. He did it three times, taking deep breaths in between so he could deliver as much air to his friend as possible, but before he made another attempt, he shook his head again. "I can't. I'm … I'm …"

Ninan knew the feeling. After holding his own breath for

441

so long, his lungs burned. Then he'd had to use energy he could hardly spare to keep breaking through the wall, and more to swim to the opening, and still more to get Wayra out. Req had done all the same things, and now was trying to lend breath to Wayra too.

"Someone else has to ..." Req wheezed.

Everyone looked at Ollan, the only one to have not fully exhausted his lungs. He nodded once and knelt across from Req, mimicking what Req had done.

Slowly he breathed into Wayra. He trembled over her, but he didn't stop. He kept a rhythm with good strong breaths and finally, before he could finish another, Wayra's diaphragm spasmed.

Ollan froze.

A gurgle erupted from Wayra's throat. Req angled her shoulders and helped turn her head so she could cough out the water, and a few coughs later she opened her eyes and stared blearily up at everyone.

She fixated on Ollan. "You ... you saved ... us."

Ollan didn't say anything; he just stared back at her with dumbfounded relief.

Ninan relaxed his muscles now that Wayra was alright. Qora was kneeling now too, hugging Wayra at an awkward angle.

This vent was a death trap, and Ninan didn't know how many more of these kinds of scares he could take.

He did know, however, that he couldn't allow the rift between him and Qora to grow any wider. The hopelessness he'd felt inside that chamber, grasping for her and wishing they hadn't been about to end things that way ... it scared him to his core.

When Qora released Wayra, Ninan held Qora to his chest and cradled her head. Nothing else mattered but the fact that they were alive and together. He wouldn't forget that ever again.

⟫⟫⟫

It must have taken half an hour, but the water slowed enough to walk through without getting washed down to the main vent, and everyone carefully made their way up to the entrance which, by the miracle of Ollan's arrival, was open. It was mostly dark outside now, and still raining, but the storm had calmed some, and the team hiked back down to Uturunku's bunker where they dried off and feasted on beans, troodon jerky, and fruit leather.

When everyone was finished eating, Ollan took something out of his pack—a chronicle papyr—cleared his throat and said, "Although I did come here to make sure you were all okay, I also have some … unfortunate news. Horrific news, to be frank." He turned to Ninan. "I didn't share it sooner because I wanted you to have the chance to catch your breath and rest a moment before I turned your whole world upside down again. But … there's something you need to know."

Ninan's pulse felt sluggish all of a sudden as he accepted the papyr with both hands.

"It's your mother," Ollan said gravely.

Scanning the papyr, Ninan felt like he was in that chamber again, with water creeping up to replace all the air around him.

… captured by Unuvian rebels …

… held hostage at the Ñiqay Arena …

… until this Fourthday at noon …

… released into the arena …

… fight to the death.

His chest rose and fell with increasing speed. He let the papyr slide from his lap to the floor, and then he stood and picked up

443

his chair and slammed it against the floor over and over until it splintered and the legs broke off and pieces of wood shot out in all directions. In the blur of his periphery, he was vaguely aware that everyone else had either flinched or gone very rigid while he lost his mind, but all he could really think about was that the horrors would never end.

Ollan opened his mouth like he was about to add some explanation to the news, but stopped, apparently thinking better of it.

It didn't matter, because Ninan already knew what he was going to say: Izhi and the Unuvians had nothing to do with this. Ninan's father was the one responsible, and the whole thing was a ploy to hurt Ninan and lure him to the execution he'd escaped weeks earlier, to end him once and for all.

Panting, he pinched his eyes closed to fight the sting behind them but it only served to force out the tears he could no longer hold back.

Qora, having picked up the discarded papyr and read over its message, went to him and held him as he choked on his sobs.

The others passed the papyr around to understand Ninan's reaction, and all were silent for a long while.

Ninan climbed out of the bunker and surfaced in the darkened forest, where the air was still moist but the rain had stopped. Mosquitoes had emerged again but kept clear of him, despite his enticing lantern light, because Uturunku had sprayed the whole team and Ollan with kukuella the second they'd returned. "The rain keeps these ones from biting," the older man had said, "but they'll be abundant afterward."

Tugging at his hair, Ninan set down his lantern and paced the clearing.

"Fourthday at noon" was tomorrow.

He should have known something like this was coming. It was the only leverage Qhapaq Apo really had left over him, since Ninan had removed his friends from Thak, and since Qora and her family had fled, and Paqari and the Razorclaws were safe in Allpa.

Mamáy, he thought.

It had been easier to take for granted the laws that protected his mother than to consider what sinister plan the qhapaq might weave to thwart those laws. Even without the blood oath, it would have been disgraceful and politically unfavorable for a qhapaq to execute one of his own quyas—but as far as anyone would ever know, it would be the Unuvians that were to blame for her death.

This was a direct call to Ninan to come forward. If he didn't, the consequence would be as promised: a fight to the death, which the quya would most certainly lose. Only trained fighters could overcome a torosaur in that arena—and sometimes, not even *they* could. Plenty of torofights ended in the torosaur's victory; that was the sport of it, not knowing if the fighter would survive. For how the whole industry treated those ceratopsian beasts, Ninan always thought the fighters *deserved* death when they got it … but his sweet mother certainly did not.

A moment later, Qora climbed out of the bunker to join him. Her eyes were rimmed red and brimming.

"I'm so sorry," she said.

They held each other for a long time before he finally said, "At daybreak, I have to go."

She nodded into his chest. "I know."

"And you know you can't come with me."

With tear-streaked cheeks, she looked up at him and nodded again and whispered, "'Leverage for villains.'"

"I shouldn't have said that. You're not a weakness. You've been my strength more times than I can count. You *are* my strength, in every moment, in everything I do now. But that doesn't change the fact that if I lose you, I will be half alive for as long as I manage to live thereafter."

"You know I won't go back to Allpa where it's safe, though," she said. "I have to stay here. I have to make sure this place burns."

"Yes. You do. Because my girl won't go down unless it's in actual flames." He kissed her forcefully, as if to impress upon her the force of his love for her, and she tangled her fingers into the hair at the back of his head and urged him closer as if to dare him to test how much she could take.

When they broke apart, he held her face and said, "I know I don't have a lot of faith, but … I have faith in *you*. When the gods didn't seem to hear my prayers, you did. As much as I want to beg you to hide until this war is over, I know you won't listen, and part of the reason I love you is because of that—because you never listen to *anyone* when they tell you not to fight. If you had, you wouldn't be here with me now. But please, for the love of those gods you believe in, survive. I need you to survive again, so that I can come back to find you, and keep you."

Qora hesitated and her chin trembled. "I don't know what I believe anymore. I used to be able to see the good in things, the usefulness, or find it if I looked hard enough. But when we almost drowned, there was nothing. Nothing I could do, not a glimmer of hope. If it hadn't been for Ollan …"

"Maybe that's where the real miracles are: in the people we love—or the people we don't know yet that we're *going* to love—who give us a chance. You certainly gave me one. And then at least a dozen more."

She seemed to consider this, then tearily said, "I'm sorry I started a fight with you here."

"Hey …" Ninan brushed her fresh tears away and released a few of his own. "What is it people say? 'I would rather fight with you than make love to anyone else'?"

She nodded. "Fighting each other is such a waste. I think our weapons would be put to better use against the New Empire."

Ninan kissed her one last time. "I agree."

"I'd lost my rhythm," she told him, "but then I simply followed the beat of my own heart."

Excerpt from *Upon the Moors of Scalebane*

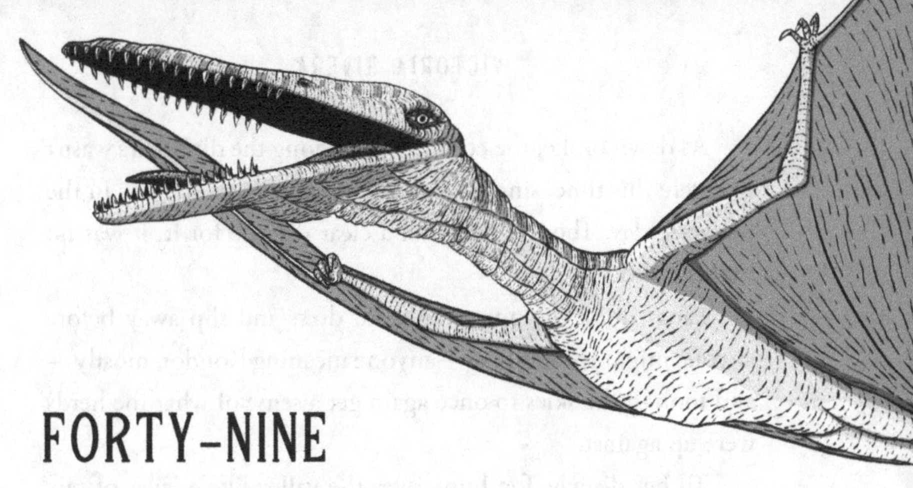

FORTY-NINE

THE FOG PERSISTED THROUGH THE NIGHT and then into the next morning. Paqari didn't even have to leave her tent to know; she could feel its chill and smell the humidity. For a moment she lay in her sleep sack, alone, dreading what came next.

Setting up camp last night with limited vision had been much worse than taking it down in the morning fog before that, but somehow everyone had managed. After the day they'd had trying to wrangle the dinosaurs under these unfortunate conditions, the herders had happily gone to rest with no attempt at evening social activity.

Feeding had been an eerie setup, with the dinosaurs prowling through the fog like ghouls of the night. The poor mammoths had been caught half blind, but the dinosaurs had been able to smell them well enough in the obscurity to attack with ease and precision.

If the group could make it to Amachakuna before the next feeding—which wasn't likely—there would be no need to witness a hunt like that again, but under these circumstances, the herders would have to give up their mounts this very evening, and either run alongside the dinosaurs tomorrow, or try to slow the dinosaurs' pace to that of a comfortable human walk. Or give up and adjust the mammoth saddles to fit the precious, godly reptiles.

As dawn broke, the commotion among the dinosaurs wasn't so severe this time, since they had already spent a full day in the fog yesterday. Though they had a clear distaste for it, it was no longer a shock.

Paqari took the opportunity to dress and slip away before anyone might speak to her—anyone meaning Kondor, mostly—and took to the skies to once again get a sense of what the herds were up against.

To her dismay, fog hung over the valley like a layer of raw white alpaca fiber, with hardly a gap to be seen.

So much for hoping it would burn off.

The princess stalled for a bit, not ready to return, but the altitude was beginning to make her lightheaded and she would eventually need to take this forecast to the others.

Back on the ground, the herders were mostly packed, and she found her own tent rolled up with her belongings put away for loading.

Kondor turned as she approached, about to heft the packs onto his own mammoth.

Her pulse kicked up. "Thank you …" she said. "You didn't have to do that."

"It's my pleasure. How'd you sleep?"

"Well enough," she told him. "If I've learned anything from joining the resistance against Qhapaq Apo—and, by extension, against my own father—it's that it's easy to wear out, but at least exhaustion can sometimes quiet the mind. Otherwise I might have been up all night worrying about today, which perhaps I should have been, because we're no better off than before."

"No?"

She shook her head. "It's going to be heavy fog for another ten miles at least."

The gladewarden took a breath and held it for a moment before release.

"I would hope this is the last of it," she added, "but it's still overcast so there's no way to guess whether it will warm up. Looks like another difficult day."

He nodded. "We'll do what we have to." Then he flinched in her direction, like he might have had the instinct to reach out to her, but stopped.

Her tone and her composure since the previous afternoon had been warning enough, she supposed, even though she'd done her best not to be outright cold to him.

"Like a wild dilophosaur, 'pretty with a frill but vicious and ready to bite.'"

Again, she had no clue what to say. One night together didn't mean anything, especially not to men like the one his herder friends had described. She supposed she felt foolish, having left his tent feeling like she'd been walking on a cloud—especially when clouds could hang low, and hide the reality of things.

They parted to tell the herders what the next several miles would look like, and then took their places at the head of the dinosaur herd. The mammoth herders, with no other mammoths to tend now but the ones they were riding, merged and rode among everyone else.

Kondor didn't try to ride close to Paqari. Most of the time there were several dinosaurs between them, and a herder now and then, especially as some rode up to make conversation with him. Other herders came to apprise Paqari of how things were going at the rear—not well, usually—but slowed and fell back as soon as possible.

Even Grimjaw and the other usual crew seemed to be keeping their distance, like they knew the princess was in a mood.

Except she was always in a mood, wasn't she? At least according to most people, even those who claimed to like her.

"Is that all I had to do to get you to stop being so scaly?"

Scaly. Dramatic. Difficult.

Unbridled, her father would have said.

Somehow this was different, though. Her usual demeanor was a mask, because it was easier to go about her life that way. Now she actually was upset.

She considered every interaction she'd had with the gladewarden, but each one looked different depending on the mental lens she used. On one hand, she could see how he might have been someone who had simply misjudged her at first, then in secret begun to like her while refusing to admit it even to himself, teased her to keep up the ruse, but then had been kind when it really mattered, and finally had given up and given in to his feelings. On the other hand, she could see a man who might have considered her a challenge and a conquest from the very beginning, trying to get a rise out of her at every opportunity and then acting chivalrous now and then to confuse her emotions, until he had finally gotten what he'd wanted, who would continue to play the game until he grew tired of her.

Gods, I'm so stupid, she thought. This was why she kept most people at arm's length.

Coming out of the mountains had finally given the herd the freedom to sprawl, but not without losing formation. The dinosaurs seemed to welcome the space, but then set about with that strange honking noise again, this time with much more urgency, and then began to meander like they'd been affected by some disease of the brain.

Herders blew their whistles but the dinosaurs ignored them completely.

Progressing in any kind of straightforward way became impossible.

Paqari walked her pteranodon quickly around one outer edge of the group to drive the dinosaurs back to the middle in the traditional way, urging the herders to do the same, until she and everyone on mammoths bordered them and had to physically interfere to deter stragglers.

At this point, the honking was so loud and persistent that the whistles were inaudible. Paqari, Kondor, and the herders couldn't keep track of all the dinosaurs, and those in rough formation seemed to be dwindling.

"We're losing some of them!" Kondor said.

Meanwhile the honks echoed and the visible dinosaurs tried to break loose and follow the sound.

"Ugh," Paqari grunted. "They're like a bunch of demented geese!"

Geese birds were rare, with long necks, webbed feet, and broad bills instead of beaks, but their migrations were notable across the continent, particularly because they would honk much like this, in a cacophonous chorus that alerted anyone below to their passing. It was some means of communication that—

The princess gasped and halted her pteranodon, closing her eyes to listen to the sound.

It started at the front, then moved backward through the herd almost like a wave.

Of course it was communication—that had been obvious— but it wasn't a communication of distress or frustration or fear. It was purposeful. Paqari herself had been the one to bring up the dinosaurs' shared ancestry with birds, but Kondor's comment that the dinosaurs in Murkroot always responded to mists and fog this way had led her to think their sounds were just a reaction.

When their view was hazy, they had a deeply rooted instinct to make others aware of their position on the landscape—an instinct that grew stronger out here.

The echo of their sound could also give them a sense of their environment by the way its ripples reflected and returned to their ears, hinting at rocky outcrops or trees or open air.

Kondor rode to Paqari's side. "What's wrong? Are you alright?"

Paqari opened her eyes. "We can use this …"

"What do you mean?"

"They know what to do and we're not letting them do it." She nudged her pteranodon to walk again, explaining her thinking as Kondor trailed her.

Meanwhile the herders scrambled to keep as many dinosaurs together as possible around them.

"Okay," Kondor said when she'd finished, "so if we let them communicate, they'll make a new formation and stay together, but … how do they know who to follow?"

"They're always willing to follow Grimjaw. If we can direct him, he'll direct the others."

"And he'll follow you," Kondor said.

Paqari grimaced. "I'm not so sure. The last couple of days he hasn't been very responsive to me. None of them have. They don't get close, they don't smell me, they just—"

"Give me your hand."

"What?"

Kondor leaned over in his mammoth's saddle and reached out to her.

She furrowed her brow but reached back, barely able to clasp his hand across the distance between the enormous beasts they both rode. If they hadn't been caught in a frenzy of reptiles right now, his touch might have made her skin burn with longing.

He strained to bring her hand up to his nose and inhaled. "You don't smell like orchids today."

"So?"

"I'm guessing you didn't yesterday either. After the night before, rinsing off in the cavern pool, and then you didn't get ready in your own tent the next morning"—he seemed to hesitate at that thought, but continued—"which means you didn't—"

"I didn't use the scent the quya gave me," she realized. "And today I left early to survey before I even thought of it. You'd packed my things by the time I got back. Is that … Is that really why the dinosaurs kept bothering me?"

"Only one way to find out."

Once she was scented again, she and Kondor set off to find Grimjaw, who was still near the front and honking like mad amid angry herders—some of whom hadn't quite given up on their whistles either.

Paqari rode ahead of the giganotosaur, even commanding the pteranodon to fly low circles around him so that he could catch her scent, which she had applied heavily.

He went quiet, following her movement with his snout.

"That's it," said the princess. "Come on you big brute." With his full attention, she turned to fly straight, commanding slow wingflaps and keeping just above Grimjaw's head to lead him on.

Grimjaw resumed honking, but Kondor relayed the message to the herders to cease any whistling that might distract the other dinosaurs.

As soon as the dinosaurs were allowed to honk an intentional chorus, those that had wandered began to return to the herd. Despite the visual impairment, they moved in unison, keeping reasonable spaces between themselves. All mammoth riders kept out of their midst to allow them to do this, now riding side by side in a line ahead of Grimjaw.

In no time, the group picked up speed and went forward like the army they were meant to be.

A while after, Paqari was able to land and walk the pteranodon. Grimjaw nuzzled her shoulder and, although Paqari's instinct was to shove him off, she forced herself to reach back and pat his snout. He growled gently … then honked right in her ear.

"Ugh!" She cringed and swatted at him.

Then she happened to glance at Kondor—who had apparently been watching her like he was suppressing a laugh—and felt a pang in her chest.

What had she been thinking, letting herself fall for a strange man from a strange land? Her decisions had been wild and impulsive lately.

She couldn't wait to get to the capital and be done with this.

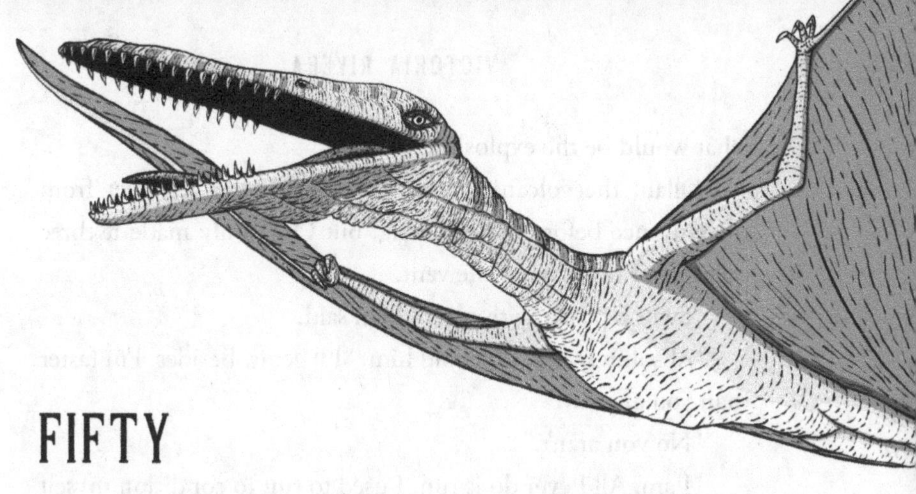

FIFTY

OLLAN HAD REPLACED NINAN on the destruction team, although he certainly was no replacement for Ninan when it came to Qora. While Ollan treasured his ability to be there for his sister when she needed him, he knew what Ninan meant to her too. He'd done his best to comfort her after Ninan had left, and stood with her as she'd watched him fly out until he was too far to see anymore.

Now it was time to get back to the business of erupting the volcano. The volcanist had gone over everything the team had learned before Ollan's arrival so that he would be up to speed. This time they wouldn't go in without a supply of heavy tools—the kinds that could smash through rock walls if need be—as well as survival supplies, and they would always leave at least one member outside to go for help in the event of another cave-in.

They had cleared all the rubble from the entrance and spent the morning running drills with an empty gearbomb. Everyone had placed their bombs in one of the designated locations throughout the vent system, then Uturunku wound up what was essentially their timer and shouted for them to go. They sprinted out of their respective places and into the main vent, up the incline and toward the breach in the flank. Uturunku rang a handbell as soon as the empty bomb's gears clicked to signal what would be the explosion.

Ollan, the volcanist, and Wayra made it a few feet from the entrance before the bell rang, but Qora only made it three quarters of the way up the vent.

"Switch places with me," Ollan said.

"Absolutely not," she told him. "I'll get it. Besides, I'm faster than you anyway."

"No you aren't."

"I am. All I ever do is run. I used to run to condition myself for hunting in case I had to outrun any reptiles I couldn't hit. I ran with Sakay to train for the Venture—and had to pass a speed test to even qualify. I ran *during* the Venture, constantly. I'm always running for my life. I'm a runner, Ollan."

He couldn't argue with that. Although he'd had to complete a series of physical tests for his military training, he hadn't done anything like that while he'd been away. Now it was all flyer riding and medium-paced treks. His legs might be longer than his sister's but he carried more weight, and she was right, he wasn't conditioned.

"Fine. We'll keep drilling."

They drilled until everyone could get out with no more than two or three paces to the exit, but no one was able to make it all the way, and Qora still came up last. Ruka assured them, however, that there should be several seconds to spare before the explosions triggered a full eruption, and Miyil suggested they call it good and not wear themselves out before the actual event. Secretly, Ollan already knew that he was going to wait for Qora, because no way would he come out of this vent without her. But that was a problem for later.

As they returned to the bunker for a break, and to get some food and additional water, Ollan heard voices coming through the trees. For a moment he worried someone from Qhapaq Apo's facility had discovered the team's location, but Gorgo's surly baritone put him immediately at ease. He hurried a few yards down the trail and found Kuy and Gorgo worn and sweating and making their way toward him.

"Kanchaya!" said Gorgo with his arms wide.

Ollan embraced both men in turn with heavy back claps, then wiped his forehead with his wrist, still rather sweaty himself. "What are you doing here?"

"We heard about the mission," said Kuy, "and we were *quite* offended that you didn't invite us along."

"I didn't exactly know what I was going to find here," Ollan admitted. "I didn't want to drag anyone else into it."

Gorgo huffed. "After what we saw on the way up the mountain, I don't blame you. This place feels like a stretch of the Grave World."

Thankfully Ollan hadn't had to witness many of the absurdities the others had described. Having bypassed the depths of the forest and gone straight to the vent, and then only having taken the shorter of the two hikes back and forth from the bunker, the worst of it was below him.

"It's not as bad up here," he told his friends, gesturing to the clearing. "Are you hungry? We were just about to eat. I won't lie to you and say the food is good, but … it's food."

Qora, Wayra, and Req were thrilled to see the two missing Razorclaws.

Uturunku welcomed them and explained everything that had been going on in the microclimate (building on what they'd already heard and seen) and described the plan. "If the two of you would like to help, we could use you to wrangle our transportation off the flank. Once we send word to Qhapaq

Izhi's operatives, they'll dispatch a pterobeast to the vent—but we were just discussing how the explosions might scare it off. Obviously we already planned to be out by that time, but if we are somehow delayed, the last thing we need is to be trapped here without a flyer."

"I thought you were worried about rebel flyers being spotted," Kuy asked.

Uturunku nodded. "Aside from Ollan's arrival—which is the only reason we're all alive right now—it will be the only other exposure that we'll risk. But considering the fact that anyone who might see us will be dead mere minutes afterward, it shouldn't be a problem."

"And Kuy and I will be able to retrieve our individual flyers from Izhi's operatives afterward?" Gorgo said.

"Yes," Uturunku told him. "The pterobeast will take us to a safety point, and from there we can assess what everyone will do next."

Some of the logistics were tricky, but ultimately the plan was ready to put into action. Now it was just a matter of *mental* preparation.

Ollan hadn't been able to look Wayra in the eye and hold her gaze for more than a second or two since he and Req had revived her. She'd thanked them both in that emotional moment, of course, and embraced them, but beyond that, Ollan wasn't sure what to say. At the time, he had only cared for her survival; he hadn't been thinking about the physical contact between them. Now, though, with the passage of time, he remembered his mouth on her mouth, the odd feeling of sharing a breath, and it stirred something inside him.

There had been a few opportunities during preparations when she had been alone, near him; his gearbomb station was closer to hers than to the others, and the team had been spread out enough on treks between the bunker and the vent for him to walk next to her out of earshot of anyone else. He'd thought to try and have a word with her then, but every time, he'd ended up either making some remark about the heat or the smell, or simply making a commiserating face at her. Part of it was because he sensed there would only be time to *start* a conversation and not finish it, and part of it was the fact that he couldn't get his hands to stop shaking.

It wasn't until they had both gone to refill everyone's waterskins (from barrels in the clearing that had collected rain) that it seemed they had some actual privacy.

They dunked the waterskins in silence at first, waiting for all the air bubbles to flow out as the water replaced them, then each took a drink. After Wayra wiped her mouth, Ollan said, "Are you doing alright?"

Wayra sighed. "Well … my throat is sore, and my chest still aches. I'll probably keep having nightmares of drowning, but all things considered, I'm fine." She paled a little, then tucked a strand of hair behind one ear. "Thanks to you."

"You really scared me," he admitted.

She chewed her lip. "I did?"

He nodded. "I mean, obviously I wasn't as scared as you were, but …"

She smiled weakly, although Ollan wasn't sure how she managed *any* kind of smile after near death.

"But, you did sort of … die."

"It certainly felt like it." Wayra exhaled sharply.

They stared at each other for a moment, because she seemed to be waiting for him to say something else and he seemed to have forgotten how to speak.

When he did manage something, it was: "Listen, I … don't really know how to say this." He dragged his fingers through his hair, pulse racing. "And I don't really know who I am right now—I'm still figuring out where I fit in my new life—so I'm not exactly in a position to be making statements, but … one thing I do know is that I … really … like you."

After a pensive beat, she just said, "Oh."

Ollan's first reaction was to be deterred by the short syllable she'd uttered, but he knew if he didn't keep going, he might never find the courage to say it again. "Not because of what happened to you—that wasn't what made me realize. I'd actually been hoping to see you when I got back to Qhispina House, after the last extraction, but the handlers told me you came here. To be clear, that's not the reason *I* came here, either. I mean, partly it was. But I had a feeling something was wrong, and I was worried about Qora and—"

Wayra took both his hands in hers—not in a romantic way, Ollan knew that, only in that comforting way she had about her—and held them firm. It didn't mean anything; it was no indication that she was taking this information well, or that she felt the same; she would have done it even (and perhaps especially) if her next words were going to be "I'm sorry but I just don't think of you like that."

Again, ignoring the potential rejection, he went on. "What I'm trying to say is, it's all terrible timing, and I don't know what will happen, but if we make it out of this alive—the volcano, the war, everything—you're one of the people I want to … spend more time with. Like I said, I'm figuring out where I fit, and I guess … I guess I would like to figure that out … with you. If that's something you're interested in."

She bit her lip, then inhaled.

Before she could reply, footsteps startled Ollan and he withdrew his hands and stepped back. Not because he was embarrassed; more so because he didn't want to embarrass Wayra, in case she had been preparing to tell him no and would then have to explain the awkward position to the other Razorclaws.

Gorgo came into the clearing and looked from Ollan to the Wayra, then raised a brow. Regardless of the fact that they stood at least two feet apart, he still said, "Sorry … Am I interrupting something?"

Ollan shook his head, perhaps with too much vigor. "Not at all."

"Okay," Gorgo replied. "Well, the old man says we're about ready. We deploy in thirty minutes."

Both Ollan and Wayra nodded.

Once Gorgo had stepped away, Ollan said, "We can talk about this later."

He couldn't help but feel as though Wayra seemed relieved. Meanwhile, he wondered if there would even *be* a "later."

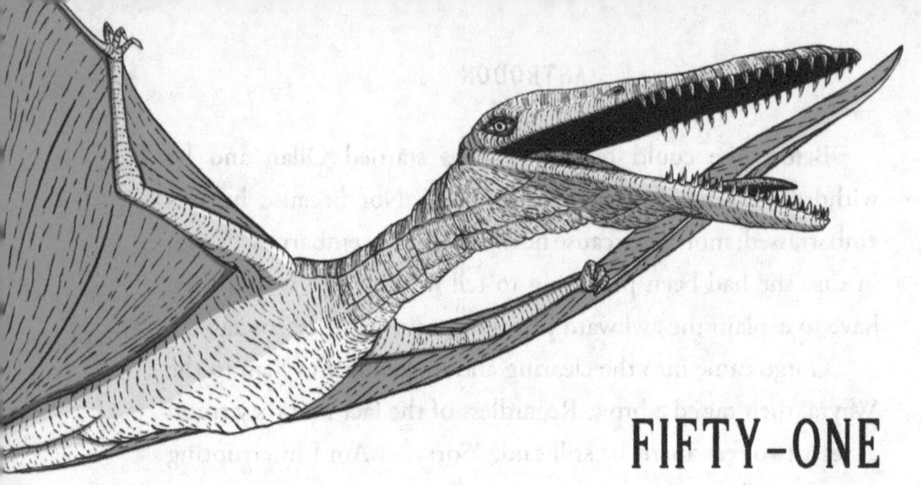

FIFTY-ONE

NINAN WASN'T SURE YET how he planned to stay alive when he knew he was about to walk into a trap. Having taken Ollan's pteranodon at dawn, he'd flown straight to the city of Ñiqay where the famed arena sat like a bowl on the land, and followed instructions from Izhi (relayed by Ollan) to the outlet of a secret passage one mile short of there. It came out through a craggy hill surrounded by a sprawl of trees, fifty-six flaps northwest of the lake as promised.

With barely more than an hour to spare before noon, he tethered the pteranodon and observed the rocky face among the plants, searching for a chiseled symbol. The Unuvian triceratops-and-shield emblem was subtle, but it marked the entrance and, upon closer inspection, revealed the fine seam that divided the facade from what lay behind.

With a push on the emblem, a panel of the rock began to revolve around a vertical axis—what appeared to be a greased metal bar affixed to the center of the panel (from the inside) that continued into the rock above as well as into the rock below—until it opened into a deep recess.

Before entering, Ninan donned a hooded cloak that Uturunku had given him from the bunker, and slipped on his strikefangs in case he encountered someone unexpectedly.

Upon entry, he found a collection of torches, one of which he took and lit for guidance. The flickering light revealed a stone-laden way through, with stones lining the walls and ceiling while limestone plaster paved the path underfoot.

The mile walk, at a jog, took Ninan approximately twelve minutes, and then he came to a point where the passage ended with another bar that ran from floor to ceiling, visually dividing a panel that was twice as wide as the first, and wooden. Pushing it would lead into the underground level of the arena, where he had no clue what to expect.

Slowly, he applied force to one side, feeling it grind slightly as one seam became a gap. He listened for a moment, but heard nothing, then continued until there was just enough of an opening to let himself through, and closed the wall behind him. Stepping back and raising the torch to it, he couldn't help but admire the expert drystone masonry, which had affixed an arrangement of cut stones to the wooden panel in such a way as to perfectly conceal it from the side he was on now. Those stones fit against the ones around them with no indication of anything amiss in the dry joints. And here, there was no emblem to give it away either; he would have to remember the exact stones that would open the passage. Ninan committed the pattern to memory for when it was time to leave, certain he wouldn't find it again on a whim. It was no wonder Qhapaq Izhi had been able to escape his citadel, with secret passages like these that even Qhapaq Apo's thorough military officers would have had to check every stone to find.

Under an arena, however, it might not even occur to them to look for one. After all, this wasn't a royalborn residence and stronghold; it was a place for public entertainment, even if Qhapaq Izhi did occasionally attend the torofights.

Further in, the darkness persisted, with only a shaft of light on the far side where a stairwell led to the main level. The whole place stank of dino ruck, even though there were no torosaurs down here; it wasn't torofighting season, but this was where torosaurs would be kept when it was—while they each waited for their turn in the ring. There must have been at least *one* torosaur, however, if Ninan's father intended to use it for a brutal execution. But where was it now?

Ninan swallowed as he held the torch over the empty corrals. One gate hung open, with its straw disturbed and a pile of ruck in the corner.

He hurried upward, peering out when he reached the top. A few guards chatted along the corridor that curved for several hundred yards around the outer perimeter of the stands. The guards were dressed like Unuvians but their posture and inflections suggested Sumaqi military training.

Carefully, Ninan continued up the stairwell that led to the mid-range seating vomitories, and made it to the third level where he would be able to see well into the arena but also where no guards appeared to be stationed. Which made sense, as they were probably expecting him to either show up on the main level or from the air on a flyer. He imagined other guards currently manning the high galleries, looking outward.

Peering out of the vomitory, he looked down the raked seating and scanned the ring below. His gaze immediately fell to a figure at the center—a woman in a red dress, wringing her hands.

His fists curled instinctively, one firming his grip on the torch he still held (because he hadn't known what to do with it just yet). The strikefangs coming off his knuckles protruded past his cloak sleeves like claws poised for attack. His breaths quickened.

Ruck—she's really here.

Despite his mother's fearful stance, she stared westward with a look of defiance on her face.

The arena had four prominent points around the ring, one for each compass direction. Ninan stood somewhere near the south point. A large portcullis marked the west point, its latticed iron drop-gate serving as the barrier between torosaur and torofighter.

Ninan took a shuddering breath at the sight of the horned reptile that waited for release. It was ceratopsian, with a stubbed horn behind its beak, and two forward-arching longhorns—one above each eye. Its color and pattern were hard to see behind the iron lattice but from here it appeared to have an overall reddish-orange tone with black horns and accents. Like most torosaurs, it also had eyespots—splotch patterns that gave it the appearance of giant eyes on its frill—the way some butterflies did on their wings.

Directly above the east point, a covered balcony extended at the perfect height for viewing the fight—not too high, but elevated from the lowborns—with seats fit for a qhapaq.

And there on that balcony stood Ninan's father.

Qhapaq Apo wasn't dressed like a qhapaq—not for this display in which he wanted to frame Unu, should any rebels happen to fly over—but rather in all black, and he waited as though he were standing on one of his own balconies, rather than preparing for the murder of one of his wives.

Ninan made note of every gate around the ring, every vomitory, every staff entry point. If he could sneak down to one of those gates (which only opened from the outside, should a fighter suddenly lose their nerve and try to leave before giving everyone a good show) and subtly get his mother's attention, and if she could run like a gallimimus, maybe he could help her escape. Unfortunately he wouldn't be able to try this until the torosaur was already charging her, otherwise it would be far too obvious from his father's vantage point. The qhapaq would notice regardless, but hopefully not until it was too late— not until Ninan and his mother were already racing for the underground passage.

He eased back into the vomitory and back down the stairwell, then took the stairs at a jog. There were still several minutes before his father set the torosaur loose, and he wondered whether he would be able to hide that long without—

"It's him!" one of the guards shouted.

Ruck.

As Ninan crossed the landing and barreled around to the next staircase, he stepped into view for an instant.

Of course his first thought was to run, but … for what? This place was a circle. All corridors led to the others. If he ran for the main exit, there would be nothing but open landscape outside and nowhere to hide. If he hid somewhere inside, they would eventually find him. The secret passage wasn't an option because he didn't want its location compromised when it was his and his mother's only safe way out. Besides, he would have to come back eventually; he wasn't going to just give up and leave his mother here.

No, all he could do was stand and fight.

Thankfully, fighting was one of the things he did best.

And now he knew what to do with the torch.

When the first guard approached, Ninan thrust the torch forward.

The guard grunted and tried to avoid the flame but it quickly latched onto his clothes once the burning oils transferred.

A second and third guard came to aid the first as he flailed, but Ninan attacked them in turn, dropping the torch and slashing with his strikefangs. The teeth cut through the guards' false uniforms and left deep stripe wounds along their ribs. He avoided any fatal punctures but didn't hesitate to stab those teeth into the second guard's thigh. The third he simply handled with a clinch and multiple knee strikes.

But then a whole horde of guards came at him from behind and he only managed to deter the first two before the rest overwhelmed him.

Once they had drawn their blades, Ninan knew it was over. There were too many.

They stripped him of his strikefangs.

A pair of them manhandled him up the stairs while the rest followed. In minutes they reached the balcony where they forced him to his knees in front of his father.

"Good work," the qhapaq told them. He glared down at Ninan. "How nice of you to arrive early, Apo-Kimsa—although I half expected you yesterday."

"I was unavoidably detained," Ninan bit out. It was only the thought of Pakasqa burning to ash that gave him any sense of satisfaction in this moment.

"Well, now that you're here, I suppose there's no need to wait. Let's go ahead and get started."

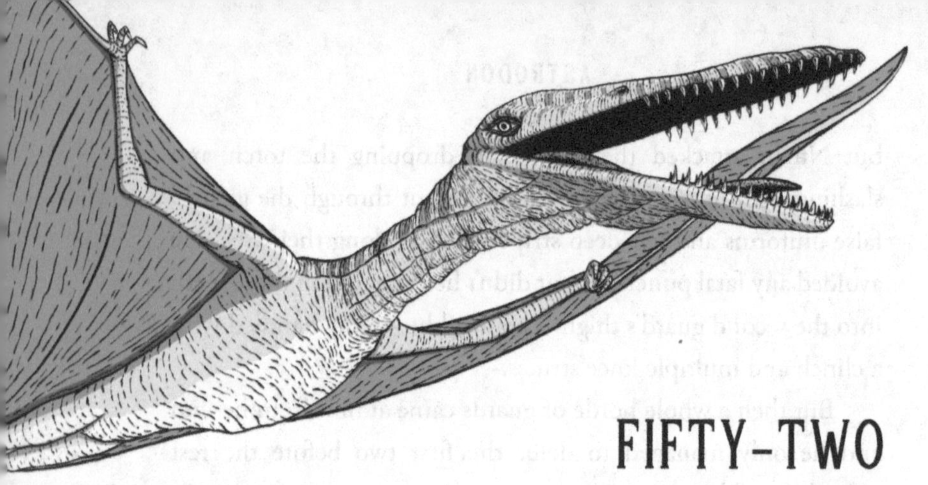

FIFTY-TWO

TWO GUARDS HELD NINAN IN PLACE while another forced his head forward. A few more waited behind, blades drawn. He wondered if yet another might come and force his eyelids open, lest he try to keep them shut when his mother faced the deadly torosaur.

This whole display was a tradition of the Kastillans that some cities in the Terrains had decided to continue, but it was rooted in an even more ancient practice, Ninan had once learned, which sent criminals, traitors, and outcasts to a violent battle with beasts or sometimes with other social outcasts.

He wasn't sure whether it was fair for criminals; perhaps it would depend on what they'd done to end up there. But it certainly was no death for the woman who had borne him.

"You may not care what suffering I inflict upon you," said the qhapaq, "but I know what I do to *her* will harm you in ways I never could."

Leverage for villains.

Although his mother stood still, the movement of the skirts of her dress in the breeze was enough to make the torosaur eagerly scrape its forefeet across the ground behind the portcullis.

The red color was one of warning in nature, a threat that had been reinforced in the torosaur's mind since it had been a hatchling bred specifically for this sport. Not even torofighters actually *wore* the color, though; they held a banner which they could conceal and reveal as needed, whose movement they could control.

"Your oath to her means nothing?" Ninan asked.

"I spilled my blood to her on the day we took the marriage vows," said the qhapaq. "Vows she broke when she fed terrenal secrets to my enemies. Now she must make a blood sacrifice to atone for her sins—and perhaps the gods will have mercy upon her soul in the Grave World."

In Ninan's periphery, one of the guards inspected the strikefangs—even tried one on, flexing to test the feel of it.

How will I get to my mother now? Ninan thought as he watched his father signal to a pair of operatives on the main level.

The operatives signaled their understanding and headed for the staff access point to control the portcullis.

Ninan couldn't breathe. What was he going to do? Even if he could get down from here, he wouldn't make it to the ring in time to stop the release of the torosaur. Should he try, though? Would it accomplish anything?

If only he could fly. The most direct path to his mother was a leap off of this balcony, bypassing the tier of seats below and crossing the dirt to where she waited. Ideally he would have never taken the secret passage but rather arrived on pteranodon, dropped in to grab her, and fled. He glanced at the guards on the high platforms, though, with their crossbows in position (probably in case any of his friends had ideas about swooping in to save him like Paqari had at the citadel) and knew his decision had been the better of two evils.

Except it certainly didn't feel like it at the moment.

The balcony wasn't that high, he supposed. Nothing compared to the one at the Unuvian citadel's main keep. This one was situated directly on top of another vomitory, and he estimated the drop to be only eight to ten feet high, although it seemed much more severe because of the vertical distance down to the ring itself.

Now that he considered it, the guards that held him by the arms kept pressure entirely from behind—because that's the direction he would be expected to go, were he to try and get out of their grasp. And behind him was also where the *other* guards stood, along with his father.

Biting his inner cheek, he eyed the drop again.

There were too many armed guards here on the balcony to fight off, but maybe he only had to worry about the ones that touched him directly. One on either side, and the other with his clammy hands on the back of Ninan's head.

A clang of metal made him focus straight ahead anyway, without anyone insisting on it. Gateway chains groaned as the guards reeled them in. The portcullis creaked. The torosaur snorted and pawed, kicking up dust in anticipation.

It was the worst moment for it, but Ninan froze. He couldn't make himself move. Suddenly he doubted himself, his plan. If he moved too soon, it might not work; if he moved too late, the torosaur would tear across the arena before he could do anything.

He flinched as the torosaur shot out before the portcullis seemed to have opened enough to allow it, metal slamming back down right after.

The quya ran, unfastening her dress as she went. She let the red material fall off the underdress beneath, and practically leapt out of it. To Ninan's shock, the torosaur went for the heap of fabric first, while his mother veered sharply out of the torosaur's path.

Not wasting another second, Ninan twisted his body to break out of one guard's grip, then thrust his fist at the other. He threw an elbow back at the first guard's nose with such force he made it crack, and caught a spray of blood just before he threw an uppercut at the guard facing him and a cross-body punch at the last. By the time the remaining guards mobilized, Ninan had leapt off the balcony.

The ground came up at him faster than he'd hoped. Before he could drop to a roll, pain shot up his legs like his shin bones had been split with an axe. As he rolled to try and shift the impact, something snapped on his right side and he tumbled heavily until he stopped on his back.

"Agh!" He clutched his ribs and coughed, inciting a new jolt of pain.

Guards shouted from above and called to guards on other levels.

Ninan forced himself onto hands and knees, wincing, and then got to his feet. The pain in his shins, at least, began to subside to a throb, but each step seemed to slow the process.

He saw his mother pick up two handfuls of dust and fling it at the torosaur's face. The torosaur snorted and screeched, but slowed at the visual impairment, allowing the quya to gain some distance. Meanwhile, Ninan staggered deeper into the vomitory and broke into a painful run through the curved corridor, knowing the guards would be ready to block him at the stairwell between the vomitory and the balcony.

But the guards would also be expecting him to go to the main level so he could access the ring.

Remembering the corrals in the underground level, he found a different stairwell and raced downward.

Guard boots struck the floor and echoed all throughout the arena, but Ninan didn't stop. The faster he went, the harder he breathed—and every breath was agony. He had to apply a certain amount of pressure to his ribs to counter the pressure from within whenever his lungs expanded.

Ninan took the final step down the stairwell, feeling like he might collapse, and ducked around the corner just as guards ran past at the top. For a few seconds he kept still and waited. When the corridor above was quiet again, he continued through the underground corridor to the west point, where it sloped to form a ramp that led up to the portcullis.

The guards that had raised the portcullis were gone, probably trying to intercept him somewhere on the upper levels.

Beyond the lattice of metal, Ninan's mother stood in the torosaur's direct path as it thundered toward her from only yards away.

"Mamáy—no!" Ninan cried.

At the last second she made a sharp turn and sprinted opposite the torosaur's movement. This technique was used by torofighters regularly, exploiting the fact that torosaurs tended to charge in a direct path with no deviation. Perhaps with enough warning, a torosaur might be able to swerve, but not on the spur of the moment.

Ninan muttered "Spirits …" through his teeth as he hurried to the portcullis winch. Unfortunately this was a two-person job, and right now he was at about half strength even for one. But he gripped it and gave it all he had.

The wheel barely moved. The mechanisms creaked. He whimpered as the pain in his ribs threatened to rip him in half.

Little by little, the wheel began to turn with a heavy groan, winding the long chain and lifting the portcullis from the ground.

The quya was already heading this direction. She would see it.

Everyone else would too—but Ninan couldn't worry about that right now; he just had to get his mother out of there.

"Gagh!" he screamed as he reeled the chain and raised the portcullis another two inches at a pace that made him long for death.

A trail of dust followed the quya, who came for the portcullis with what could only have been blind faith. She wouldn't know why it was lifting, or who was behind it, but it was her only way out.

Ninan managed to make eight or nine inches of space under the portcullis before any guards realized what was happening. His screams certainly did nothing to avoid attention, but it couldn't be helped. Whatever had happened to his ribs after the jump seemed to quadruple in intensity while he kept control of the winch. Tears streamed down his cheeks and sweat dripped from his hairline, but his mother was almost there.

And so was the torosaur.

It focused its direct-path charge on the quya again.

Ten inches.

Ninan tensed every muscle he had, and pressed his elbows against himself to fight the pain. He cried out once more.

Eleven inches.

His mother's footsteps went *pat-pat-pat-pat* on the dirt.

The torosaur's feet went *thud-thud, thud-thud, thud-thud* behind her.

Still eleven inches.

The torosaur was closing in.

Please, gods, Ninan thought with no actual expectation that any god would hear him.

Twelve inches.

Flattening herself, the quya wriggled under the portcullis, its sharp spikes tearing her underdress at her back.

Her last foot came under just before the torosaur approached.

Ninan dropped the gate and heaved the quya up as the torosaur slammed into the portcullis, horns coming through the gaps in the lattice and its head bending the metal. The torosaur roared and stamped.

"Apo-Kimsa …" the quya choked out.

"We have to go," he told her through an equally choked breath.

They hurried down the ramp and through the underground corridor. Ninan's muscles burned and his side throbbed like a war drum, but compared to what he'd just been doing, it felt almost blissful.

"How did you get in?" the quya asked while they ran.

"Qhapaq Izhi told me about a secret passage. That's how we'll get out. It's undetectable; my father won't even know to have the guards look for it."

They raced around the next curve toward the corrals, no doubt with guards headed down to them this very second.

"Are you alright?" Ninan asked when he had a second to glimpse her wild hair and the blood and dirt on her underdress. She was barefoot, too. A royalborn and a quya, but Qhapaq Apo had left her like *this*.

"All things considered, yes," she replied. "But your father's cruelty knows no bounds. His intention was for you to watch me die today, and then he was planning to take you straight to Allpa, where he would force you to watch him overthrow the last independent Terrain—before he killed you."

Slowing at the information, Ninan said, "Today? He's going to attack Allpa *today*?"

Four days still remained until the cession deadline.

"First thing tomorrow. He has everything in motion," his mother told him. "He'll justify it with more lies. I'm so sorry."

Gods, where did it stop? This man would destroy every last good thing in Runaqa.

When they reached the wall where the passage was hidden, Ninan stopped and embraced his mother—a woman forced to obey royalborn men her entire life, who had then risked that life to try and thwart her husband's evil plans. The only member of his family who had truly loved him and cared for him had been subject to a punishment that was too cruel even for most criminals.

He looked over his mother's shoulder at the stones on the wall. Mentally he counted them and determined the right spot.

A sick feeling spiraled inside of him, and he knew what he had to do.

Ninan pulled back and wiped his mother's tears. Then he removed the cloak he still wore and helped her into it.

"Follow the passage to its end," he told her. "When you come out, you'll find a tethered pteranodon. Get on it. Fly to the Allpan capital. Tell Quya Urpi everything you know so she can prepare."

She shook her head. "Why are you talking like you're not coming?"

For a moment he just stared at her. Surely she knew why.

"I have to kill him," Ninan said. "I know my brothers will only take his place, but they're nothing when compared to his villainy. I'm the only enemy he'll let near him—because he thinks he can still control me."

"Apo-Kimsa ... you're my *son*. My only child. I can't leave you. Your father is dangerous."

"You said yourself he won't try to kill me until I've seen him take Allpa. I'll have time." When she opened her mouth to protest again, he added, "You know I have to do this—and if you don't get somewhere safe, he will keep trying to use you to make me cooperate, and eventually it will work and then this will all be for nothing. So … please, Mamáy …"

Her eyes welled.

He pushed open the passageway and guided her into the darkness. "There won't be any light, but the passage only goes one way, with no branches. Hug the wall. It's only about a mile."

She turned back for a final embrace. "I love you, my son."

His voice broke. "I love you too, Mamáy."

Shouts from further down the corridor told him his time was up. He kissed her cheek and closed the wall, and felt along the break to ensure nothing would show.

Weaker now than ever, he clutched his side and hurried around the next bend so that the guards would not find him anywhere near the passage. He even crept into the next stairwell and made it a few yards through the main-level corridor before the guards caught up with him.

"Where's the quya?" one of them demanded as the others took Ninan and bound his wrists.

"I don't know," Ninan said. "She took a wrong turn. We got separated. I was trying to find her; that's why I came up. Please don't hurt her …"

"That's for the qhapaq to decide," said the guard. He ordered a few others to keep searching.

Ninan hung his head as the guards marched him back to his father.

Water may cleanse, but only fire purifies.

From "Forgers of Earth" by Hatun Walla

FIFTY-THREE

"**THIS IS IT,**" Qora said to Ollan, Wayra, Req, Kuy, and Gorgo. All but Kuy and Req each held a gearbomb. The brassy, metal containers housed several gears fitted together like clockwork, each with a winding key to set them in motion.

Uturunku, Miyil, and Ruka had already taken position throughout the vent, and Qora wanted a few minutes with only her brother and the Razorclaws at the entrance. It was warmer today, and dry, but still clouded, lending an eerie feeling to the atmosphere.

"We might not survive it," Kuy said, "but if we go down, we make sure all of Qhapaq Apo's people—and mutant dinosaurs—go down too."

Wayra nodded, although Qora saw the twinge of pain in her expression at the mention of all the animals that would be killed in cold blood. "People all over Runaqa are counting on us."

"We won't let them down." Ollan held out his hand, palm up.

Qora placed her palm down on his and clasped it.

Req added his, then Wayra hers, then Kuy and Gorgo theirs.

Gorgo nodded. "Let's smoke that bastard."

They dispersed and took their places.

In the deepest of the gearbomb detonation points, Qora set her lantern down and tried to calm her thumping heartbeat

as she turned over the bomb casing. It was midday now—
"Fourthday at noon"—and she wondered whether Ninan had
found his mother.

The ground here had fractures veining through it, which
implied pressure underneath, which implied that there was
something eager to break through. As the volcanist had said,
the more pent-up pressure they could release, the more reactions
would occur, building even more pressure and stimulating the
volcano as much as possible.

After the collapse at the entrance, and after breaking open
the water chamber the day before, Qora knew how volatile every
crack in the vent could be. She took a shuddering breath in that
thick, odorous air, and said a silent prayer.

It seemed like an eternity waiting for Uturunku's signal—
especially since he had to wait for Kuy and Gorgo to get all the
way out to stay with the pterobeast. Qora was already poised
with her legs slightly bent (one in front, one behind) and her
upper body angled forward and her elbows at her sides, with the
gearbomb between both hands.

Despite her eagerness, the metallic clanging of the bell still
came too soon and her fingers slipped when she first tried to turn
the bomb's winding key.

Be precise or do it twice, her mamáy's voice whispered in her
mind.

Once again, there would be no second chance for this.

She focused.

She wound the bomb and set it on the ground and leapt out
of the crevice, legs alternating and slicing the air as she made her
way up the branch to the main vent.

Like she'd practiced dozens of times, she leaned into her
strides, pushing against the upward slope. Lanterns lined the

walls every few yards, set up in advance to show the way.

The ground was mostly dry now that the internal heat had evaporated all the water that had washed down to the shaft. The upper chamber of water that had fed the lower chamber had fully emptied and even stopped dripping sometime last night, leaving a pool of water on the lower chamber floor but not enough to spill out the hole again, which was a relief.

Now the only problem Qora faced was the fact that the incline seemed significantly steeper than it had during drills, which she realized may have worn her muscles and drained her energy as the team leader had suggested. Or maybe it was just because she knew that this time, her life truly did depend on her speed, and the pressure was building in her mind the way it would soon build in the volcano's core.

But she pushed on, breathing fast and hard, heat swelling in her body. Her wristbow bracer trapped sweat along her forearm, but she'd worn it anyway; it had seemed silly to have a vest with pockets full of bolts and not the weapon to go with it.

Up ahead, figures emerged before her—every member of the team except Uturunku. The older man had been in charge of one of the detonation points closest to the entrance, so maybe he'd already made it out.

Ollan fell back so Qora could catch up to him. She gestured for him to keep going, but of course he didn't listen. Req and Wayra fell back too.

"You're all insane—just go!" Qora said.

It didn't matter now, though. They were all running together in a cluster, panting and huffing, and no one was going to outrun her from here.

The light from the outside, although clouded, grew brighter as they neared the opening. It wouldn't be much longer.

Stride after stride they pressed on and Qora was starting to feel the relief already.

Almost there.

They were close to three quarters of the way through, going strong, and—

CRACK.

A fracture formed along part of the floor. Req tried to overstep it but it caught the toe of his boot. He lurched forward and hit the ground with a grunt.

Everyone stopped so that Ollan could hoist him up, but Req took one step on that injured foot and cried out.

Wincing, he said, "Ruck, I think it's sprained."

Ollan then supported him in a limping run, but this significantly slowed their pace.

"You can't get stuck in here because of me," Req said.

Wayra scoffed. "Like hell we can't."

Precious seconds ticked by before the opening came fully into view. The volcanist and team leader came running back in, apparently after having made it out and realized the rest of the team was missing.

Before they met in the middle, a series of blasts echoed up the vent.

Some were a half second apart, others came a second or two after.

The vent shuddered.

Ollan adjusted Req's arm around his shoulder and tried to pick up speed.

Wayra took Qora's hand as they stuck close to the men.

The volcanist and team leader raced back outside.

Rock cracked from somewhere in the depths of the vent. Smaller rocks broke loose from the walls and ceiling, raining down on everyone.

A sickening groan rolled forward. Tremors shook the ground beneath Qora's feet, forcing her and her friends to stagger.

A flash of heat and steam chased them up.

A *BOOM* sounded outside and from above—no doubt the ash and gas and pulverized rock shooting up from the shaft through the crater, what the volcanist had described would happen.

A wave of pressure slammed against the flanks from the outside, shaking everything within.

High-pitched animal screams came at Qora's ears.

The diffused light from the already cloudy sky diminished to an even darker shade of gray. Qora imagined the ash clouds layering against the sky to add to the obscurity.

New cracks formed along the vent walls, snaking alongside the fleeing team.

Dust and rocks and heat and moisture spewed at their backs.

The volcano rumbled and quaked.

Qora and her friends hurried to outrun the cracks that were quickly becoming fissures.

Just a few more yards now. Come on. Please.

One of the fissures spread past the team, then veered down the wall.

Everyone remained together until a large rock broke from the ceiling above Qora's head and she halted suddenly—releasing Wayra's hand—to dodge it. In the second it had taken her to duck and cover, the spreading fissure snaked across the ground in front of her.

"Qora!" Ollan said over his shoulder.

Her friends and brother had already gone several paces ahead.

Req released Ollan—standing on one foot—so that Ollan could go to her, but Ollan skidded to a stop as the fissure widened.

More rock broke off and fell into the deepening rift.

Qora knew she had to jump while she still had the chance. Every rumble of the volcano seemed to split the rift another inch. She stumbled toward the edge trying to keep her balance as another tremor shook the ground and threatened to knock her over. The heat made her dizzy and she had to squint as new showers of rock and dust peppered her face.

Somehow through the noise and the haze, Ollan's voice broke through.

"Qora."

She clenched her fists and focused on his face.

With all her energy, she leapt.

Her foot caught on the crumbling edge, but Ollan caught her by an arm and dragged her onward.

One final wave of heat urged them the rest of the way out.

The upper third of the volcano was partially collapsed. Previously hidden side vents further out along the flanks burst open and shot out gas and tephra. The summit billowed more ash and gas into the large mushroom cloud already formed above it, while streaks of purple lightning crackled and snapped in its midst.

Kuy and Gorgo wrangled the pterobeast as it reared at the effects of the volcano ripping apart from the inside out. Finally, Kuy subdued the pterobeast with a dominite crystal as all nine team members climbed into the gondola.

No—not nine. There were only eight of them.

"Where's Uturunku?" Qora said.

The volcanist flashed her a grave look.

"Inside," the team leader said.

"What do you mean, 'inside'?" asked Wayra. "Why?"

Miyil replied, "He wanted to make sure our efforts were

enough to fully erupt the volcano. All our bombs were on the upper third. He said there should be at least one that made it to the bottom of the shaft."

Qora's stomach lurched.

"I must atone for what I've done."

Uturunku had never made it out—hadn't even tried. The man must have waited until the other bombs were seconds from going off and dropped another down to the very bottom. He would have been standing at the center when—

"Rise!" the team leader told the pterobeast.

As the pterobeast flapped its wings for takeoff, a new blast in the volcano launched another substance from the top—a ground-hugging cloud that shot down the slopes.

Pyroclastic flow.

It came so fast, Qora's breath caught in her throat as she stared up at the mass of ash and heat moving toward her.

With only maybe twenty yards to spare, the pterobeast rose on eager wings and swept the team out of the cloud's path.

Heat still suffocated their feet through the gondola floor until the pterobeast gained more altitude, and they all gripped the harness ropes desperately as they watched the scene unfold below.

Trees collapsed under the moving cloud. Mutant reptiles screamed for an instant and then cut off. Boulders *melted*.

The rim at the top of the volcano bulged with red-hot liquid, cracking the rock around it before a guttural roar set it loose. It spilled over in wide streams and poured down the flanks. Side vents—including the one the team had just evacuated—oozed additional streams, painting the dark mountain.

Dangling together, bodies close, everyone leaned against one another. Qora thought of Uturunku's sacrifice, wondering if it was what had produced such severe consequences. Indeed nothing had survived that death cloud, and now the lava came after to sweep up the mess.

She thought of her mother's advice again—"if the fire burns too hot, forge your weapons in it"—and sighed. In this case, the fire itself had been the weapon ... and the enemy had never seen it coming.

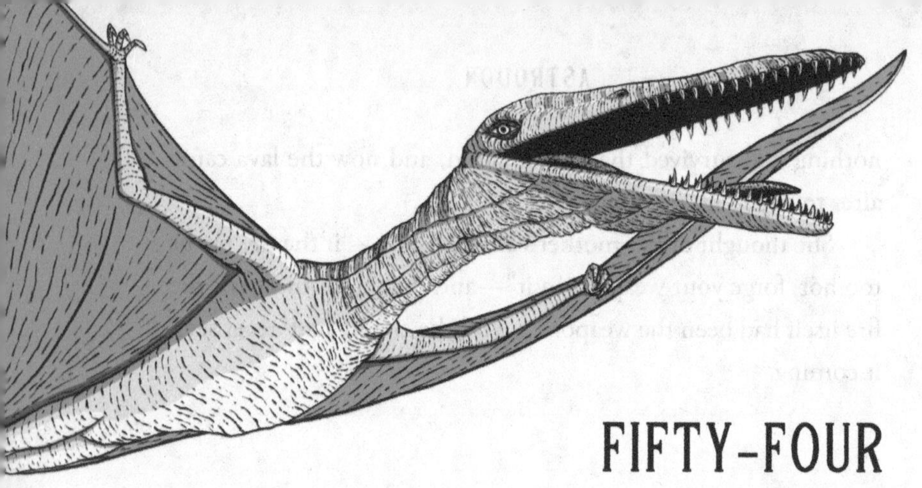

FIFTY-FOUR

OLLAN GAVE THANKS to every god he could think of as the team landed at the safety point in the hazy afterglow of the erupted volcano. Even from miles out, the whole world smelled of smoke and char, but Ollan heaved a sigh of relief and hugged his sister and his friends on the ground. He tried not to linger with Wayra, for fear of causing more tension between them; they still hadn't spoken about his confession, due to the mission and all that had been riding on it. Recovering from the mission would take time as well; adding any other mental or emotional tasks on top of that wouldn't do either of them any good.

"A lot of that will end up in far-off places." Ruka pointed to the smoke. "You might even see it back in Allpa. From the look of it, the upper-level winds will carry most of it the opposite direction, but lower-level winds could take some home with you."

Ollan remembered times when the volcanic region had been especially active and, even being more than a hundred miles from Qhusi, had hazed the sky where his family had lived. It thrilled him to think Qhapaq Apo might soon be able to suspect—from the smoke alone—that Pakasqa was burning.

Everyone was filthy and ash-smudged and exhausted, but they broke into stunned laughter and—some of them—tears. They took a few minutes to drink and rest, not sure what to make of the burning behemoth in the distance, and then it was time to return to Qhispina House.

Several hours later they arrived ready to clean up and collapse on one of the quya's feather mattresses, but once again a life in this place during this era could not have been so simple.

Quya Urpi and Qhapaq Izhi thanked them for their service and gathered them all into the grand salon to convey the most recent news.

Ollan braced himself.

"I've received word from the princess," said Quya Urpi. "It seems there have been several delays during the migration. Everyone is fine," she clarified, "without illness or injury, but we are not to expect them for at least two more days."

"Oh," Ollan replied. "That's alright then, isn't it? They'll still arrive before the cession deadline."

The quya seemed to have to steel herself before she answered. "Yes, they will still arrive before the cession deadline. However, there's been another development: Qhapaq Apo has accused us of attacking one of his strongholds in northern Sumaq. I don't know whether the attack is a fabrication, or whether some unaffiliated rebels tried to aid our side without considering the consequences, but regardless … the Sauroguard is on its way."

"No …" Qora choked. "We're not ready."

"We're not," the quya agreed. "But we'll have to be. I have all my people working nonstop to prepare the castle. I'm grateful that we had as much time as we did to build new walls and fortify the old ones, to research Sauroguard weaknesses using the specimens some of you have helped collect, and to condition my armies and amass a good supply of dominite. Beyond that, all we can do is our best."

Qhapaq Izhi addressed the group. "You've done well. We

will stand together and not back down."

The quya nodded. "That said, there's someone I should introduce you to—someone who brought us more specific, vital details on the threat we now face." She whispered to one of her attendants to "fetch our honored guest."

Within a few minutes, the attendant escorted another regal woman into the salon. She was petite with a kind face.

Everyone stood when she entered.

Then Qora released a barely audible gasp, then bowed.

The others exchanged confused glances but followed Qora's example.

"This is Quya Illari Kallpa," said Quya Urpi.

Ninan's mother. But, did that mean—

Qora's eyes brimmed when she went back upright, and Quya Illari came to her at once and drew her into a gentle embrace.

"Don't worry," said Quya Illari. "He's still alive." She pulled back and held Qora's face as though she were her own child.

This only made Qora cry harder.

"My son chose to stay and fight his father," the quya continued. "I tried to stop him but, I'm sure you know how he can be."

Qora erupted with a sad laugh that seemed almost involuntary, then wiped her eyes. "Yes …"

The group gave them a moment to comfort one another, and then Quya Urpi said, "We should discuss where you would all like to be when the Sauroguard arrives. Where do you feel your talents will serve us best?"

Ollan looked at his friends, who looked back with weary faces. It was a loaded question, after what they'd endured thus far. "How much time do we have?" he asked.

Quya Urpi deferred to Quya Illari for that.

Ninan's mother replied, "The Sauroguard will begin its advance at dawn."

There is no blade more cutting
than a woman's angry gaze.

Allpan proverb

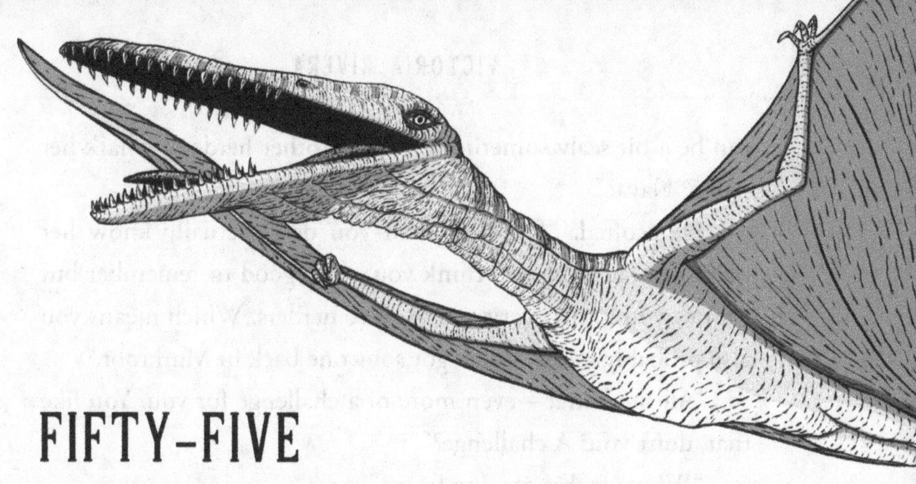

FIFTY-FIVE

FINALLY THE HERDS CAME OUT OF THE FOG—and just in time for the sun to break through and burn off the misty blanket they'd left behind.

Paqari sneered at the sky like its whims had been intentional. It had, after all, cost them an extra day, which meant that now they would face the problem of what to do about the food supply.

Their coordination had allowed them to move smoothly and without too much more delay, but not with any increased speed. This meant that they still had twenty miles to go and would have to stop for another night.

They would ride another mile, however, before having to discuss it, Paqari decided. She wasn't ready for the fallout yet. For now she wanted to enjoy the victory of making it through the fog.

Kondor seemed to have other ideas though.

He steered his mammoth up next to her, then waited a beat. "Have I done something to offend you, princess?"

She sighed. "You mean because I haven't slept in your tent again, gladewarden?"

"Look ... I didn't *expect* anything to happen again, but I'd be lying if I said I didn't *hope*—"

"I can't be the only girl on this trek with a wild streak. Suri can be a bit scaly sometimes. Or that other herder—what's her name? Naya?"

He scoffed. "Don't pretend you don't actually know her name. You act like you think you're too good to remember but I know you know every one of these herders. Which means you also probably know Naya's got someone back in Murkroot."

"All the better—even more of a challenge for you. You like that, don't you? A challenge?"

"Where is this coming from?"

"I guess I'm just 'vicious.' You know—always 'ready to bite.' Right?"

Kondor narrowed his eyes.

"Don't look so confused," she said. "If you go around discussing your intended conquests, people are going to talk."

"I didn't say anything to anyone."

"Oh no? Not all those times when Suri rode up for a chat while I was in the air?"

"Half the time she was complaining about Chinbo—mostly because she'd love the chance to stay in *his* tent, but he's dull as a pachyceph and too busy carving figurines to take a hint—and the rest of the time she had to listen to me tell her how bad I had it for *you*."

"You mean how badly you wanted to *tame* me?"

"I couldn't if I tried," he argued. "And I never said any such thing. I did say you're like a wild dilophosaur—and I stand by that."

Paqari pursed her lips and flared her nostrils, nudging her pteranodon to speed up.

The gladewarden matched her pace. "Maybe I like that about you. Not because you're a challenge but because *you challenge me*. There's a difference."

494

"I'd like to believe you but I'm afraid your reputation speaks volumes."

"If you were to read those volumes, you might find that my first few years as a gladewarden in a new city were difficult—which I implied to you the other day—and that I poured myself into a night life among my peers to try and find my place. Yes I dallied some, and sometimes with elusive women, but I had no control over what people said about it." He huffed and shook his head. "For someone who reads so much, you sure have trouble with subtext."

When he rode off, she didn't follow him.

The irony sat like a stone in her stomach. She knew what it was for people to talk about her when they had no business doing so. Her own reputation in Tisqu may have accurately reflected her character to an *extent*, but it was nowhere near the full story.

She thought about this for a long while, and soon it was time to stop the herd. The landscape stretched out into a vast expanse of grass, which swayed in a warm and gentle wind.

Herders gathered at the front again and Paqari said, "Well … I think you all know what I'm going to say."

Every face looking back at her was morose. Kondor halted his mammoth at the back of the group.

"Our daylight is running out," she continued. "These dinosaurs have had a long journey and they need nourishment. I'm afraid the time has come to accept the inevitable: We have to let them eat the mammoth mounts."

"And then what will we ride?" said Chinbo who, once again, had been whittling while he rode. He clutched his knife and his mammoth's reins in one hand, and what looked like a wooden feather (with such realistic detail it could have come from an avian dinosaur) in the other.

"You know exactly what," said Paqari with a glance at Grimjaw.

"But you know we can't do that," said Naya.

"You can and you have to," Paqari told them. "It's not a negotiation. You can't match the dinosaurs' pace on foot. The dinosaurs can't go without food. There's no other option—unless you want us to leave you here in the wilderness until gods know when, while your own food supply is almost gone too."

Suri folded her arms. "You come from a land where people treat dinosaurs like slaves, so I guess it's natural for you to be cruel and inconsiderate. We wouldn't expect you to understand what a compromise of morals it is for us to climb on the backs of these reptiles, even for just a few miles. As if it wasn't enough to ask us to bring them this far in the first place …"

"I am trying to help make all of Runaqa safe for everyone, including your precious dinosaurs," Paqari argued. "From the first moment my people went to yours with our plea, we made it clear that we understood what a moral sacrifice it would be. I'm not standing before you pretending that this isn't hard for you, or that it's not a lot to ask, but sometimes morals must be bent."

"What kind of moral is it really, though," asked a male herder from the middle of the group, "if we bend it whenever it's convenient? If we were as morally flexible as you are, the Tail would be just like the Terrains."

"That's not what I mean," said the princess. "What I'm saying is, this is a different context. We can't always follow the rules, and that doesn't make us amoral. Intention matters too."

The herders slowly broke into a racket. They wouldn't ride the dinosaurs and there had to be something else they could do and the princess could never understand and this whole thing was a mistake and the elderboughs should never have agreed to this …

Paqari tried to shout over them, to defend her points, but no one was listening.

"If you'll just calm down …" she said.

Then it was, "Why have we been listening to *her* this whole time?" and "We should put it to a vote!" and "She might be a princess in Tisqu but that's nothing to *us*. If anything, we answer to Grimjaw."

Finally a louder, deeper voice overpowered them all.

"Enough!" Kondor said, riding forward. "I won't hear another word of this!"

The herders quieted and stared over at him.

Kondor scrubbed a hand over his jaw and sighed. "You're all so stuck on the old ways. I get it—I really do. Our traditions are longstanding, and they bring us peace. We respect the dinosaurs, and in return, they are loyal to us. What we have at the Tail is unique on this continent, maybe in this very *world*, but … that doesn't mean we shouldn't adapt. Because of the destruction up north, we've had to adapt our ways to bring our godly beasts to the fight. The elderboughs made an exception because it serves the greater good. Now we have to make another exception so that we can finish what we've started, so that all these torturous days will have meant something. We did not come this far just to give up this close to the end." He looked at Paqari, then back at the herders. "If you truly honor our dinosaurs, and all dinosaurs everywhere, then give them nourishment. Provide them the strength to do what they came to do!"

It took the herders a minute to absorb what Kondor had said, and then slowly, one by one, they dismounted and began to remove the mammoths' packs and saddles.

Paqari felt an overwhelming warmth in her chest as she watched the herders accept the gladewarden's instructions, and she nodded once at him in silent thanks.

He nodded back.

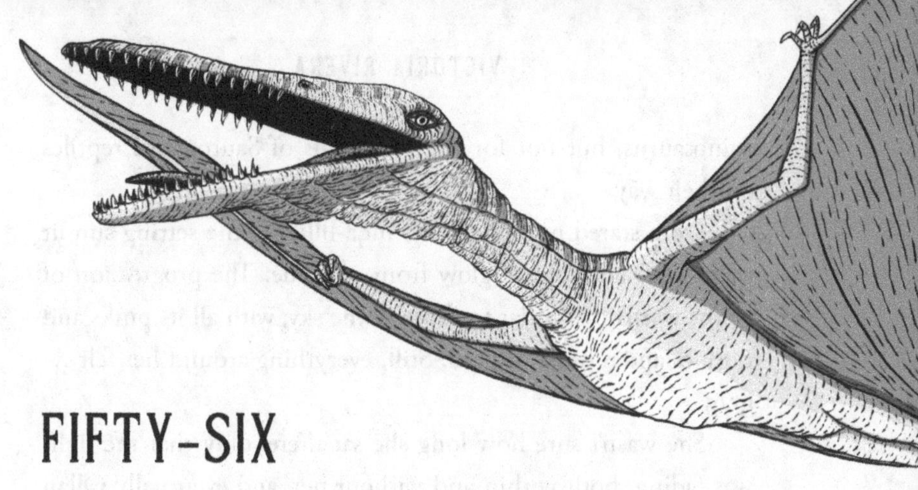

FIFTY-SIX

QORA SAT ON A BENCH in the Allpan castle's expansive flower garden with her knees drawn up to her chest. Everyone had agreed to give her a moment alone when it had been clear their attempts to console her might not be what she needed right now.

Her thoughts spiraled as she considered the dangers that Ninan had faced to rescue his mother, and the fact that he had willingly gone with his father who was ready to kill him whenever the time felt right. The ache in her chest seemed to spread by the second.

War preparations were lacking. The giant theropods would not arrive until well after the Sauroguard decimated the capital. Paqari might be stuck somewhere. Ninan was a prisoner.

No matter what she did, things only got worse. Whenever she and her friends made progress, something else erupted. Where were the gods in whom she had put her faith? Was anyone watching over the righteous? Or was it really just up to her to take care of herself and the people she loved, until she ran out her luck and finally lost everything?

Her mamáy's phrase that "even grass has a blade" might be true, but a blade like that was no match for metal. Try as she might to make a cutting edge out of whatever she had on hand, that would only get her so far. It was enough for the Venture spinosaurus, but not for the thousands of Sauroguard reptiles on their way.

Qora stared numbly at the inqa-lillies as the setting sun lit them with an ethereal glow from one side. The progression of colors wasn't dissimilar to those in the sky, with all its pinks and purples and a burst of gold. Still, everything around her felt … gray.

She wasn't sure how long she sat there, only that the light was fading, both within and without her, and eventually Ollan came to find her.

He sat beside her without saying anything for a moment. Maybe he didn't know what to say, or maybe he appreciated the silence too. Or maybe he knew exactly what he wanted to say but he still wasn't sure of his place with her. Qora had dispelled the notion that she didn't need him, but that didn't mean he would be able to play the same role he once had. At least, that's what she imagined he was thinking.

Finally, he said, "I know it's usually Mamáy coming at us with all the words of wisdom but … sometimes I think about Papáy, and the things he used to say."

Qora hadn't thought about their papáy in a long time. Whenever she did, she felt as though her memories of him had faded; she couldn't picture his face so well anymore, and it only reminded her that she hadn't ever had much time with him. Not that any amount would have been enough. He'd died when she was eleven, and even when he'd been alive, he had always worked so many hours to keep everyone fed and clothed, it had sometimes felt like minutes a day that they'd seen one another. But she was always grateful for the way he had dedicated his life to his family's care.

She shifted slightly to look at Ollan. "Like what?"

"Do you remember," Ollan replied, "that time when we had to re-thatch the entire roof? Which also happened to be during shearing season? And somehow the closest well was dry too, so we had to haul water from the next one out, which was—what—close to a mile?"

"Gods, yes. That was ... quite a month. We had that infestation of mice, too! That's when we got the compies." She almost smiled, but her lips couldn't quite form the shape. "And then we were trying to grow a bit of our own food, so there was the garden to tend ..."

Ollan nodded. "Everything went wrong at once. We all had to pitch in. There was one day—one that was so bad, I'll never forget it—when my skin was blistered from the sun, and my hands were blistered from the shears, and I had a crick in my neck from the bucket yoke. You were just eight years old and up to your elbows in alpaca fiber, Hakan was crying nonstop, Mamáy was *so* pregnant but still crouching to pull weeds. I'd had about enough and I started to say so, but Papáy put a hand on my shoulder and ... do you know what he told me?"

Qora shook her head.

"He said, 'Son, I know you're tired. I know you're spent. I know you've got nothing left, but ... we're not done yet. We can't stop until we're done.'"

With a teary gaze, Qora thought of how her papáy had gone to work most days on the drystone crew, how he had often worked until his fingers bled and then gone home and worked some more, patching up the house, fixing broken furniture, rounding up escaped animals. If anyone had had a right to want to quit, it had been him. But he'd still taken time to sympathize with his son during that moment of despair.

"You think he'd say the same thing now?" Qora whispered

as she held back a sob.

"Without a doubt."

Qora squeezed her eyes shut to release her welling tears. "I keep … holding on, and trying to be strong. I try to have faith, even when it all seems lost. I keep thinking that if I just hold on a little longer, a miracle will happen, that it's just a matter of time. But, gods … I feel like I've been doing that for years."

"Me too," Ollan admitted. "Not quite like you, but I certainly understand the sentiment."

"I keep trying to look for the miracles. Like the way I came out of the Venture with exactly what I set out to get; Rimaq recovered from theropox and I paid my fine. Or how I met Ninan. Or how, later, I got *you* back, which I never thought possible. How we managed to win favor with the Tail to get the giant theropods on their way to Allpa—late, but still. How this very morning we destroyed Pakasqa. Miracles happen every day. It's just … sometimes I wonder whether those will matter, if we lose so many other things along the way and if everything around us falls apart."

"I think they do matter."

"But are miracles real? Or are they just products of good luck and hard work and a strategy that manages to overcome the opposition of the moment?"

"I think people think miracles are, essentially, when the gods grant a wish. But I would say miracles are when your grit finds the right grooves, when you're doing all that you can do and then the patterns of nature—either human nature or the features of the natural world—align with that. For the most part, I think we can make them happen, if not for ourselves then for others."

Ninan had said something similar.

"Maybe that's where the real miracles are: in the people we

love—or the people we don't know yet that we're going to love—who give us a chance."

She looked at her brother with the weight of his lost four years on his shoulders, and having been responsible to help take care of their family at a young age. He had given her a chance. He had taught her to shoot—to survive. And he had come for her in the volcano vent.

"Anyway," he said. "We're not done yet. We can't stop until we're done. I don't know who, if anyone, or what, if anything, is watching over us, but I know we've got to do something worth watching."

Qora imagined gods looking down from the High World, not so different from passengers in a pterobeast gondola, seeing everything from above and all the patterns in the land below— hidden routes and dinosaur tracks and patchwork crop lands and volcanic explosions and serpentosaurid trails …

"Something worth watching …" she repeated.

Suddenly a plan began to form within her mind. It was only the seed of an idea—but an idea that was perhaps the craziest she'd ever had. Her chest swelled. She stared at Ollan with what must have been a wild look in her eye.

He raised a brow. "What?"

"You're right. We're not done yet. We're just getting started."

May your tears water the barren soil
to sprout the seeds of hope.

Qolqese blessing

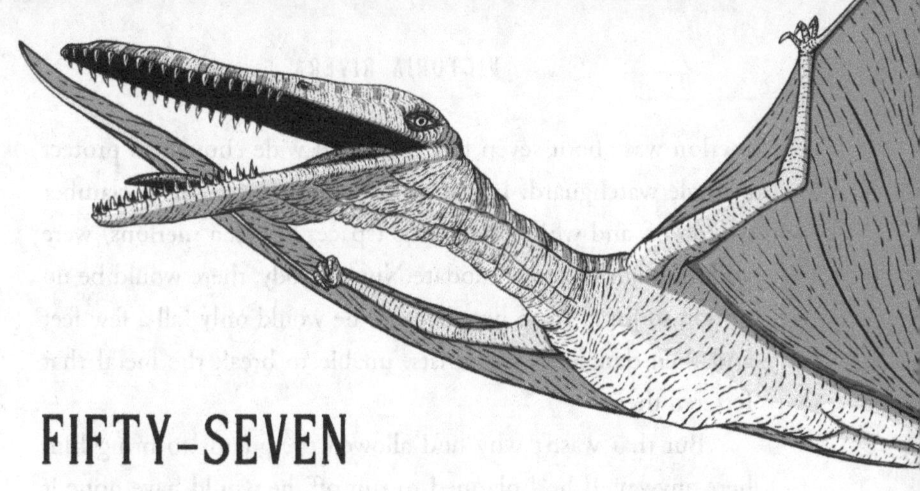

FIFTY-SEVEN

SOMETIME AFTER MOST OF THE NIGHT in a dank cell, guards opened a creaking hunk of a door on strained hinges and dragged Ninan out. His ribs on one side throbbed violently, and he kept his breaths as shallow as possible to avoid worsening the pain. It was still dark outside, however, as the guards manacled his wrists. He hissed through his teeth when they shoved him into a pterosaur gondola.

After a few hours in the air, the pterosaur landed at the base of an Allpan watchtower that Qhapaq Apo had already overthrown, with Qhispina House in view in the dawnlight. Ninan stared at it, feeling like he'd failed the quya and all the forces that assembled there. But they had *assembled*, from what he could see, which meant his mother had made it safely there to warn Quya Urpi.

A strange haze tinged the sky, and he might have thought it was only light tricks at this early hour, had it not also carried the faint scent of smoke. Had the pyroraptors set grasses ablaze on their way here?

The guards marched Ninan up the watchtower's spiraling stairs and chained him to one of the battlement merlons.

It was a long chain—with each end connected to one of his manacles—that draped around the outside of the merlon. The merlon was about seven feet high, and wide enough to protect a single watchguard. It was most definitely too tall to clamber on top of, and while the crenels (spaces between merlons) were wide enough to accommodate Ninan's body, there would be no option to jump from here because he would only fall a few feet and then dangle by his wrists, unable to break the metal that fettered them.

But that wasn't why he'd allowed the guards to bring him here anyway. If he'd planned to run off, he would have done it at the arena. Still, if he wanted to get close to his father again, he would need to free himself somehow, and that was where he hadn't thought too far ahead. It wouldn't have mattered even if he had though; there hadn't been any way to tell where he would end up, what weapons might be available to him, or who would be keeping watch on him. By its very nature, this was something he would have to do on instinct, when opportunity arose. If he couldn't manage those circumstances, maybe he didn't deserve to survive.

The watchtower had a view of the castle on one side, and a view of the battlefield leading up to it on the other. There was just enough length on Ninan's chain that he could move to see everything—depending on which gap he looked through—and he knew that was no mistake.

Four guards remained at the tower with him, including the one that had been admiring his strikefangs on the arena balcony. In fact, that guard wore the strikefangs right now, and sneered whenever Ninan happened to glance his way.

Another hour or so later, when Ninan sat on the floor with his back to the battlements, dying to take a full breath but afraid his ribs would protest if he tried, another gondola arrived, carrying Qhapaq Apo.

The sneering guard ordered Ninan to get up.

With no energy to argue, Ninan got to his feet, grunting, and directed his attention northeast, opposite the castle. That's what his father surely wanted.

Ninan was already in position when his father finished ascending the tower.

"Apo-Kimsa," said the qhapaq. "You will now have the privilege to witness the marvel I have created. While you may not believe in the divine will that certifies my power, perhaps now you will reconsider—although, it makes no difference whether you do or don't, because one way or another, the empire will rise again … and I will control its every move."

Thousands of figures crept over the horizon, first in a thin line across the width, then advancing to reveal more numbers behind. They were too far away for Ninan to differentiate their features, but his heart pounded wildly at the sight.

In no time, the reptiles would blanket the entire plain.

It was really happening; the war had begun.

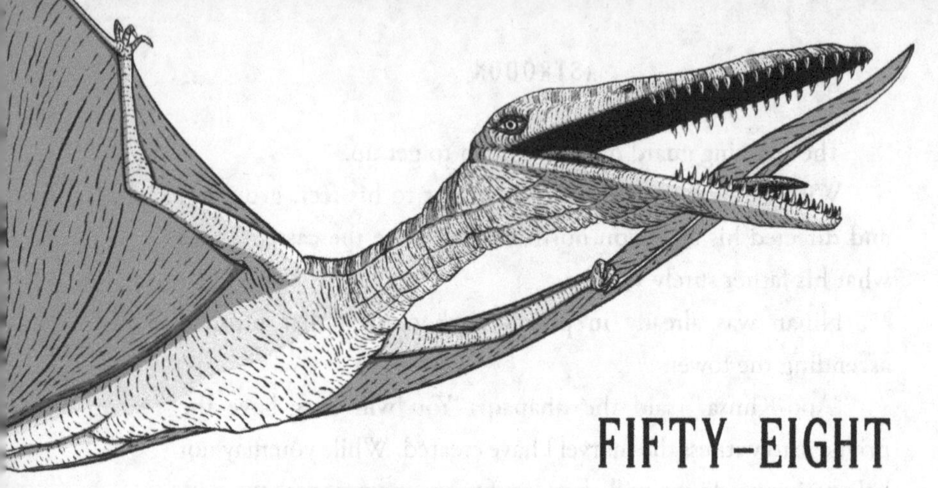

FIFTY-EIGHT

THE CASTLE WAS IN TURMOIL when Qora and the Razorclaws loaded the last of the dominite and equipment onto their pteranodons. Around them, guards, officers, soldiers, and handlers worked to get everything in position for the Sauroguard. Qora hoped her plan would be able to aid them.

In her preparation, she had been able to focus on this new mission instead of constantly worrying about Ninan. Of course she did still constantly worry, but she'd managed to relegate it to the back of her mind rather than deal with it at the forefront.

In the breaking dawn, Ollan helped Qora secure everything and stood back to observe. He was wearing his new military uniform, but with the jacket still open over his undershirt.

"I wish you were coming with us," she told him.

He gave a forced smile. "Me too. But this is another one of those times when I have to let you do what you need to do—and besides, I have a spanner squad to command."

"You don't have to *let* me do anything," she argued. "I want you with me. Not once have I felt like you were holding me back. Not once have you overstepped. My skills have changed, and so have my responsibilities, and you have recognized that and treated me like a teammate and a friend every step of the way. *And* you've been the brother I needed. So please ... don't act like I want you to back off."

Her brother sighed. "Alright. I'm sorry."

Somehow in all the chaos, Quya Urpi still came to bid them good luck. "You have everything you need?"

Kuy nodded. "Yes, Your Majesty. Thank you."

"Mister Kanchaya," she said to Ollan. "Why aren't you dressed?"

"Apologies." Ollan began to do the buttons on his uniform jacket. "I'll be ready in just a moment …"

The quya frowned. "No. I mean dressed for *this* task." She gestured at the pteranodons.

"Um." He stared at her, mid-buttoning, then glanced at the Razorclaws. "I don't understand. I have to command the spanners."

"I have plenty of military officers at my service," said Quya Urpi. "Dauntless revolutionists are much harder to come by. I'll need every one of you in order to accomplish your sister's plan. And let's face it: You don't belong with the Bolt Corps. You're a Razorclaw; it's time we stop pretending otherwise."

Req scoffed. "Who's pretending otherwise? I already considered him one of us." He looked to the others for confirmation. "Didn't you?"

Wayra, Kuy, and Gorgo all nodded.

Ollan's eyes glistened like he might cry.

"Excellent," said the quya. "I'll divide your squad between the other boltmasters. You've trained them well. Now don your gear, Mister Kanchaya."

He smiled incredulously and bowed. "Right away."

She smiled back. "Godsspeed."

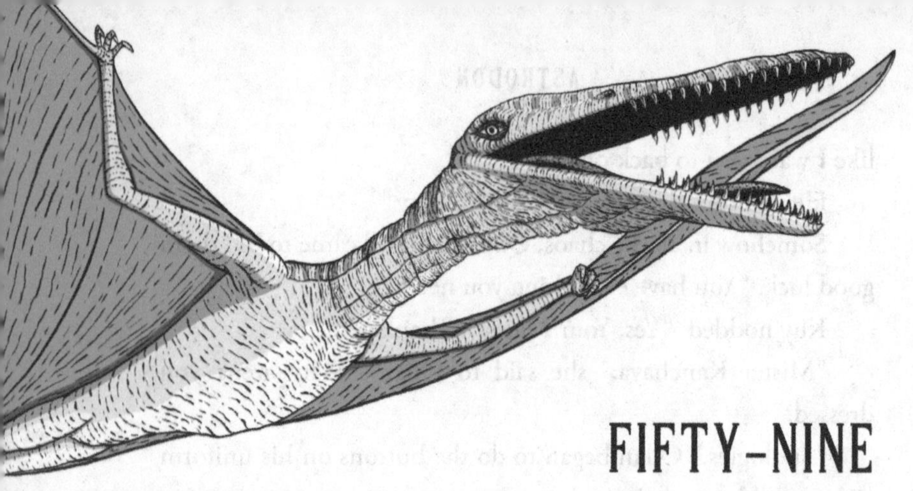

FIFTY-NINE

NOW DRESSED IN EXTRACTION CLOTHING AGAIN, Ollan hurried back toward the pteriary where the Razorclaws would be loading a pteranodon with supplies for him.

"You're a Razorclaw; it's time we stop pretending otherwise."

He let the words linger in his mind. Although he had been working with the Razorclaws for some time now and even been treated as an honorary member, it had never felt permanent. Their missions had necessitated his help and he had gladly provided it, but until now he had always imagined he would go on to fulfill a different role somewhere else. That's where his position with the Allpan Bolt Corps had come in, he supposed. It had made the most sense, considering his background. And yet, that background was so far in the past now, it hardly seemed a part of him anymore. He wasn't a soldier. He wasn't a miner either, despite having spent more time in the mines than in the military. But a Razorclaw? For real?

One corner of his mouth twitched up.

It felt … right.

Ollan was so exhilarated by this that he went charging into the connecting corridor and had to come to an abrupt, skidding stop when Wayra intercepted him.

"Wayra," he said through a pant. She was supposed to

be at the pteriary with the others, getting ready to leave. "Is everything okay?"

She nodded. "It's fine. Everyone's ready and waiting."

"Right. Sorry. I was on my way. I know we need to leave as soon as possible, I just—"

"I didn't come to tell you to hurry," Wayra clarified. "I wanted to, um …" She closed her eyes for a second and took a breath. "We haven't really had a good moment to talk—about what you said yesterday. Not that now is the best moment either …"

Ollan cleared his throat, mouth suddenly going dry. This was it. This was where she was going to tell him what a good friend he'd become. They worked well as a team—a team that he was now truly a part of—and it would be tricky to maintain a dynamic that was anything more.

In time, he might be able to accept it. It had been inevitable that he would feel something for her, with the way she always opened her heart to new friends so easily, and the way she could nurture the souls of humans and animals alike. She was skillful and loyal and beautiful. But he could learn to appreciate those things in friendship alone, he told himself—eventually.

"You don't have to say anything," he told her. "I can't imagine how much pressure I must have put on you. Especially at a time like that, with such an important task ahead of us. Honestly, you can pretend it never happened. Really. No hard feelings. I do care about you, maybe in too many ways, but, because of that, I don't want to ruin what we already have, or for you to feel like you need to explain yourself, or console me, or …"

He realized Wayra was gradually coming forward, and that sometime during his ramblings she had stepped into his immediate space.

She reached up and put a hand to his cheek and met his gaze.

Of course she would try to console him even though she didn't have to. He was like a frightened reptile, and she was here to make sure he knew everything would be alright.

But then she tilted her face up and came forward again until they were so close he could see the flecks in her eyes. His insides went wild at the proximity, heart thrumming so fast he could hardly stand still.

Wayra seemed to study him for a moment before her lips parted. She leaned in and brushed her mouth against his with a featherlight touch that was somehow more erotic than if she had kissed him full on.

Not wanting to scare her off, he waited.

Finally she pressed her lips into his, and he knew it was alright to press back. He grasped the loose waves of hair that skimmed her shoulders.

The kisses were experimental at first, but soon became more exploratory and less timid. Ollan forgot for several long moments where he was and where he'd been headed, completely consumed by this and only wanting to get more and more lost.

When they were both flushed and breathless, they came apart and Ollan smiled. "If that's your way of saying you just want to be friends …"

"I think I have enough friends," she told him.

SIXTY

PAQARI HAD RISEN EARLY with Kondor and the herders. It had been a strange feeling to have no mammoths with them.

The herders had then set about saddling the dinosaurs, with much hesitation—not only because of their reservations about it, but also because it wasn't something they'd ever done before.

Some of the dinosaurs had held still for it while others had twisted back to sniff the strange things being strapped to their backs. A few had flailed and fled. Reluctantly everyone had agreed it would be best to use dominite to help the dinosaurs cooperate, especially when the spinosaurs' back sails made it necessary to saddle their necks instead, which had required them to lie down on their bellies similar to the sleeping pose.

There had been much grumbling about the dominite, but Kondor had reminded the herders that at least it would keep the dinosaurs calm. While it wasn't ideal to bend their will, it was better than having to manhandle them into submission.

The saddle straps were thick and long, with multiple buckles, while the saddles themselves were so heavy they required at least four people to lift them. Adjusting to different sizes and body shapes had taken some time. With dominite, however, the herders had managed it within a couple of hours.

Thank goodness they hadn't had to prepare *all* the dinosaurs as mounts, only enough to carry the herders, some of whom doubled up and rode together.

They hadn't bothered with reins or bits because the dinosaurs weren't trained to follow commands anyway. Herders were just along for the ride, wherever the dinosaurs were willing to go.

Kondor rode Grimjaw and Paqari stayed on the pteranodon, and then there was nothing to do but advance on the last stretch of grassland toward Amachakuna.

Steering the dinosaurs was another challenge, but Kondor suggested they use a method similar to what they'd done for the fog: Paqari would urge Grimjaw onward, and they would allow the rest of the herd to follow by their instincts. Occasional whistling helped to avoid stragglers, and then it was just a matter of the herders adjusting to the new height, angle, and gait.

When only about fifteen miles remained, a flyer and rider came at them from the opposite direction, similar to the day Qora and Ninan had been called away. Paqari tightened her grip on her own pteranodon's reins and tried to suppress the sinking feeling in her gut.

It was the same messenger as before, from Qhispina House.

The group allowed him to land and walk his flyer alongside them.

"I'm glad I found you so close to the capital," he said. "However, I'm afraid it's not close enough. The Sauroguard is coming."

Paqari's blood ran cold. "What? When?"

"Now. From what our watchguards have told us, troops were about ten miles out and not paced much faster than you, but they started moving at dawn," he explained. "Which means we have minutes before they arrive. The quya is tending to preparations but asked me to see if there was any hope we might receive the giant theropods earlier than expected."

"I told her two days," said the princess, "in case we experienced other delays. Thankfully we did not, but at our current pace, we won't make it for another three hours."

The messenger nodded. "Understood. Would it be possible, however, to … hasten the dinosaurs? I'm aware they can't keep a quicker pace for a long journey, but perhaps in an emergency …"

From here to the castle, the land was flat with no obstacles but for a sporadic tree or two, and the Kuchuna River at the end, which should be no trouble to cross with the dinosaur's long and powerful legs.

Paqari looked to Kondor for advice.

"There might be some way to speed them up," Kondor said, "but we'd probably have to startle them. That's risky. I don't know how we would control them or keep them together. Not to mention it's difficult to startle an apex predator; not much intimidates them."

"We can't force it with dominite either," Paqari thought aloud. "Only if they were trained to follow charge commands, which they're not. Right now we're operating off their group instincts and a whiff of perfume."

Kondor huffed his frustrated agreement. "Even if we could get them straight to battle, they don't have the fool's silver in their systems. They'll be susceptible to Apo's dominite."

Right. Paqari hadn't even considered that yet. The plan was to get them to the capital with plenty of time, allow them some rest, and lace their watering troughs an hour in advance of a potential attack. Trying to organize something like that for three hundred dinosaurs at the last minute when the whole castle was under siege would be impossible.

They all thought for a moment.

The princess couldn't believe this was really happening. Yes, she had known it was coming, but not so soon. She'd still maintained hope that something would stop it before it started. Now the dinosaurs were going into battle late and unprepared.

"I'll fly with you to the capital," Paqari told the messenger. "I need to see what we're dealing with, and speak to the quya."

Kondor cast a worried glance at her, but she inclined her head slightly in response. He knew it was necessary.

With that, she swept up and out alongside the messenger until the herd shrank behind them.

It only took four minutes to cross the expanse by air, which, once again, made Paqari scowl. Migrating land animals had felt like chiseling script into stone instead of just writing with ink on papyr.

And then she saw the Sauroguard on the horizon: thousands of dinosaurs spread far and wide, organized by species, marching with the order and obedience of human soldiers, but with built-in scale-and-scute armor. They were living weapons, enticed by dominite, a wave of disaster headed straight for the castle.

The majority of the Allpan Guard covered the grounds leading up to a new defensive wall, while many defended the wall by its walks, and others manned contraptions from the castle spires.

One look at the setup, though, and Paqari knew the castle wouldn't be able to defeat what was coming. They needed the giant theropods. Honestly, she didn't think that would be enough either—but it would certainly be the only thing to give them a chance.

The same lowly tail
that drags upon the ground
may yet thrash like a royal whip.

Sumaqi proverb

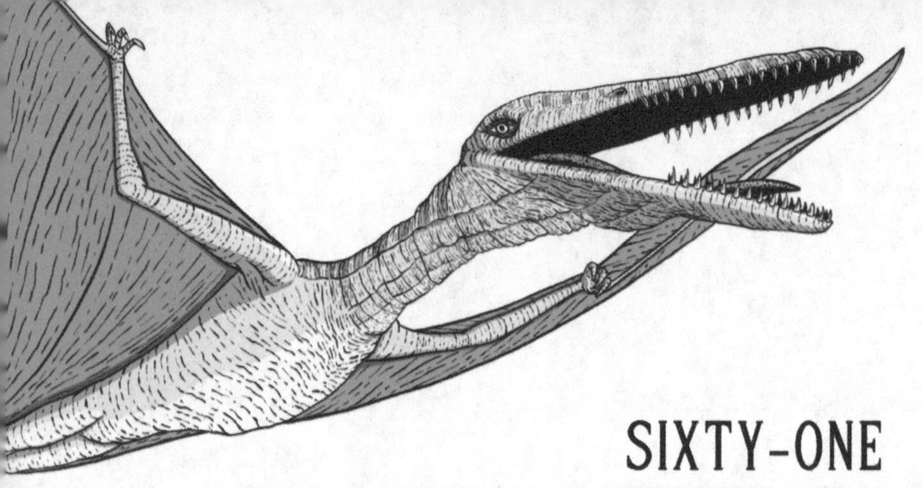

SIXTY-ONE

QORA AND THE RAZORCLAWS flew past the hot springs, where the grass was scant in favor of splotched minerals—pale calcium deposits and reddish iron stains—that hosted shallow, misshapen pools of water. Steam sent up scents of metal and sulfur.

A few miles beyond that, they came upon a more sunken area, surrounded by tall, waving grasses—a place that would have been practically invisible when approaching it at ground level. The only indication that something was different here would have been the clusters of shrubs that implied more water. That water, however, was minimal and stagnant, surrounded by browning reeds and mud that was half dried and cracked at the edges. Curved grooves marked the earth, winding impressions that overlapped like a diagram of tree roots.

The impressions were the same kind Qora had seen in the fields around the Pakasqa volcano; there was no mistaking them.

Qora and her friends landed on a bare stretch, their pteranodons' foot-claws striping the packed mud as they each came to a halt.

The air was sour with a blend of reptilian musk, wet earth, and rot.

Insects buzzed over the water. Frogs croaked nearby. The occasional bubble rose in watery mud and burst.

Qora shuddered as she observed the location. Despite its implications, she couldn't see the very thing she'd come for, but she knew it was there, lurking, ready to kill.

"Do you see any?" Wayra whispered.

Everyone shook their heads, but no one else made a sound, not even the pteranodons. They seemed to sense it was best not to.

It was like they were being watched.

No—they *were* being watched, Qora thought. Most certainly. A place like this was perfect for predators to watch and wait as prey wandered closer in desperate search of water, drawn here by necessity.

Then that very water shifted somewhere.

Qora sucked in a breath and held it.

A shape began to emerge, slowly and deliberately. Scales glimmered as a thick rope of muscle unwound itself in the murk. One green eye rose above the surface, its slit widening.

The grass twitched now too, revealing another body whose muscles contracted and expanded as it crept forward.

Curves bulged on the banks.

And suddenly Qora became aware of them *all*.

A heap coiled among the shrubs; something half submerged in a shadowy pool; a long mass partially burrowed into the mud; another green eye; a black, flicking tongue.

She released her breath in a careful, controlled manner.

"Gods, they're everywhere," she murmured against the lump in her throat.

They were even bigger than the serpentosaurid that had tried to strangle her during the Venture. The quya had informed her that the Allpans called these "megaboa," and rightly so, as their bodies were some three feet in diameter at their thickest parts, and stretched to around forty feet long.

"What," Req said through his teeth, "have we gotten ourselves into?"

"Dominite—*now*" was all Qora said in response, without taking her eyes off the reptile that watched her from the water.

Everyone withdrew large dominite crystals from their pockets, holding them like torches against the dim early morning.

The glow emanated from each crystal and combined, spilling onto the ground ahead of where the reptiles lay.

One by one they slithered from their hiding places, fixated on the crystals, disturbing the reeds and grass and mud, and sending ripples through the water.

By all logic, the pteranodons should have stirred or flinched. Apparently it wasn't uncommon for enormous snakes like these to strike flyers of any size that came to drink from murky waters. But the dominite soothed all the reptiles within range.

Locking her elbows to keep her arms from shaking, Qora sat still on her saddle in the midst of at least a dozen megaboas that all raised their heads and flicked their forked tongues as if trying to better sense the dominite. She hoped they didn't sense the scent markers the team had packed on utility belts around their hips—kept at the ready for when it was time to use them on the battlefield. That scent would spur an attack, and Qora was sure the wristbow bolts in her vest pockets wouldn't be enough to protect her.

"Unload," she told everyone.

Everyone had two packs: a small one and a large one. The small pack only held a couple of defense weapons, survival supplies, and a firestick (in case the team ran into trouble out here and needed to signal the quya for help). The larger, heavier pack was attached by ropes to the saddle straps around the pteranodons' bellies.

Once everyone had detached their *large* packs, they removed the outer material to reveal tight-woven rope-net sacks underneath, full of more dominite crystals. Then they dropped them to the ground.

"Rise!" the team said in unison.

The pteranodons flapped high and dangled the dominite sacks over the megaboas. The megaboas converged, hissing and rearing up, their muscular bodies like sauropods with no limbs.

Qora and her friends kept the dominite just out of reach, then turned back for Qhispina House, drawing the megaboas onward below and behind.

Daring to look down, Qora caught a glimpse of the megaboas slithering in unison, now almost twenty in tow.

With a dominite supply like this, these reptiles were at the team's command. Of course the supply also drew smaller reptiles from the grass and little pterosaurs from the few trees along the way, but none of these seemed to tempt or distract the megaboas, who only had one goal in mind at the moment.

They were so enticed that, as Qora suspected, they even slithered past the hot springs despite their aversion to the sulfuric scent.

Although the team had to slow down because the megaboas weren't going nearly as fast as the pteranodons could—ten miles per hour, maybe, compared to the pteranodons' sixty—they were following at an unnatural speed, ignoring all their instincts for energy conservation in favor of chasing the high. It would probably kill them if they kept it up too long, Qora thought. She hoped they could make it the few remaining miles to the castle without any issues—and perhaps having worked up a raging appetite.

Either way, it was an incredible sight.

"I don't know who, if anyone, or what, if anything, is watching

over us, but I know we've got to do something worth watching."

Qora straightened her shoulders and said, "Alright, friends: Let's put on a show!"

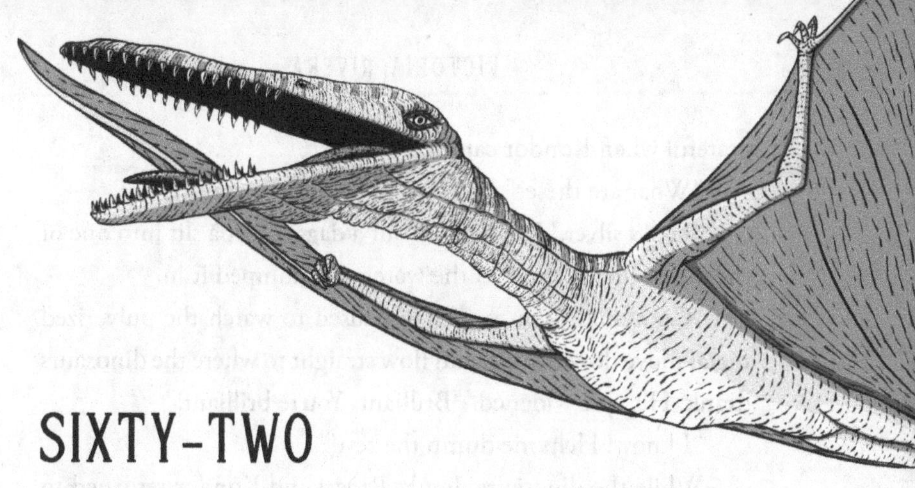

SIXTY-TWO

ONCE PAQARI HAD SEEN THE DOOM sweeping toward the castle, she'd begun formulating a plan. She leaned forward on her pteranodon to keep as flat as possible for better aerodynamics even though she was sure it only made a fraction of a difference—but every minute counted, didn't it?

Especially considering the very heavy packs on the pteranodon's back.

Soon she landed back with the group as they followed the river toward the castle.

"How bad is it?" Kondor asked.

"Bad," the princess admitted. "But if we hurry, I think we can make it."

"Hurry how?" he said. "We can't get them to move any faster."

Paqari ignored him. "First things first, we need to pull over right next to the river. It's watering time anyway." She told all the herders to get the dinosaurs into the usual routine.

Once the dinosaurs were lined up along the bank and had begun dipping their snouts, she flew to a spot upriver, dismounted, and took down the saddlebags, which contained smaller burlap sacks that were full and tight against their seams. They were much heavier than she liked to admit, so she was grateful when Kondor came to help.

"What are these?" he asked as he lifted one off.

"Fool's silver." Paqari took out a dagger, cut a slit into one of the sacks, then took it to the water and dumped it in.

"Good gods, you're—" He paused to watch the pulverized metal move downstream and flow straight to where the dinosaurs drank. His eyes widened. "Brilliant. You're brilliant!"

"I know! Help me dump the rest!"

While the dinosaurs drank, Paqari and Kondor returned to the herders.

Paqari picked Suri out of the group and said, "Remember back in Murkroot, you said you tried several whistles on the dinosaurs? You said there was one pitch they really didn't like— one that made them 'race off in a big mass' together? You said it tapped into some stampeding instinct that was only possible in short bursts?"

"Yes ..." Suri replied.

"You're going to have to recreate it."

Suri's brows rose. "What? I can't make a whistlemute that fast. It would take me *hours*."

Paqari found Chinbo and dragged him over by his shirt sleeve. "He's got the supplies and the skills. You've got the experience. Get to work."

"But—" Suri protested.

With a nod at the dinosaurs as they lapped up the silver-laced water, Paqari told her, "I'll give you fifteen minutes."

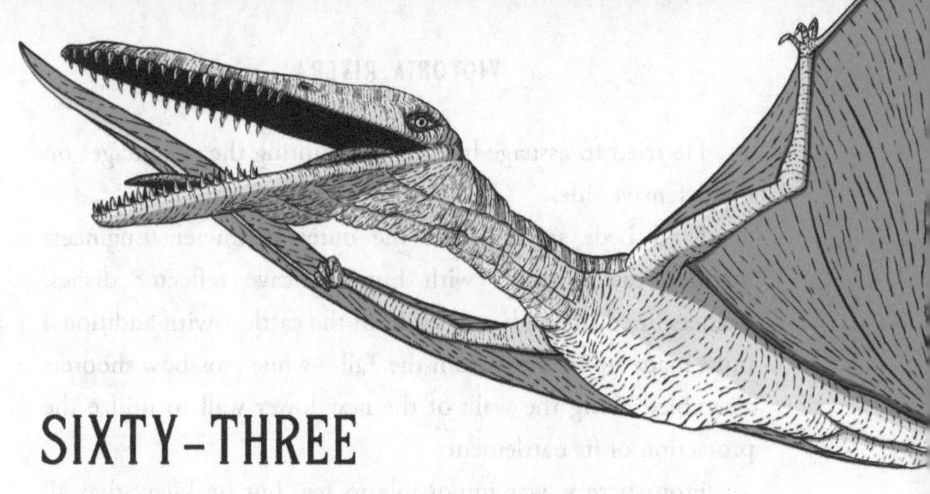

SIXTY-THREE

NINAN OBSERVED THE QHISPINA HOUSE CASTLE, hoping its defenses were sufficient, although now that he'd seen the extent of the Sauroguard, he doubted they were.

The giant theropods had not arrived, that much was clear; he wondered what had gone wrong, whether his and Qora's leaving the migration had made things worse. The group might still be coming, thinking they had three more days. There hadn't been sufficient time to warn them that the Sauroguard was coming early, and besides, what could they have done to speed up anyway?

Gods, he hoped Paqari and Kondor were all right. And Qora. He still didn't know the outcome of the mission at Pakasqa, but he knew it was better not to think about it. It would only make him anxious, and he had no power in this moment, chained up like this.

That faint, smoky haze he'd sensed earlier now filtered the light and formed a halo around the sun. Suddenly he began to question his assumption that the pyroraptors had set distant fires. Volcanic eruptions could also spread smoke far and wide. Maybe, just maybe, a successful volcanic eruption at Pakasqa had done so too.

It doesn't guarantee the team's survival though, he reasoned.

He tried to assuage his fear by counting the advantages on the defensive side.

Sand beds spread from the outer perimeter. Engineers manned castle towers with huge concave reflector dishes. Archers lined the high wall walks of the castle—with additional units made up of those from the Tail—while crossbow shooters assembled along the walk of the new lower wall to utilize the protection of its battlements.

From here it was impossible to see, but he knew that all defenders had been fitted with earplugs to guard against the screams of the scutellosaurs, and special airway masks to block the noxious gas of the hypsilophodons.

Defenders on the ground wore greased greaves to deter the troodon sticky-silk webs. They would also be carrying extra-sharp, serrated blades to cut those webs, if needed.

All defensive gear would have been tested on the captured reptiles to ensure its strength, or at least that had been the plan as far as Ninan had heard before he'd left for the migration. He didn't know whether the extraction team had managed to capture one of every specimen.

The trained smilodons would come last, kept inside the ramparts until defenders could take down the reptiles that might damage the smilodons' senses.

If Ninan had to guess, there were also hidden dinofelis traps along the final stretch, leaving only enough field space for the Allpan Guard units to spread out safely in defense.

All external watchtowers were occupied by Sumaqi forces, and so was the rocky outcrop halfway between here and the castle, which surely would provide a clean, elevated view of what was about to unfold.

He watched the Sauroguard inch closer and closer until

finally they filled every crevice of his view of the ground.

Beastlords, wearing their signature dominite-crystal collars, rode triceratops among the units, shouting commands. They carried scepters tipped with large dominite crystals too—although they had to wear thick helmets that covered their ears, with masks that obscured all but their eyes, in order to protect themselves from the sounds and scents of their very own reptilian soldiers.

Qhapaq Apo flew above the units on a pterobeast—not a pteranodon, but a full-sized saddled pterobeast (draped in red caparisons with gold tassels, embroidered with Sumaq's spinosaur-and-shield emblem) whose figure blackened everything below with its shadow. He held a dominite scepter as well, but the crystals at its tip pointed out from the center like a burst of purple rays, and he wore gilded armor and his famed gilded crown that was the likeness of a spinosaur skull fit to his head.

Below, hypsilophodons took the lead, darting forward and spewing their noxious gas as they approached the castle. The front lines held their ground with shields and smilodon-tooth spears, faces masked against the scent, while crossbow units shot in coordinated waves and archers aimed high for arcing shots that rained on the scutellosaurs that followed.

Even from all the way back at the watchtower, Ninan had to press hard against his own ears when the scutellosaurs screamed.

Catapults from behind the wall launched dozens of muters at once—the same bombs the Razorclaws had used in the Aquchay to dampen the sound of their arrival. The resulting particles canceled the brunt of the sound, giving the archers a chance to shower arrows again and take out as many dinosaurs as possible.

This repeated several times, screams and muters and

arrows, screams and muters and arrows, until the majority of the scutellosaurs were pierced clean through—which took some effort because of their thick scutes.

While the Allpan Guard was forced to exhaust a large amount of ammunition, pteranodons flew over and spewed acid.

Shield units on standby united to form shelters, covering groups of shooters.

Ballistas shot barbed nets into the air that flung open to catch pteranodons or at least knock them off course. The nets that missed fell to the ground and hindered land reptiles instead. Archers aimed for the acid pouches in the flyers' throats and burst several before they could build pressure again.

Muters shot out again.

Air squads flew out from the castle dropping firebombs over the Sauroguard, taking out clusters as the copper balls struck and the internal chemicals met to explode. From the equipment packs, Ninan could tell that the riders were also armed with hushdust, which would only work on the beastlords (not the reptiles) except that the beastlords' masks would easily prevent inhalation, rendering the substance useless here. Qhapaq Apo had prepared for that, it seemed.

Huge reflector dishes bounced light from the castle's defense towers, with engineers angling them to try and catch the sun at its low, rising point. They did their best to bounce the light at the beastlords and their crystals, in hopes of degrading the dominite in increments, but this would unfortunately not be very effective until the sun rose higher.

Mononkyus came next, racing forward in a horde. Their small statures allowed them to slip between the cracks of the front line's defenses, and they punched their long claws at defenders' legs.

The reinforced greaves protected the defenders, however,

and many simply kicked the mononykus away.

Defenders on raptorback came out from reserves on both sides of the castle, their megaraptors prepared with fool's silver and thus immune to enemy dominite. They speared attacking dinosaurs and charged oncoming troops.

All the Allpan defenders carried their own dominite, which distracted some of the Sauroguard, but most often the beastlords' dominite collars won out.

Just when Ninan was beginning to think there were no dinofelis traps, emerging therizinosaurs began to drop as though the ground had fallen out from under them.

Their weight, Ninan realized. Every reptile that had come forward thus far had either been relatively small, or had flown over—not sufficient to break the traps' hidden surface grates. Even though these therizinosaurs were small compared to their parent species, they were still as tall as grown men, with much more meat on their bones. They screeched when they hit the pit spikes, their venomous claws gone to waste. In seconds the pits were full to the brim, while the reptiles behind simply trampled their dead and rushed on.

Crossbow units fired new waves of bolts, striking several hundred therizinosaurs, but each seemed to require at least five or six bolts before it would fall. Many reached the front-line defenders and began to slash.

The armored defenders slashed back with their swords and stabbed with their sabertooth-spears to keep the therizinosaurs at bay. Additional defenders matched enemy claws with strikefangs.

Troodons came after and discharged their sticky silk at the defenders' legs, but the oiled greaves kept the strands from adhering properly. That was, until the beastlords switched tactics and commanded the troodons to aim high, trapping arms and weapons instead.

Some defenders managed to kill enough of the surrounding reptiles that they were able to cut their comrades free.

Irritators swept in after, emitting their vibrations that affected the entire human body—not just the ears—prompting the Allpan Guard to catapult another wave of muters that only partially canceled the effects.

Defenders faltered. Velociraptors scuttled in between to make their way to the wall, gathering sand on their sticky foot pads, which limited their vertical progress to a few inches before they slid back down.

Ninan silently praised the defense method, but wished there were something for the larger and more powerful reptiles that would be as effective.

Then came the dracorexes, with little arcs of electricity between their cranial horns, charging the defenders. If Ninan remembered correctly, all the Allpans' protective metal should be lined with rubber. It wouldn't do anything against blunt-force trauma, but it would temper the electric shock.

Dracorexes bent their heads forward. Defenders held out their spears to impale them, but dozens of dracorexes broke through, knocking their foes to the ground as electricity buzzed and sparked and moved along the metal layers of armor.

With much of the front lines dead, deterred, or distracted, ankylosaurs thundered up to the wall to swing their enormous club-tails at the stone.

"No ..." Ninan whispered. This was it. They were going to breach the wall. And then any of the hundreds of mutant reptiles the defenders had not managed to kill would filter into those holes, followed by units of pyroraptors, oviraptors, and finally the color-morphing megaraptors.

It was too much. Maybe if the giant dinosaurs had arrived on time, the castle would have stood a chance.

What had he been thinking, getting himself chained to this tower? Now all he could do was watch everything fall apart. Not that he could have made much of a difference, but at least he wouldn't be stuck here like an idiot. He hadn't stood close to his father for more than a minute, let alone made any attempt to end him. The qhapaq continued to soar over the battlefield on his pterobeast, far out of reach, shouting directions at the beastlords.

Ninan was so helpless in this position that his father hadn't bothered to leave him with more than two guards. There wasn't much he could do with his wrists bound in iron; he certainly couldn't fight anyone off, and there was no pool of acid to corrode the chains like last time. Both guards were watching the brutality with rapt attention.

With his head swimming at the action—clanging blades and crossbow clicks, thundering footfalls, sizzling electric currents, the occasional scream of a scutellosaur, the faint, lingering stench of troodon gas wafting backward on the wind—Ninan had to brace himself against the battlements. His father was going to win.

It was only as he closed his eyes for a moment, his ears tuned to individual sounds in the cacophony, that a distant hiss caught his attention. The guards began to murmur, pointing northward.

Ninan followed their gaze to the grasses beyond the castle—where at least two dozen megaboas slithered at an ungodly speed.

Nets full of dominite dangled from pteranodons, baiting the giant serpents.

And leading this unconventional brigade were Qora and Ollan Kanchaya.

"Gods in the High World," Ninan remarked.

His heart leapt.

Maybe Qora was right. Maybe everything on this earth *was* available to help them in this fight. Her ability to find the things that were good and useful in her environment had given her an edge time and time again. Bioluminescent fungus to provide light in the darkness; a floating pterodactyl nest to carry her on the river and forego the impassible jungle; vindictive serpentosaurid beasts to terrorize the enemies that had dared to threaten her refuge.

If it weren't for her insight, even *he* wouldn't have had a chance; she'd seen the goodness in him, too. Because of that, he was hers now. Forever.

"Are you seeing this?" one of his guards shouted down at others on the ground.

Qora and the Razorclaws spread out over the Sauroguard, from the castle wall clear back to where Ninan watched from the tower, drawing the megaboas. It was Kuy and Req who came closest, but they were too focused to see Ninan there lurking between merlons.

They pulled up the dominite nets by the attached ropes and secured them to the saddles. Then they withdrew a large supply of—

Eggs?

Kuy chucked eggs at the Sauroguard reptiles and then at the beastlords and even at some of the guards at the tower's base. Req did the same. The eggs smashed open and spilled a greenish, oily substance.

"Those creatures are very scent-motivated and scent-repelled. They'll be all over anything with dryosaurid musk ..."

The eggs must have been blown out and refilled, Ninan

thought. It was a brilliant delivery method, with eggs in abundance and easy to break.

Instantly the megaboas rose up on their thick bodies and slammed their heads forward, fangs bared at anything the oil touched. They swallowed beastlords whole and tore Sauroguard reptiles in half.

"Ruck!" said the guard who still wore Ninan's strikefangs.

Both guards raced down the tower stairs with weapons raised.

Up at the defensive wall, megaboas bit into the Sauroguard reptiles. They sent others fleeing in droves and slithered through their midst, hissing violently. Blood dripped from their mouths.

Qhapaq Apo swooped low to swing his dominite scepter in front of them, distracting them momentarily from their task. He shouted at the pteranodon beastlords to withdraw their spitters from the castle attack and come to his aid.

Qora aimed her wristbow and fired at a pteranodon's throat pouch just before it geared up to spew. The pteranodon let out a garbled squawk.

Alone on the tower, Ninan wasn't going to waste the opportunity. He took one look at his chain and pulled it taut with both hands so that it hugged the merlon and wrapped the extra links around his wrists.

The pain in his side seared as he walked up the wall, using the chain as an anchor. Halfway up, he tugged the chain, which scraped against the stone as it slid higher. A few more vertical steps, another tug, another step. He cried out at the sensation that he was being ripped in half, but landed on top of the merlon on his knees with a grunt and a pant. No one paid him any attention.

From this point, he looped up the chain's slack from around the merlon and tossed it inside the battlements with a clatter before climbing back down to the floor. He leaned out through a crenel and shouted to his guards.

"Hey!"

It took several tries to get their attention as they swung their swords at a megaboa. The one wearing Ninan's strikefangs looked up to see Ninan displaying his newly mobile chains.

The guard swore and dipped back into the tower.

By the time the guard ascended, Ninan had positioned himself strategically.

The second the guard set foot in front of him, Ninan came from behind and wrapped a section of chain around the guard's neck. He held it tight with one hand and snatched the guard's blade with the other. The strikefang teeth jutted off the guard's knuckles as he grasped at the chain to try and get his fingers under it for some relief, but Ninan held it until the guard blacked out, then slowly lowered him to the floor. It took some digging but he found the guard's keys and unlocked the manacles, rubbing his wrists.

"That's what you get for taking what's not yours," Ninan muttered as he removed the strikefangs and slipped them over his own knuckles. Looking down at the tower's base, he spotted a Sumaqi pteranodon. Looking up, he caught sight of his father flying toward the rocky outcrop.

This was his chance.

Ninan stumbled down to the bottom of the tower and came out to see a megaboa rearing its head at Sumaqi officers, who had gathered around it with swords. It was so much thicker than the serpentosaurid that had woken him with its nightmarish hiss in the jungle.

Sprinting past, he climbed onto the pteranodon and commanded it to rise to the skies.

And then Kutiq saw her crest the hill on the back of a baryonyx with her army behind her. She raised her golden spear—and for the first time, Kutiq believed the gods were real.

Excerpt from "The Slayer Queen of Wilamaya"

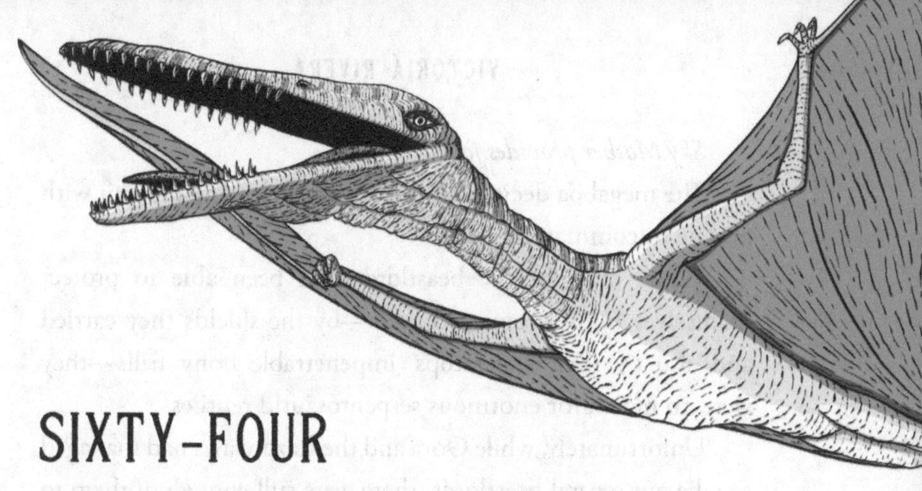

SIXTY-FOUR

QORA FLEW CLOSE ENOUGH to the castle to see Quya Urpi standing on the balcony of the main keep, directing the waves of retaliation like a symphony conductor. Qhapaq Izhi and Quya Illari stood at her sides. The royalborns appeared to be having an intense discussion as they observed what was happening on the battlefield.

The sky was hazy with smoke from Pakasqa that had traveled all this way on the wind. The volcanist had rightly predicted that some of it would follow; not a lot, but enough to remind Qora what a victory smelled like, and to make her crave another.

Swooping over a unit of oviraptors, Qora chucked an egg at their beastlord. The shell fractured on contact, spilling the dryosaurid glandular oils all over his armor.

One of the megaboas hissed and struck the spot.

"Dryosaurid glandular oils make a strong salve. It stinks as badly as the musk."

As soon as Qora had thought to involve the megaboas in battle, the way to focus their strikes had been clear. Megaboas aggressively hunted dryosaurids—the crocodilian variety that were often found in their habitats. Last-minute preparations had been intense, utilizing hundreds of eggs from the culinarium as to mark targets with the appropriate scent.

Sky Mother provides for us.

The megaboa decimated the beastlord, leaving his unit with no one to command it.

While most of the beastlords had been able to protect themselves from arrows and bolts—by the shields they carried and also by their triceratops' impenetrable bony frills—they were no match for enormous serpentosaurid reptiles.

Unfortunately, while Qora and the Razorclaws had managed to take out several beastlords, there were still enough of them to shout orders at the reptiles, whose numbers remained high.

While the smaller theropod dinosaurs feared the megaboas, the ankylosaurs were not intimidated. Even megaboa fangs couldn't get through their plates—and so they proceeded with orders to smash their club-tails against the stone wall.

Arrows and bolts bounced off the ankylos' armored backs, save for a few that caught the gaps between plates and spikes. This only served to slow the ankylos, but did not put an end to their destruction. Bolas went flying at their legs, exploiting the tails that made the ankylos top heavy and throwing them off balance. A few tipped over, mid-swing, while others continued to batter the wall until the stones began to crumble.

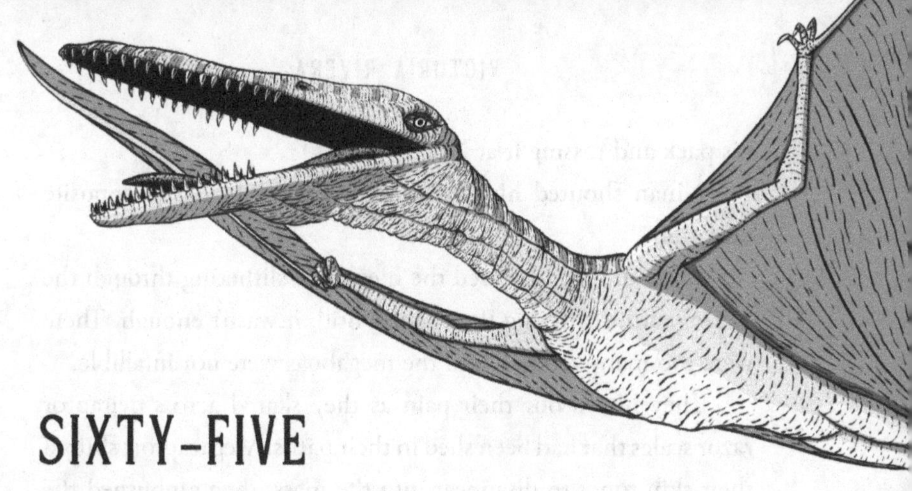

SIXTY-FIVE

NINAN ANGLED DOWN TOWARD THE OUTCROP, keeping his father in his sights.

Qhapaq Apo landed his pterobeast, which was excessive in size for a single-rider mount—comically so—but the man would have accepted nothing less for going off to battle. Anything smaller simply didn't convey his dominance.

Guards followed on pteranodons and accompanied Qhapaq Apo to this new vantage point, which provided a much closer, wider view.

Now mostly out of range of the chaos and its dangers, the qhapaq and his guards removed their masks.

Glancing at some of the Allpan air squad riders and their hushdust, Ninan veered back over the battlegrounds.

He flew up to one of the riders, who flinched at the sight of a Sumaqi pteranodon and raised a longblade.

"It's me!" Ninan said. "You might have seen me before, at Qhispina House. Apo-Kimsa Kallpa!"

The rider squinted, then lifted his brows. "Ninan? The rebel prince ..."

"I need your hushdust." Ninan pointed his head at the unmasked guards on the outcrop.

"It's yours!" said the rider, removing a powder cannon from

his pack and tossing it at Ninan.

Ninan shouted his thanks and flew back in the opposite direction.

As he did, he observed the megaboas slithering through the Sauroguard, scattering their ranks. Still, it wasn't enough. There were too many reptiles, and the megaboas were not infallible.

They hissed out their pain as they skated across oviraptor razor scales that had been shed in their paths. Megaraptors shifted their skin tones to disappear into the mass, then ambushed the megaboas three or four to one.

When pyroraptors spewed their fire breath, the megaboas recoiled at the flames. Therizinosaurs, upon their beastlord's word, slashed with a fury, leaving striped gashes laced with venom on the megaboas' twisting backs.

The few pteranodons that were not spitting acid at the castle defenders came to defend against the megaboas too, leaving wounds that deepened fast and ate through the flesh to reveal the large vertebrae underneath.

The Allpans finally released the smilodons through portcullises that slammed shut the instant all had gone through. The smilodons pounced on the megaraptors and the troodons and the hypsilophodons with such rapid maneuvers that few had the chance to strike back.

Eventually, however, the dinosaurs began to overwhelm them with sheer numbers, and gained more ground as they employed their special features.

Like every other defense the quya had, no matter how brilliant, this was going downhill fast.

But the Sauroguard would have taken the castle in minutes, Ninan reminded himself, had the extraction team not provided specimens for the quya to prepare against, and had Qora not dragged the megaboas into battle.

It was another one of those times when Ninan knew he was supposed to be grateful for apparent mercies, yet was still left to wonder why the situation necessitated mercies at all. A delayed failure was still a failure.

Then the catapults groaned one after the other and sprung forward with a *CLANK*, flinging out hundreds of tubular objects that each streaked the air with smoke. When they landed among the hordes of reptiles, the smoke accumulated fast. It blanketed everything on the ground with thick plumes that smelled of sugar and saltpeter.

Smokers, Ninan thought. The kind he'd learned to make in Thak. He gave silent thanks to Pidru and Tamya and all his friends that must have helped to generate the supply.

Megaboa heads rose above the smoke.

The Razorclaws flung the rest of the scent tags blindly.

The smoke inhibited all other reptiles, but the megaboas could still follow the dryosaurid scent without needing to see, giving them an upper hand.

One of the pteranodon beastlords flew out and dropped beside Qhapaq Apo, spoke to him for a few seconds, and then flew out again, putting a trumpet to his lips and blasting a fanfare.

Ninan pulled back among the Allpan air squad as the Sauroguard pteranodons withdrew from terrorizing the castle and assembled in a strange side-by-side formation across the battlefield.

The beastlord shouted directions at them: "Up! Down! Up! Down! Up! Down!"

As if in a winged march, the pteranodons flapped in unison, sending out huge gusts that swept across the expanse below—

pushing the smoke in a swirling mass straight back toward the castle.

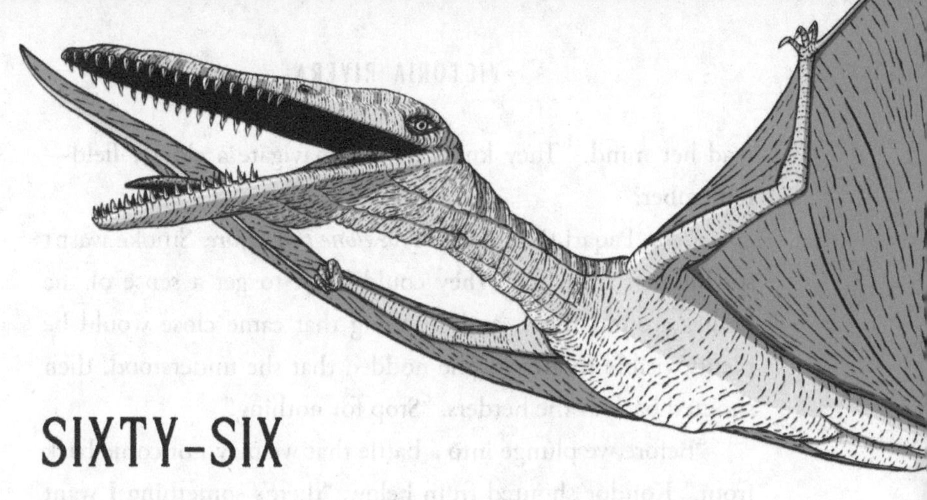

SIXTY-SIX

PAQARI FLEW AHEAD OF THE GIANT DINOSAURS as Suri blew the new whistle from the back. The giant dinosaurs thundered across the grassland in a mass, so swiftly that it reminded Paqari of the gallimimus on the Qhispina House grounds. That was the first time she'd been so close to Kondor, after he'd rescued her from death by trampling.

She looked over her shoulder at him now as he rode Grimjaw with a determined gaze. Even though he must have never imagined he would be riding a giganotosaur at top speed, he did it with a rogue sort of confidence, which looked good on him.

As they crested the gentle slope of land that came up behind Qhispina House, smoke spread across the view.

"What?" Paqari thought aloud. It wasn't unreasonable to see smoke, she supposed, with fire-breathing pyroraptors among the Sauroguard, but this was … a lot. It was thick and concentrated in one area, and it seemed to be coming in a tidal-style wave toward the castle.

If only Paqari had arrived with the dino herd a few minutes earlier, they might not be racing into obscurity. It would be difficult to fight when they couldn't clearly see the enemy.

"It's alright!" Kondor called up to her as though he could

read her mind. "They know how to navigate a cloudy field—remember?"

Right, Paqari thought. *They've done this before.* Smoke wasn't so different from fog. They could honk to get a sense of the bodies around them, and anything that came close would be plenty visible to attack. She nodded that she understood, then shouted back at the herders. "Stop for nothing!"

"Before we plunge into a battle that we may not come back from," Kondor shouted from below, "there's something I want you to know, princess!"

She fell back a bit, flying low and level with where he sat on Grimjaw's hulking form, her pulse pounding in time with the rhythm of the stampede. Last time they'd spoken about anything besides the migration, she'd shown herself to be presumptive and insecure. Kondor didn't deserve that. If she'd wanted to know more about his past, she should have asked.

He went on: "I think you're brilliant, and stunning, and—yes—ferocious. Somehow, even though you were raised in a prim little castle, your heart is wild and wayward. Every day since we left Murkroot, I've been fighting what you make me feel, until finally I gave in—and once I did, I regretted nothing. Yet you seem to think I never cared, that this was all some kind of game to me ... except that that couldn't be further from the truth. When it comes to you, princess, I am *dead serious*. Do you understand?"

Although Paqari pursed her lips, she couldn't keep from smiling.

"I'm sorry," she told him, "for thinking the worst of you."

Just like with the fog, it had been difficult to see things clearly, but there were other ways to navigate. If she were to follow her instincts, as the dinosaurs had, they would have told her not to fear, and that moving forward would only take her to new and wonderful horizons.

"All's forgiven," said Kondor. "Besides, I thrive on your spite."

And then they crossed the river and plunged into the smoke.

"The Astrodons" from *Myths and Legends of the West*

When the earth was filled with all manner of reptilian beasts, the gods saw fit to introduce another kind. And thus they brought forth beasts which bore hair and fur upon their backs, and which did give milk unto their young from their bodies. The gods called them "mammal," and the mammals multiplied in great variety.

But the dinosaurs and other reptiles did not wish to share their kingdom. They fostered a spirit of enmity, and so set about to terrorize their animal brethren. Many of the mammals developed speed and agility to evade the reptiles, while others adapted to hide among leaves or beneath the ground. None dared to challenge the great reptiles—that is, until the astrodons.

The astrodons did assemble together in darkness, which they did not fear, for their teeth did emit light like unto the stars. And thus, they prowled the territories of the dinosaurs and advanced upon them under the cover of night.

And the dinosaurs did see the glowing teeth of the astrodons, and said to one another, "Those are but stars on the horizon that have fallen and lost their way. We have no cause for concern."

But the "stars" grew as the astrodons neared, and by the time the dinosaurs became aware of their true source, the astrodons had overwhelmed them.

The astrodons, however, did not desire to destroy the reptilians, but only to convey a simple lesson—that no creature is infallible, and that all must live in tolerance of one another.

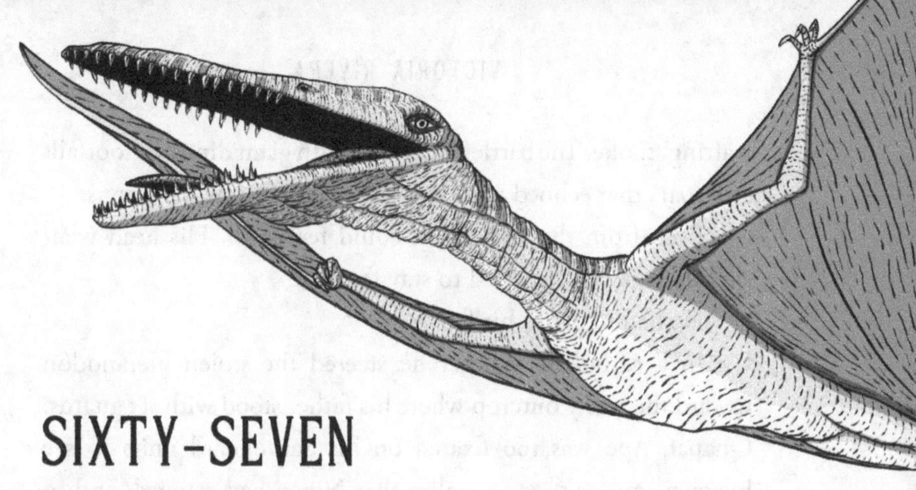

SIXTY-SEVEN

GIANT DINOSAURS CAME BURSTING THROUGH the smoke like beastly angels born from the mists of the High World. Kondor and the herders, to Ninan's surprise, rode on the dinosaurs' backs, while Paqari flew in on a pteranodon.

The shocking arrival of the giants put the Sauroguard reptiles on the defensive even though the giants had yet to attack.

Scutellosaur screams and blasts of pyroraptor fire and the hypsos' noxious gas all converged on the giants, inciting retaliation. The giants lunged at the Sauroguard, clamping their enormous jaws on the other reptiles and sinking in their teeth.

Ankylosaurs abandoned their work on the holes that had begun to form in the wall, now swinging their club-tails at the tyrannosaurs, spinosaurs, and giganotosaurs.

The mononykus simply fled the scene, while troodons spit their sticky silk to try and ensnare the giants' hind limbs. Dracorexes thrust their horned heads at the giants and zapped them into a frightening rage.

Beastlords tried to lure the giants with dominite, but the giants ignored them; somehow Paqari must have used the fool's silver on them, although Ninan wasn't sure how she'd done it with such short notice.

It was a mess of firestreams and cracks of electricity and

wafting smoke. The battlefield shook with giant dinosaur footfalls and roars that echoed wide and the irritators' low vibrations.

Even from the air, Ninan could feel it all. His head went slightly fuzzy but he tried to stay focused.

He had to get to his father.

In a turbulent manner he steered the stolen pteranodon toward the rocky outcrop where his father stood with six guards. Qhapaq Apo was too fixated on his Sauroguard units to see his own son, or to even realize that Ninan had escaped, and so instead of flying in a direct path, Ninan veered into a wide arc, out of any potential sightlines, and flew behind the outcrop. Before the shadow of the pteranodon could alert the guards to his presence, he aimed the hushdust powder cannon and dusted the guards.

Just as he'd distributed enough to put the guards to sleep, his father turned abruptly. The qhapaq's gaze rose to where Ninan hovered behind him.

The guards collapsed.

Qhapaq Apo raised his dominite scepter with its splay of crystals glowing bright.

Ninan's pteranodon locked its attention on the dominite, following the movement as the qhapaq pulled back.

Ruck, Ninan thought.

Completely out of control, Ninan gripped the saddle pommel to remain seated as the pteranodon flew over the outcrop's front edge. The powder cannon fell from his grasp and plummeted some hundred feet to the ground.

Ninan's father walked backwards to draw the pteranodon onto the flat rock and commanded it to land.

Once it had, there was nothing more to do. This pteranodon, which Ninan had snatched from the Sumaqis, would not disobey.

It had trained with the Sauroguard—not to mention that the qhapaq held a massive collection of crystals atop that scepter.

With no other choice, Ninan dismounted, dizzy from the flight and from enduring the pain that split his side whenever he raised his right arm. He faced his father.

"It's a shame," said the qhapaq, "that you inherited my ingenuity and my cunning … without the proper vision." He glanced at the watchtower where Ninan had been chained.

"I inherited nothing from you," Ninan spat. Although he knew it wasn't true. He had the same nose, similar cheekbones, perhaps the same sense of adamance and the same refusal to play by the rules.

The main difference was that his father was in a position to *make* the rules too, and to do so in such a way that he could bend everything around him to his will.

"You could have been a great man," said the qhapaq. "Instead you play games. You evade authority. You cheat and you steal."

"Cheat and steal," Ninan repeated. "You're right; I guess I am a little like you. Except you cheat the forces of nature, and you steal lives and dignity from the people who should prosper under your rule."

"I wouldn't expect you to understand the complexities of what I must do. In your small mind, you believe that someone in my position ought to be noble, when the only way to succeed is to be ruthless. The great mountains that form upon the earth do not—*cannot*—care for all that is destroyed to create them. Rocks collide and tilt and fold, shattering all that existed before, because the gods themselves know that this process is *necessary*."

Ninan clenched his fists at his sides, strikefangs pointed down. "It's *necessary* to destroy in order to make room for better things, is it?"

The qhapaq narrowed his eyes and tightened his grip on the dominite scepter.

"So when my friends erupted the volcano at Pakasqa," Ninan continued, certain now that volcanic smoke was the source of the sun's halo, "destroying the entire habitat that made these monstrosities possible"—he gestured at the battlefield where reptiles raged and reared—"you agree it was for the best?"

When the qhapaq said nothing, only watched his son with a subtle tick in his jaw, Ninan said, "That's right. They triggered an eruption—to spill fire and destroy everything below, and make sure you never breed another mutant reptile again. I'd say that's for the best, but ... what do *you* say, Father?"

Without taking his attention off Ninan, the qhapaq made a hand signal high in the air. An instant later, one of the airborne beastlords landed.

"Yes, Your Majesty?"

"It's time," said the qhapaq. "Release the skyfire."

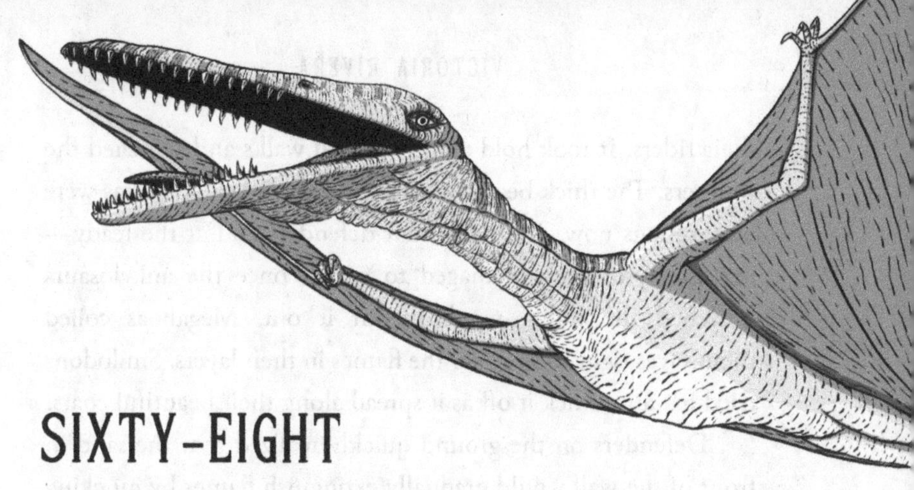

SIXTY-EIGHT

THE ECHO OF THE WORD "SKYFIRE" volleyed across the battlefield as one commander passed the message onto the others.

Ollan paused in the air, slowing his pteranodon so that it flapped rapidly to stay in one place.

Skyfire?

A trumpet blared several times. It was different in pitch and pattern than the fanfare that had drawn the pteranodons into formation to waft the smoke.

Hundreds of pterodactyls soared toward the chaos at the castle wall—as if from nowhere.

They came in shades of black, with faint markings on their heads and bodies. Even though they were only half the size of their pteranodon comrades, their dark emergence made Ollan break into a sweat.

One of the airborne beastlords flew above and shouted, "Destroy!"

The pterodactyls opened their elongated, toothy snouts and spat a dark liquid that caught fire mid-air and stuck to every target like flaming tar.

Where defender armor had been sufficient to keep pyroraptor flames from catching, this substance clung to it without mercy. It burned through the giant dinosaurs' scales and terrorized their riders. It took hold along the wall walks and scorched the shooters. The thick beams of the catapult and the ballistas were bonfire logs now. The water that defenders had at the ready—in case pyroraptors managed to get in once the ankylosaurs breached the walls—wouldn't put it out. Megaboas coiled themselves tight to smother the flames in their layers. Smilodons tried in vain to lick it off as it spread along their beautiful coats.

Defenders on the ground quickly realized that the sand in front of the wall would gradually extinguish flames by mucking up whatever made them stick, but this was a temporary solution that worked only for those in that zone.

Shooters fired at the pterodactyls. Crossbowers focused firmly on those that flew low while archers moved around to get better angles on those that flew high. When possible, all aimed to shoot into the pterodactyls' mouths, as trained; some shots came close, but few landed perfectly on these moving targets.

Ollan took shots from the air with his own crossbow, swerving to miss a fiery stream that came straight for his face. Qora fired her wristbow several times, reloading fast from her vest pocket-pouches. Between the two Kanchayas, they took down five of the flying demons, but there were still so many more.

Other Razorclaws chased the pterodactyls on pteranodonback, trying to slash at them with longblades, only managing to nick a wing or a tail. The scales were thick and near impenetrable. Bandits joined the fight, bringing with them additional fighters from their extended crew. Allpan air squads dwindled.

Once again, the qhapaq had unleashed a new evil for the resistance to defeat, only this time Ollan had no clue how they were going to do it.

He thought of the bestiary with the missing page—and mentally filled it in.

Pterodactyl (Skyfire)
Feature: adherent incendiary expulsion, fortified scales
Vulnerability: unknown

"You must be like unto the serpent, who will shed her skin when she has outgrown it."

Shaman Sisa Achirana

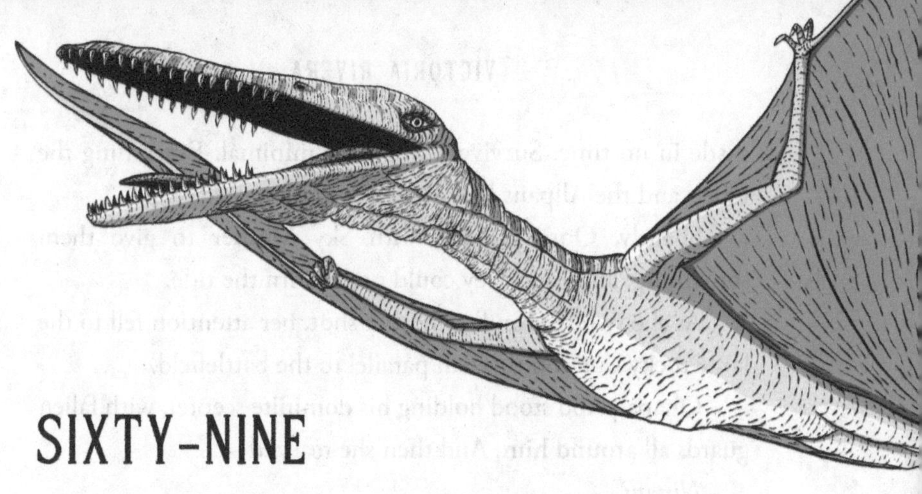

SIXTY-NINE

THE WHOLE WORLD SEEMED TO BE ON FIRE. The volcano had been one thing, Qora thought, with a sweeping scorch that had ended everything in its way at once. But this was a targeted sort of cruelty, prolonged for every victim. Dinosaurs and human defenders alike cried out in agony when they went up in flames. Paqari and Kondor had brought the giant dinosaurs in the nick of time but it still hadn't been enough—and neither had the megaboas.

The efforts had nearly allowed them to fight on even ground, but of course Qhapaq Apo was no fool; of course he'd had one more trick up his sleeve.

Qora flew hard to get under a cluster of pterodactyls and fired her wristbow at their bellies. She had no confidence that this would work on a breed created explicitly for the purpose of war, but she had to try.

A few of her bolts stuck, knocking the pterodactyls off their flight path. The throats were narrow and the scales around them were thick, but she aimed for those too, when she could, even though she rarely so much as skimmed one.

Flaming streams zipped past her several times, once so close that the heat grazed her cheek.

If they kept going like this, the qhapaq would overtake the

castle in no time. Survivors would be minimal. Everything the rebels and the Allpans had done would be wasted.

Silently, Qora pleaded with Sky Mother to give them something, anything they could use to turn the tide.

As she swooped in for another shot, her attention fell to the large rocky outcrop that ran parallel to the battlefield.

Qhapaq Apo stood holding his dominite scepter, with fallen guards all around him. And then she realized—

Ninan?

"Spirits," she whispered.

He was alive!

His position on the outcrop didn't lead her to believe he was out of danger, but at least he was here! At least she could see him. At least he was in one piece.

Relishing the sight of him, she lost focus on her task. She missed her shot by an embarrassing margin, and failed to keep aware of her immediate surroundings as she loaded a new bolt.

Another pterodactyl came at her from behind. She knew this only by the rush of air beneath its wings that stirred the hairs on the nape of her neck—and then by the searing heat that struck her back.

"Aggghh!" she screamed.

With no thought for any other aspect of her safety, she let go of the pommel and shucked off her green vest, dropping it as the flames spread across its panels. It fluttered to the ground in slow motion, charred fabric alight.

Her eyes welled and a pulse of heat flared between her shoulder blades.

The vest portion of her jacket was all she'd had left. She knew that was an exaggeration, but it felt true. A thin layer of hope, the essence of all she'd become in this fight—not just the battle below but the battle she'd been fighting for months, for years—and now it was on fire, soon to be a pile of ash in the grass.

Even more fitting was the fact that, while a fire had ignited inside of her that made her want to rain bolts on Qhapaq Apo, she only had a single bolt left in her wristbow. One little bolt.

She locked eyes with the qhapaq, who had seen everything and sneered back at her.

Maybe one bolt was all she needed.

SEVENTY

BEFORE THE "SKYFIRE" HAD ARRIVED, Paqari had been carrying the herders one by one, on her pteranodon, to the safety of the castle. Riding the dinosaurs had been sacrifice enough for them; while the giant dinosaurs were strong in battle, the herders were a gentle people not trained to fight. Kondor, however, had refused to let her take him until the others had gone, and in the end refused to even go at all. He *was* trained (he insisted) to some extent for conflict, and though she tried to remind him that the conflict for a gladewarden in Murkroot—or probably anywhere at the Tail—was nothing like this, he had remained on dinoback. The princess suspected he was too fond of Grimjaw and couldn't bear to leave the giganotosaur to his own devices.

Not wanting to watch from the sidelines, Paqari then flew up to the ballista tower where both giant weapons were aflame, surrounded by injured operators trying in vain to douse them. There was still a good supply of copper-cased firebombs behind them, which would now be very difficult to launch.

"Allow me," she said, gathering several into her pteranodon's pack. "I'll deploy some of these myself."

The princess flew off again, throwing firebombs at oncoming acid-spitters and skyfire. Whatever substance the pterodactyls ejected made for twice the incendiary effect when the firebombs struck them, although Paqari missed several and the bombs exploded on the ground instead. Meanwhile, Kondor fired his wristbow at anything that came close to Grimjaw, then held fiercely to the saddle pommel for balance whenever the giganotosaur lunged at an opponent.

As soon as there was a break in the madness to do so, Paqari delivered half her firebombs to Kondor, and together they defended the ground and the sky immediately around them.

It was probably a futile effort, she thought, but they were both headstrong and didn't plan to let that go to waste. They would go down fighting if—or more likely *when*—it came to that.

That was, until an irritator's vibrating growl sent both Kondor and Grimjaw into a disoriented stupor, making way for a dracorex to charge Grimjaw. The electricity sparked between the dracorex's horns just before it slammed its head at Grimjaw's chest, collapsing him on the spot.

〰〰〰

"You're …" Ninan rasped at his father as they stood above the violence and bloodshed. "You're evil incarnate."

Ninan's whole body—except for his ribs—felt numb, and so did his mind. Despite the perpetual threat of this battle that had been looming for months, he still couldn't believe he was actually watching it unfold before him.

He had allowed his father to trap him for the second time, unable to control the pteranodon that would allow him to fly away to aid his friends. But of course it was part of the task he had set for himself. Once again, he was the only enemy allowed to stand directly in front of the great Qhapaq Apo.

"I am *power* incarnate," said the qhapaq. "Look at what I've done! Look at all that I can do! I have created new life, brought things into existence that no one had ever before witnessed. Now you can see that not only is my leadership sanctioned by the gods, but I *am* a god! And for once"—he sneered and spoke through gritted teeth—"you will respect me."

Qhapaq Apo swung his scepter and struck Ninan across his fractured ribs.

Crying out, Ninan fell to his knees.

He slammed his eyes shut against the blinding pain. Nausea crested in his gut. His breaths quickened, each another dagger in his side.

His father tossed the scepter to the rocky ground with a clatter, then drew a sword.

⟫⟫⟫

Ollan and the Razorclaws took down pterodactyls one at a time. Wayra swooped in close and cut one's head with her blade. Kuy positioned himself to stab one from underneath. Req, however, took a flaming hit to the shoulder and flew straight to the strip of sand, where he flung himself down and shoved himself into a small mound to stifle the fire.

The princess had had the right idea chucking firebombs at the pterodactyls, Ollan thought, before she'd abandoned the whole thing and gone to aid a fallen giganotosaur with Kondor. If only the pterodactyls weren't spread far and wide, it might be possible to get more than one or two within a firebomb's blast radius.

⟫⟫⟫

Qora wove between enemy flyers, keenly aware of the single

shot she had left. Ninan was on his knees in front of his father, whose blade was drawn at his side. She was too far away to hit the qhapaq, and in her haste to get in range she flew against a Sauroguard pteranodon. By its bulging throat, she knew the pressure had already built and she swerved to miss the spew of acid; it landed on her saddlebag instead. The acid hissed as it ate through the leather; if she didn't detach it fast, it would eat through to her own pteranodon's scales. She strained to unfasten the buckle until the strap went loose and the bag dropped to the ground with a *whumpf*.

Then a skyfire pterodactyl dove toward her and opened its mouth. It happened too quickly for Qora to react in time. She held up her forearms to block the streaming fire, bracing herself for the agony of the burn, but thinking that at least it wouldn't touch her face. Just as it was about to spew, a bolt came at it from the side and pierced it clean through, knocking it laterally.

Qora lowered her arms.

Ollan lowered his crossbow.

"Thank you," Qora breathed.

"No problem. Are you—agh!"

A second pterodactyl's fire spit splashed across the weapon, flecking Ollan's hand.

"Ollan!" Qora shouted.

His now-flaming crossbow plummeted. He screamed at the fire that stuck to his wrist and fingers.

There was nothing he could do but press his skin tight against the saddle, which spread the substance but smothered the flame. Qora looked on, helpless, as he winced and waited for the flame to die.

"We have to find a way to gather them," Ollan choked out. "To get them all in one place. Paqari has firebombs; if we time a launch just right ..."

"Get them all in one place," Qora repeated in her mind.

The words struck her because gathering pterodactyls had once been one of her greatest fears during the Venture.

"They're drawn to bright lights and loud noises."

Mentally, she could still hear the screech of the wild flyers approaching at the riverbank—the time she had drawn them by accident, and the time she had called them reluctantly but on purpose, using a firestick. The same kind of firestick she and the Razorclaws had carried this morning (and still currently kept in their packs) to call the quya in case anything had gone wrong with the megaboas.

Skyfire pterodactyls were not wild, so she couldn't be sure their instincts were the same—but there was nothing to lose.

On the outcrop, Ninan stared at his father with a weary, hopeless gaze, and Qora wanted to go to him, to use her last shot to save him. But with Ollan injured and without a weapon, she was going to need that shot. Firebombs only worked on impact, and the fatal blow would need to detonate somewhere in the midst of all the pterodactyls, which meant it would need to be in the air. Someone would need to throw it—and Qora would need to bust it open with a bolt.

Maybe the explosion would be enough to get the qhapaq's attention and give Ninan an advantage.

Except Qora had to gather the pterodactyls first.

She reached for her saddlebag, only to remember it was somewhere on the ground. But Ollan still had his.

☽☽☽

Paqari stood guard with firebombs at the ready while Kondor

examined Grimjaw.

"I think his heart stopped," he told her, pressing his hand to Grimjaw's breastbone.

The princess had blasted the offending dracorex on her way to land beside Kondor, but more death wouldn't bring back the giganotosaur if he was truly gone. She found herself not willing to consider that possibility yet. It was a dinosaur, for gods' sakes, but his lifeless form filled her with sadness and rage.

She glanced up as Qora swooped toward her.

Before the pteranodon's claws had even rustled the grass, Qora said, "I'm sorry about your friend but we need a firebomb—now."

))) (((

With his wrist wrapped in a torn strip of his shirt, and feeling like it had been burnt down to the bone, Ollan dismounted his pteranodon and stood at the center of the battlefield. Dinosaurs and smilodons and megaboas continued to fight around him but he took the firestick out of his saddlebag and raised it high.

Paqari circled above with a firebomb in hand.

Qora hovered a ways off, wristbow in position.

Ollan pulled the sparkcord.

The three of them held their breath.

))) (((

Ninan bowed as his father swung the blade back to prepare for the cut that would end their feud. Even with the pain that ripped down his side, Ninan knew he had the skill to block that blade at the hilt and maneuver himself to safety. Or better yet, he only had to throw a punch with one of his strikefangs. It would be easy, he told himself. But for some reason, he hesitated.

This man was still his father. Some deep and desperate part of Ninan still wanted this man to love him, to take pride in him. And Ninan was not a killer; not if he didn't have to be.

But he *did* have to be—didn't he?

The qhapaq had caused so much suffering and death. What was one young man's soul if it meant saving the world from this monster?

In the span of a few seconds, Ninan gathered his courage.

When his father was about to swing forward, a pyrotechnic squealed into the air and exploded in red sparks.

Qhapaq Apo paused mid-swing and turned to look.

All his precious Sauroguard pterodactyls flocked to the spot.

The image of the pterodactyls at the Amaru riverbank flashed in Ninan's mind.

Paqari flung a firebomb upward from above the swoop.

As it peaked and fell, Qora aimed her wristbow. She waited for what felt like a beat too long, but then the weapon clicked and the bolt zipped up at a perfect diagonal to strike the copper casing.

The impact forced a fiery blast that engulfed the pterodactyls from the center of the mass outward.

Ninan felt the *BOOM* in his chest.

All pterodactyls in the center of the swarm were blasted to bits on the spot. Those on the fringes caught fire fast, pierced by shrapnel and torn to pieces by the blast force. The substance in their throat pouches seemed to ignite from the inside, spreading flames to anything else in range—sparing no reptilian victims.

Qora and Paqari had already flown away. Ollan sprinted from his spot before the bodies—or what was left of them— came hurtling down.

Teeth bared, Qhapaq Apo turned back to Ninan and raised his blade once again, but this time, Ninan was ready to do what he had come to do.

He thrust a strikefang at his father's core.

The smilodon teeth cut through with ease.

Ninan felt a new pain in his own body, something that had nothing to do with his ribs and everything to do with his father's choked expression.

The qhapaq grunted, dropping his blade and holding onto Ninan for support. He looked directly at his son, but somehow also looked past him as he rasped, "After all that I've … built? After all that I've … *created*?"

With tears in his eyes but no mercy left, Ninan yanked out the strikefang and removed the qhapaq's trembling hand from his shoulder.

The qhapaq staggered backwards, each of his faltering steps an inch closer to the edge of the outcrop. "I created *you*, too—remember?"

Racked with sobs, Ninan managed to stand firm. "And of all your creations … I was the one you could never fully control." At the last second, before his father went over, he added: "I guess that's why I was your downfall."

(AMANCAY drops her bloody sword with a clatter, falls to her knees before KING INTI)

AMANCAY: It is done. The scalebrute has taken its last breath.

KING INTI: Now you see, Amancay, that the monster was not Shadow itself; he simply blocked the light.

Amancay and the Scalebrute of Saqrampa, Act III, Scene VII

SEVENTY-ONE

THE SMOKE DISSIPATED, revealing endless heaps of flesh. Blood oozed from torn cavities and organs. Strings of sticky-silk lay strewn about. Razor-scales stuck up from between blades of grass. Pools of acid continued to eat away at their craters in the ground. Flames lapped at the air from burning bodies and supplies. Scattered dominite crystals faded as the sun beat down on them.

The surviving megaboas slithered back toward their habitat. Sauroguard dinosaurs wandered the landscape with few beastlords still standing to command them and little dominite to keep them in formations. Wounded beastlords staggered through the field as Allpan guards emerged to capture them and hold them for trial. Animal handlers, using a new supply of dominite, dispersed to round up stray dinosaurs; the surviving pterosaurs would be more difficult, but a few of the handlers took to the sky to try to lure them down.

Qora flew to Ninan, who had picked up his father's dominite scepter and flown down to where the qhapaq's body lay. She found him kneeling beside the gilt-armored corpse, clutching his side, face streaked with dust and tears.

He looked up when she landed and dismounted, then stood on shaky legs and embraced her. His body trembled with silent sobs, but she held him and he held her too, and she had the suspicion that if either of them were to move another muscle, they might both collapse. For now, they held each other up; it seemed they always had.

〉〉〉

It had only been a few minutes, but Grimjaw still had not woken. Paqari racked her brain for a way to revive him. Kondor mournfully stroked the giganotosaur's forelimb.

"There's one thing we can try," Paqari told him. "It's going to sound odd, and you might not want to do it, but if he's already dead it won't matter." She scanned the grass for some stray dominite.

"Whatever it is, I trust you," said Kondor.

Within a few seconds, Paqari had found a crystal and also located a wandering dracorex the handlers had not yet rounded up. She ran to the dracorex and waved the crystal until the dracorex fixated on her, then lured it over to Grimjaw and motioned for Kondor to get away from the body.

Using the same commands and hand signal that the beastlords had, Paqari said, "Charge!"

The dracorex built up the electricity between its horns, tilted its crown forward, and rammed into Grimjaw's chest.

Grimjaw jolted in response—what seemed to be reflexively—but then his eyes flew open and his jaws parted and his chest inflated.

"Limbs above ..." Kondor went to the giganotosaur, who howled like he'd been woken from the dead—because, in a way, he had—and tried to get back upright.

Paqari released a sigh and wiped the sweat from her hairline.

"I don't understand," said the gladewarden.

The princess smiled faintly. "Along the Tisquvian coasts, there are beds of electric eels. Once in a while, someone gets shocked ... and sometimes it's enough to kill them. Three summers ago I accompanied my father on a sea voyage, and one of the crew went overboard. The man encountered an eel, and that was that—or so we thought. Other crew went after his body, found him floating like driftwood, but as they hauled him through the water, the same eel shocked him again ... and immediately he woke. As soon as we returned home, I scoured my library for an explanation, and I learned that an electric charge can stop the heart. Fortunately, in some cases, it can also *start* the heart, if done correctly and before the lack of blood to the brain causes any damage."

As Grimjaw lumbered about, Paqari couldn't be sure he wasn't brain damaged—or whether he was just recovering—but when he leaned toward her and nuzzled her shoulder, she figured he was probably fine. She patted his enormous snout. "You're very welcome. And thank you for your service."

Kondor shook his head like he couldn't believe any of this. He took her by the wrist and drew her over to him.

She put her arms around his neck and met his gaze. "So you really forgive me?"

"For thinking I'm a callous rogue? Yes. For making me lose my wits every time you're around? Well, that's going to be a little more difficult."

Rolling her eyes, she stretched up on her toes until her face was level with his, and kissed him.

〈〉〉〉

The Razorclaws and their bandit friends went about the

gruesome task of putting fatally wounded dinosaurs out of their misery. Ollan accompanied Wayra, whose red-rimmed eyes hinted at the toll it was taking on her to do this. So much suffering, so much loss. Innocent creatures used as weapons, with no thought for their sentience, for their capacity to feel fear and pain.

He paused to embrace her. It was all he could do, but he hoped to be the one to comfort her for a very long time.

ɔɔɔ

Ninan and Qora flew back to the castle together, with the qhapaq's corpse secure in their pteranodon's beak. They landed on the main keep's balcony from which Quya Urpi had commanded her forces, and deposited the qhapaq face up onto the tiles.

It was an undignified treatment, Ninan realized, but there was no better way to handle it. The man had fallen a great distance and they hadn't been close enough to a building to carry him in with their own strength. His dead eyes stared up at them.

Quya Urpi came out with Quya Illari to meet them.

Ninan went to his mother and fell into her arms. Together they shed more tears as she cradled his head against the crook of her neck.

"It's done," he told her in a whisper.

"It was necessary," she replied. "And we will all be better off … because of you."

Qhapaq Izhi came to let the quyas know that most of the surviving Sumaqi guards and beastlords were in custody (aside from a few that had fled) and that he had dispatched messengers to tell the other Terrains of Qhapaq Apo's death and failed attack. "Once everyone has recovered, many public appearances will be in order. The masses must be made aware of the lies they have been fed about Apo-Kimsa's death and Quya Illari's capture."

Ninan nodded. For once, he would make a public appearance without pretending to be something he was not. He would finally reveal the truth about why he'd competed in the Venture, about the coercion that had led to his arranged engagement, about his willing escape from the wedding, his time in hiding, his aid to the rebellion, and even his final moments with his father. There was no more room for deceit. He would set the record straight. He would need time to process all that had occurred, but when he was ready, he would make sure that Sumaq—and Runaqa— were never the same again. For the better.

With that, he leaned over his dead father and put his fingers to the man's eyelids and closed them.

𝄢𝄢𝄢

At night, Qora stood on the balcony of her bedroom—hers for as long as she wanted, Quya Urpi had said—and looked out at the grounds below washed in hazy moonlight. There were no corpses out there, not from this side of the castle, and for a moment Qora relished her ability to turn her back on all the bloodshed and pretend it had never happened.

But of course, it *had* happened. Nothing could change that.

It had taken all day for the quya's forces (and everyone else willing to help) to clear the brunt of the mess, but it would take months to put everything back in order, and even then, the land and the people would always bear certain scars. Many people were lost in battle, along with smilodons and several of the giant dinosaurs from the Tail; others were maimed or injured but would recover in time.

After a brief ceremony, the Tailfolk had allowed the Allpans to make use of the bodies of their fallen dinosaur friends so that nothing would go to waste. Bone marrow had been harvested to quickly heal major wounds, as Qora had experienced herself when she'd returned from the Venture. She still couldn't understand those mystical bones and their power, but once again, she felt Sky Mother's hand in her life.

She looked over her shoulder at the sound of knuckles rapping on the door frame. Ninan was standing in the open doorway, smiling sadly. He had dark circles under his eyes, and he walked in with one hand resting on his side. The physicians had wrapped his torso to help his cracked ribs heal, and given him some oral medicine for pain, but he would be sore for many weeks, maybe longer.

He came to her and stood beside her on the balcony, slipping an arm around her waist, then looked up.

Stars twinkled, somehow still visible even though the volcanic haze lingered in the atmosphere.

Qora could tell that Ninan was looking at Astrodon.

"Your father must have seen Runaqa a bit like this, I think," she said, gesturing at the sky. "One big space to conquer, and everything in it small. Except nothing out there is small; it only looks that way from a distance, when a man doesn't understand his position—when he believes he's the center of the universe." She thought about her conversation with Ninan at the Tail, when they'd been stargazing.

"He certainly did believe that." Ninan scoffed.

"He thought we were just little lights, but when he got closer, he found out we were fiery giants. Each one of us."

After a pensive moment, Ninan said, "Is it alright if I feel like I'm just sort of … suspended up there with nothing to hold onto?

If I don't have the same faith that you do in our purpose here?"

"Of course it's alright. It's like you said: You like to look at star patterns because it's a way to make sense of them, because even though they're mythical, it's nice to recognize something in the void. That's what faith is to me—trying to recognize something, anything, in this void. I don't think it's really about gods; I think it's about being human together, and trying even when all seems lost, fighting for what matters to us, even though we don't know why we exist to have wants and needs to begin with, showing reverence for the beyond and for all that is bigger than us. Maybe more than anything, faith is defiance—an act of rebellion against chaos. It doesn't really make sense that we exist at all, yet … here we are, miracles incarnate. You're my miracle, at least."

Ninan pulled her tight against him. "And you're mine."

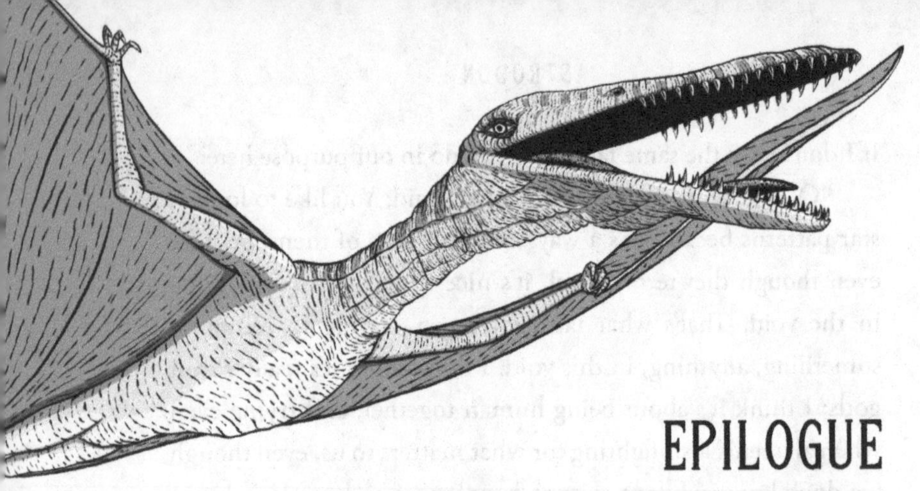

EPILOGUE
ONE YEAR LATER

NINAN AND QORA PAUSED IN THE CENTER of the Kallpa House ballroom as the music stopped. They separated, bowed to one another, then turned and acknowledged their guests, who applauded their dance.

The guests then dispersed, raising their voices with remarks to one another, while a few made their way to the couple.

"You look beautiful," Paqari told Qora.

Qora's green wedding dress was both alluring *and* fitting for the Raptoriva, Ninan thought.

Ollan and Wayra, hand in hand, joined Paqari for greetings.

"Congratulations," Ollan said before kissing Qora's cheek, then shaking Ninan's hand.

"Thank you," said Qora. She accepted a hug from Wayra, then asked, "How's the sanctuary?"

A large portion of Allpan lands had been set aside to hold the last of the Sauroguard reptiles. They would live out their days on open habitats that felt natural, where wild game could run through for them to hunt, but they would be protected and also contained and separated to avoid breeding. Everyone agreed that they must be allowed to die out peacefully, so that no one could ever use them to terrorize again.

"It's wonderful," Wayra said. "The dinosaurs are doing well. We don't usually have to use dominite anymore to keep them calm. That's *one* good thing about all their Sauroguard training: They're primed to learn commands and follow. Now that they trust the handlers, we're able to care for them as needed."

She and Ollan had been working with the quya to establish the sanctuary, and Ninan sensed that Ollan had finally found his place. Wayra of course was right at home with reptiles, but Ollan's motivation to do this work was less obvious. Qora had said a few weeks earlier that she thought maybe Ollan *related* to the reptiles, as he too had been displaced, forced from one way of life to the next, and left to make sense of it. Maybe the sanctuary was cathartic in that way.

That was understandable. Being able to participate in healing this broken world was helpful to personal healing as well. Ninan had experienced that himself.

He and Qora had spent most of the past year making public appearances—like another tour, except that they'd set their own terms. Their purpose had been to connect with their people on a personal level, to convey the truth, and to build trust, while also addressing troubled regions to determine where people might need the most assistance. They had even worked to rebuild communities like Thak, to which some of the families had returned now that the Terrain was safe.

Safe for most people, at least.

Not everyone had accepted Ninan's return. In light of Ninan having killed Qhapaq Apo himself (regardless of the qhapaq's many war crimes) and another rebel group's assassination of Apo-Huk, those loyal to their former leader and his first heir were not happy with the change in government plans. There had been street riots in Qhusi, and death threats too.

Apo-Iskay had been tried and also found guilty of war crimes, namely his hand in staging the "rebel" attack that his father had used as an excuse to advance on Allpa, which had killed hundreds of civilians in the process. These acts stripped him of his title and inheritance, but again, there were those who maintained that he was the rightful heir to Sumaqi power. Some of the highborn loyalists, like Qhapaq Apo's chief attendant Mullu, refused so adamantly to serve another leader that they even went so far as to take their own lives.

Ninan was the only one left to replace his father, but there would always be some contention over the matter. In the meantime, he had asked his mother to act as regent for a few years until he was ready to lead Sumaq himself. For now, he wanted to continue his work with the people, and enjoy his time with Qora.

He and Qora were young, of course, for marriage. Qora had since only turned nineteen, and Ninan twenty. They might have waited, but Ninan didn't see the point; he knew he only ever wanted her. Besides, when it was time for him to be crowned qhapaq—a concept he still couldn't fathom—he wanted Qora by his side, both physically and legally, to rule with him in equal measure. In all things, she was his partner.

More than anything, he wanted a family, one that loved as families should, which he had found with Qora and with all their friends and allies, and he wanted to cling to that with everything he had.

"Perhaps you two would like to borrow the *Velosaura* for a honeymoon voyage," Paqari said.

Ninan scoffed. "I appreciate your generosity, but I never want to set foot on that ship again. Speaking of, I heard you had it docked down at the Tail. Is that true? You negotiated it away from your family?"

"I did," Paqari said. "Kondor came with me when I renounced my title and we sailed it all the way to Brinegrove. My mother was absolutely scandalized. I wasn't sure whether she was happy to see me go so she wouldn't have to deal with me anymore, or whether she would have preferred to keep me there out of spite. Either way, I doubt I'll be invited to my sister's coronation."

Yet another unusual political shift: Paqari's sister as quya of Tisqu. Due to Qhapaq Achik's close affiliation with Qhapaq Apo, the Tisquvians had ousted Paqari's father from power. Paqari's younger brother had been heir by law, despite the fact that their mutual sister was first born, but the people had seen fit to make a few changes in the wake of Quya Urpi's defense against the New Empire. It seemed a female leader could do great things— especially when she ruled with compassion and wasn't afraid to rally all the help she needed to preserve her people's freedom.

As far as other leadership across Runaqa, Qhapaq Izhi had redeemed and restored his citadel, along with his power, and the Qolqese monarchs would remain in place, as would Quya Urpi.

Kondor stepped up and handed Paqari a drink, then took a sip of his own. "Congratulations, Ninan and Qora."

It was strange to see him in fine threads and gold buttons, instead of his usual woolly vest and gladewarden gear, but he'd cleaned up well. The way Paqari ran her fingers down one of his jacket lapels hinted that she thought so too.

"Better not spoil her too much," Qora said, nodding at Paqari's drink. "She might remember her fine upbringing and not want to go back with you."

Paqari rolled her eyes. "Don't worry. It's not that bad. I've realized I quite like being up in the trees. Especially in Brinegrove where I can also look at the sea."

"'Not that bad,'" Kondor repeated, "because we built her an enormous house with big windows facing the water, and because she's made a deal with a book merchant from Anglonsa to send her a regular supply of literature for her library.'"

Last Ninan had heard, Paqari had managed to maintain a bit of her inheritance when she'd left Tisqu, and worked out a material trade with the elderboughs to ease the burden on some of the Tail's industries. This had allowed her to exchange her Tisquvian wealth for Tail wealth, which gave her the means to continue a fairly nice lifestyle abroad.

Meanwhile, Kondor had taken a new gladewarden position in the same seaside city to be near her, and Paqari now spent her time teaching at the Verdurian Institute, where she was employed to speak ad nauseam about her scientific interests. It seemed the princess, who had often doubted her ability to adapt to the world beyond her island, had carved a new place for herself.

The giant dinosaurs that had survived battle had been returned to the Tail via Allpan cargo ship (once ships large enough could be built to carry them), a much better method for everyone involved. Word had it that Grimjaw lived in Brinegrove now too.

Qora asked Paqari about the latest book she was reading, and then someone tapped Ninan on the shoulder.

He turned to see Pidru and Tamya, and embraced them one by one as they offered congratulatory statements. They and their mamáy were among those who had returned to Thak, but Ninan had insisted that they live with him at Kallpa House. Again, he would keep his family close—and they were indeed his family.

Other families originally from Thak had chosen to remain

in Allpa, while the Allpans supplied local laborers to assist them. The quinoa was thriving, which had prompted Quya Urpi to build additional communities to try their hand at growing more varieties under the guidance of Sumaqi experts.

Quya Urpi was making conversation with some of the Sumaqi diplomats but would make her way over soon.

Tamya gushed about Qora's dress and all the ballroom decorations. Then all the mothers arrived—Ninan's, Qora's, and Pidru and Tamya's—with greetings, along with Hakan and Rimaq.

Hakan sheepishly asked Tamya if she would like to dance.

The two of them went off with all the awkward mannerisms of adolescence. Ninan had learned after the battle that it had been Tamya and Hakan that had organized production of the thousands of smokers launched to blind enemy forces. Heroes in their own right. He wondered what they might accomplish together as they grew, and vowed to ensure a better world for them.

It wouldn't be easy. While the great war was over, there would always be battles to fight. The world was advancing every day, and people were always creating new ways to secure power. Just last month Ninan had received news about the continent of Emborica and the weapons they utilized there—handheld metal things that could blast projectiles faster than a blink.

It wasn't enough to do away with things like the Venture, or to improve the working conditions of terrenal industries, or to change laws and build morale among the people. Just as Ninan and his friends and the Allpans had prepared against every possible threat—seeking information, researching and developing weapons and resources, extracting specimens for study, calling on all potential allies—he and Qora would have to do the same for Sumaq. They must always be alert, aware, and proactive. They must never forget how evil would always lurk in the shadows, waiting for an opportunity to strike.

At the moment, Qora was all smiles. For once, she didn't carry the weight of so many fates on her shoulders. For once she could be a young woman bathed in the love of all those she cared about. Ninan remembered the raptoriva as she'd broken free from her tether and flown across the gorge; he recalled the feeling of watching her soar, knowing she could do anything, and now watched Qora in her green dress with the same elation. He took her hand and held it tight.

Qora could do anything too—and Ninan was glad she'd chosen him to do it with her.

ACKNOWLEDGMENTS

Another big thank you to my babies for being so patient with me while I finished this trilogy! Thank you for being so excited for me, for asking questions, for visiting me at in-person events while I promoted books 1 and 2, for not making me cry too much when I had to leave for writing conferences (okay, I did anyway), and for always looking out for dino merch because you know how much I love it. I'm so excited for you both to be able to read these books one day.

Nano, my love, thank you for taking care of me during the final push and for all your support so I could get things done. I know it's been a lot—not just book 3 but all my writing and publishing endeavors. Despite being a woman of many words, I sometimes still don't know how to express what I feel when it comes to real people in the real world, so I'll just say: page 207, paragraph 3, lines 3-6, and also page 573, paragraph 2, last two sentences. Te amo.

To both my writing-friend Kristins (who luckily spell their names the same way so I can pluralize that), thank you for your guidance, encouragement, and for always being willing to talk bookish business and nerdery with me.

Brooke! Thank you for checking in on me so often to see how I'm doing and for always asking how my writing is going. You always make me feel like my endeavors are valid, even when I worry that something "doesn't count."

Once again, thanks to my artists, Dan and TrifBookDesign, for helping make these books so visually beautiful.

Finally, thank you to my superfans who kept asking when book 3 was coming. It means so much to me that my work means so much to you. You're the best! ❤ ❤ ❤

ABOUT THE AUTHOR

VICTORIA RIVERA is a graphic designer and mom of two kiddos. She has a bachelor's degree in English and has worked as a copy editor, proofreader, and designer at newspapers and magazines.

She was born and raised in Oregon but currently lives in northern Utah and misses the rain.

When she's not writing, she enjoys doing DIY projects, playing Beat Saber, rage-cleaning to good music, and reading (obviously).

For updates on books, **subscribe to her email list at www.toririv.com**. Follow her on **TikTok (@tori.riv)** for a glimpse into her day-to-day activities and other bookish things.

If you enjoyed this book, please leave a review on Amazon
and/or Goodreads. Your feedback is greatly appreciated!

www.ingramcontent.com/pod-product-compliance
Lightning Source LLC
Chambersburg PA
CBHW011312310726
48973CB00011B/2892